For DANIELLE

CONTENTS

BETWEEN TWO FIRES

Christopher Buehlman

PART I

Now in these days the Lord God had turned His face from the business of men; and the angels who had remained loyal to Him said to one another, we must look after the children of Adam. And they did so, as best they could.

Now also the third part of the angels who had rebelled looked upon the earth, and saw the hand of God withdrawn from it; and the air was cold in the valleys of men, and the sea was also cold.

And one of the fallen angels, whose name was Uzziel, said, it was for man's sake that we were cast down, for we would not bend our knee to him; let us test the Lord and see what He will do if we afflict their mightiest kingdoms with hunger. And this angel rose from the waters of the sea and made rain; and the spikes of wheat and the ears of barley were heavy with that rain, and they fell into the mud, or withered, or went to rot; and the livestock were made sick, and they died in great numbers; and in their turn, the children of Adam knew hunger; and men devoured all there was, and there was no more. And many died. And some would go into the deadyard and eat of the newly buried. And the babes born during those years who lived to be children had only twenty-two teeth.

And the Lord made no answer.

Now another of the fallen, whose name was Beliel, said, it was for man's sake that the war began in Heaven; so let us try them with wars in their greatest kingdoms; and he rose through the wells of a king who ruled a mighty island, and blew pride into his mouth; and when this king spoke, he swore that he would have the crown of an even greater kingdom, which he would take with the sword. And so he came upon his neighbor's shore under arms and with banners. Now the greater king, seeing that his land was in peril, sent out a mighty host in armor of iron and silver; and they rode against the men of the island, who shot them with arrows, even through their armor, and they died. And so the long war began.

And the Lord made no answer.

So it came that the first among the fallen, whose name was Lucifer, said, our old enemy sleeps; if we do not seize this hour, we will come to the End of Days as He has written them, and He will grind us under His heel, and destroy us forever; let us rise against Him now in all our numbers, and pull the walls of Heaven down, and shake out the souls of the just; and let us seize our brother angels by the throat, and cast them down into Hell; and let us live as once we did, upon the Great Height.

But some were fearful of the power of the angels of God, whose numbers were greater, and whose generals were Uriel, and Gabriel, and Michael, who had broken the back of Lucifer and sent him into the hot coals in the belly of the earth to blacken his face with soot and know he was lower than the Lord.

And some were fearful that God would wake from His drowsiness and rack them with pains and fires even they had not learned to endure, or destroy them utterly.

And the first among the fallen spoke to them, saying, then let us test Him one more time; it is for man's sake that we were insulted, for his sake that we were driven out, and for his peace that we are mortared under; let us break the roof of Hell with our fists and murder the seed of Adam; for if God will not rouse Himself to save His favorite creature, His sleep is deep, and we may catch Him by the hair, and cast Him down.

And one of the fallen, whose name was Azzazel, said, shall we kill them with fire or with cold?

And Lucifer spoke to him, saying, neither of these.

What then, said the wicked angel.

With a Great Plague, answered Lucifer.

And so it was.

And the years that had passed since the Lord had come to be born among men were one thousand, three hundred forty eight.

ONE

Of the Donkey

The soldiers found the donkey on Friday. It was lame and its ribs were easy to count; it was too weak to run from them or even to bray at them, but it didn't seem to have the disease. It was just old.

It looked at them hopefully from beneath a willow tree, swishing its tail against the flies. The fat one, and nobody knew how he stayed fat, took his war hammer up, meaning to brain it, but Thomas stopped him. He pointed at the barn. It would be smarter to walk it to the barn first, where they could shelter against the coming rain. Godefroy nodded his agreement.

The four men had been on the road in their rags and rusty armor without a good meal for many weeks, living on spoiled food from houses, watercress and cattail tops from ditches, worms, bugs, acorns, and even a rotten cat. They had all eaten so much grass that they had green piss. The disease was ruthless here; it had killed so many farmers that there was no bread even in this fertile valley. There were not enough hands to swing scythes, nor enough women willing to gather for the threshing, nor any miller to grind, nor bakers to stoke the ovens. The sickness, which they called the Great Death, passed mysteriously but surely from one to the other as easily as men might clasp hands, or a child might call a friend's name, or two women might share a glance. Now none looked at their neighbors, nor spoke to them. It had fallen so heavily upon this part of Normandy that the dead could not be buried; they were piled outside in their dirty long shirts and they stank in the August sun and the flies swarmed around them. They lay in weed-choked fields of rye and oats where they had fled in delirium. They lay pitifully in the shadow of the town church where they had crawled hoping that last gesture would lessen their time in purgatory, stuck like glued birds to the limestone where they had tried to cool their fevered heads. Some fouled in houses because they were the last and there was no one to put them out. Those with means had fled, but many times it dogged them even into the hills and swamps and manors and killed them there.

The soldiers made a fire in the barn just near a small creek and a still house. The wood was damp and smoked unpleasantly, besooting the unchimneyed barn, but soon they were carving meat from the donkey's haunches, running sticks through it, eating it almost raw because they couldn't wait for the fire to do its work, licking their bloody fingers, nodding at each other because their mouths were too full for them to say how good it was.

The sun was setting orange beneath a break in pewter clouds that had just begun to spit rain when the girl poked her head in the barn door.

"Hello," she said.

All of the men stopped chewing except Thomas.

She was a bad age to meet these men; just too old to be safe and just too young to know why. Her flaxen hair, which might have been pretty if it were not greasy and wet, hung damply on her neck, and her feet were growing before the rest of her, looking too big for her sticklike legs.

"Hello," she said again.

"Hello, yourself," Godefroy said, leaning his lanky body toward her like a cat sighting on a bird.

"You're eating Parsnip," she said matter-of-factly.

"It's donkey. Would you like some?"

This last would have sounded friendly except that Godefroy patted the rotten beam he was sitting on. She should sit near him if she wanted food.

"No. She was tied up in the woods to hide her, but she must have gotten loose. Her name is Parsnip," she said.

"Well," Thomas said, "that's lucky for us. We're not supposed to eat meat on Friday, but parsnip is perfectly permissible."

The others laughed.

"The mouth on you, Thomas," Godefroy said, lingering on the final *s*, which Thomas's half-Spanish mother had insisted on pronouncing. "To the whoring manor born."

"Is it Friday?" the fat one said. Both Thomas and Jacquot, the one with the drooping eye, nodded.

Only Thomas kept eating. The rest watched the girl. The girl stood there.

"Come sit near me," Godefroy said, patting the beam again. With his other hand he brushed back a wick of his stringy, black hair. He wore jewelry that didn't seem to belong on such a dirty man. Her eye fixed on a cross of jasper on a gold necklace; something the seigneur's wife might wear.

"I need help," she said.

"Come sit here and tell me about it."

Nobody wanted strangers close these days; she began to realize there was something dark in this man's mind.

the word is rape he'll rape me

She thought about turning and running to her tree, but an angel had shown her these men, and pointed to the barn. She knew it was an angel because his (her?) pretty, auburn hair didn't seem to get wet in the rain, and because he (she?) looked like something between a man and a woman, but more beautiful than either; it just pointed and said, *Go and see.* When angels spoke to her, and she had seen perhaps three, they spoke the same Norman French she spoke, and she found that odd. Shouldn't they sound like foreigners?

She put her faith in the angel even though it was gone now. It was that angel whom she saw most often, and she liked to think it was hers.

She didn't run.

"I need help putting Papa in a grave."

"Silly bitch, there aren't any graves any more. We're in a grave already, all of us. Just stack his bones outside. Someone will get him."

"Who?"

"How the devil should I know? This is your sad little village. Maybe some nuns or monks or something. Anyway, everyone else is just putting them outside."

"I can't lift him."

"Well, I won't lift him. I didn't live this long to catch it by hauling around dead serfs."

"He's not a serf."

"I really don't give a shit."

"Please."

"Forget it, girl," Thomas said. "Go back in the house now."

This man was different; he didn't frighten her, even though he was the biggest of them; exotic with his long-ish dark hair; handsome despite a nose that had been broken more than once and a round, pitted scar on his cheek. He had more armor than the others, some on his legs and shoulders, as well as a longer coat of mail. But over his chain mail hood he wore a peasant's big straw hat with a horn spoon through a hole in it; he was clearly dangerous, but also just a little ridiculous. He had spoken gruffly, but in the way that a man barks at a child to make the child act swiftly when there's trouble.

She liked him.

"Wait a minute," Godefroy said, dismissing Thomas, and now addressing the girl. "How much is it worth to you?"

Brigands. That was the word for what these men were;

men who were soldiers before the war with the English, but who now traveled the roads, or hid in the woods and robbed people. Even before the plague had come, her papa had spoken with their neighbors about what to do if brigands came.

Now they were here and no one could help her.

Why had the angel left? Why had he pushed her toward these thieves?

"We only have a little silver," she said, "and some books."

"I don't want silver."

"The books are very good, most of them are new ones from the university in Paris."

"Books are for wiping my ass with. I want gold."

"I don't have any."

"Of course you do."

Godefroy got up now, and Thomas stopped eating. Godefroy went over to her and pointed two fingers at where her pubis would be beneath her dirty gown.

"Right there," he said. "Haven't you? Haven't you got just a little gold there already?"

The fat one was the only one who laughed, but it was hollow. None of them liked this about their leader: his taste for the very green fruit. She had the fine bones and small build of a child, but her gaze was more than a girl's; she was probably just on the eve of her first bleeding. If she lived, she would be tall next summer.

"Christ crucified, Godefroy, let her alone," Thomas said.

"That's only for my husband."

"Ha!" Godefroy barked, pleased at this touch of worldliness. "And where is he?"

"I don't know."

"He shouldn't leave you alone."

"I mean I don't know who he is. I am not yet promised."

"Then I'll be your husband."

"I should go now."

"We'll all be your husbands. We're good husbands."

"She could have it," the fat one warned, eating again now.

"I'd rather get it from her than her papa."

"Leave her alone," Thomas said, and this time it wasn't a request. He put his straw hat beside him. He tried to do it casually, but the fat one saw it and, also trying to be circumspect, spat out the overlarge piece of donkey he had just taken and set the rest on his leather bag.

Godefroy turned to face Thomas.

The girl slipped out the door.

"What if I don't want to leave her alone?" Godefroy said.

"She's just a scared little girl in a dead-house. Either she's full of it and you'll breathe it in from her, or she's shielded by God's hand. Which would be even worse for us. Save your 'husbanding' for whores."

"The whores are all dead," said Jacquot.

"Surely not all of them," said Thomas, trying one last time. "And if one whore in France still has a warm *chatte*, Godefroy will smell it out."

"You make me laugh," Godefroy said, not laughing. "But I need to fuck something. Go get that girl."

"No."

Thomas stood up. Godefroy backed up a little in spite of his nominal leadership; Thomas had white coming into his beard and lines on his face; he was the oldest of the four, but the muscles in his arms and on either side of his neck made him look like a bullock. His thighs were hard as roof beams and he had a ready bend in his knees. They had all fought in the war against the English, but he alone among them had been trained as a knight.

Godefroy noted where his sword was, and Thomas noted that.

Thomas breathed in like a bellows, and blew out through clenched teeth. He did this twice. They had all seen him do this before, but never while facing them.

A drop of sweat rolled down Godefroy's nose.

"I'll get her," Jacquot said, proud of himself for thinking of a compromise. He went out of the barn into the rain, pulling his coarse red hood up. He held the hood's long tail over his nose and mouth against the smell pouring out of the house as he pushed the door open with his foot. The sun was almost down now, but the house was still full of trapped heat. The smell was blinding. Wan light coming from the polished horn slats in the windows shone on the rictus of a very bloated dead man who had stained his sheets atop a mess of straw that could no longer be called a bed; he had kicked hard at the end of it. His face was black. His shirt rippled; maggots crawled exuberantly on him, as well as on two goats and a pig that had wandered into the single-room dwelling to die.

The girl wasn't here, and even if she had been, Jacquot didn't want to find her badly enough to stay in that hot, godless room.

He would have preferred to go back to the barn then, but his failure would only put Godefroy in a worse humor. So he went around the back of the house, thankful for the cooler air, and whistled for her. He stood very still and looked around carefully. His patience was soon rewarded; he noticed her white leg up in a tree. Ten minutes later and it would have been dark enough to hide her.

She was up in her tree, whispering for the angel and asking it to come back; but then she wasn't sure anyone else could see them, or that they could do anything or lift anything. Or even that they were real. She had only started seeing them since the Great Death came on.

She thought that the ones she was seeing were lesser ones; that the famous ones like Gabriel were preparing for Judgment Day, which must be soon. Gabriel would blow his horn and all the Dead in Christ would get out of their graves; she knew this was supposed to be a good thing, but the idea of dead bodies moving again was the worst thing she could imagine; it frightened her so much she couldn't sleep sometimes.

If the angels were real, why had she been abandoned now?

And why weren't they helping anybody when they got sick?

Why had they let her father die so horribly?

And now the man with the drooping eye had seen her.

Why did her angel not strike this man blind, as they had done to the sinners of Sodom and Gomorrah?

"Come down, little bird," Jacquot said. "We won't hurt you."

"Yes you will," she said, gathering her leg up under her gown as well as she could.

"All right, we will. But not much and not for long. Maybe just a night and a morning. Then we'll be on our way. Or, better yet! We might take you with us. Would you like that? Four strong husbands and passage out of town?"

"No, thank you."

He leapt up onto a strong, low branch, almost high enough now to reach her foot, but she climbed higher. She was much lighter than he. He would lose this game.

"Don't be trouble," he said.

"Don't rape me," she said.

"It won't be rape if you agree."

"Yes it will. Because I'll only agree to avoid being hurt."

"So there we have it. You'll agree to avoid being hurt. Very well. Come down or I'll hurt you."

He dropped back down to the ground now.

"You don't mean it," she said.

"I do."

"You're not a bad man. I don't believe you are."

"I'm afraid I am."

"But you don't have to be!"

"Sorry. Already am. Now I see a bunch of lovely stones by the stream. What say I go get them and throw them at you until you come down?"

The foliage wouldn't allow for much stone-throwing, and he wasn't sure he could make himself throw a stone at her in any case, but he said it as if he meant it. He sensed he had to get her to the barn quickly.

"Please don't."

"Then come down."

"It's the other one. He's the bad one. Tell him you couldn't find me."

"He has a temper."

"So does my father."

"He's dead."

"No, he's not."

"Enough games. Come down or I knock you down with stones."

She was crying now. He thought she would call his bluff, but soon she probed for a lower branch with her long, ungainly foot. He helped her down and felt her trembling. He felt sick about what he was doing, but hardened his heart. He decided to talk to her about it while he hoisted her up on his shoulder and walked back toward the barn.

"I know this seems awful, but it really isn't. If God wanted order and goodness in the world, He shouldn't have made things quite so hard on us. We're all dead men, and women. He wants chaos and death? He gets them, and what say do we have in it? All we can do is try to have a little fun before the mower comes for us, eh? And he will come for us. If you relax, you might not have such a bad time."

"You're just saying these things to make yourself feel better," she said, breathing hard in fear for what was about to happen.

"You're a smart girl. Too smart. This world's not made for smart girls. Here we are."

So saying, he used his free hand to open the barn door.

"Mary, Mother of God," he said.

Godefroy was breathing his last, rough breaths facedown in the dirt with a hole in his head that was pouring an arc of blood like a hole in a tight wineskin. His hands were shaking. The fat one was slumped against the wall and looked like a sleepy child with his chin on his chest, except he was drenched in blood and the head sat wrong because it was barely attached. His hand was off just below where the chain mail ended. It was nearby, still clutching his wicked hammer. His killer had put the sword exactly where he wanted it, and with great strength.

"Put her down," Thomas said.

"I will."

The sword's point poked Jacquot's woolen hood and settled just behind his ear. He knew the man wielding it could drive it through both hood and skull as easily as into a squash.

"Please don't kill me," Jacquot said.

"I have to, or I can't sleep here."

"I'll leave."

"You'll come back and cut my throat at night out of love for Godefroy. He is your cousin."

"On my mother's side. And I didn't like my mother."

"Sorry, Jacquot."

"You could leave."

"I'm too tired. And you would find me."

"No."

"Put her down so she doesn't get hurt."

"No."

"Do you really want your last earthly act to be trying to hide behind a girl you nearly raped?"

Jacquot put her down, then put his hands over his eyes. But while Thomas was trying to work up the will to strike, the girl stood in front of the smaller man.

"Don't kill him," she said.

She looked up at Thomas, and he noticed how very light and gray her eyes were. Like the flint in the walls of the barn, but luminous. Like an overcast sky on the verge of turning blue.

Thomas lowered his sword.

The rain stopped.

"Don't kill anybody else again."

TWO

Of the Honey and the Broken Cross

T homas and the girl slept in the barn on separate piles of rotten hay with the droopy-eyed man tied up in the donkey's old stall. He didn't make trouble in the evening because he knew how close to dying he had been, but near morning he forgot and woke Thomas up.

"What?" Thomas growled.

"My undershirt. Would you help me so I don't soil it? I have to shit."

"Just shit yourself."

"You only have to move the shirt a little."

"I don't care if you shit yourself. You don't deserve any better."

"This is my only shirt."

"There's a stream. Jesus, you're a woman. Shut your hole."

"So you'll cut me loose when you leave? So I can wash my shirt?"

"Not if you don't be quiet."

The droopy-eyed man was quiet for a minute.

Then he wasn't.

"How can you sleep with all the birds going? And with those two lying there dead. Did you close their eyes, at least?"

"No. They'll want to see Jesus coming."

"At least the rooster's dead. There's one happy thing. Will you leave me my sword and crossbow?"

"I don't know."

"Because if you don't, it's just like killing me."

"No, Jacquot, it's not. Killing you would be just like killing you, and I'm still tempted."

"You could bury them. You could wrap them in a cloth, bury them and leave a shovel. That way it would take me a long time to get to them. You'd have a head start. Or, if you wanted time, you could break the . . ."

Thomas got up.

"I'm sorry. I'm nervous. You know I talk when I'm nervous. I'll be quiet now."

"It's too late."

He went over to Jacquot and punched him with his mailed fist until the man lost consciousness and loosed his bowels.

The smell offended Thomas, so he walked over to the barn door and breathed in the morning air, which was cool and good. A very few stars were twinkling in a clear sky just beginning to lighten in the east. It was too light to see the comet, and he was glad for that. He didn't want anything else to worry about just now.

The girl was making noise in her sleep, just sounds at first, but then she said "Papa . . . Papa . . . They see you through the painting. The little boys . . . are devils. Get away from it." Thomas woke her then, his huge hand swallowing her shoulder as he shook her.

She looked warily up at him at first, and then she remembered him as the man who had protected her. Then she remembered more and looked like she might cry.

"No tears," he said. "And no talk of devils."

"I'll try not to cry," she said. "But I'm not sure I can stop."

"Just try."

She stood up now, brushing straw from her tangled hair.

"And who spoke of devils?"

"You did, in your sleep."

"I know I was having a bad dream, but I don't remember devils."

"Stop saying it. You call their attention when you speak of them."

"Yes," she said. "I think that's true."

Thomas walked over to where the fat man's severed hand still clutched the war hammer. He tried to unwrap the stiff fingers, then gave up and grabbed the hammer above them, bringing it over to where Jacquot's crossbow lay. The girl thought he would smash the bow, but instead he smashed the crank lying next to it, beating it into junk.

"Why not the bow?" said the girl.

Thomas looked at her standing with her delicate arms and legs and thought how odd it was that children were small, and that they found this normal. He could not remember being small. What must he look like to her, standing so far above her, holding that murderous hammer? What did it feel like to know you lived or died at the whim of the giants around you?

"Why not the bow?" she said again, a little louder.

"It's too beautiful. Italians made it and it can punch a bolt through chain mail as if through eggshells."

It was indeed a beautiful thing, its polished cherrywood handle paneled with carved ivory depicting the Last Supper.

"He'll kill you with it."

"Then that's my problem."

"Mine, too."

"How do you figure?"

"I'm coming with you."

"Horseshit."

"I am."

"We'll talk about that in a minute. But he can't load the crossbow until he finds another manivel. He's not strong enough. I'm not strong enough. Hell, Samson's not strong enough."

She walked closer to him.

"Don't swear."

"Balls to that. I'll swear as I please."

"It's..."

"What?"

"Ignoble."

"Well there's a big word. You can read, can't you?"

"Yes. French and Latin. Not Greek."

"Anyway, what's this about you coming with me?"

"Why don't you take the bow?"

The bow would have been useful for hunting if Thomas had any skill with it; he did not. He missed almost every deer, quail, and rabbit he ever shot at with bow or crossbow, and he didn't like spearing frightened deer that the hounds had cornered. The only thing he liked to hunt was boar, because a boar would turn and fight you until you drove the spear in deep enough. That was something Thomas had a gift for.

"It's ignoble to kill from far away."

"Our Lord said not to kill at all. What's the difference?"

"Our Lord also said to render unto Caesar what was Caesar's. My sword belongs to my seigneur. Or did, until the English feathered him at Crécy. Feathered me, too, but I lived. God, in His wisdom, made me a fighting man."

"Yet you ride with a man who kills from far away. So what were you doing on the road with these men?"

"Well. That's another matter."

"I'm asking."

"You were asking about the bow, and I was trying to tell you."

"You could sell it."

"It's his," Thomas said, indicating Jacquot. "He needs it. He's not strong."

"Neither are you if you ride with him."

"What a pain in the ass you are! Anyway, I don't ride with him. Not anymore. You settled that."

She looked down at her feet, using her toe to move a straw around in the dirt.

"What were you doing coming up to us? That was stupid."

"I needed . . ."

"I know. Your dead father. But girls shouldn't come up to soldiers. You know that now. Right?"

"I know that now."

"Good."

She used her big toe and the next one to lift the straw until she lost her balance, then picked up another straw and started the game again.

"But if I hadn't come up to you, I would be alone."

"You are alone."

"No. I'm coming with you."

"What a pain in the ass! Three pains in the ass!"

"Don't swear."

"Christ's holes, little girl. Christ's bleeding, whoring holes!"

"Bury my father."

"No."

"He called me his little moon."

"What?"

"His little moon. That's what he called me."

"I'll catch it!"

"I didn't. You won't."

"I will."

She looked at him now.

"Then maybe you'll go to Heaven if you catch it doing something good."

Thomas went to speak but didn't.

He hung his head and nodded.

The work was going to be awful. So he made the man with the drooping eye do it. Thomas stood outside the house with his sword over his shoulder, looking in, while Jacquot broke the legs off the family table and then, using the sheet beneath the dead man, pulled him onto it. He was half hysterical with fear; he had wrapped the tail of his hood around his face and wedged a pomander of lilac and lavender in next to his nose to keep the evil air out.

"A lot of good the pomander did them," Jacquot said, heaving the corpse onto the board. He was barely audible through the cloth and over the flies. "I mean, by Saint Louis and his whoring oak tree. If this goddamned thing worked, he'd be out here dancing a jig with us. Instead he's reeking to God's feet, and ready to split for the worms in him, and I'm next. You've murdered me, making me do this."

"Shut up."

Jacquot grunted as he pulled his burden over the threshold of the house.

"So we waste half a day burying a stranger and leave our friends like animals?"

"Our friends *were* animals. We're doing this for the girl. Now shut up."

"What are you going to do? Punch me out again? Then who'll roll this geezer into his hole? You will, that's who."

"You're giving me a headache."

"Who's got a headache? You weren't beaten half to death last night. You didn't shit yourself and then dig a grave and then..."

He stopped talking when the little girl approached him. He had the corpse ready to dump into the shallow hole, but she came up to it and put a small cherrywood cross in its hand.

"It fell out," she explained simply.

Then she amazed and horrified both men by kissing the bloated figure on the cheek.

"Good-bye, Papa," She said. "Now Mother will look out for you and this knight will look out for me."

"Are you quite done?" Jacquot said.

She nodded. He tilted the table and Papa fell in the hole, breaking open like rotten fruit. The girl didn't watch this, but she did watch Jacquot's face as he watched it.

"It's okay," she said. "That's not really him anymore."

"No shit," he said, and coughed into his face cloth, which he was about to remove when Thomas motioned to the dirt pile.

"Oh, come on. Let me take a rest."

"After you shovel."

While the man with the drooping eye sweated and complained and by and by filled the grave behind the little house, the girl went back inside and soon returned bearing over her shoulder a tied sheet full of goods she clearly meant to salvage.

"Where are we going?" she asked Thomas.

"Well, I am going south, or maybe east. I haven't decided."

"What is there to the south, besides the pope?" she said.

"I don't know. I only know it's not the west."

"What's in the west?"

"More of this," he said, gesturing to the still, broken land around them.

"All right then. South," she said.

"One town," Thomas said, holding up a thick, callused finger. "I'll take you along until we come to the next town, and keep you safe until then. But if you cry, bitch, or moan on the way there, I'll leave you flat. If you behave tolerably, I'll dump you in the lap of the first live abbess or even whoring novice nun I see."

She squinted her eyes at his profanity, but he moved his finger closer to her face, saying, "And I'll swear as I please. By the Virgin, by her sour milk, by the hair of dead pigs, whatever the devil puts in my mouth. And the more you complain about it, the worse I'll get."

She narrowed her eyes yet further at him, which made him think her papa had a slow hand for hitting.

"Don't pull a face at me. Hand me that sack you brought out."

"Why?"

"It's too heavy for you and we don't have a horse," he said, snatching it out of her grasp.

"You could have had a donkey."

"What?"

"You ate my donkey."

He grunted at her and began pulling things out, starting with a sextet of yellow beeswax candles.

"Fancy," he said. "No serf has wax candles. What did your papa do?"

"He's a lawyer. And he keeps bees. Kept bees, I mean. He traded honey and comb for them with the chandler. Soon after people started getting sick, some apprentices came and burned the hives up, saying that the bees had brought it here, flying to sick towns, and towns where Jews were. Later, they came back starving and asking for honey, but Papa told them they burned it up, so they threatened to kill him, but only hit him. But he wasn't hurt much. Only he did have some left."

"So he did," Thomas said, tasting his finger as he pulled out a sticky pot. And then another one. He darted his eye to Jacquot, who had already seen the pots and was coming over quickly, forgetting that he was still holding the shovel.

Thomas stood up and leveled his sword at the man, who remembered the shovel, dropped it, and dropped to his knees, clasping his hands before his chest. He opened his mouth as if waiting for communion. Thomas stood over him with the honey pot and the sword.

"Please?" Jacquot said in the smallest voice he could muster.

"All right, all right, baby bird. Stop your peeping," Thomas said, sheathing his sword. He tipped the pot of thick, amber stuff and held it over the smaller man's mouth so a string of it fell slowly in. Jacquot made glad noises and swallowed it, grinning, getting it nastily in his beard. But there wasn't a second dripping, even though he opened his mouth expectantly again.

"Dig."

"It's done."

"It's almost done. Dig."

Thomas pulled a large book from the girl's pack.

"What's this?"

She just looked up at him.

He squinted at the letters and sounded them out.

"Thomas Aquinas? Really?"

She nodded.

"Can't you read?" she asked.

"Not Thomas Aquinas."

"I thought knights could read."

"Who said I was a knight?"

"You look like a knight."

"You haven't met many knights. Most can write enough so they don't have to draw a chicken for a signature, but nothing... scholarly."

"Thomas Aquinas is Papa's favorite. Because he could have been a lord but chose to renounce the world. Although I much prefer Saint Francis."

"I thought Aquinas was fat."

"I don't know."

"He was. He was great and fat. So he might have renounced tits on women, but then he ate cakes until he got tits of his own."

"You shouldn't mock a great man."

"Even his book is fat. It weighs as much as a calf."

"I'll carry it."

"You'll begin by carrying it and then I'll carry it. If your papa loved it, leave it with him. And this? What the hell is this?"

He held up a small deer-bone instrument of sorts with a stem and a bulb at the end. She took it from him, took it to the water pail, and put some in. Then she blew into the stem and it chirped agreeably, sounding just like a bird.

"Leave it," he said, taking it from her.

He was about to snap it, but she put her hand on his.

"Why? It doesn't weigh a thing. And it makes me happy."

"Making you happy is not my job."

"I know. That's why I want the whistle."

He grunted and gave it back to her.

"Don't you do anything but grunt?"

He grunted again.

She answered him by blowing into her toy, managing to look both innocent and defiant, the whistle sputtering out its cheerful birdsong.

"But you're leaving this," he said, displaying for her a cross of wood and lead.

She stopped chirping.

"No," she said.

"The real one weighed less."

"It was given to us by a Franciscan."

"For a fistful of silver and a long leer at your mother, if I know my Franciscans."

"Please don't talk dirtily about my mother. For all your other swearing, please don't do that."

"Fine. But this goes."

So saying, Thomas stood and chucked the cross into a muddy field. No sooner had he thrown it than the girl took off on her broomstick legs and fetched it out of the mud, clutching it to her breast, further dirtying her once-white gown. He took it from her and threw it again. She ran again to fetch it.

"Goddamn it," he said when she brought it back. He took it from her again and threw it against a tree, where it split into two pieces. The girl looked at him and sobbed and put her wrist to her mouth.

"It's just the weight of it," he said. "We'll find you a smaller one."

Still she sobbed.

"Don't cry for the thing. It's just junk."

"I'm not crying for that."

"Jesus, what then?"

"Just for a moment. I saw it."

"You saw what?"

"Your soul."

"Souls are invisible."

"Not always."

"Yes, always. But not for you, eh? Well, how was it? Horns and little goat's feet? Am I a devil?"

"No. But there's one near you. There's always one near you. They want you."

"A witch. Jesus Christ bleeding, I'm about to go on the road with a small, weird witch."

She wiped tears from her cheeks with the insides of her wrists. She looked like a wild little peasant brat. Who would ever agree to take her in?

"Do you have a comb in that bag?"

"No."

"Is there one in the house?"

"Yes. It was my mother's."

"Bring it. And start using it."

THREE

Of the Tower and the Looted Church

An old tower stared down at them from a hill with its narrow windows; some minor seigneur's keep inherited from Norman days, not unlike the one Thomas had left behind in Picardy. In better times a horseman might have ridden out from this one and charged them a toll for use of the road, but horse and horseman were likely in the bellies of the crows that cawed down at them from the battlements. The shadow of the tower crept down the hill of burnished grass toward them, and Thomas thought they might have three hours of light left.

"What's this town called?" he asked the girl, fanning himself with his hat.

"Fleur-de-Roche," she said. "Would you like to know my name as well?"

"No."

"Is it because you don't want to feel affection for me?"

"I don't."

"But you might if you knew my name and other things about me so I wasn't just 'girl.' Is that why?"

"Shut up."

It was a small town, but bigger than the one he had found the girl in. Down the hill from the tower, a stone church dominated a collection of shops and a few score houses. Blue jabs of chicory grew wild in a field lying fallow, while all around it untended barley and spelt waved in the warm breeze. The harvest festival of Lammas had come and gone uncelebrated here.

He looked back up at the tower. It would be useful to get up that hill and survey the road and the town. The tower was compelling, but risky. The heavy door seemed to be ajar. An invitation? It would be a delightful ambush spot if anybody had the inclination; nine chances in ten said it was empty—it was that tenth time that caused so much grief.

I'm not carrying anything worth robbing

The girl looked up at him, her hair more gold than flaxen now that it was dry, now that the sun shone on it.

Yes you are

Thomas left the girl near the road, handing her his straw hat. He fitted the conical helm that hung from his belt on top of his chain hood, then hiked up the hill to the foot of the tower, unsheathing his sword and yoking it over his shoulders.

He might have gone in to search the tower, but he didn't want to pass the two dead scullery women sitting near the gate. The crows had been at them and they grinned black-eyed at him, their heads touching almost tenderly. He walked along the wall with the crows mocking him until he came to a point where he could see the road they had just traveled. He sat down in the shadow of the wall for several moments and watched the road, making sure nobody was following them.

It was unlikely that Jacquot had gotten loose so quickly. Thomas had found him stuffing his underpants with the gold chains from around Godefroy's neck and the silver coins left in the fat one's leather bag; another beating had followed, mitigated by the girl, but then Thomas had decided it would be fitting to leave Jacquot tied to the tree he had fetched the girl out of. He also posed a wooden sign around his neck, which the girl wrote upon in charcoal at Thomas's instruction.

do with me

as seems right to you

to do with thieves

That was what Thomas commanded her to write, at least. She translated this somewhat liberally.

we thieves shall do

the same to you

if we catch you

Jacquot's crossbow had been hidden in the tree near him, hanging like evil fruit with the little sack of quarrels. He had bitched at them while Thomas bound his limbs with rope the girl got from the house, crying that it was too tight, that he wouldn't live the night out, or that wild dogs would come and eat him.

"What dogs? They're all dead. You're more likely to be eaten by starving farmers."

Then Jacquot had switched tactics and reminded Thomas what good times they'd had together dancing brawls and dansas at the Candlemas feast near Évreux.

"You passed out and I had to carry you back to camp. You're the one who had the good time."

Jacquot said three would be better than two if there was trouble.

"Not if one of those three causes the trouble."

Then Thomas had turned his back.

"PLEASE!" Jacquot had yelled, causing the girl to stop.

"Mightn't we . . . ?" she had started, but Thomas cut her off.

"If you go back, you're his to take care of."

She had hung her head and kept walking.

As the girl and Thomas were nearly out of earshot, Jacquot had finished by calling out nastily "God bless you both for this," and then shouting until he was hoarse.

As they passed a house with a yellow-green, newly thatched roof, a woman coughed wetly from inside and then launched into a loud *Pater Noster* punctuated with more coughing. The girl went toward the window, but Thomas plucked her back by the sleeve.

"I know her," the girl said, "she puts out a table on feast days and sells cakes with honey and walnuts. She's nice."

"The plague doesn't care about nice. Stay away from there."

"I can't remember her name."

"She doesn't have one anymore."

The girl looked as if she were about to cry, then crossed herself and they moved down toward the church.

"Do you know anyone else here?"

"The priest is Père Raoul. Papa brought me here to see mystery plays in the spring. It was Adam and Eve, and then Lot's Wife. The players always invite the village priest to take part; Père Raoul played the serpent, and then the wicked man of Sodom, and then the devil. He had a pair of red horns. I think he liked being bad as long as it was for pretend."

"Do you know where his house is?"

"No."

"If we find him, I'm leaving you with him."

Fresh graves pocked the churchyard, and just past that a big pit yawned with a heap of dirt near it. Thomas knew what was in the pit. Every town had something similar. The first dead had been given Christian burials, and then the ones who had buried them needed burying, and then there were so many a pit was dug, and then there was nobody willing even to take them to the pit.

"Everyone's dead here," she said.

"Maybe. More likely that they're hiding. I would hide from strangers, wouldn't you?"

She shook her head no.

"No, I guess we know you don't do that."

Thomas pulled his scarf up over his nose and mouth as they passed the pit and went to look in the church. It was a simple church with a dirt floor. The cross and everything else of value had been taken from the altar.

"I think your priest is dead," the big man said, looking back at her.

The girl knitted her brow.

"He was so good. Why would God kill good priests?"

"The plague kills everything. Only the priests who won't visit the sick have a chance of living."

"Then he's dead," she said.

"Looks like I'm stuck with you for a while longer. We'll sleep in the church. Maybe nobody died in here."

During the night he heard the girl speaking, but not in French. Latin. He thought he heard her say "Avignon." He thought about shaking her, but instead got up and went outside to walk in the cool air and look at the stars. A comet had appeared last week, near Cygnus, and he looked to see where it was moving. It would not be long before it cut the neck of the pretty swan in the east. He knew it was wicked, a plague token in a sick sky, but it was so beautiful he couldn't stop looking at it. There had been others before it. Three at once had shared April's sky, one so bright it washed out the stars near it; this was before the plague had come to Normandy, but it had already started spreading elsewhere, and everyone was talking about Judgment Day. He remembered the tales of the travelers they met, and often robbed; an earthquake in Italy, dwarfed by the earthquakes and freak storms that punished India; how the earth had cracked in the land of the Mongols, all the way down to Hell, and it was Hell that burped up this pestilence.

The comets had been just another indication that something in Heaven's mechanism was sprung. Several of the other brigands under Godefroy had melted away before the sickness pared them down from twenty to the four they had been when they found the girl's donkey. They had thought to save their souls by quitting the pack of thieves, but doing so had probably saved their lives. The company had gotten sick after robbing merchants with a wagonload of furs; no sooner had they abandoned one sick one to his death than another started whimpering in his sleep from a swelling in his armpit or groin.

Twelve died in two weeks.

He thought further back, to the days after his injury and betrayal, when he first came to Normandy, meaning to damn himself and grow rich. A whore had warned him not to take the road from Normanville to Évreux that particular spring night because she knew men who lay in ambush there. Thomas paid her to take him on that road, which smelled of all spring's gaudy notes, but honeysuckle most of all, and to introduce him to those men.

To Godefroy.

The most feared brigand in Normandy, for a year or two.

The man he had just killed.

When Thomas went back in the church, the girl was sitting up.

"We are going to Paris. And then to Avignon," she said.

"The hell we are."

"I have to go to Avignon. I'm not sure why. I have something I have to do. And you have to make sure I get there safely."

"I don't like your dreams. Someone's going to call you a witch and turn you over to the church."

"Do you think I'm a witch?"

"They'll put the tongs to you. Would you like that?"

"You didn't answer my question."

"I don't know if you're a witch."

"What does your heart tell you?"

Thomas put his hands on his hips and walked in a slow circle, his head down.

"My heart lies," he said.

"Something lies to you, but it's not your heart."

"Stop that weird shit. I don't want to hear it."

"We have to go to Avignon. But first we go to Paris. There's something in Paris we need."

"What we need is to stay in the country. Those big cities are tombs, and they're hungry. Going to them is stupid."

"Yet we have to go."

"Says who?"

"Père Raoul."

He threw up his hands.

"What, the dead one?"

"Yes, he is dead. He died in his little house with his blanket over his head. He came to tell me."

"Horseshit."

She knitted her brow again.

"I'm going to sleep a little more," she said.

She lay back down on the packed earth as if it were settled.

"If you see your dead priest again, tell him he can go to Paris and Avignon alone. After he fucks himself."

"He won't be back."

"Good."

She curled her knees up kittenishly and was almost instantly asleep.

Thomas waited until he heard her soft snoring and then quietly gathered his things. The girl was a liability; he would have a better chance on his own. He could travel faster, hide more easily; if he needed to do something brutal, he wouldn't have her knowing, flint-colored eyes on him, making him hesitate and perhaps dying because he had. This world wasn't made for children, particularly girl children, and most particularly those without fathers. That wasn't his fault. If God wanted her protected, He could do it Himself. He was about to leave her in the church when he saw something red by his foot. It had not been there before. When he saw what it was, he crossed himself for the first time in months and flung it out-side. Then he put his gear down. His heart was pounding in his ears.

The item that had bothered him so was a crude painted mask with horns on it. The kind a country priest would wear to play the devil in a mystery play.

FOUR

Of the Monastery, and of the Best Wine Had in Seven Years

They marched together for two days, and on the first day they saw no people and ate only green stems, a parsnip she pulled out of the ground (using the end of her dress wrapped around her hand), a grasshopper she managed to catch, and a very little honey. They were making for Paris, though the girl couldn't say why. Despite the devil's horns Thomas had seen the night before, he thought about abandoning her no less than a dozen times, and, to that end, he hardly responded to her attempts to speak to him. She had a pretty voice, and decent manners, and he would easily feel affection for her if he let himself, but he determined not to.

With limited success.

"Where were you born?" she said as they crested a hill under a pleasantly warm, blue sky.

"Picardy."

"What town?"

"A town."

"A big town?"

"Just a town."

"With what name?"

"Town."

"This town. Is it near a mountain?"

"No."

"A hill, then?"

"No."

"A lake?"

"No."

"Farms?"

"No."

"All towns are near farms."

Thomas scowled down at her, but she deflected this with a look of unperturbed precocity. The intelligence in her eyes goaded him, reminding him of someone else.

Someone who had hurt him.

"Then, yes," he said.

"Near farms."

"Yes."

"Good. Now we're getting somewhere. Trees? Is the town near trees?"

"I guess."

"I want to revisit the question of the hill. Because you didn't seem sure."

"Yes, it was near a hill."

"But you seemed sure about the mountain. So no mountain."

"No."

"And the name?"

"Town, I said."

"No town is named Town."

"Mine was. Townville-sur-Cunting-Town. What did your papa do again?"

"He was a lawyer."

"It shows. Now shut up."

"You'll never get a wife being so mean."

"I already had one."

"What happened to her?"

"I killed her for talking."

The girl giggled at that.

"And is she buried in Townville-sur-Town?"

"Shut up."

"I suppose you killed your children, too."

"All of them."

"What were their names?"

"Boy, boy, girl, and shut up."

They saw the monastery on the second day, and only because they went into the woods to forage. They got less than a fistful of sour berries between them, but, as they were about to leave, Thomas spotted a hare and chased it down a footpath that led farther into the woods. The hare got away, of course, but the woods broke on a small hill, and from the hill he saw the low stone walls and the thatched roof, and what looked like a garden.

"Oh, sweet Jesus, let our luck be in," he said, and the two of them went to the gate. It was a simple gate of interwoven sticks, standing open. A wooden sign over the gate said, in burned-in Latin:

This gate opens

to all who enter

in Christ's peace

He drew his sword and went in.

She followed behind him, with her hands clasped as if to pray, and then moved past him and headed directly for the little stone church, ignoring his "Ho! Wait!" He let her go, shaking his head at her, and then assessed the grounds.

It was a small monastery, home to no more than twenty brothers from the look of it. Only the church and the outer walls were stone; the cloisters and dormitory were wattle and daub. Another hare, or the same one, darted from the garden, but Thomas didn't even try to lunge at it, instead making straight for the earthen cellar where he suspected the buttery would be. It had already been emptied. Considerately, respectfully, and quite thoroughly emptied.

"No luck at all," he said, and suppressed the urge to spit.

The dormitory was empty, except for ten straw beds, several of which bore the stains of plague on them. He backed out quickly.

He found the girl kneeling outside the church, praying silently into her clasped hands, her cheeks wet.

"Why didn't you go in?" he said.

She just looked at him and wiped her cheeks.

And then he smelled them.

He peeked in the door, waving flies away from his face, and saw four puffy corpses lying in the nave, wearing their off-white, undyed woolen habits. Three were lying on their backs, and the last one, an old man, was curled like a baby near them. He had his eating knife in his hand, and his habit was open on one side. The floor was sticky under him. He had died trying to burst one of those awful lumps. Flowers were strewn on the lot of them.

"Cistercians," Thomas said.

Fresh dirt mounds out back covered the first brothers who fell, but only four. If they had been buried one to a grave, and if all the beds had been filled, a few were unaccounted for; probably those who had emptied the buttery. Maybe they thought they would go to another abbey. Thomas didn't envy them trying to travel unarmed with the last cart of food in the valley.

When the girl finished her prayers, Thomas said, "No food. They got the stores, and emptied the fishpond and the dovecote. They had an oven, but it's been cold a long while. The garden where they grew food is all turned up. All they've got is damned herbs and flowers."

The girl went to the herb garden and motioned for Thomas to follow. She handed him a bucket from the well and walked him through the garden, filling it with flowers and greens she tore expertly with her small, white hands. He started grabbing at everything, but she stopped him before he grabbed one green stem. She shook her head at him urgently.

"What? Why?"

She used her finger to write *monkshood* in the dirt.

He furrowed his brow to read it, sounding out each letter. Monkshood.

Poison.

"Oh. Thank you. So, what, you're not talking?"

Not here.

"What, because it's a monkery?"

She nodded.

"You didn't take a vow."

Yes I did, she wrote. *By the church. In my heart.*

It was taking him so long to read this that she just pointed at the church and placed her hand over her chest.

He grunted.

"Is this vow for the rest of your life?" he asked.

She shook her head.

"Just while we're here?"

She nodded.

"In that case, we are definitely spending the night. Maybe a week."

She reached into the bucket and threw some damp leaves at his face. One stuck on his forehead and she laughed in spite of herself and her temporary status as maiden Cistercian.

They ate their bucket of greens and bright flowers. Along with the buttery little crowns of calendula, which he remembered now from his mother's garden—she used to mix it with chickens' grain to make their egg yolks darker and, she said, better for the blood—Thomas kept picking out one broadish leaf, nodding his head as he tasted it.

"What's this one?"

Sorrel, she wrote.

"It's good. Like a lemon, but good. And this?"

Lovage

"This?"

Comfrey

"This one I know. Don't eat it all. And get more of it in the morning, if there is more. It's good to pack in a wound to stop bleeding."

Yarrow

"How do you know all this?"

Mother, she wrote, and a smile broke so gently on her face that Thomas bit his tongue viciously to keep from weeping for his own.

They slept in the open air of the cloisters, near statues of St. Bernard of Clairvaux, St. Genevieve of Paris, and the Archangels Michael and Gabriel. Thomas woke up in the middle of the night and went to look at his comet. It was across Cygnus's neck now, and seemed to be reddish at the tip, as if there were a tiny vein of blood in it. He rubbed his eyes and looked away, but when he looked back it was still there. He noticed a second comet now, close to it and very faint.

"Just kill us all," he said. "What are you waiting for?"

He slept hard after that, and dreamed of monks singing plainchant. He woke in the peach light that came just before sunrise. The air was chilly, and the girl was still sleeping.

The air smelled of juniper, though he saw no juniper bush.

It also smelled of wildflowers.

Both of them had been covered in flowers.

They met travelers the next day: a cloth merchant from Bruges, his family, and two Flemish men-at-arms, with five horses between them. All seemed to be in good health. Thomas would have been glad to meet them two months before, with Godefroy and his band of killers behind him; the horses were young, the cart promised excellent pickings, and Godefroy would not have bothered this woman.

The two parties stayed fifty paces apart and Thomas and the merchant each shouted news about what lay behind him. The news was not good in either direction. Then the man offered to buy food. Thomas said he had none to spare, and would have said the same had the girl's sack been full of sausages and peas; money wasn't what it used to be. The merchant looked at the sack. The older of the two Flamandes suddenly looked nervous, and Thomas guessed that he was afraid the merchant might order them to search the sack. Neither man wanted to tangle with Thomas. The merchant, who was in fact assessing Thomas, finished this, saluted him, and moved his party on.

The bridge Thomas wanted to cross was said to be just on the other side of a river town called St. Martin-le-Preux, but as he and the girl approached the town, they came to an overturned and wheel-less handcart, on the bottom of which someone who was not a confident letterer had painted, in what looked like blood:

go back

As this was the only bridge they knew of, they continued forward, although Thomas traded his straw hat for the helmet and carried the sword naked across his shoulders. The girl took her bird whistle out, poured a little of her water, and began to make birdsong with it.

"Stop that," he hissed.

"I just don't want to surprise anyone. And I thought this would let them know we're friendly."

"I'm not friendly."

"But I'm friendly, and I'm the one with the whistle."

He was just about to take it from her when a priest walked out to meet them, easily visible in his white linen alb, holding in his hand a horn lantern. It was still light enough to see, but the priest kept the lantern near his nose and mouth.

He came from a hidden recess in the woods near which the skulls of animals had been nailed to trees.

"Stop. Please," the priest said, holding up one delicate-looking hand.

Thomas was glad to keep his distance; he turned his head to left and right to make sure nobody was moving on their flanks. The priest now looked to the right and left as well, wondering if the soldier had confederates skirting up the sides.

"You don't have to be afraid," the girl called out to the priest, but Thomas pinched her arm.

"Speak when I tell you to," he told her. Then he called to the priest, "We're not sick."

"Do you promise?" the priest said.

"On my word. Are you alone?"

"Oh, yes. Quite alone."

The priest lowered his lantern.

"I'm not sick, either."

"We saw your sign."

"Sign?"

"Go back."

"Ah. That will have been the militia," the priest said.

"Where are they?"

"As I was their confessor, I fear they probably bypassed purgatory on their way straight to the cauldron."

"Dead?"

"Some time ago."

"We just want to cross the bridge."

"That's problematic."

"Why? There's no toll, is there?"

"There's no bridge. When was the last time you had wine? And I mean good wine."

Thomas smiled broadly, showing teeth in surprisingly good shape for his age. Teeth he would be very glad to stain purple.

The people in the town near the river had burned the bridge to try to isolate themselves, but the Death was on both sides and found them anyway. A peddler had paid a farmer to sleep in his barn, against the orders of the seigneur, but the next morning the farmer found him there with his face frozen in pain and fear, and muck from the horrid buboes staining the pits of his shirt. The farmer had seven children, who worked and played in the fields with neighbor children and helped out at the widow's alehouse. Soon half the families on the east side of town were stricken, along with the widow. The die-off started, as it always did, with those who were good enough to minister to the sick and bury the dead, and with those who gathered at the alehouse, including the militia. When the churchyard was full, families dumped the bodies in the river and the eels fed on them.

Then something else moved in that also liked to eat what the eels grew fat on. Fishermen who speared or cast nets for trout, eels, and pike began to disappear, even when they went in groups of two or three.

Nobody knew what was happening until a young boy sprinted back to town and said that his father and uncle had been eaten by a "great black fish or snake" with a "flat mouth" that hid in the murky shallows. It had lashed at them with the end of its tail and pulled the men in, then tore them with spines, and then its great, froggy mouth had opened and clamped down on their heads, swallowing each of them whole in several fast gulps. The boy had stood transfixed until he saw that it was slithering up the bank toward him, and then he had run screaming for the road. The monster would have caught him, but his panicked flight had startled his uncle's mule, still tied to its cart, causing it to buck and catch the thing's attention. It wanted the mule more than the boy, so it coiled all around the poor animal and bit its head off, dragging the body, cart and all, back down the bank and into the river.

"How long was it, boy?" the priest had said.

"I don't know."

"Think. You saw it take the mule. So of course it was longer than a mule. As long as three mules perhaps?"

The boy shook his head.

"How many, then?"

The boy held up eight fingers, then corrected it to nine.

Several of the men in town who were still healthy and still brave enough to leave their houses met up at the alehouse and drank until they had the stomach to go down to the river and look for it. They took their axes and wooden flails, their clubs and scythes, and they swore to Saints Martin and Michael and Denis to cleave the thing in two or die in the attempt. The priest, who drank with them, witnessed these oaths, and agreed to come with them, and to hold over the men his processional crosier with its agonized Christ. All their boozy courage left them when they went to the banks and saw the wreckage of the cart, and the piles of shit the thing had left on the bank, all full of boots and bones and broken tools, and even the shredded cuirass of a man-at-arms. Even with the bridge down, it seemed, some were trying to cross the river. But they were not making it to the far shore.

"This is beyond our power, brethren," said the priest. "God forgives us the oaths we make in ignorance. Let us return to town before we make the thing stronger on our fat and our blood."

None of them protested.

"What about the seigneur?" asked Thomas, leaning toward the priest over his modest table. "If he's well enough to issue orders about letting in strangers, he should have enough spunk to buckle on his armor and put a sword in that thing."

The priest smiled his distinctive, sad smile, making the well-used lines around his eyes deepen. He was probably a year or two older than Thomas, but drink and soft living made him look closer to fifty than forty; faded speckles of wine on the chest of his alb, only muted by his attempts to clean them, testified to the death of the town laundress. Despite his woolly eyebrows and masculine chin, there was something womanish, almost wifely, about the cleric's aspect.

"Our lord is what you might call . . ."

"A frightened cunt?"

"If no more generous term occurred to you. He has shut himself and his retinue in the tower. His herald comes down on Fridays and reads his proclamations, which are ignored. He never gets off his horse. A man confessed to me that he intends to throw a slop pot at the herald the next time he comes, and asked me to pardon him in advance. I told him that gesture would put him one slop pot closer to Heaven. Better the herald should get a faceful of shit tomorrow than an axe handle across the nose next week. That's where things are heading. We starve down here, unable even to pull fish from the river now, while our master has the water mill and ovens and has hoarded back enough grain to keep himself fed until doomsday."

"So, a week's worth, then?"

The priest laughed and went to pat Thomas's arm in fellowship, but Thomas pulled his mailed arm back with the sound of money being withdrawn from a card game. He waved a cautionary finger but was still laughing. As was the priest.

The priest noticed the salt stains on the knight's dark garments and the rust stains on his light ones. Had he had a page and squire? A wife? Or had he been this dirty before the Death came?

"Who is the girl to you?" asked the priest, gesturing where the girl lay sleeping on a straw pallet. "And don't say your daughter."

"I don't know who she is. But she sleeps a lot."

"Maybe she's hoping to wake up from this bad dream."

"If so, she's smarter than both of us."

"I don't know what smart is anymore. More wine?"

"With pleasure."

"Good, isn't it?"

"The best. Black as a woman's heart and sweet as her . . ."

"Yes?" the priest said, amused.

"Other heart."

The priest tipped the small cask of wine so the last of the pretty, red liquid spattered out of it and into the serving jug.

"The wine is from Beaune, but it comes via Avignon, from the private stock of His Holiness."

"But how . . . ?"

"Where my younger brother is a steward of sorts; one of those who dresses His Holiness, or was. His office now is less. Formal."

"But, still . . ."

"My very handsome younger brother. Eight years my junior, but seems younger still. A certain cardinal is . . . fond of masculine beauty. And this pope is known for his generosity. Even when it comes to vices he does not share."

"Ah."

"Indeed."

Thomas laughed.

"So you drink the fruit of your brother's damnation?"

"Just the one barrel. I believe God has it within His heart to overlook my overlooking."

"You had only one barrel of this? Why drain it tonight?"

"Why not? The desire came on me suddenly. It's the last wine in town. I should have used it up at Mass, but there is neither wafer nor bread to go with it. I think the monks who made my wafer are all dead."

"Cistercians? Half a day from here?"

"Yes," the priest said hopefully.

"They're dead. A few may have fled."

"Ah," the priest said. His Adam's apple bobbed as he swallowed hard twice, and his eyes moistened. He nodded. He looked as if he wanted to reach out for Thomas's hand, but he didn't.

"Anyway, nobody comes now. I haven't even been in the church in two weeks. I'm as scared to go there as they are."

"If you don't go to church, how do you know they don't go looking for you?"

The priest looked down at his hands, where the fingers were grabbing each other.

"They know where I live. Some still come for confession; they shout their sins from the path and I shout back their penance from my window. Though even that's been nearly a week. No more Mass, in any event. And the wine may serve a holier purpose in your belly."

"Oh?"

"I was hoping a cup or two might extract some knightly oath from you. You are a knight? Or were?"

"I was. I still am, I suppose. But it feels more like I was. It feels like a long time ago."

"You could be one again."

"I doubt it. I have done things."

"Things?"

"I was cheated of my holdings."

"The English?"

Thomas shook his head.

"Worse. A Norman. Le Comte d'Évreux, who treated with the English after our loss at Crécy. My keep was near Givras. I . . . despaired of justice. I took to the road and lived by the strength of my arm. I sought out even worse men than myself. I wanted revenge on him. I still do."

Thomas fell silent.

"Do you want to make confession?"

"No."

"Not to me, eh?"

"I just don't want to."

"I wouldn't blame you if it was me."

"No, it's . . . No. There's no point."

"Kill the abomination in the river and God will make you a knight again."

"I'd rather He got me another goblet of this."

"No," the priest said. "You wouldn't rather a goblet of wine than your honor back. Your joking is pleasant, but it doesn't hide the hole in you."

Thomas turned his eyes away from the priest's warm gaze.

He only just managed not to cry. He did this by angering himself at God for making him suffer and pay for sins he had been backed into. God ringed you round with hounds and cornered you, then speared you with your back against a tree. When Thomas spoke, he turned down the corners of his mouth, and his words came out as a quiet growl.

"I'll kill the whoring thing."

FIVE

Of the Thing in the Murk

T homas slept poorly; the wine had given him a burning stomach, and when he slept he dreamed of wading in mucky water, looking for things he had dropped. He gave up at first light, still belching sour wine, and began to put his armor on.

"Christ, it tasted good going in."

He had slept in his filthy padded leather gambeson, as he had for months now, so he started right in putting on his armor, starting with his *cuisses*. He had finished buckling his second thigh piece when he stopped. The priest was sleeping heavily on his short bed with his knees drawn up and his ankles crossed. Thomas shook him awake. The smaller man looked frightened at first to see the large, strong shadow over him, but then he remembered he had a guest.

"Good morning," the priest said.

"How deep is the river?"

"The river?"

"Where your monster is. How deep? Thighs? Tits? Chin?"

"Well . . . chin. On me. At the deepest. Perhaps to your shoulders."

"Shit," Thomas said.

"You're really going to the river, then?"

"I said I would."

"What we say and what we do are . . ."

"Well, I do what I say. Which is why I don't say much."

Thomas stood for a moment, considering the heavy, rusty mail coat in his hands.

"You're wondering about your armor."

"Yes."

"You only half believe there's a monster in the river. And you don't want to drown looking for it."

"I know of men who have been pulled under by their armor. That's real. The thing you described? I don't know. It seemed possible last night that a monster might be eating men in your river, though I've never in my life seen a monster. So this morning . . . Can such a thing exist in sunlight? And yet it seems these are the end days, and I think Hell has opened its doors."

"I think that, too."

"Spines, the boy said?"

"Spines."

Thomas considered the priest's soft hands and kind, almost comical face, what with his wild gray eyebrows and long head. He didn't seem sick, though he was likely a bugger; not that Thomas had known many of the latter.

"Help me with the rest of this."

The priest stood and helped Thomas wriggle into his mail shirt and buckle on his shoulder pieces.

"You should scour all that," the priest said, smiling and showing Thomas his orange hands.

"Later. If your big eel eats me and shits me by the river, it should have rust for its spice."

"What, saffron? It's nearly that color."

"Who can afford saffron? Mix it with blood and we'll have paprika."

The priest laughed.

Thomas put his surcoat on over everything; it was filthy and blue and had no coat of arms on it.

"Now get me your sword; you'll want me to bless that."

"Where is my sword?"

He had propped it against the wall, but now it was gone. As was the girl. Thomas banged the door open and went outside, where the sun was now rising, peering tentatively under a scud of clouds that would soon swallow it. He saw the girl sitting by a tree with his sword unsheathed next to her. She had blood on her gown. He stomped over to her, took the sword up with one hand, and yanked her up by the arm with the other.

"Jesus whoring Christ," he said, looking at the cut on the meat of her hand. It was half the length of her smallest finger and not very deep, but it was still bleeding. "Do I have to watch you every second? Can't I just sleep without you doing something stupid?"

"I'm sorry," she said meekly.

"What was your idea, touching my sword? Nobody touches my sword but me."

"I ... I wanted to clean it for you."

"Well, don't! This is what you get."

He bent her arm around hurtfully to show her dripping hand to her.

"I want to help."

"You bleeding all over my things doesn't help me, you, or anybody. Understand?"

She nodded, trying not to cry, and he noticed he was still holding her wrist, which suddenly looked very small and fragile in his big hand. He let it go. She wanted to rub it, but she was embarrassed and hid it behind her instead, looking up at him. He was about to bark, *What do you want now?* at her, but he thought about it and saw that she was hoping to get some kind word from him. He fished around in his head for one.

"Go ... go see the priest," he said, as gently as he could. "He may have a cloth to bind that little cut. And put some yarrow in it, since you know what that is."

She obeyed him.

He picked up his sword and saw that her blood was smeared on its point and the well-notched edge that had bitten her.

"Clumsy little witch," he said.

It got darker.

A drop of rain fell in Thomas's eye.

The priest went with Thomas, wearing his chasuble and a threadbare golden stole, holding the crosier over his head while the girl walked beside them swinging a censer with frankincense and rosemary in it. At the priest's suggestion, Thomas held his sword by the blade, inverted so the quillons made a cross of it. The rain was light now, little more than a mist, but the road was muddy enough to coat the soldier's boots and the priest's simple shoes. The girl had left her shoes behind because she felt God liked bare feet better than shoes for holy work.

Two men from town came with them; one a skinny, heavily bearded young man with an ancient boar spear; the other a fat, blond farmer with blond porcine bristles on his jowls, armed with a billhook for hedges. Both wore straw hats. The smaller one looked scared, as did the priest. They had both been to the river to see the thing's signs. But not the farmer. The farmer was piss drunk. Thomas reminded himself to stay well away from him if a fight started, because he was stout and thick-armed and likely to gut friend and foe alike. Among the bitterer lessons of brigandage Thomas had learned was that farmers were strong, often stronger than the horsemen who despised them, and that they lived so close to starvation that they would fight like bears to hold on to what crumbs and bits of wood or leather they owned.

If the priest hoped their procession would draw fresh recruits from the houses they passed, he was disappointed. A few women peered at them from windows, all crossing themselves, and, on the outskirts of town, one bare-ribbed dog looked up at them briefly before going back to breakfast on the foot of a corpse leaned up against a sheep wall. The body had a flour sack over its head at least, but it had stained the sack and it stank even in the cool rain. Sheep's bones littered the field past the wall—sheep had fared as poorly as men in this scourge—and the seigneur's keep came into view around a stand of alder trees.

The pilgrims marched up to the gate, where Thomas pulled a leather cord that rang a bell up on the battlements. He waited the time it took the swaying, fat farmer to piss against the wall—the priest admonished him with his name, Sanson, but was waved away with the man's free hand—and then Thomas rang the bell again. After a third tug on the cord, a very pale young man with plucked and redrawn eyebrows looked down at them from the wall. He held a crimson woolen cloak squared over his head, presumably to protect fine clothes they couldn't see from their angle.

"If you're not here to buy grain, then go your ways," he said.

"Good herald," the priest said, "Please let us speak to Guillaume."

"Guillaume has fallen. I am seneschal now. You may speak to me."

"Then I will say a Mass for Guillaume, and rejoice in your good fortune. We have not come here to buy grain, which you know we cannot afford, or to rent your mill, for we have nothing to grind, or your oven, for we have nothing to bake. Rather, we offer your master the chance to win God's love in battle."

"Go away," he said simply, and disappeared.

Thomas felt his anger rise.

"HERALD!" he shouted, making the beardy man near him flinch.

No answer came from above.

"Whoreson ass-sniffing HERALD!"

The herald reappeared.

"Who has the insolence to speak that way to me? When

you speak to me, you speak directly to my lord!"

"Then tell your lord to get his little prick out of his wife and help us kill the thing in the river."

"You common bastard!" the herald yelled. "I'll have you know we still have men-at-arms in here."

"Then tell them to stop husbanding their hands and come down to the river. Something is killing your people."

"It's called the plague, you idiot," the herald said, more quietly, and disappeared again. Thomas's worst insults didn't bring him back this time. So he grabbed the cord and yanked with all his might, grinning at the sound of the bell coming loose and clanging down stone steps somewhere above them.

The five of them gasped at what they saw. Tracks in the muddy bank, like a snake would make, but much larger, had beaten under all the grass close to the river, and crisscrossed and looped between here and the town. It was visiting the town now. The piles of foul shit the priest had described were still there, full of bones and clothes. A woman's severed leg lay white but mud-spattered just by the bank. This was nothing less than a visitation from Hell. The priest, quite pale now, began to pray psalms in Latin, and he urged the girl to swing the censer, which she did. The man with the big beard started shaking. Thomas said, quietly "Priest. If it goes badly for us, run like a young man, and take the girl. She'll try to stay, but don't let her." The priest never stopped praying, but nodded, which Thomas didn't see because he kept his eyes fixed on the milky gray waters of the river.

The former knight went forward at a crouch, with his sword at the ready. The stout, drunk farmer with the billhook came next, and the beardy one barely walked forward at all, staying close to the priest and the girl. Thomas was as taut as wire.

Step.

Step.

Step.

He froze when something moved in the water near the pilings of the collapsed bridge, something like an oily black arm, but the width of a draft horse's chest. He wasn't entirely sure he had seen it.

Then all of them said some variant of "My God" when its head broke the water's surface.

White-eyed and flat-headed, like some giant cross between eel, newt, and frog, it laid its head on the bank and felt around with long whiskers around its mouth and eyes until it found the woman's leg. Its tongue darted out and latched onto the leg with a thatch of evil little hooks at its tip, pulling it under the water with it, bending a growth of sweetflag rushes. They sprang back up. The water foamed and then flowed gently again, as if none of it had happened.

Those white eyes, a grandfather's blind eyes.

The small, beardy man dropped his boar spear and ran so fast his hat blew off him.

The stout one stood openmouthed, then vomited. But he didn't run. Rather, he followed Thomas right up to the edge of the water, which flowed gently now and showed no sign of the thing.

"Please, sir knight. Please protect me in this fray."

"Wipe your chin," Thomas said.

Now what?

He was so heavily armored he dared not go far into the water, but, when his slapping the water with the flat of his blade and his shouts of "Ho! Ho, there! Bring your foul ass out of the water and fight me!" failed to rouse it, he ventured first one leg and then the other into the softly flowing murk. The big farmer stood near him, wide-eyed, shocked sober, his arms so tense the end of the billhook quivered.

"Hand me that boar spear," Thomas said. The farmer did as he was told, fetching and handing over the wickedly pointed spear. Thomas put his sword in his left hand and began to use the spear to probe the water in front of him. He jabbed at it viciously, hoping to goad the thing into surfacing. It didn't.

Thomas went a little farther in.

He looked at the burned pilings, wondering if it nested down there, curling itself around them. Perhaps he should wade over there—he could use them to help him keep his head above water.

The wind blew harder, and the rain came now, threatening to snuff the girl's censer, which she still swung dutifully. The priest's Latin prayers were harder to hear.

Thomas alternated between stabbing the water with the spear and slapping it with the sword's flat, until it seemed to him that he was wasting his time.

"What, you only kill mules and fishermen? You only take the legs off fishwives? Come and get me! Me!" he said, his voice cracking a little. Rain poured into his armor and down his face, making him blink. Relief that the thing didn't want to fight him blended with shame at that relief, but then relief won out. Perhaps a few more stabs at the base of the pilings and then he could say he'd done his best. He slapped the surface of the river halfheartedly again, then began backing out of the mucky water.

And tripped.

He put his booted heel down on a submerged log in the mud behind him; the log slithered out from under his foot at great speed, causing him to fall into the river and hurl the sword behind him. He thrashed in the water and sputtered, getting to one knee with difficulty, cocking his spear arm.

Part of the thing coiled through the water in front of him.

He lunged at it with the spear, twisting his body into it with the brutality that hours in the tiltyard had made as natural for him as walking. The spear stuck deep; that lunge would have impaled one man and killed the man behind him, but this was no man. The thing coiled rapidly away from him, wrenching the spear from his grip. He stood up with great effort, the sodden chain mail trying to drag him under, and launched himself toward where the sword had fallen.

He saw that the girl was looking for it, too, up to her thighs in dirty water, her little limbs white against the river and darker sky. She bent down fully into the water now, her face submerged as though she were hunting turtles. He tried to yell *Get back!* at her but could only cough, so he reached into the water, grabbed a fistful of her blond hair, and jerked her up and toward the bank. She had the sword by the blade, getting cut again as she fell and dropped it. He saw where it fell, though, and saw her clambering through the mud and up to the bank. The priest was running to fetch her. Thomas grabbed the sword and wheeled around to the river, sensing he had had his back to it for far too long a fall of seconds.

"Watch! Watch!" the priest was yelling over the rain.

He turned to see the thing slithering toward him just under the water, its flat, froggy head as big as two tournament shields, its obscene whiskers trailing behind it, the spear making an S pattern in the water where it was still stuck in the thick of it. It was easily twenty paces long, the water rolling over it hypnotic, almost beautiful.

Its head broke the surface now and its whiskers flicked forward and whipped him. Thomas heard splashing to his right but ignored that, keeping his eye on the monster and bringing his sword up. It opened its mouth wider than it should have been able to, showing its sickly white inside and rows of teeth the length of long fingers. Thick, clear liquid poured from it. It coiled its body up behind its open mouth in preparation for the strike as Thomas readied himself to die plunging his sword down its throat. Something flashed at the edge of Thomas's vision, and he saw the billhook come down with great force on the side of the thing's head, opening up a white, blubbery wound in it and making it hiss. The billhook fell again and again; the farmer was going at it like he was hacking down a tree, his red mouth pursed with the effort. Thomas struck it with his sword now, cleaving a horrible wound into its nose and mouth, from which it recoiled, doubling back on itself under the water with a great splash.

Once it was out of reach, it broke the surface again, rearing up to show its white belly, on which pairs of backward-facing, curved, black spines the size of paring knives were arrayed like teats. It hissed at them and the spines flexed and oozed black fluid all over its belly. It had oily fins on the sides of its neck ending in more spines. Now its tail rose up out of the water, and the farmer crossed himself and whimpered. The tail had a human hand at the end of it. So white it was nearly translucent, bright against the black sky.

A fucking hand!

The tail slithered forward now, and the hand groped the side of the thing until it found the spear stuck in it, which it pulled out. Thunder grumbled behind it.

The farmer started whimpering an *Ave Maria*, and it cocked its head, listening, its whiskers whipping excitedly. Thomas banged his fist heavily on the stout man's shoulder to shut him up, but he only prayed louder. Without warning, a ripple went through the thing and the end of its tail lashed like the end of a whip. The hand released the boar spear and it flew at the farmer as though it had been shot from an arbalest. It would have skewered him right through his praying mouth had not Thomas shoved him. As it was, it laid open his cheek and his temple and he screamed horribly.

Then the creature did the worst thing Thomas had seen yet; *it opened its mouth and exactly imitated the farmer's scream.*

It moved toward the men again. The farmer just kept screaming, even as it mocked him, holding his hand against his head where the blood ran out thin and fast in the rain.

Thomas had never been so afraid. *I can't I can't I can't*, he thought, even as he drove his legs forward through the muck to meet it. Thomas swung hard at its head, but he only hit it a glancing blow as it lunged past him and grabbed the screaming farmer, cutting off his screams as it took the man's head and shoulders into its mouth with a violent, wet slapping sound. It contracted the muscles in its neck now and lifted the heavy farmer out of the water, pointing his kicking feet at the sky and trying to swallow him in repeated gulps, *BAMF, BAMF, BAMF*, like a pelican taking a big fish.

Thomas saw the end of the farmer's billhook sticking out of the water. He sheathed his sword so not to lose it, then sloshed over to grab the pole arm. The thing was having trouble getting the farmer down. Thomas slashed at it with all his considerable strength, gouging tears in it that would have gutted an ox. One of these, driven high, opened a hole near the lump the thing was trying to swallow, and Thomas was treated to the sight of the farmer's white face turning as he went farther into its gullet. It could no longer ignore the strong man tearing at it, though, so it turned its blind face toward him, the other man's feet sticking out of its mouth. It lashed its whiskers at Thomas to find him, then slithered the tail-hand up around his leg. It dropped its head and neck into the water now and slithered more of its coils around the nuisance who had been chopping at it. It foamed the water with its spasms as it continued trying to swallow its meal, but now its back half was free to fight.

Thomas dug at it underwater with the point of his weapon, gouging it so its oily blood floated up, but then the awful white hand was on his face, grabbing his cheek excruciatingly, digging for his eyes. He wrenched his head back and forth, then drove the weapon into the riverbed so he could find the shaft again. He was not strong enough to pull the hand away from his face, however, and he felt something sharp scrape his *cuisse* as the thing constricted around his leg.

"*Whoring spines*," he squealed crazily, standing wide and struggling to keep his footing, now jerking the hand's thumb back as he would to break a man's grip. With the other hand he found the knife on his belt and began to saw where the hand joined the tail. His knife bit deep, and it withdrew the hand to save it, then jerked, pulling Thomas underwater.

He felt sure he would die now, but he didn't give up.

He wrestled and arched, and managed to get half his sword free, though it was no easy task with the black coils around his legs and those evil spines scraping his chain mail, and he bent into a coil of it and started using his weight behind the half-exposed blade to cut. It thrashed, jerking him around madly on the muddy bottom, though his head broke the water and he managed to get a breath in him. His sword came out of its scabbard and he held on to it for his life. It was then that one of the spines on the bottom of it found purchase and punched through his armor at the groin, where a few snapped links of chain he had meant to have mended allowed a small opening. It was enough. He ground his teeth together against the pain and nearly lost the last of his air, but instead drove his sword into it hard, causing it to release him entirely. He broke the surface of the water and got heavily to his feet just as the thing's head came up, its first meal now down nearer the middle of it, but it was Thomas who moved first, lunging at its neck.

He got there before it could face him and leaned into his sword, driving it through the monster, and driving the monster down until he felt his point bite rock on the other side. He pulled the sword half out and changed the angle, leaning into it again and using the strength of his legs against the river bottom to push like a plowman and slit a huge gash in it, through which black, stinking fluid now poured. It thrashed violently, but Thomas held on even though the world was beginning to get dark. He summoned what felt like the last of his strength and pushed the sword toward where he hoped a heart was.

It punched through something. The thing shuddered and turned on him now and bit him, taking his head and neck into its mouth as it had done with the peasant, but, though the pressure on his chest was terrible, its strength was ebbing and its teeth did not pierce his chain. Thomas screamed hoarsely in the darkness of its mouth, and then couldn't scream anymore as it took him underwater. Water and foul issue flooded its mouth and Thomas began to black out. Then it shuddered again and vomited Thomas into the river, along with the dead farmer, someone's head, the woman's leg, and any number of eels.

Thomas fought to keep his head above water, praying the priest would haul him out. But he was alone and dying, with his armor heavy on him in the river. He would have to save himself. He heard it thrashing, and then the thrashing stopped. He thought it was dead but didn't think he had the strength both to turn and look at it and to keep from falling into the water. He hauled himself to the shallow part and nearly collapsed, but he knew he would still drown if he did. So, with his leg going numb from the thing's spine in his groin, and the river and black sky seeming to spin around him as if he were a bead in a toy top, he crawled through the mud on his three good limbs until his face was far enough out of the water so he knew he would not breathe any in.

His legs were still in the water. If it wasn't dead, it would drag him under. But he didn't care now.

Something was banging on his armor and his helmet.

Hail.

It was hailing.

So this is the end of the world, he thought, feeling nauseated, hoping to pass out.

And he passed out.

SIX

*Of the Marriage on the Bank and the Visitation
in the Stable*

The woman stumbled down the muddy road, trying to remember how to get to the river. She had lived in St. Martin-le-Preux her whole life, but the fever made her forgetful and she kept losing her way. The hail had woken her up from what might have been her last sleep, and when she woke she had such thirst that only the river could slake it. Besides, a devil was in her house. Not the Devil himself, but a small one. A goat kid with a twitching tail that climbed on the bed with her and tried to steal her breath when she got sleepy. It leapt away when she woke, and hid in the shadows, waiting for her to get sleepy again. She would cheat it this time; she knew it wouldn't follow her to the river. She went out into the hail and took a beating from it, but it stopped soon and turned to cold, stinging rain.

She got terribly lost even though she knew the river was close, and she slapped her palm on several doors, some of them doors she recognized as belonging to friends, but nobody opened to her. She cried against the wall at one house and a gentle voice from inside, her sister's voice, said "Go on, now, Mathilde. I still have the two children and you mustn't give it to them. Go on." So on she went. Her children had died of it, and her sweet, old husband, and his brother, and she was the last one in the house. She had paid a young boy to care for her when she knew she had it, but he had left after one day. All he did was bring her things she asked for; but he refused to empty her slop jar and still he wanted a week's farm wages for the first day. She paid him, but he saw where she got the money from and took the coffer in the night, leaving her with nothing. The boy had worked with her husband. Learning to be a cobbler. Now he had his master's money, but little good it would do him in Hell; he was already sweating with the first fevers. It was after he left that the little goat had come.

The woman had no wimple on and her pale orange hair hung greasily about her shoulders. Her eyes were red and swollen. Windows closed as she passed them, and it began to make her angry. She wanted to stop and have words with the betrayers who were abandoning her, but her throat hurt like it had pins in it, and if it came to a fray, she didn't want anyone touching her left armpit, which had grown a painful swelling the size of a crabapple that gurgled at night and seemed to speak to her.

She had to get to the river.

At length, she remembered a turn between two houses that she had passed several times, and she stumbled downhill, laughing and crying at the same time at the sight of the water. She didn't care if the water was clean as long as it was cold. She would wade into it and might even put her head under to stop the heat in it.

That was when she saw the knight, lying on his stomach with his feet in the river. She knelt next to him and drank, coughing half of it back up; something foul was in it. Foul and oily. But her throat felt better.

She looked at the knight and saw that he was strong and beautiful, and dead. She cried for how beautiful he was. Even his scars were beautiful and perfect, the pit on his cheek where God had put His finger to mark him as holy. She lay down next to him on her side and took off his helmet. He still wore a chain hood, but she could see his hard, beautiful face better now. Her husband's wedding ring was on a cord around her neck, and she took this off, and breathed on it, and pushed it onto the knight's finger, though it wouldn't pass the second knuckle because his were soldier's hands.

"I marry you," she said, "I marry you now, knight."

She cried and kissed his still mouth, tenderly at first, then with her tongue. His mouth was warm. He was breathing. She became confused about whether he was dead. Perhaps not, but, like her, he would be soon. Everyone would be soon. She used her hair to clean his brow, and she stroked his face with her hand.

"My husband is in Heaven with his first wife, but I will go to Heaven, too, and you will be my husband there. And I will be a good wife. I will show you. I will dress for bed," she said, and took off her sickness-stained gown and one of her muddy hose. She got tired unrolling the second one and draped herself across the knight's armored back and died there.

And that was how the priest found the armored man and the pale, dead woman, nude but for one stocking, her back covered in plague tokens the color of eggplant, as if a little goat had danced upon her and bruised her with its hooves.

"Where am I?" Thomas shouted from the bed, his eyes wild.

"You're in my home," the priest said, looking down at him. "You've been hurt."

The priest was holding a lantern near his nose and mouth. It was night.

Thomas began to remember. The creatures in his dream had not been friendly, so he took a moment trying to remember if this priest was. Frogs. Now he remembered. Frogs had come, latching onto him, feeding on him, covering his face and hands. He had been watching from outside himself as spiny little frogs ate him. He shuddered, then kept shuddering. The pains in his head and in the corner of his groin were distinct: one was leaden and dull, like an old rusty lock set at the top of his neck, and embraced his temples; the other was hot like someone had taken a coal from a brazier and tucked it at the top of his pubis. Everything on him felt clammy and sticky. He sneezed.

He looked up at the priest again and saw the half of his face that was brightly lit by the lantern he held close to it. Three superficial scratches jagged across his cheek.

"What have you done with her?" Thomas said, and sat up heavily, looking at the priest with dangerous, murky eyes.

"Nothing, friend. She's . . . oh, the scratches. She gave me those when I pulled her away from you. On the shore. Really, I was pulling her away from the . . . There was a . . . a young wife, Mathilde. A good woman. With Christ now, if any of us are. You may be sick."

"Where is the girl?"

"I persuaded her to sleep in the stables tonight, but she will come back when she wakes up. She sat on that little stool near you until an hour ago. She's quite faithful."

Thomas looked under the threadbare sheet that covered him and saw what the thing in the river had done to him; an awful hole a few inches above the base of his *verge* wept into the hair there. All the skin around it was swollen, and a separate swelling was coming in near it, where the leg met the groin. The whole area was a misery.

"So I have some uncleanness in me from that thing, as well as plague."

"It seems so."

"Did you give me last rites?"

"Three hours ago."

"I'll try not to sin."

"You're in no condition to sin, except perhaps unclean thoughts."

"Not having any. Hurts too much down there."

"You're safe from lust, at least. Having any temptations about gluttony?"

Thomas shook his head.

"And it's hardly sloth for a sick man to rest. Don't worry. I'll look after your soul. As for the body, that's in God's hands."

Thomas nodded.

"You killed it, you know."

Thomas made a pleased sound and his lids got heavy.

"It floated downriver like an old empty sock, leaving its awful guts behind it. It was an awful, murderous thing, and you killed it with your own hand. It was worthy of a saint."

Thomas slept.

He woke up again just before dawn, to the sound of labored breathing. Not his own. Someone was suffering, trying to breathe with pierced lungs. He hadn't heard that sound since the catastrophe at Crécy, when he lay with a broken leg and an arrow through his face, listening to his seigneur breathe his last breaths, sucking bloody air in around the ashwood arrows that had punched through his chain hauberk in three places. He always loved his lord for not moaning, as other men did. As Thomas did. He knew in his heart that his lord, the Comte de Givras, had died awake, gritting his teeth, using his last strength to keep from making an unchivalrous noise. The comte was not as strong in the arms as Thomas, almost nobody was, but he was tougher. He died a better death than Thomas was about to, fouling his sick-sheets in bed.

But now that horrible breathing.

Outside his window.

A shadow passed.

He got to his feet and found that the right leg was completely numb, as if it had fallen asleep, and it was all he could do not to crash to the floor. He was sick and dizzy and his nose was running into his beard, but he got his sword and moved past the sleeping priest. He opened the door in time to see the form of a man limping toward the stables.

Where the girl was.

"You!" he said, but coughed at the end of it.

The figure didn't turn.

Thomas tried to run at it, but now his woodish leg betrayed him and tumbled him onto the ground, where he blacked out. He came to not very long after, and went farther toward the stables, where he saw the girl and the figure talking over a lantern. His eyes were tearing, and he couldn't see well, but it looked like a man. A shirtless man with long spines. Thomas lurched toward the couple, but the world spun again and he went out.

He woke again moments later, or thought he did, to find the spined man helping him into bed. Except the man was bleeding all over the bed and laboring to breathe, because he was full of arrows, not spines.

"Seigneur!" Thomas tried to say, but it wasn't his lord.

He didn't recognize the man, a short dark-haired youth with protuberant, drilling eyes that looked almost luminous.

The man exhaled a shuddering breath, spraying a small amount of froth from his chest wounds, then pressed hard with his thumb on Thomas's forehead, forcing him to fully recline. It hurt. The man wheezed and coughed horribly and limped out of the room.

Thomas still felt the imprint of that hard thumb.

He slept.

But not before he muttered, *"Sebastian. Saint Sebastian, help me."*

SEVEN

Of the Battle of Song-of-Angels

I n the morning, the girl told the priest that the three of them were going to the shrine of the Virgin of the White Rock, ten miles north. She was granting miracles to some, and she would rid Thomas of the plague.

"But, child," the priest said, "This man cannot travel. And the bishop heard rumors of this shrine many years ago, and visited it and declared that, while it was a holy place and Christians should pray there, they should expect no miracles."

A saint had told her. She bit her lip, wondering if she should let them know one spoke to her. It seemed better to keep that secret.

"A higher power than the bishop says the shrine is healing people. And we can take the knight upon a cart."

"If I had a cart."

"Go to the almond orchard and pray. God will show you a way."

"No," the priest said forcefully, "We must stay here. If God wants our friend to live, He will bestow that grace upon him wherever he is."

Her insides fluttered as though a small bird were near her heart. Words came to her. She closed her eyes and said them.

"Matthieu Hanicotte," she said, calling the priest by his

true name, which he had never told her, "you say these words because you fear to leave your little home. But I turn your words upon you; if Death means to take you, he may do it here as easily as on the road. He is already in this house."

A chill passed through the priest, and he said meekly, "Watch over our friend. I am going to the orchard."

The dead man's cart was in good repair, and the three of them were soon upon the road to Rochelle-la-Blanche, a hill village where granite was quarried. The priest drove the fine cart, while Thomas lay feverish in the back of it. The girl held a cross over him with one hand and lay her other hand upon his burning chest. The priest was certain she was a saint. He had no other way to explain his discovery in the orchard.

The cart's owner had broken his neck trying to stand on the wheel of the cart and beat the last almonds from a high branch. The body was still warm when the priest found him. A chill had gone through Matthieu Hanicotte, and for a moment he had wondered if the girl was diabolic in nature. He thought not. Then he had a moment to wonder whether God had slain this man to provide them a cart, or if He had merely directed Matthieu to the scene of this sad event, already foreordained. What was the difference? Everything served God's will, and here, at last, after months of senseless deaths and unending tears, was a tragedy that bore some fruit. The priest had blessed the man, then cried and thanked God for at last revealing His face to him. For all those thanks, however, the mule was stubborn, and it had taken the priest nearly half an hour to get it moving.

But now the mule was happy to pull.

As they got closer, they passed others bearing the sick and dying to Rochelle-la-Blanche.

It was midday when they saw the town.

And the mob that was heading there.

Nearly thirty peasants, mostly men, were marching on

the town, several of them pulling a small, empty cart by hand. They were all armed. When they noticed the priest's cart coming up behind them, they turned.

"A mule!" one shouted.

"Get the mule!" said a woman with a two-pronged wooden pitchfork.

"It's a priest," another said.

"Fuck him, we have a priest, too. And we need that mule," said a man in gaudy yellow stockings.

Père Matthieu felt a shock of ice in his heart, and he nearly froze with fear. The knight could have made the mob think twice, but he was dying. Then an idea came to Matthieu and he leapt to his feet, standing tall in the cart, and, though his knees shook, he kept his voice firm.

"He who wants the plague, come and take this mule. For plague is upon this man you see here. He who wants his soul in Hell, come and take this mule unlawfully from one of God's priests, and stop us on our pilgrimage."

This halted their frightening surge toward the cart.

Now the woman with the wooden fork said "Come with us, Father. Help us take the Virgin back."

"What?" said the priest. He now noticed a stocky, cow-eyed priest among the farmers; he was holding a pewter candlestick like a club, and he seemed abashed to have encountered another of his sort. He shook this off and spoke.

"Yes, brother. We're taking our Virgin back. She was stolen from our village, Chanson-des-Anges, by those bastards of Rochelle-la-Blanche during the Great Hunger of '17. Since then God has smiled upon them and pissed upon us for not defending her. Help us in our rightful suit."

"Shame on you, brother," Père Matthieu said.

The girl stood now, wide-eyed, and said, "You've got devils with you. Right now, with you."

"In your hearts!" Père Matthieu said quickly, suddenly scared this mob might decide she was a witch. "For the devil is in any heart that moves a man to hurt his neighbor. Yet will he leave you in peace if you will put your weapons down and turn from your sin. This is your last chance."

"You're not from here," the club-wielding priest said viciously and suddenly, as if the words weren't his, and began toward the cart. The girl's gaze stopped him.

"I see it," she said quietly. "I know what's at your elbow."

It was the cutting of a marionette. The stocky priest began to cry then, blubbering incoherently. The woman with the fork came now and grabbed him by the shoulder.

"To Hell with them," she said. "Let's get Our Lady back. Chanson-des-Anges!" she said. The crowd echoed her cry, and they lurched toward the village, pulling the weeping priest with them.

Even though it took place at Rochelle-la-Blanche, the battle would henceforth be known as the battle of Chanson-des-Anges, because the attackers shouted that again and again. They shouted it as they waded into and pushed aside the crowd of sick and penitent pilgrims that surrounded the statue. They shouted it as they broke the arm of the priest of Rochelle-la-Blanche, who threw himself in front of his Blessed Lady to defend her. They shouted it as they broke the pretty, white-stone statue from its nook in the white rock beside the church, leaving a piece of her foot. They shouted it at the group of men who began to form in the market square nearby, now six, now a dozen, shouting and pointing and summoning others.

Then one in the Chanson mob said, "Do not let them gather!"

Nobody was sure who said it, because only the girl could see the foul thing that spoke those words.

A stone flew. Then a brick. Someone shot an arrow. Then the invading mob rushed at the outnumbered men in the square, and a horrible melee began. The Rochelle townsmen scattered, but more were coming. The Virgin must have been working true miracles here. More healthy men were gathering than the priest or the girl had seen in one place since the sickness first came. Now a hunchback in a blacksmith's apron ran toward the Rochelle men, dragging a box, from which they began to pull swords, axes, and hammers.

"Defend the Lady!" someone said, and the Chanson-des-Anges mob fell back toward their cart, where the Virgin of the White Rock lay awkwardly on her side, and formed a ring about it. The men of Rochelle surrounded them. They were reluctant to start killing, but then someone in the square held up the body of a little blond boy whose head had been busted by a brick.

"Perrin!" one screamed. "They killed little Perrin!"

The twenty or so defending the cart screamed defiantly "Chanson-des-Anges, Chanson-des-Anges," as if daring the thirty well-armed farmers, tradesmen, and granite workers to slaughter them.

They took the dare. The two groups bludgeoned, stabbed, cut, and gouged each other while dust flew and screams rang out. When, at last, the people of Chanson were nearly overcome, the woman with the fork dropped it and picked up a fallen hammer, jumping up into the cart with the Virgin.

"If we won't have her, you won't either! Fuck her," she said, and smashed the Virgin's arm from her body.

Back in Père Matthieu's cart, the girl screamed.

The fighting stopped and everyone watched, stunned.

"Fuck her! Fuck her!" the woman screamed, wide-eyed.

The hammer fell again and the Virgin's nose was busted.

Two more strokes and the statue, once so beautiful that men wept to see her, was nothing but rocks. White dust covered the Chanson woman's face.

Something laughed, but only the girl saw what.

"Death!" screamed a Rochelle man.

And Death answered his summons.

None from Chanson-des-Anges was left alive.

The last one, the cow-eyed priest, was killed with the

same brick that killed the little boy.

Afterward, the survivors took the wounded off and the people of Rochelle-la-Blanche cleared as far away from the killing field as they could. The girl tore herself away from Père Matthieu and walked through the twisted bodies, toward the ruin of the Virgin of the White Rock. She was shaking and weeping, looking far smaller and younger than she had. She bent near the cart and picked up the statue's arm, hugging it to her.

The priest helped her up into his cart now, where Thomas lay very still, breathing his last. He had the impression that something with a cold, fishy mouth was tugging at him. His bladder loosed and he breathed out, his chest rattling. He did not inhale.

The girl took the Virgin's hand and forearm up and pressed the two stone fingers, held out in benediction, against the knight's forehead, just where he had felt St. Sebastian's thumb the night before.

She pressed hard.

The thing with the fishy mouth left.

Thomas gasped and opened his eyes.

And then he slept.

Thomas woke up and thought something was horribly wrong. A dream in which his mother wove at her loom and sung a *chanson de toile* about a common woman who loved a great seigneur dissolved; now an angel was rubbing his head with a cool cloth; he had died, he was sure of that, but under no circumstances should he be in Heaven.

He turned his eyes to look at the angel, and saw that it was only the girl. Her very gray eyes were on him, waiting to see if he would speak.

"I died," he said.

"Almost."

"You . . . saved me?"

"God did. With the hand of the Virgin. It was her last miracle."

Thomas coughed, but less horribly than he had before the end.

"I stink," he said.

The priest, who was near the hearth, said, "Not like you did. What's stinking now is just the bedstraw. Some of your sickness went into that, I think. One thing you never get used to is the way the sick ones smell. As if we needed any further proof this curse fell from the heavens to show us how corrupt we are." He went back to stirring the pot on the fire.

"What's there to eat?" Thomas said.

"Oh, he has an appetite, there's a hopeful sign. Of course, having received last rites and lived, you're supposed to fast perpetually now. And go barefoot. And remain chaste."

Thomas grunted.

"But I won't tell anyone if you won't. 'What's to eat?' he says. Nothing but the worst soup in Christendom; grasses, flowers, twigs, some fungus from the sides of trees, a blighted radish, and, the best of all, four baby birds I broke free from their eggs. I was hoping just to get the yolks and whites, but the chicks were nearly ready to enter this sad world. Now they're in soup. You'll have to eat one, bones and all."

"I've had worse."

"Well, I haven't. I'm just a soft priest in a cozy village. Or was. At least there's a little salt. I spared a pinch of salt so we could choke the rest down."

The girl changed the water in Thomas's cloth and rubbed his temples again. It was so cool and so good. He closed his eyes and breathed a long, contented sigh. This was the best he had felt since . . . since something awful happened. What? Something in a river.

"What I can't stop thinking about," the priest went on, "is wine. I never thought it would just run out. I thought men would always make wine, as bees make honey and cows make milk. That I would one day find nobody, not one person, with a skin or cask or pitcher of wine to sell, had never occurred to me."

"I pray for you, Père Matthieu," the girl said.

"That I'll find good wine?"

"That God will fill you so full with His love that you will not need wine."

"That's a fine prayer, girl. But, if it's no trouble, ask the Lord to send me a little wine along with His love. I promise to be grateful for both."

Thomas got better slowly, but more quickly than any of those few the priest had seen survive the plague. He took walks in the priest's yard, slurped bad soup, cracked the few stray almonds left in the cart, and savored the last of the girl's honey.

By the end of August the girl was asking if he felt well enough to travel.

"Let me guess. Paris, then Avignon."

"Yes."

"For mysterious reasons that will come to you later."

"Yes."

"It must have to do with the pope."

"I don't know."

"Because the pope lives there."

"And you lived in Picardy. Was everyone who came to Picardy coming to see you?"

Thomas furrowed his brow.

"Hey, priest. Is this little girl a witch or a saint?"

"A saint, I think," Père Matthieu said.

"But you're not sure."

"No, actually, I'm not."

"Would you like to go to Paris with us?"

"No."

"So you'll stay here, then."

"No."

"Which is it?"

"I'll go to Paris. You asked me if I would *like* to go to Paris. I would not. But I'm out of food, wine, and parishioners. So, like it or not, I have to leave my pleasant little house. If she's a saint, this is a holy pilgrimage. If she's a witch, I might try to mitigate her wickedness."

They left on the first day of September.

On the third of September, against the wishes of his wife, the seigneur of St. Martin-le-Preux at last gave in to the yapping of his herald and seneschal, who claimed the priest was harboring a coarse man who had insulted the lord's honor and broken his bell, as well as having provoked the foulness in the river to kill numerous peasants, on one of whom it seemed to have choked and burst itself.

The lord reluctantly sent his last three men-at-arms down to search the priest's house, but they found that the priest had left. Knowing the priest's brother to be a servant in the house of His Holiness in Avignon, the men searched the house for treasures Père Matthieu might have left behind. One of them poked in the dirt of the yard with his pole-arm. One went through his trunk, his pot, and his few tools.

The other turned up the straw of the bed.

The next day, this man had a fever.

Four days later, everyone in the castle was dead.

The new seneschal was last, crying at his own image in a polished piece of brass, trying with a shaking hand to paint fine eyebrows on the ruin he had become.

EIGHT

Of the Feast, and of the Night Tourney

T he castle was deceptive in its proximity; it floated on its pale green hill for the last half of the day, seeming as distant as a celestial body, and then at dusk it was upon them, with its proud white walls and turrets. The banners of the seigneur flew from the square keep, and men walked at ease atop the gatehouse, where the drawbridge was down in welcome. Perhaps the plague had spared this place.

"Let's stop here and see if we can get a meal," Thomas said.

"I have to get to Paris," said the girl.

"And still you won't say why."

"I don't know yet."

"I counter what you don't know with what I do know. We are hungry, and being fed is better than being hungry."

"Not always," she said.

"Yes, always," said Thomas.

The priest said, "I don't see what's wrong with fortifying ourselves, if they will share with us. I have a little coin."

The girl shook her head obstinately, but Thomas stopped the cart and looked for a long while at the strong castle, imagining where an attacker would place siege engines and try to dig tunnels if he came up against this toothy stone beast. The hill was steep, the ground was tough-boned, and the walls were well built and hung with wooden hoardings from which defenders could work all sorts of evil against attackers. The English would have the Devil's own time trying to get in there, if they came.

"Let's goooo," the girl whined, sounding less like a witch or a saint and more like a brat who needed the back of a hand.

"Shut up," Thomas said. "A rider's coming."

Just as the sun went down, a man on a delicate-looking Arab horse issued from the open gate, pluming dust behind him.

The priest smoothed his robes and held up his crosier. The girl knitted her brow. Thomas, seeing the splendid livery of the herald shining even in the failing light, suddenly remembered that he was in a cart, and felt ashamed. Carts were for peasants, not men-at-arms. He got out of it and stood, holding his hand up in salute.

The herald of this castle was every bit as sunny and pleasant as the one in St. Martin-le-Preux had been haughty and contemptuous. His voice broke out of him like birds from a copse of trees.

"Greetings to you, friends in God's love. Are you come to see the tourney? Or," he said, looking at Thomas, "to compete in it?"

"Neither, friend," said Thomas. "We are on our way to Paris."

"Paris? Have you heard no news from there?"

"No."

"Perhaps because nobody is coming out alive. The Scourge is carrying off three hundred a day there. Death reigns in that city, and there is no law. And there is no food."

"There is little food anywhere."

"Our tables are well kept."

"And the plague?"

"It has come and gone. We were touched, and then it sputtered and went out. Our seigneur has ordered us to be merry and gay, and to fear no strangers. And to make music. He has ordered fife, drum, and viol players to play at every hour, even through the night. He believes the sickness, like a dog, bites those who fear it."

"The dog I saw bites everyone and can't hear music."

"I can only speak for what has happened here, my lord. Many fell, but now none fall. And jolly music plays all the time."

"I am no lord."

"A pity. You might have broken a lance tonight. In the night tourney."

"I thought tournaments were forbidden by the king."

"The king's arm has grown short."

Thomas smiled, showing his white teeth. "I would like to see this tourney," he said.

"Can you ride?"

"I have no horse."

"But can you ride?"

"Well enough."

"We might find one for you. You look like a man who has spun a quintain or two, and, if the truth be told, we are not so well provisioned with knights that we will turn our noses up at any worthy horseman. Our lord has called for a tourney, and we shall make one as best we can. Will you fight?"

"No!" the girl said, and Thomas shot her a cold look.

"Yes," he said.

"Excellent! In that case, I have the privilege of inviting you to my lord's table this evening. Are you hungry?"

"God, yes," the priest said.

The girl would not go to the castle.

Thomas commanded, the priest entreated, and in the end she skittered up a tree.

"For Christ's sake," Thomas said. "Get down from there."

Nothing.

"We've been eating twigs and earwax for a week. Now we

have the chance to really fill our bellies, and you do this."

Nothing.

"Stop being headstrong and get in that cart! It's getting dark. Goddamn it, don't make me leave you out here. And don't think I won't."

Nothing.

"Suit yourself," Thomas said, and turned to follow the herald, who was politely waiting just out of earshot. The priest sat in the cart alone, torn between the two of them.

"Go with him, Père Matthieu," she said from her perch. He could see only her feet.

"But . . ."

"I'll be safe here."

"It's not safe."

"I'll be all right. I know how to sleep in a tree without falling out. Go. You want to."

"Yes."

"He needs you," she said, and disappeared farther up into the tree.

The priest nodded and drove the cart behind the herald's horse, upon which Thomas was now also mounted. The pale grass of the hillside was punctuated with thistles of the brightest purple, each flower of which seemed to have been issued exactly one bumblebee.

"Simon will show you to your chambers," the herald said, indicating a sullen but brightly liveried boy who met them once they were inside the portcullis.

"What is the name of this place?" Thomas said.

The herald smiled pleasantly, as if this were a joke.

"Supper will be in an hour."

The serving boy had spoken very little, but had ushered them to a small but cozy room with a real bed in it. The most he said to them at once was, "The sire invites you to go wherever you wish before supper."

Thomas, who had been grinning broadly ever since they slipped between the strong walls of the castle, nevertheless decided to strip his armor, stay in his chambers, and close his eyes so he might be fresh for the meal. The priest went off to explore.

Two men came and asked for Thomas's armor.

"The herald said you might want this cleaned?"

Thomas hesitated while the wary man he had been since Crécy struggled with the man he was before. The earlier man won out. Thomas handed over his gear and was given a handsome green robe with cloth-of-gold stars to wear to dinner. He hung it from a nail and lay down to sleep in his stinking long shirt.

The priest crawled into bed beside Thomas an hour later.

"What did you think?"

"A magnificent fortress, really! The tapestries! In the old style, but such colors. And such a mighty tower. I went atop the battlements and felt that, had it been daytime, I might have seen all the way to Avignon, and beyond. I tell you, I think I'll see the Afric shores tomorrow."

"You lie, priest."

"I embellish. But the height was astonishing. In the morning, I'll have to get the boy to take me to the chapel."

"I would have thought you'd go there first."

At this, Père Matthieu's face sank.

"I tried. I got confused in all the halls and couldn't find it."

The boy showed up just before the feast and shook them both awake from where they snored on the bed. They followed him to the Great Hall, which rang with the sounds of music and cheerful speech as they approached. Thomas felt ten years younger than he was, up on the balls of his feet with anticipation. The tangy, earthy smells of cooked meat and pastries brought water to their mouths as they rounded the archway and saw the hall.

"Thank you, my God, my merciful God, that the world is still sane and happy here at least," whispered the priest, as he caught sight of wine going from a jar with a mouth like a lion into a lady's goblet. The herald strode over to them and embraced Thomas before announcing them both.

"Sire, I present Sir Thomas of Picardy, and Père Matthieu of St. Martin-le-Preux. Sir Thomas has agreed to try his skill at arms tonight for our amusement and his greater glory."

The lord of the castle, a stunted but ferocious leonine man with little black eyes, looked up from his conversation with a Germanic-looking knight and grinned a black-toothed grin at Thomas and the priest. A plump, black-haired young woman with a high forehead sat next to him, seeming half-asleep and indifferent to everything.

"Any man who has hardened himself with the practice of arms is welcome here. Next, any woman at all. After that, certain musicians and priests," he said, following his jest with a roar of laughter that others around him quickly mimicked. "You are the fourth man. Now we can have our little sport tomorrow. I hear you ride a mule."

Thomas bristled at that but said, quietly, "My horse has died."

"That wouldn't stop a proper horse! Well, then, you shall have one of mine. Have you an armorer?"

"I have only my armor, my sword, and this priest."

"You can use my armorer. And my priest, if you like. Yours looks like a bugger."

"Is there a priest who isn't?" asked the German-looking fellow, who turned out to be a Frenchman. The whole table laughed, as well as the hurdy-gurdy player, who had stopped turning his handle while the lord spoke.

"Did I tell you to stop playing? Your job is to keep the plague out, not stand there and laugh at our jokes like they're meant for you to hear. Turn that goddamned thing. And make it pretty. Or I'll break your hands. Is there anything sadder than a hurdy-gurdy player with broken hands? Maybe a Jew who sneezes at the sight of gold."

Everyone laughed, except Thomas and the priest.

The lord noted this, said, "How dull," pointed at them, and flicked his hand. Little Simon sat them at one of the far arms of the great U-shaped table. The hurdy-gurdy played loudly, and conversation resumed. Kitchen women brought a basin around from person to person so hands might be washed, and then the herald announced, "Sir Théobald de Barentin and his squire, François." Simon placed them at the other arm of the U, across from Thomas and the priest.

This Théobald looked familiar; he was a little younger than Thomas, with sandy hair, a small patch of beard on his chin, and clever bug-eyes made for mockery. The squire was a dandy. Théobald saw Thomas looking at him, winked quickly, then whispered something to the squire. The squire snickered.

Thomas's hand dropped to where his sword hung on its belt. He just rested it on the pommel. This gesture was not lost on Théobald, however, who winked again, even more provocatively than the first time.

Thomas grinned at him, suddenly boyishly happy at the probability that he would be swinging a weapon at this man in the coming hours.

The food was beyond belief in its variety and in the skill of its presentation. The first course to appear was announced by the herald as "Cathar delight." Pastries in the form of a small tower were shared out until a breach formed that revealed, within the tower, a painted almond-paste statue of a nude woman tied to a stake amid "flames" of crystallized honey and ginger that were to be broken off and sucked. The woman was crudely made, her chest flat, recognizable as a woman only by her vivid golden hair.

"I'll have you all know, my great-grandfather was a famous killer of heretics," the seigneur boasted, "but he might have spared this one." The flames were all gone, so he lifted the woman out and licked her sticky belly shamelessly, then bit off her legs.

Fruits and cheeses came next, served in bowls painted with images of men and women copulating. The priest ate hungrily from them, and when Thomas pointed out the figures, the priest shrugged and said, "perhaps this is as close as I get to being fruitful and multiplying." Thomas kept looking at him, amused by his moral flexibility. "At least the sinful painter was a man of talent, wouldn't you agree?" he said, and Thomas laughed.

"I wonder how the girl's getting on," the priest said now.

"As well as she deserves," Thomas said. "I will not be governed by her in every little thing. If she wants me to go to Paris, fine, but she'll learn to stay where I say and eat where I say."

"Eating from these bowls may not be a sin. But I should have stayed with her," the priest said.

"What, up her tree?"

"I could have sat beneath it."

"You still can. No one's keeping you here."

"Yes," the priest said, then looked up at where the hurdy-gurdy player had come very near, staring at him while he played loudly and smiled. A woman filled the priest's goblet with thick, red wine. Père Matthieu did not leave.

Now vases and amphorae heaped with roasted eels and lampreys were brought to table, but Thomas thought of the thing in the river and could not bring himself to try these. He did notice Théobald of Barentin greedily heaping eels upon his platter; when he saw he had Thomas's eye, he bit into one of the long fish, said "Vengeance at last!" and laughed, though Thomas had no idea what he meant.

The main course came next.

"Three Kings," the herald intoned, and women brought out a huge platter piled with venison and other exotic meats, and several boats of garlicky brown gravy. Peacock and pheasant feathers accented it artfully, and topping it were three large, roasted monkeys sitting on cedar thrones, wearing capes of ermine. They wore golden crowns, which the cook, a man with narrow eyes and very long fingers, proudly tipped back, letting steam rise from their open skulls, into which he placed three elegant spoons. The chamber burst into applause, and one fleshy woman actually wept, though whether for the beauty of the display or the pathos of the monkeys was unclear.

The seigneur practically leapt from his chair; he took the spoon from the central monkey's head and slurped the delicate meat, contorting his face in ecstasy.

"Priest!" he said, "How do you say 'This is my brain'?"

The priest looked flabbergasted.

"Well?"

"Er ... in Latin?"

"No, in cunting Flemish. Latin, Latin! What else do you ask a bugger priest about?"

"Well. *Hoc est cerebrum meum.* But that's uncomfortably close to ..."

"A monkey may speak Latin, may he not?"

"If a monkey may speak at all, I suppose."

The lord slurped again from the spoon, then said, "*Hoc est cerebrum meum*," in the squeakiest monkey voice he could muster. Now he dipped the spoon back into the monkey's head and walked a spoonful of brain purposefully over to the priest's lips. "Say it," he commanded.

"I'd rather not," the priest said, squirming uncomfortably.

The nobleman pressed the spoon against the priest's lower lip.

"Say it!"

"My lord," Thomas said evenly but with a steady gaze.

"I ... I ... forgive me, but no."

"My *lord*," Thomas said, scooting his chair back a little. Across the hall, Théobald de Barentin scooted his chair back as well.

The hall was silent now.

The seigneur shot Thomas a look that made him suddenly see a lion killing an old man on sand with a hooting crowd looking on. The image left as quickly as it came.

"Very well," the seigneur said, in a mildly conciliatory tone, "the priest need not speak Latin for us. But he shall have no brains until he does. And no wine until he has brains."

So saying, he turned his back and walked the spoon back toward the Three Kings.

The priest cleared his throat.

"*Hoc . . . Hoc est cerebrum meum*," he said quietly.

The lord turned on his heel now, grinning mildly, and steered the spoon for the priest's mouth, which he opened, accepting the spoonful of salty, garlic-scented meat.

It was the best thing he ever tasted.

His goblet was filled.

At just that moment, the seigneur noticed that the hurdy-gurdy player had stopped playing to watch the standoff. He grabbed the little man's closest arm, dragged him to the table, and, in three nauseating blows, broke his hand against it with a heavy pewter mug. The musician screamed and ran off, dropping his hurdy-gurdy, which broke as well.

"Where's the viol player?"

"Sleeping, sire," the herald said. "He played all last night for us."

"Wake him."

Thomas and the priest ate to bursting. Thomas ate no monkey, but he did fill his trencher with cuts of strange meat he drenched well in the intoxicating gravy. "What is this?" he asked a serving woman.

"Deer, ram, wild boar," she said. "It is all roasted together."

"Tastes boarish, but strange bones for a boar," Thomas said.

"Perhaps I am mistaken. My lord has beasts from many

lands in his cages, and they are eaten when it pleases him. Or perhaps it is a Jew."

The man next to Thomas laughed so hard at this he nearly choked.

The viol player, while pale with exhaustion, was very skilled. He looked Moorish, and moved his hips in strange and sensual rolls while he drew across the honey-sweet strings. Thomas was becoming drunk, and the priest was drunker. He noticed Père Matthieu watching the musician distractedly.

"Jesus Christ, you are a bugger," Thomas laughed, though there was no laughter in his eyes.

"No! Just. The music. I am enraptured with it. I have never heard its equal," the priest said. A fat drop of sweat fell from his nose. "Or, almost never."

Thomas noticed the bored gaze of the woman who sat beside the seigneur upon him now. The fire from the hearth and many torches made her headpiece twinkle hypnotically. She was beautiful, more so than he had noticed before. He raised his goblet slightly in salute to her, which she answered by dipping her thumb into a monkey's head and putting that thumb into her mouth. Thomas saw her tongue flicker for just a moment and knew that the wound he got in St. Martin-le-Preux was completely healed.

"I think the lord's daughter likes you," said the man next to Thomas.

"Daughter? She's past a maiden's age. Where is her husband?"

"She is newly widowed."

"How newly?"

"He was killed at Crécy."

"That was two years ago."

"Are you quite sure?"

"I was there."

"Oh, well. Seems like yesterday. She was quite attached to him. We all were."

"What was the knight's name?"

"You know, I have forgotten. I'll just ask her. Euphémie! Ho!"

The woman turned her head slowly and looked at the man. Her eyes were very large and green.

"What do you want, Hubert?"

"What was your husband's name?"

"My husband?"

"Yes, you know. The very tall, handsome one who gave you several stillbirths, then went off to die in Picardy."

"Ah. Him. His name was..."

"Horace?" barked her father.

"No."

"It was Pierrot?" suggested the viol player with a decidedly Aragonés inflection, never missing a stroke on his instrument or a turn of his waspish hips.

"No, you silly hedge-cock, I would never spread my legs for anyone named Pierrot. No, it was..."

She opened her mouth now and issued a deep, manly belch. One heartbeat after it was finished, the whole room erupted in exuberant laughter.

Thomas was sloshily offended.

He banged his fist on the table. Nobody noticed, so he banged his wooden goblet on the table, splashing wine all over himself and the priest. The laughter died off to a trickle.

"You go too far!" he shouted at his fellow celebrants. "You injure the memory of a worthy man." He was swaying.

"Oh?" said the seigneur, amused and intrigued. "How so?"

The wine-sotted soldier could not answer, and almost cried, remembering his lord's hard death.

The man next to Thomas said, "Please forgive him, sire. He was also at the cursed defeat of Crécy, and I think his heart was broken there. Perhaps he knew the man in question. Sir knight," he said, turning to face Thomas, "while you were serving under our noble king, did you have the honor of knowing a tall, handsome chevalier named..."

At this he belched even more forcefully than Euphémie

had.

Everyone laughed.

Thomas went to backhand the man, but fell, causing the room to laugh harder. He got to his feet, feeling nauseated.

"I will not dine with you troop of pigs," he said, and looked around for the priest, who was passed out now with his head on his arm and a puddle of drool under his face. He jerked at the priest's robe, but the priest did not awaken. Thomas left him where he was and lurched in the general direction of the door, followed by the viol player, who used his music to dramatize Thomas's struggle to make an indignant exit. The room was hysterical. A woman gasped for breath near him: "Oh God, oh God, I think I pissed myself!"

He kicked backward at the viol player, catching him in the knee and making his face contort in pain, changing the music from a racy celebration of the drunk's progress to a lament for all unjustly injured musicians.

Thomas got to the doorway and went out into the darker hall, still hearing laughter and music behind him. He felt his way along the wall for support, realizing now he had no hope of finding his chamber without the boy who had brought him here.

"I'll sleep in the whoring stable, then," he said, and kept moving.

He felt his way along the straight wall for what felt like an hour, passing many exquisite tapestries with bizarre motifs. One stopped him and made him stand swaying before it, trying to comprehend; it seemed to show a noblewoman from the previous century bathing an infant; but she was holding it by its legs head down into the tub. Bored angels in clouds above received the infant's drowsy, winged soul, while at the bottom of the tapestry, black devils with tusks coming from the bottoms of their mouths, and even stranger devils in a great variety, received the ecstatically grinning soul of the mother. A lionish thing with human hands felt the woman's breast. Next to it, the largest of the devils had twelve eyes and a round, fiery mouth. It seemed to stand on owl's legs. Its black hand was between the legs of the woman's soul, two fingers in her up to the knuckle.

"Filth," Thomas slurred.

Just then the candle to the left of the tapestry flickered and a spill of wax overflowed its sconce, spilling suggestively on the floor.

"More filth."

He remembered that he had to find the stable and go to sleep there, so he continued on. Soon he came to an open, well-lit archway he hoped might lead outside. Instead, he entered the Great Hall once again by the same door he had pitched out of. Everyone was looking at him, deeply amused but silent, as if they had been waiting to surprise him. He felt his way to his seat, pulled it forward, and sat down again next to the unconscious priest. He put his arm on his head and slept.

An instant later, someone was shaking him.

It was the man next to him, the man he had tried to strike.

"Sir knight, sir knight," the man was saying in a hushed voice.

"What?" Thomas slurred.

The man's mouth was so close to his face he could see the texture of his green little tongue and a dark shred of meat between two of his asymmetrical teeth.

"You passed out. You mustn't sleep at table."

Thomas shook his head and sat up, profoundly confused.

He was about to point out to his neighbor that the priest was sleeping and nobody had bothered him, but when he looked he saw that the priest was awake and having his goblet filled again.

"Everyone is toasting the heroic deeds of the war with England. You don't want to miss it, do you?"

"No," he said thickly.

The serving woman now filled his goblet. He saw that her

nipple was out over the top of her garment and had the nearly irresistible urge to lean forward and lick it.

Across the hall, Théobald de Barentin had taken to his feet and was looking at Thomas with his protuberant eyes.

"And let us not forget our friend, Sir Thomas . . . of Picardy?" he said. "Although I cannot remember what town in Picardy. But I believe I met you near Cambrai, ten years ago."

Thomas felt his face flush, and he resisted the urge to look down.

"Yes, it was you!" the other man continued. "Your seigneur, the Comte de Givras, a worthy man with ridiculously large mustachios, was camped near the Count of Hainault as the English drew their battle lines across from us."

"You are correct, sir knight. I was there. Let us speak of something happier."

"Forgive me, I must continue, it's just too good! This Thomas was not yet a knight, though he had thirty years behind him. Still, his manners were so coarse and his birth so low, his seigneur, again, a wise and worthy man, had not yet bestowed upon him his belt and spurs. Now, imagine! This great battle was about to start, and, suddenly, a noise went up from all the men on both sides. The Count of Hainault hastily knighted some dozen of his young squires and men-at-arms so that they might fight and perhaps die in the holy state of Christian knighthood. This man's lord, looking at his brawling, overmuscled squire with white hairs coming into his beard, took pity upon him and knighted him as well. Only the battle hadn't started yet. A hare had leapt between the legs of the French army, and they had been cheering at that. A hare! The battle never started. Our king decided to remove himself, and everyone went away. Only here were all these sad bastards knighted because of a hare. The Knights of the Order of the Hare! And one of their illustrious number is with us tonight!"

"I have fought many actions since then!" Thomas roared.

"All in our king's service, no doubt."

"Get yourself *fucked*, and your shit-nosed girl of a squire.

I don't have to answer to you. Where have you fought? In a whorehouse brawl? For the right to plow your whore mother without paying?"

"Ah, there's that rare strain of nobility that made your lord so proud to knight you. And you know perfectly well where I fought. You're just too drunk to remember."

"My nobility will show itself on the field," Thomas said, waving off the girl who tried to fill his cup again. "And not in perfumed words to impress teenaged serving girls."

Théobald bowed.

"Ho-ho!" the seigneur said. "Now I would not miss the night tourney for anything. Not cunting *anything.*"

He smiled with his mouthful of black teeth.

Night.

The blackest hour of it.

Thomas found himself in bed, but he was not sure how he got there. His head hurt miserably. A small wax candle guttered in a nook, making the shadows on the stone walls hop nauseatingly. He would have done anything for a cupful, or even a palmful of water. The figure next to him shifted.

"Père Matthieu," he whispered.

The figure shifted again, pulling the blanket half off itself, revealing the very pale, moley back of the lord's daughter. Something growled from the lower half of the bed. He looked up to see a tiny dog curled between his mistress's feet, growling a warning at him. He growled back at it, then reclined. The room smelled like hot cunt and red wine vomit. He checked over his side of the bed and confirmed his suspicion that he had been the source of the latter.

Fragments of the night's events came to him in watery flashes:

Her open mouth coming to kiss his, her teeth graying toward the black of her father's teeth, her pear-green eyes half-lidded as her tongue flicked forward, her breath with its notes of garlic, fecundity, and rot; his two fingers sunk in her up to the knuckle; her wheezing beneath him and digging into his shoulders with her fat little fingers, her legs curled up so she made a football of herself. She had bitten one of his nipples so badly he wondered if he might lose it.

"So this is Hell," he muttered.

He glanced at his borrowed robe, which was hanging from a nail near his head. He noticed the cloth-of-gold stars on the sage-green fabric and saw that they looked very much like the stars in the actual night sky. He found the constellation of the swan. Then he found his comet, with its little bloody vein. And the smaller one near it.

He was afraid now.

He did not want to touch the robe, so he put on his soiled long shirt and inner leggings. When he sat gingerly upon the bed to put his boots on, the little dog uncurled itself and stood yapping and growling at him as if it were in pain. Soon it was, because it made the mistake of biting Thomas's arm, for which he grabbed it, absorbing two more little bites, and flung it against the wall. It made a great noise. He didn't look to see if it had roused the woman on the bed, because he didn't want to see one of her large green eyes fixed on him; he was grateful to hear her chortle softly and then snore.

He took his sword and left.

Soon he was lost again in the labyrinth of stone halls, dripping candles and sputtering torches. At last he felt cool air and went outside into the night; other people, still dressed in finery from the feast, were moving in the dark courtyard as well, and some now came through the same door he had just used. The woman from his bed was one of these, her headpiece perched on her high forehead again, the wicked little dog in her arms, her green dress shining.

How did she get dressed so quickly?

She ignored him as she moved past, then turned her head and said, "You'd better find your armor. And I hope you ride better than you fuck. Théobald outclasses you miserably there." Everyone around them heard and laughed.

He stood there, headachy and confused, while the crowd flowed past him. He looked where they were going and saw pennants flapping in the cool night breeze over a grounded constellation of lit lamps and torches.

The tournament field.

He felt a tug at his elbow and saw the boy, Simon, standing there.

"The armorer wants you."

Run! Get out of this place!

Armorer.

How long had it been since he'd had an armorer?

In his confusion, he followed the boy to a lit tent. The two men who had taken his armor before were within, ready to suit him in his mail and plate; it had all been scoured and shone marvelously. A tournament helm sat on the arming table.

Thomas's mouth stood open.

"Don't just gawk at us. And don't get too attached to it. Sir Théobald will smash it all into junk, like as not, and you with it. He fights with a mace, and he's quick as a fish from a dead man's skull."

Thomas nodded at them and let them begin.

He noticed his surcoat, cleaned now, and emblazoned with a heraldic image that had not been there before. Two fleurs-de-lys and a hare.

He chuckled.

Yes, this was Hell. And if all that was left for him to do was fight, he would fight to frighten Lucifer.

"Fuck it," he said. "Just fuck it."

"That's what we say, Sir Thomas," the older armorer said. "And if it won't let you fuck it, cut its throat. Hey, Jacmel, pass us down his sword. He'll want that cleaned, too."

The other man handed him the sword, and the armorer only half unsheathed it before he sheathed it again and put it down on his arming table.

"Christ! What the hell is on this thing?"

"I killed something foul in a river."

"Well, I'm not touching it. Hey, Jacmel, you want any of this?" he asked the other one. The other one shook his head. The first one tossed the sword at Thomas's feet, and they finished buckling him in. A horse whinnied outside the tent.

"That'll be your horse, Grisâtre," the first man said.

"I thought he was riding Belâtre," said Jacmel.

"Oh, right. The seigneur is riding Grisâtre."

At that, trumpets sounded and the herald spoke, though Thomas could not hear what he was saying. Then the crowd roared. The tourney had begun.

He went out of the tent and saw the mottled charger he was meant to ride. A gray-haired, long-headed squire in an ill-fitting jerkin and loose hose held the reins, and the man was so drunk he could barely stand. A second look at the ridiculous squire showed him to be Matthieu Hanicotte, the priest.

The sound of something punching through armor came from the tournament field, and the crowd loosed an impressed *HOOOOOOAAAAA!*

Thomas's borrowed horse turned to look at him, and Matthieu motioned toward the saddle. Thomas mounted.

"Are you yourself, or a devil?" Thomas asked, putting on his tournament helmet.

"I don't know," he slurred, "but I'm fairly sure there's a devil out there."

A horrible shriek came from the field. The crowd went, "*HO-oooooooo,*" the way a crowd will when something awful has happened to a man. The squire-priest grabbed a lance from where it leaned against a rail and handed it to Thomas, taking up two spares as well. Thomas looked down the shaft at the point; it was a war point, sharp and deadly, not the blunted quartet of knobs one used in tourneys.

"So be it," he said. "Let's go die, priest."

"I wish that were all we risked here," Matthieu said.

He turned the horse and brought it onto the trampled sod

of the list.

"Oh, for Christ's sake," he said under his breath.

Two horsemen were on the field, and a third waited on the far side.

What must have been a hundred torches burned, and burned the image into his mind; the German-looking Frenchman from the feast was sitting dead in the saddle, a lance through his side. His helmet was off. The seigneur, also *sans* helmet, circled his horse around him, then spurred it close, using a one-handed war axe to split the man's head laterally, from nose to the back of his skull, the contents of which flew all over the sand.

The crowd screamed its approval.

Then a monkey came from beneath the stands, a monkey of the same sort as the three that had been roasted for supper, and began to pick from the sand and eat what had flown from the man's head. When he had gotten all there was to be found on the sand, he scampered up the horse and up the armored body of the half-headed German Frenchman, and began to eat directly from the bowl of his remaining head.

"*Hoooooooooo!*" went the crowd.

Now the monkey kicked his heels against the armor of the dead knight he straddled, and the knight's body jerked and spurred the horse, who trotted off the field to eat grass. The knight's body slid heavily out of the saddle, and the monkey scampered beneath the stands again.

The crowd went silent, then began to chant, "Next! Next! NEXT! NEXT!"

The lord, still circling on Grisâtre, pointed his gory axe at Thomas.

Thomas suppressed a shudder.

I can't, I can't, I can't, he thought, then spurred his horse forward to take his position at his end of the list.

"Lance, or sword?" Thomas shouted at the seigneur.

"LANCE!" he bellowed, "But not me. Him!"

Théobald de Barentin was in position now, placing his

tournament helm and taking his lance. He sat a whitish horse that couldn't wait to run. His dandy squire handed him his first lance.

"READY?" screamed the lord, raising his axe.

Théobald raised his lance.

Thomas raised his.

The axe fell.

The chargers started off, Thomas's more heavily, and the two made for each other. At French tournaments, a barrier normally separated the jousting knights to prevent collision, but this was open like a German field. Thomas reined his horse to keep it on the right side, his lance pointed crosswise, but the horse stubbornly made right for its oncoming counterpart. At the last minute, the other horse corrected and the men shocked their lances into one another. Thomas felt his glance solidly but harmlessly off Théobald's chestpiece, rocking him back with the impact. Théobald's point, however, gouged into Thomas just below the left hip, dislodging several links of chain and digging a hotly painful furrow into him. He gritted his teeth and tried unsuccessfully not to grunt, reeling but staying upright in the saddle.

Both men had kept their lances, so they wheeled their horses around and repositioned themselves for another charge. Neither waited for a signal from the seigneur this time; they both made for each other.

This time, however, Thomas felt his horse slowing beneath him. He swore at it and spurred it, but Belâtre kept losing speed, even as the other knight loomed larger and more dangerous through the slit in Thomas's helm. The horse stopped altogether.

"You *whore!*" Thomas said to his mount even as Théobald's point dropped and slammed into Belâtre's chest. The horse screamed, reared, and threw Thomas off. He landed heavily on his back, sending a wave of pain down his legs all the way to his heels. He sat up to see the dying horse topple on its side, kicking its legs in the air. No sooner had it landed than at least a score of dark shapes rushed from beneath the stands and swarmed over it. The monkeys. Only this time Thomas wasn't sure they were monkeys. Whatever they were, they dragged the horse away, already disemboweling it.

"Forgive me, Sir Thomas," the seigneur said. "I didn't know my horse was a fucking coward."

Thomas crabbed his way to his feet. Why wasn't his squire helping him up? He removed his borrowed helmet and looked back down the list. He saw Matthieu now, lolling against a rail, his head tipped back. The viol player from before was pouring wine down his throat, his free hand rubbing the older man's crotch.

The lord barked, "On foot!" and now Thomas turned and saw the other knight stomping toward him, swinging a flanged mace, his helmet also off.

"Right," Thomas said, and drew his sword.

He moved first against Théobald, running at him and lunging his point at the other man's face. The knight spun and sidestepped at the same time, bringing his mace around into Thomas's back, breaking a rib. Thomas let the momentum take him forward so he wouldn't be in jeopardy from a second blow. The armorer was right. Théobald was fast.

As a fish from a dead man's skull.

He heard the armor moving behind him and sensed the mace passing only half a hand's length from where his head had just been.

But Thomas had tricks, too; he planted his foot and spun suddenly, crouching at the same time, driving his point at the other man's middle. It struck home, and, even though the mail stopped it, the force pushed the man back and sapped the strength from his mace swing so that, when it landed on Thomas's shoulderpiece, it hurt but didn't damage.

His back was in agony.

Did water just come from Théobald's armor?

Thomas didn't have time to pull back for a proper swing, so he chopped short across his body, hacking at Théobald's inner arm to try to knock the mace out of it; he knocked the mace arm wide, but his foe kept his weapon, letting the momentum carry it over his own head, and backhanded into Thomas's arm, which went numb.

Salt water got into his eyes. Théobald was definitely leaking salt water. And his armor was now finely coated with rust. Thomas didn't actively notice these things; without hesitation, he switched hands and licked out with the sword point, which caught the other man between the knuckles of his mace hand, opening the links of his chain mitten and making him drop the mace.

Now Thomas saw the exposed hand and how white it was. So white it was almost translucent.

A fucking hand!

He lashed out with the blade again and caught Théobald across the side of the head. Seawater, not blood, gushed from the wound. It stank. Théobald looked amused. He opened his mouth and a scream came out, but it was not his scream. It was the scream of the fat peasant who had died in the river. It was the scream the thing in the river had mimicked.

Thomas recovered from his stupefaction and swung hard now with his working arm. Théobald, who was getting puffier and whiter by the second, raised his arm so it caught the force that had been meant for his neck. The armor saved the arm from getting severed, but the bones in it were broken and he careened sideways. More water gushed from him.

An eel slithered out of his leg armor to writhe on the sand.

The sky was not as dark as it had been.

Théobald scrambled for his mace now, picking it up with the badly broken arm; Thomas struck him across the back, breaking his scapula. Unconcerned, Théobald lurched up and the mace head backhanded Thomas across his own numb arm, which was also broken.

The opponents paused now and looked at each other.

Théobald grinned at Thomas, and thread-fine marine worms sprouted from his lips. A small fish ate one of his eyes from the inside.

And he stank, and he stank.

Théobald de Barentin, Théobald...

Dead at the battle of Sluys.

He fell into the sea when an English ship rammed into the ship he was on. He was the best fighter in Normandy, but he was not stabbed or shot with arrows. He just slipped on the wet deck and fell into the water, where his armor pulled him under.

Thomas's lord had told his men before they met the English at Crécy, to remind them that no death was inglorious when suffered in the field.

Light was coming into the sky.

"Hurry!" screamed a woman from the stands, and the cry was picked up by the other spectators, all of whom were beginning to rot now. Some yelled "Kill him!" or "The sun!" The lord of the castle shouted "HURRY!" as well, and tried to shout it again, but the word changed into the roar of a lion. Thomas spared a glance at him, and saw that he was growing taller, stretching out of his armor, so that his skin showed between sections. His head was a lion's head now, but lumpy and corrupt, balanced badly on the ungainly stack of flesh and armor he had become.

A devil.

A devil from Hell and a court of the damned.

The thing that had been the seigneur started taking jerky steps toward them.

Théobald lashed madly with his mace now, and Thomas blocked or avoided all but one blow, which he stepped into at the last instant to avoid taking the head of the mace; instead he caught the shaft across his jaw, which broke.

"Hurry," screamed the mob, which had begun running off the stands toward the combatants.

Thomas shoved his sword into the face of what used to be Théobald de Barentin, and it shuddered and stopped moving. Thomas yanked the sword out of it but fell on his side. The lion-devil roared, standing over Thomas.

The crowd of finely dressed corpses moved closer. One of the monkey-things tugged the armor off his foot and bit it.

Thomas held his sword up.

The sun's crown came over the edge of the land, just one brilliant orange diamond's worth.

And it was all gone.

Everything.

Thomas was lying in a cow field, holding up his sword, dressed in his rusty armor. Neither his arm nor his rib nor his jaw were broken. A rusted plow stood where the lion-devil had been, one of its spars hanging at the angle of the axe it had just been holding. A dead sheep lay in exactly the position the corpse of Sir Théobald had assumed when he collapsed. A small Norman tower, long abandoned and crumbling, stood where the mighty castle had been when they first saw it at dusk. The priest, lying facedown in his robes, was breathing heavily in sleep.

"A whoring dream," he said.

He got to his feet and stretched.

He saw a mound of dirt and walked over to it, having a long piss against it. He realized he had to shit as well, and walked around the dirt mound to see if he could find an ass-wiping plant. What he found instead was a common grave. The last corpses were recent and had not been shoveled under very well. A woman's moley, nude back stood out at him. Also, the herald; the small boy, Simon, in bright livery; and the Moorish musician. A little dead dog had been tossed in as well.

The sunrise was among the most beautiful he had ever seen. He got to his knees meaning to thank God for it, but couldn't think of any words to say.

The girl walked over to him, brushing a leaf out of her hair.

"Are you ready to go to Paris now?" she said.

"Yes."

PART II

Now the great plague had stilled the hearths in the countryside, and darkened the windows of the cities of man; Death's hand sat upon the brow of the king and also the farmer; Death took the beggar and the cardinal, the money changer and the milkmaid. The babe died on the breast, and sailors brought their ships to port with dead hands. And the wickedness of man was laid bare, so great was his fear of this pestilence; for the mother fled her children and the son nailed shut his father's door, and the priest betrayed his flock. Still other men said, "God is gone from us, or never was at all; let us do as we will, and take pleasure as we may, for all is lost." And so the wicked went in bands and took the daughter's maidenhead, and killed others for their sport. And some shut themselves away in walled towns, and let none pass; when the bread was gone, they drew lots, and some were given to the butcher that the rest might live. Some righteous men and women yet held faith, but they were scattered so far that none could see the other's light, and it seemed the darkness had no end.

And the Lord made no answer.

Now devils walked the earth, at first in dreams and then in flesh, and Hell had dominion in diverse kingdoms. Those men who died in furtherance of evil yet walked as shades, and even those who died in goodness might be raised by devils and abused. Sacred places were turned rotten, and holy men abased, *so the seed of Adam could take no comfort, and the prayers of men and women would not strengthen the angels of the Lord, who were grown frail.*

And the Lord made no answer.

Now the greater devils who walked the earth were Ra'um and Oillet, and Bel-phegor and Baal'Zebuth, whose agents were flies. Two thirds of the fallen had gone even to the walls of Heaven, where a great war raged, a war of bent light and thrown stars and noises that killed; a war of great limbs locking, and the spear, and the sword, it was a war of tooth on wing; a war of machines whose effects were abomination, a war of shaken walls, a war of hammers that, though turned, broke the arm that held the shield. For the strength of the angels of God was reflected strength, and the source was grown distant; yet the fallen had sat long in the coals of their exile and grown hard, and their strength was their own; and their generals were Lucifer and Asmodeus and Astaroth and Moloch; and the angels who resisted at the gates were Michael and Zephon and Uriel and Rafael, for Gabriel had gone to look for the Lord.

But the Lord made no answer.

Some few angels of God slipped from Heaven by stealth, and hid themselves, whether in the fields or in the cities, and worked against the fallen angels as best they could, and to save the lives of men, though they did these things in secret, for their powers were grown weak upon the earth. Certain treasures from Heaven they hid in the earth as well, in case the walls were breached, and among these were pots of oil and scents from Heaven's gardens, and nectar, and gold from the tails of stars; and also they preserved certain tokens from the time God walked among men, and among these were His sandals, and His crown of thorns, and the nails from His wrists and ankles, and also the spear that pierced His side.

It was the hour of the fallen angel.

And God had stopped the fountain of His love.

And it was said that He had gone to make a new world and new angels and new men.

And the walls of Heaven would fall.

And all these now struggling above and below would perish.

NINE

Of the City of Paris

Paris first announced herself with a column of smoke rising over a hill. They knew they were close, as they had been following the river from the west, and Thomas and the priest wondered if the whole city might be burning. When they crested the hill, Thomas felt ashamed of his naïveté; the city dwarfed the fire, which was outside the walls in any case. A fire big enough to burn that city would have rivaled the furnaces of Hell, and the smoke from it would have blackened the bottoms of the clouds.

All that was burning was a wheat field, and the fire was at its end, burning itself out against the banks of the Seine. Several houses had been reduced to blackened skeletons, as had two cows. One calf lowed from a hillock, barely visible from behind the curtain of white smoke that surrounded it; the fire would spare this beast. The octet of ragged figures around it, however, would not. Already they were testing the smoking earth to see if it would burn them through the rags and bad shoes on their feet. Already they were hefting their axes and daggers. They didn't look like farmers. Thomas scanned the fields and saw a pair of legs jutting from a patch of unburned wheat. Murder, then. Thomas was suddenly sure these men had set the fire. He should have waited and watched longer

before they approached; but it was too late now. Several of
the killers looked at the cart as it passed, but nothing in the
cart could possibly interest them as much as the calf. One of
them looked at Thomas, and he met the man's gaze, not in
threat, but to let him know he would fight if he had to. The
man quickly assessed that they could take the cart, but not
without cost. He looked back up the hillock. Now Thomas
lowered his eyes in shame to remember that, had things fallen
out differently, he might be standing in that group, along with
Godefroy and Jacquot, waiting to carve the dead man's calf.

I saw it.

What?

Your soul.

Thomas remembered the last winter with Godefroy,
when his were the most feared brigands in High Normandy.
In the better months they had restricted themselves to robbing merchants, particularly on the roads leading south and
east toward the Champagne fairs, trundling away carts laden
with food and wool on the way down and gold and spices
on the way up. December came, however, with rain and sleet
in its fists and breath that numbed them to their feet. Food
ran scarce and their reputation now worked against them
—what merchants traveled then did so under arms. Villages
set watches for them and hid their grain in caves and under
clever hidden doors and pits in the fields. Their very few coins
and other small goods went down wells or in coffers buried
under straw. They hid themselves, too, because they knew
that Godefroy, whom they called "the black cat," would stop
at nothing, even torture, to learn where they hid their meager
treasures.

And their livestock, which, to Godefroy's mind, included
daughters.

In response, Godefroy learned stealth.

Near Gisors, just before the Christmas feasts began, the
brigands stopped outside a village they would all remember,
though they never knew its name. Two men stayed with the

horses; the rest waited until almost sundown and walked two miles through the woods to the most isolated farmhouse. Everyone inside was likely to be asleep; peasants slept long hours in the winter to save strength. The thieves muddied their faces and crawled on their bellies until they were close enough for Jacquot to shoot the guard dog. The windows were hung with sheepskins to keep the heat of the fire in, and the cold thieves coveted the warmth nearly as much as the food they hoped to find.

Thomas grabbed the sheepskin and yanked it down, rolling awkwardly through the window with his sword drawn. A calf lay in the middle of the dirt floor, with a goat and two children sleeping against it. They woke up at the sound of Thomas's heavy feet, and stared at him; they thought a devil from Hell had come to them, and they weren't far wrong. The others leapt in as well. One of the children cried out and the rest of the house woke up, all in one room, six adults on a moss-stuffed bed. An old man at the end reached for something on the floor, but a nearly toothless little killer named Pepin leapt the calf and the children in two steps and stabbed the man's belly. He dropped whatever it was he'd grabbed for and palmed his wound, huffing "Oh, oh."

The only other men, probably an in-law and a hired man, froze and offered no fight; they were soon shamed by an old woman who swung at Thomas with a fire poker. He ducked it and shoved her down, where another man sat on her. She yelled and this man punched her until she stopped.

Godefroy noticed that one of those on the bed was a decent-looking girl of perhaps fourteen. Probably already married. He yanked her off the bed by the foot while Pepin hovered over the rest of them with his knife.

They took the girl and the beasts out; Thomas carried the goat over his neck, and Jacquot led the calf, but the real prize was a milk cow on the other side of the house. They butchered her that night in the hills, along with the other animals, smoked the meat, and rode off before the local lord could muster sufficient men to deal with them. Just before they left, they let the girl stumble back into town, mostly intact on the outside.

Thomas had argued with Godefroy about the girl, but in the end had walked away.

The meat had gotten them through January.

The family, of course, would have been reduced to begging from their neighbors, perhaps even forced to sell their land.

As the brigands left the house that night, the old woman had gotten up and yelled after them from the doorway. Her words were slurred from her newly broken teeth.

"God will see you in Hell! You're the Devil's now. May you choke and die and go to him sooner."

Normally some of them would have jeered back at her, but her words fell on them with the weight of a proper curse. Robbing peasants felt much more sinful than robbing merchants, but winter didn't care about such sensibilities.

In February, they robbed another farmhouse, and this time the men fought. Pepin was killed. As were the men. Godefroy ordered the house burned. A dark-haired little boy just in pants stood bewildered near the blaze, saying, as if there had been some mistake, "We live here. We live here."

Not six months later the plague had come, killing most of the thieves.

And everybody else.

Nothing matters anymore.

Thomas shook away his ghosts and turned his eyes now to Paris. Her walls were the faintly yellowed white of bones, and her turrets stood proudly, each a lazy bowshot from its neighbor. He could see what must have been the Louvre, the king's fortress, strong and white, cut from the same stone as the city walls. The spires of cathedrals poked at the sky, and the roofs of the shops and houses tumbled against one another. Even dead, if she was dead, Paris made a lovely corpse.

And yet Thomas wished she had burned. He would have embraced any excuse to keep going, as they had been, on small roads or no roads, meeting few living souls, foraging as best they could. How long could they live like that? Until winter. But what then?

"I don't care," Thomas said, at the end of this chain of thoughts, and neither of his cartmates pressed him for what he meant. There was a great deal in this world not to care about.

The Port du Louvre was the closest gate, and, luckily, one of the few that remained open; the provost of Paris, on the authority of the king, who had long since fled, had shut most of the other gates in a vain attempt to close out the scourge that was killing the city. Rare carts bearing food were allowed in; anyone at all was allowed out; strangers could enter so long as they appeared healthy.

The guards on the top of the wall did not appear healthy. They were underslept, ashen, and cranky, though not energetic enough to cause much mischief. They told the girl to display her armpits, neck, and groin to them, but did not care to make Thomas strip down his armor, and likewise told the priest to keep his robe on. The priest shook his head at them. One of them apathetically tossed a small stone at the priest. They waved the cart through.

"Now would be a good time to tell us what you're looking for," Thomas said. The girl nodded. She looked frightened. She didn't look like she knew anything about why they were here.

"The first thing is to find lodgings," the priest said.

Nobody alive wanted them, and the dead didn't answer.

They wound through the narrow, muddy streets, at turns disgusted by the filth beneath their feet and awed by the soaring spires of churches or the houses of the very rich. On some streets the houses and shops were so close they nearly touched heads together over the muddy paths, throwing everything into shadow. Some bodies, at least, were being picked up in tumbrils pushed mostly by desperate-looking fellows who had as much to fear from hunger as from the murderous, stale air around the dead.

Nobody answered at the inns on the Right Bank, or, when they did, it was just to tell them to go away. Most of the people who had gold had already piled their possessions in whatever they could still find with wheels on it and headed for the countryside. The only medical advice that proved sound against this sickness was "run far and stay long." Yet even that worked only if you were lucky or well-informed enough to run where it hadn't struck yet. And if you were not already sick. The only thing that slowed its spread was the speed with which it killed; once it was in you, you had a day or maybe two before you were too sick to travel. Or hours. Thus it spread from town to town at the speed of a leisurely walk, but it missed nothing.

So they went south on St.-Denis until they got to the bridges that crossed the Seine onto Île de la Cité, the island at the heart of the city. The larger of these bridges, the Pont aux Changeurs, was for wheeled vehicles and beasts and had shops along the sides, none of which were occupied. Likewise, nobody was bothering to collect tolls. Between the shops on their right they could make out the smaller bridge, the Pont aux Meuniers, which was only for pedestrians and had thirteen water mills at its base. Both bridges were wooden. The celebrated stone bridge, the Grand Pont, had collapsed during a winter flood fifty years before. At the time, that had seemed the greatest calamity Paris could suffer. Now the mills at the base of the pedestrian bridge regularly spat out corpses that citizens living close to the river had jettisoned rather than waiting for the cart to come.

On the island, they rode past the strong, white walls of the royal palace, atop which several archers were laughing, firing their bows at something on rue St. Barthélemy. As they cleared a stack of empty, ruined wine barrels, just near St. Barthélemy church, they saw the target; a very fat dead man with thirty or forty arrows stuck in him, and more stuck in the mud or lying with their points broken off from hitting the stone building behind him.

They would have to cross the field of fire.

"Please don't shoot us, brothers," the priest called to them.

"We don't shoot priests," said one of them.

"Well, *he* doesn't," said the other.

"Hey, Father! Make a circle with your arms! A big circle!"

The others laughed.

They were drunk.

"Yes, and put that bastard driving the cart in the middle of it."

"Shut up. He looks like a knight."

"Knights ride horses."

"A glass of cider says he's a knight."

"All the more reason to fling a shaft at him. Maybe he's one of the eunuchs that let the English shame us at Crécy."

"Don't let Sir Jean hear you."

"Fuck him, he went with the king."

"You may pass, but hurry up."

"Yes, hurry!"

Thomas urged the mule forward.

For a long moment the only sound was the clop of the mule's hooves on the muddy street.

"You wouldn't," one of the archers said.

"I dare you," said another.

Thomas said "Don't look at them."

An arrow whistled behind their heads and stuck in the dead man's open mouth.

"Phillipe! You did it."

"I work better with obstacles."

Past the palace and St. Barthélemy church, they went right on rue de La Vielle Draperie, and then right on La Juiverie, named for Jews now absent, having been expelled from the city yet again nearly thirty years before. Soon, seeing the twin square towers of Nôtre Dame off to his left, Thomas tilted his head back and spat toward the great cathedral, watching the white spittle arc and separate in the air; he imagined it was a stone tossed by a trebuchet and that it would knock a hole in the gorgeous round window over the doors, but it just fell in the mud.

They were coming to the southern part of Île de la Cité, where the Hôtel Dieu stood near the Petit Pont that led to the Latin Quarter. The Hôtel-Dieu would have let any poor travelers stay one night, as was its custom, had the great hospital not been overwhelmed with those dying of plague. A staggering heap of bodies lay outside awaiting removal, two of them *filles blanches*, young nuns in white who had been taking care of the sick. A glimpse through an open door revealed a hell of vomiting, coughing, and sobbing with a very few wretched figures in white trying to ease the torments of far, far too many.

The girl sobbed and the priest held her. Thomas's hand jerked with the long-suppressed reflex to cross himself, but he did not do that. He ground his teeth and shook his head.

As they approached the bridge to the Left Bank, the girl sat up from where the priest had been holding her and looked at the gray waters of the Seine rushing under it. A dead sheep floated by but didn't keep going on the other side. The priest wondered if it had caught on debris down by the piers, and if that debris included people, and surprised himself by not feeling anything about it. On the other side, at the entrance to the Latin Quarter, they passed a painted wooden statue of Christ up on a pedestal of stone, at the foot of which a feverish woman grinned, sweating, with a dead cat cradled in her arms.

Thomas looked up at the long-headed Christ and said, not wholly under his breath, "You're dead, too, aren't you? If not, get off that whoring thing and do something. Or at least whoring wink at me. You can do that much, can't you?"

It didn't wink.

But the woman did.

They wheeled along in the butchers' quarter, where the mud stank with the blood and viscera of slaughtered animals, a few of which were still being butchered despite the paralysis that gripped so much of the city. A man grinned a nearly toothless grin at them as he cut the throat of a suckling pig he had just tied up by its feet, its blood jetting on his stiff leather apron and into the pail he had placed beneath it. He called out the price of the pig, but they couldn't hear it over its squeals. The men of rue de La Bucherie seemed to be doing better than the dyers on Gobelins, just nearby, where nothing was moving at all.

They got lost again in the labyrinthine streets and began to despair of finding lodgings. The sun was so low that only infrequently did it finger its way between the buildings to throw cool, golden light on the mud. Just such a shaft of light illuminated the foot of a masculine-looking woman. She sat in the doorway to a leaning timber building with flaking paint. A sly-looking young man stood near her, cleaning his nails with a rusty knife.

"You look lost," she said to them.

The priest looked first at her greasy blue stockings, then up at her tangled hair, and finally at her face. She had the look of a wary mastiff. She also had a moustache that might have better suited a thirteen-year-old boy.

"We are," he said.

Thomas noted that she was a big woman with strong hands and shoulders, old enough that the man near her might have been her son, and that she wore a fine hat, a rich man's floppy felt hat with a gold pin. Doubtless there were more fine hats than living heads to fill them in this city, and after a point it could hardly be considered looting to liberate them.

The girl noticed her eyes. They seemed kind to her, despite the woman's rough look. Out of nowhere, she wanted the woman to hold her. It had been so long since she had smelled a woman's skin that even a dirty woman's embrace would have been welcome. She was still disturbed by the sight of the dead young nuns near the hospital and she wanted a woman to hold her and tell her that the whole world didn't yet belong to Death, masculine Death with his hourglass and his holes for eyes. Death with his bony arms that only embraced to take you away, like a lamb from market. Like the pig on La Bucherie. How did Heaven come into all of this? Heaven was life, not death. Heaven was a woman holding your head in the crook of her arm and looking down at you. Heaven was a warm hand on your cheek and the smell of soup with garlic on the fire.

How could people enjoy anything in Heaven with their noses rotted off and their ears full of mud and worms, and no cheeks, and no hands to lay on cheeks?

She had never felt so alone, or so confused.

"Maybe I can help. What are you looking for?"

She thought she smelled garlic coming from the building.

"A bed," the priest said. "A stable. Anything."

"You're in luck," the woman said. "I own a few buildings in this neighborhood; the renters all died in one just down the street, you see it there by the big puddle, with the blue door. But it's dry and it's got two decent beds. How much have you got?"

"How much do you want?" the priest said.

"Ho-ho!" said the woman. "You're stumbling around this dead city an hour before dark with your heads up your asses, lucky anyone says a word to you, and you want things done your way. Are you going to tell me how much you've got?"

"Well, no, but I will tell you what we're willing to spend."

"I'm sure it's not enough. But tell me. I could use a laugh."

The last of the sun slipped off her foot and now winked on a silver spoon hanging from her belt.

"Ten deniers."

"Ha! That's a country priest for you," she said to the young man, whose nails didn't really look any cleaner for all his knifing under them. "First time in the big city, eh?"

"All right, all right. How much?"

"Three sous."

"Is this room perhaps in the royal palace?" Thomas said.

She narrowed her gaze and jerked a thumb at him, looking still at the priest.

"I don't like him."

The priest said, "He's a bit gruff at first, but he has a good heart. How about one sou, five deniers?"

"I'm not the one who has to bargain. It's three sous."

"How do we even know you own the room?" Thomas said.

"If he talks again, I've got nothing else to say."

The priest looked imploringly at Thomas, who shrugged and turned his gaze away.

"Will you show us the room?" said the priest.

"I'm not getting up. I don't step and fetch for you."

"What about this young gentleman?" Père Matthieu said, indicating the sly young man.

"He's busy."

"May we have the key?"

"When I get the money."

"May we at least see the key?"

"You may see it and have it when I get the money."

The priest went to the cart and got the coins, which he reluctantly put in her mannish hand. She made them disappear, then rummaged in a moldy pouch on her belt and produced a small brass key, holding it up before the priest.

He took it and frowned at it.

"It looks like a coffer key, not a proper door key."

"Oh," she said, "Am I a liar now as well as your servant?

Then give it back to me and go your ways. Go and sleep in shit for all I care."

"I'm a priest, you know."

"Then pray for a room."

"Never mind. We'll take it. But it had better be what you said."

"Fine."

The woman now produced a little piece of ginger and began to chew it.

The girl salivated despite herself and asked, "Do you have any more ginger?"

The woman shook her head and flicked her hand at them.

They left.

Maybe sixty yards away, they stopped the cart near a big depression in the road in which a puddle had formed. The priest approached the blue door the woman had indicated and went to fit the key, which was clearly too small, into the lock, but the door opened anyway.

The room was mad with flies.

Three badly decomposed bodies lay in the room, which stank miserably from them, but also from mold (the roof had fallen in), urine, and feces; several piles of turds lay near the open window—clearly people sat over the ledge to shit or pissed freely through the opening. The dirt floor was also littered with animal bones, eggshells, fish scales, and all other manner of refuse. They had been sold the right to sleep in the neighborhood morgue, latrine, and dump. The priest gagged, the girl moaned, and Thomas went to the cart and got his sword, drawing it from its sheath. He ran the sixty yards back to the stoop, but of course the woman and her companion were not there.

He kicked in the door and went into the building, where a young woman grabbed up a child he had knocked over with the door; the child screamed and held his head. An older woman he didn't recognize stood frozen near the fire where she had been stirring garlicky pottage, and now a man grabbed up a meat cleaver. He stood in front of the women and the child but was too scared of Thomas to move forward.

"What do you want! Get out!" he pleaded, gesturing impotently with the cleaver.

"The ... the old woman on the stoop. She cheated me."

"What woman?"

"She sold us a bad key."

"What! You hurt my son! I don't know about a damned key!"

"You're hiding her," Thomas said, but didn't believe himself. The old trickster had nothing to do with these people. The money was gone.

A thin-limbed man with a strangely protruding belly came from upstairs with a sword, but he froze, too.

Rob them! Make them give you what they have!

Thomas shook that wicked voice out of his head.

The man from the stairs licked out toward Thomas with his sword, but he was scared and kept himself well out of range to hit or be hit back.

"Get out!" said the man with the cleaver, his face very pale now. "Get *out*!" said the mother, still holding the hurt child. The woman at the pot threw a ladleful of hot, oily pottage at him.

Thomas could see in the young father's eyes that he was working himself up to take a real swing at him with the cleaver, and there would be blood if that happened. A lot of blood.

"I'm sorry," he said, backing out the door.

An old man looked at him from a window across the narrow street but then moved into the shadows, saying feebly, "Go away. Leave them alone."

Confusion, anger, and guilt wrestled in him.

"Whore!" he screamed. "You rotten old whore!"

"Shut your hole," a deep voice said from a high window.

"You're a thief!"

"You should know about thieves around here!" Thomas rejoined.

He spat on the ground and stomped back to the cart.

Nobody followed him.

Thomas returned to the cart just as the priest was about to throw the useless key into the street, but the girl said, "May I have it?"

"Whatever for?"

"It's pretty."

Her simplicity made Père Matthieu embarrassed for his anger at having been cheated. He gave it to her, and she smiled up at him.

"If it made you smile, it's not completely worthless," he said, smiling back at her.

"I'm glad you two are so goddamned happy," Thomas said.

"You have food on you," said the girl.

"Never mind that. Now what?"

"I suppose we sleep in the cart," said the priest.

"All right. Let's pull it away from this shithole of a neighborhood first."

A few minutes later, on another street, the girl pulled a green ribbon from her sack and tied the key around her neck, then sat back, looking at the last, orange light of the sun on the rooftops. That was when she saw the angel. It was neither male nor female, but both somehow, and more beautiful than either gender. It asked her to sing a song for it.

"I don't know if I feel like singing," she said.

It asked her to sing anyway.

The light was on its beautiful hair and the whole street suddenly smelled like pine trees and juniper.

She sang.

Hey little robin, hey-ho

Do you sing for me, hey-ho?
In your Easter best
With your pretty red chest,
Do you sing for me, hey-ho?

Hey little robin sing-hey
Do you fly to your nest, sing-hey?
To your house of sticks
And your pretty little chicks,
Do you fly to your nest, sing-hey?

"Hey down there!" said a man from a second-floor window. "I know that song. Are you from Normandy?"

The girl nodded.

"So am I. My mother sang us that on our way to church. I haven't heard it in twelve years or more."

"My mother sang it to me as well."

"Are you healthy?"

The girl nodded and showed him her neck.

"All three of you?"

"On the blood of our savior," said the priest.

"You shouldn't be on the street now. It's nearly dark."

Thomas stopped the cart.

"Do you know what happens after dark?" the man continued.

"We have no place to go," said the girl.

The man looked back over his shoulder and exchanged a few words with someone. Then he looked at them again.

"I'll feed you, the three of you, if you'll sing it for me again."

Jehan de Rouen was a woodcarver. He sold wooden statues of Christ and the saints, but especially Mary, from his first-floor shop, and he and his wife lived above this. His success meant that they did not share their house with another family, as most merchants were obliged to. The workshop was neatly kept except for the odd piles of shavings, and the priest felt bad about bringing the mule inside.

Jehan insisted.

While his guests sat down to table between the kitchen and the workshop, Jehan fetched a bottle of pale spirits, setting out a bowl and pouring some in. He gave it first to the girl.

"Do you recognize that?"

She made a face but nodded.

"Papa likes that."

"Everybody's papa likes that in Normandy. It's made from the best apples in France."

He shared the bowl around. It made a pleasant little fire in their bellies.

The priest set in praising the artisan's figures. Thomas, who recognized their long-headed style, said "Did you make the Christ on this side of the bridge?"

The woodcarver flushed with pride, hoisting up his very heavy brown eyebrows, which hardly thinned over his nose.

"I did."

"A marvelous figure," said the priest. "A welcome reminder of Christ's love after the misery at the Hôtel Dieu."

"Actually, the abbey commissioned it, hoping it would keep the plague out. But we've had plague. And worse."

"Worse?" the priest asked, not incredulously, but hoping for specifics.

"You'll sleep in my workshop. Keep the windows closed and barred. If you use the slop jar, don't open the windows to throw it out until morning. They don't come every night, but it's been nearly a week. They're due."

"What are due?"

"If you hear something heavy treading in the street, pray hard but quietly, and stay away from the windows. And if anything knocks, don't open."

"What knocks?"

Jehan darted his eyes at the girl, then shook his head and

took a deep breath.

"What comes?"

"We don't know. Nobody who sees them lives."

Jehan's wife, Annette, brought out stale bread trenchers with the last of their thin soup. "Don't be shy about finishing it; we've had ours," she said. Overcome with emotion at her kindness and her plain, handsome face, the girl kissed her hand. The wife stroked her hair. The girl suddenly felt the hurt in the woman, how it mirrored her own hurt. One had lost a daughter, the other a mother. Each saw a flicker of the dead one. It was bitter but very sweet and good. Annette took her head into her bosom, tentatively at first, but then with great emotion, and cried down into her hair.

"What are you called, little bird?"

"Delphine."

They cried together and held each other as the priest looked at Thomas and Thomas looked down, deeply ashamed.

In their weeks together, neither man had ever asked her name.

The liquor was soon gone, and the embers of the fire were cooling. After a hushed consultation with his wife, the woodcarver took his hat in his hands and asked Thomas and the priest if the girl might be allowed to sleep in the bed with Annette; Jehan would make his bed on the woodshop floor with the other men. They nodded.

"Thank you," Delphine said, and went upstairs.

The priest and Thomas looked at each other, each thinking the same thing.

She's home.

This is her home now.

When the men were all settled on the tightly packed dirt floor, Jehan spoke to them in a whisper.

"It's not that nobody has seen those that knock; it's that

what they've seen is so awful."

"Go on," Thomas said.

"Maude, a widowed hatmaker on the next street, heard the knock and didn't open. But she heard her neighbor, Humbert, open for them and then yell. Her house is old and she could see out through a space between the beam and plaster. She said a stone man had Humbert by the hair and bit his nose off. Then it went in, and a stone woman after it. The whole family was killed: bludgeoned and bitten. The work of the Devil."

"It was dark, yes?" the priest said.

"Course it was; they only come at night."

"How could she be sure it was stone? Maybe these were just thieves."

"There was stone dust and bits of stone in the house from where Humbert's son tried to fight them. And I reckon you could tell a stone man from a man of flesh even in the dark. And what thieves bite people to death?"

"Hungry ones?" Thomas said, but neither of the other men found that funny.

His sorry joke hung in the thick darkness of the workshop for a long moment, until the mule took a relaxed and abundant shit on the woodcarver's floor. Thomas started chuckling, and soon the priest and Jehan were chuckling as well, and then the three of them were trying unsuccessfully to bite back laughter like naughty boys in church.

"What's so funny down there?" Annette called.

"Oh, nothing," Jehan said. "One of our guests said he enjoyed his supper."

They laughed themselves to sleep.

Nothing knocked for them that night.

Morning came. The sky was a bright gray that neither threatened rain nor allowed for the possibility of sunshine, but it was welcome after the night the men had spent huddled on the workshop floor listening for the knocking of God knew what. Thomas was up first, and he opened the window enough so that he could try to scrub the worst of the rust off his armor. The sound woke the priest, but the woodcarver snored on, the scent of his Norman apple brandy still spicing his exhalations.

The priest sat close to Thomas and spoke quietly into his ear.

"What are you going to do if the girl stays?"

"She'll stay, all right. She's already spreading rushes with the woman and helping her kill fleas on the coverlet."

"So what will you do?"

"Same as before. Push on."

"Where?"

"Hadn't thought about it yet."

"I have. I think I still want to get to Avignon."

"Your catamite brother?"

The priest winced at that, but nodded. There was something flinty about Thomas this morning.

"You might come with me."

"In your cart?"

"How else?"

"I might take the cart and leave you here."

"I couldn't stop you, of course."

"I know."

"Don't talk like that. What's gotten into you?"

"I'll talk as it pleases me to talk. And don't look so wounded about the cart. Just because you went out to the orchard and found it doesn't make it yours."

"I'm not contesting that. I just thought . . ."

"Well, don't think. I do better alone, that's all. I don't know how I found myself tagging behind that little witch in the first place. Or with you. I'm damned already, as are you, though you don't realize it because you've got your robe and your cross and your Latin. I just . . . don't want anybody's eyes on me. If I have to do things to survive."

"I see."

"No, you don't see. What you don't see is that you're a common bugger priest. And she's just a skinny little girl who wants her mother. And I'm an outlaw knight who's been formally cut off from the sacraments of the church. Death means Hell, so I'm going to keep death off me as long as I can. And I'll do that better in the country than I will in Paris or Avignon."

The woodcarver stirred, but then went back to snoring.

"You're . . . you're excommunicate?"

Thomas nodded, then stood up from the floor without the use of his hands, as a fit young squire might have; as if his anger made him youthful. With his brow creased and his eyes set belligerently he looked thirty, not forty. He looked like figures of Mars. Or Lucifer. He got his sword and sharpening stone and squatted nimbly back on his heels.

"When?" the priest said.

"Does it matter?"

"I'm just curious. It's . . . It's so final."

"I thought I'd let you know before you cried too hard about parting company with me."

"Why did they do that to you?"

"What do you want, the given reasons? Or the real one?"

"Given, first."

"Heresy, sodomy, blasphemy. The usual things to turn a petty lord's village against him."

"You don't strike me as a sodomite."

"Oh, but heresy and blasphemy sit well, do they?"

"Perhaps blasphemy. You do have a colorful way of expressing displeasure. But why did they really excommunicate you?"

"To get my land. Why else?"

"Blasphemy is serious."

"This from the man who took communion from a monkey's head."

"That really happened?"

"If we both remember it, I'd say yes."

The priest's face reddened with shame, and then he looked forlorn.

"Don't take on so," said Thomas. "Nothing cunting matters."

"That's the way a man talks before he damns himself."

"It's not the first time I've said it."

"Tell me what happened."

"Is our host sleeping soundly?"

As if to answer the question himself, Jehan the woodcarver exhaled horsily with his lips, making a sound like "Plah."

The priest looked back at Thomas.

"Tell me."

TEN

Of the Battle of Crécy

It had rained. Just a quick August shower and then it was gone and everything smelled like late summer with just that hint of damp and rot. The farms in Picardy were stubbled where the wheat and barley had already been mowed. The ground was moist and Thomas could smell the good, black soil of his home province, even over the equally pleasant nose of horses and oiled steel.

His lord, the Comte de Givras, had sued for the pleasure of being in the first line of knights to charge the English where they set themselves on the field at Crécy, which meant he sued for Thomas's right to be there, too. They drew up in the first line of attack along with Alençon, the king's brother, and came up to the edge of the field, looking at their adversaries.

The invaders under King Edward of England had backed themselves up a terraced slope between two copses of trees with a flat field before them. At least, it looked flat on the approach. A bank with a drop the height of a man revealed itself as the French host drew up; to attack the English lines, the knights of France would have to ride around to where it flattened out, which was only about eighty yards from another run of trees, and then mount the hill.

It was a funnel.

It was a trap.

The crossbowmen, mostly little Genoese mercenaries whom the French called "Salamis," went out first at the king's command. They were bitching because the big shields they hid behind while reloading hadn't come forward yet, and their hempen strings were wet from the rain; besides, it was late in the day and they would have to shoot uphill and into the sun. They wanted to wait for their *pavisses*. They wanted to wait until morning, when the sun would confound English arrows. King Phillip told them they would have worse than arrows to deal with if they didn't do their work tonight. But, as the French were all about to find out, the king didn't have anything worse than arrows.

The Salamis came running back after about ten minutes, more than a few of them bloodied and stuck with feathers; Thomas would always remember how one had an arrow stuck straight through his hand and was waving it about as if it were on fire and he might put it out. A French knight yelled, "They've switched sides!" and another yelled, "Cowards!" and soon the impatient knights were riding over the Genoese through that narrow pass to get at the English. Some even struck down at the fleeing men, but Thomas's lord did not, so neither did Thomas.

They rode hard at the line of English knights, who were standing at the top of their tawny slope like bait. They were standing with their poleaxes and swords, confident the French would not reach them in any shape to hurt them. They were flying the banner of the dragon, as the French were flying the sacred red oriflamme, which the Valois king had fetched with great ceremony from St. Denis; both banners meant the same thing—no quarter. Thomas's seigneur wanted at the English king, whose camp sat by a large windmill, or at his son, the Prince of Wales. He wanted to punish them for the insult of their small numbers; the French had them three to one, as men-at-arms went. Most knights, lords of manors and castles large and small from the breadth of France, had only contempt for the rows of farmer-soldiers arranged in wedge formations between the English knights, but Thomas's blood wasn't so far above theirs. And he had a bad feeling. The archers were standing like dogs at the crouch with their longbows strung and little fences of arrows stuck into the ground at their feet. They were waiting. Thomas guessed that they had picked a landmark to range their first flight, and that they would loose when the French vanguard passed it. Now the hill got steep and took the speed out of their charge, the horses sweating and blowing hard from their nostrils. Thomas looked at a knobby shrub jutting out, and thought, *That's it*, even as Alençon's horse drew beside it.

The English archers, rough plowmen from Lancashire to Kent with overmuscled right shoulders and no feeling in the first three fingers, sank into their hips and pulled their heavy bowstrings back to their ears. As did the pale, dark-haired Welsh bowmen in their parti-colored green and white. Some five thousand archers in all.

They loosed.

Thomas couldn't hear the slap of all those bows through his padded aventail and helm, but he saw the arrows rise like a swarm of flies and then come down. He had no visor. Many of those who had them didn't push them down in time. The arrows fell hard with a noise like hail on tiles, but also sick and wet where one slammed through chain mail or into horseflesh. Men gasped and swore and screamed, but the horses' screams were worse. They bucked and reared and bit at the arrows sticking in them. Some turned their haunches and ran, while others lay down and refused to move again. Many fell and pitched their riders. The French line was dissolving, and they weren't halfway to their enemy. Thomas saw that his lord was riding crooked in his saddle, and then he saw two shafts sticking out of the older man, both in the chest; the older man would have fallen but for the deep saddle and high pommel made expressly to keep knights cinched in place. Thomas raised his lance and couched the butt in its fewter, reaching out to grab the reins of the comte's horse; and then an arrow went *whung* on his lord's conical helm, and he felt a hard slap on his face, like from his mother's spoon in the kitchen. Suddenly he was leaning back, almost out of the saddle, looking up at the clouds. But his eyes weren't focused right because there was something white in the sky.

Fletching.

He had an arrow in the face.

He sat up and the pain hit him so hard he dropped his lance and almost passed out, but he didn't. The horses had both stopped. His seigneur was slumped to one side, in danger of falling. Thomas tried to speak, but only blood came out of his mouth—the point was in his tongue. What was left of the French line, maybe four dozen knights and the Comte d'Alençon, was bulling toward the English, their backs receding as they rode to die.

As the remnants of the French vanguard closed, the English began to touch off crude cannons, sending brass and stone balls whizzing into men, sending limbs and scraps of armor and fabric in all directions, sending gouts of smoke skyward. The banging cracks, like near thunder, further terrified the injured horses. One knight to Thomas's left, whose surcoat blazed with three crescent moons argent, tried to regain control of his mount, which was kicking madly with a half dozen shafts in him. The horse kicked Thomas's leg and broke it even through the greave, then, his eyes as wide as goose eggs, threw his rider off and stamped the man's helmeted head into the mud again and again with his front hooves, destroying it utterly. Then he lay down and died on what remained of his master. He was not alone; one Englishman would later say the dead horses were lined up like piglets to suckle.

Thomas grabbed again for his lord's reins, using the rowels on his spurs to guide his own horse, and turned them both away. The Comte de Givras groaned, as if in disappointment, and another shaft caught him in the back. Thomas spurred them both for the French lines, but the next wave of knights was charging at them, shouting "Saint-Denis!" and "Glory!" They were beautiful in their surcoats of many colors, a flock of exotic birds heading for birdlime. Some of them were dying already, as the arrows were falling their way now.

Only the fact that the archers preferred charging knights to retreating ones saved Thomas and his Lord from being riddled; the volleys had also opened up big enough holes in the ranks for the two men to pass through, although one knight in robin's-egg blue glanced against Thomas so hard he knocked him into his seigneur, who nearly fell again. He was shaking his head, ashamed not to be dying on the field. But he was certainly dying.

His little page, Renoud, and Thomas's squire, André, ran up with a barber-surgeon, who helped the injured men off their mounts. Thomas was nauseated from pain and all the blood he had swallowed, and the eye above the arrow wouldn't stop tearing.

The surgeon used a pair of shears to cut the arrow on the comte's back so he could lie down to die; the Comte de Givras was a more important man than Thomas, but the surgeon attended Thomas because he saw that he might live. He pulled the big man down and wedged a stone between his back teeth to keep his mouth open, then cut the corner of his mouth forcing the shears in to snip the shaft. He got the point out of the tongue—nothing had ever hurt Thomas so badly—then pulled the shaft up out of the cheek. His hands were slimy with blood, and his grip kept slipping. He would have stitched Thomas, but someone had him by the sleeve now, shouting "The king's musician is hurt, the king commands you!" and he was gone.

The page held the seigneur's hand as Thomas heard his awful breathing; he was drowning. He died clenching his teeth and shivering. He was awake until the very end and knew what was happening to him, but he did not cry out. Thomas did, as much to see that the great man was dead as for his own pain.

It was the worst day he had ever known.

With the squire's help, Thomas sat up and watched the second wave fail, too, though some had gotten close enough to exchange blows near the banner of the Prince of Wales. Soon they were finished, and a lull followed. Now bare-legged Welshmen ran from the English lines and stuck knives into the eyes and visors of the stunned knights on the ground, killing them as easily as boys hunting crabs.

Thomas's eye was hemming itself shut as the injured side of his face swelled. Men who passed them did not recognize him. Now a man wearing the king's livery came and took both Thomas's warhorse, who was lathered in sweat and stooping his head, and his mild-mannered palfrey, who always did a side-to-side dance when he smelled lettuce. He never saw either horse again.

The sun went down and still the beaten French rallied again and again to ride into the gloaming. Thomas had a moment's hope when he saw the windmill near the English king on fire, its great spars turning ablaze like a slow wheel in Hell; but the English had burned the windmill themselves to give their archers light to murder by.

It had been dark for an hour when the call went up to flee. There would be no more French charges; the English were coming down from their terraced hill, and there was nothing to stop them. Thomas was suddenly aware of being alone— he did not know where his squire was and could not remember the last time he had seen him. The cries of wounded men being killed on the ground grew closer, as did the rude, choppy language of their killers, confident now, calling out to one another. Thomas sat up as best he could with his sword pointed behind him, ready to take the leg off a Welshman before he died. He heard hooves and wondered if an English knight was about to spit him. He turned his head. Here was his squire with a horse, a tired old nag from the baggage trains. Thomas tried to speak but wept when his swollen tongue touched his palate. André made a shushing gesture and, with some effort, got Thomas up, and then on the nag's broad back. He leapt in front of his master and took Thomas's great weight on his back as he took the reins and they cantered away from Crécy-en-Ponthieu. The night was very dark. The nameless horse sometimes pitched to avoid the body of one who had tried to flee but succumbed to his wounds; so many had died that Thomas could not comprehend it. The plain below the English position would be known as the valley of clerks, for it would take an army of men with pens and field desks to record the names and titles of the French dead.

It was at the town of Amiens where Thomas convalesced, his squire having paid a surgeon to see to him.

"A good thing it was a bodkin point on that shaft," the surgeon had said as he put first wine and then egg white in the punctured cheek. "A broadhead would have never come out. As it is, I'm scared that tongue will sour and kill you, so I'm tempted to have it off. But then what would you pray with?"

Before he pulled the tooth whose roots were knocked loose by the arrow, then stitched the tongue and face, the surgeon told the squire to hold Thomas's head still. Thomas grunted something.

"That's what they all say," the surgeon growled, "but he'll hold you just the same. And if your lordship bites me, I'll yank a good tooth as well."

It had taken less than an hour, but it was the longest hour Thomas could recall.

The ten minutes he took to set the leg seemed merely purgatorial after the hell of little pliers fishing in his cheek for loose bone, and the dip and bite of the curved needle in his tongue.

"You'll not be so pretty now, but you may live to thank the Virgin, if she saves you. The pain's a good sign. I'll come around again tomorrow night. Splash some more wine on that around suppertime, but no supper for you till Tuesday, and then only broth and raw eggs. God felt so bad about throwing man out of the garden, he gave us the chicken, which gave us the egg. Wouldn't surprise me to find out angels' blood was egg whites. God rest you, sir knight."

The squire stayed with Thomas for two weeks while the arrow wound toyed with his life, first reddening around the margins, then running clear, then slowly, very slowly, beginning to heal. When he was out of danger, though still not well enough to travel, he sent his squire home to tell the lady of the manor he was alive. The seneschal, who had been watching for Sir Thomas, stopped André at the gate and told him what had happened.

The squire turned around quickly and rode hard for Amiens.

André stood in the little room with his hat in his hands and his hood thrown back. He measured his words and spoke them slowly, pausing before the worst ones.

"Sire . . . Your keep and the lands of Arpentel are . . . forfeit to the Comte d'Évreux, of Navarre and Normandy. Your seneschal made to stand against him and prepared for siege; but your wife, fearing the comte's cruelty should he breach the walls, treated with d'Évreux and let him into your keep. And, it seems, after very little struggle . . . her bed. Your son, however, has been declared by the comte the lord of the manor and stands to inherit when he comes to majority. D'Évreux, in the interval, is regent and protector, and your rents will go to him, save enough for your lady to keep a modest household."

Thomas shook his bandaged head and said words that sounded like "the king."

"The king is weak now. The lords of Normandy scheme against him, and treat with England. King Phillip gave our fallen lord's lands of Givras to the Norman to keep him from rising in plain revolt. And now he has seized yours, which border Givras. Because he can. Because you were faithful to your seigneur, and he was faithful to the defeated king, you have been . . . moved aside."

Thomas shook his agonized head, his eyes tearing.

"Further," the squire said, "you are declared excommunicate. The bishop of Laon himself has ordered it, against the protests of your priest. They will strip you of your spurs in absentia, empty the chalice, and lay down the cross; if ever you return and try to claim your land back, the priest must deny the people the sacraments as well."

Thomas made a sound that might have been, "When?"

"The ceremony is tomorrow."

And so Thomas had healed. When his money ran out, he went west to Normandy and sold his soul to Godefroy, watching always for the heraldic crest of the man who had ruined him, Chrétien, Comte d'Évreux: the gold-on-red wheel of Spain quartered with a barred field of fleur-de-lys. Thomas agreed to stay with the brigands so long as they stayed in High Normandy; Godefroy agreed that they would often visit the comte's domain. Thomas swore that this grasping lord with lands in Spain, Normandy, and Picardy, who had his piggish eyes even on the crown of France, would die in the mud at a brigand's hands.

He swore it, spat on a cross, and flung it down.

Since God had permitted his excommunication, he would earn it.

Thomas never thought himself the kind of man to take part in theft and killings, and to permit rape, but, in the name of revenge, he became exactly that kind of man.

For a time.

ELEVEN

Of the Market on rue Mont-Fetard

"**W**hat became of your squire?" said the priest.

"I've no whoring idea. I sent him off rather than take him to Hell with me, but he's like to have found another hell. Probably married an English girl and hung a mess of brats off her dugs."

The woodcarver's eyes were open now. Thomas turned his gaze upon him.

"How much did you hear?"

"More than I shall soon forget."

Thomas breathed in, as if to exhale some oath, but he had mellowed with the telling of his tale. He suffered the priest to put his hand on his shoulder, then hung his head. Now the woodcarver sat up and put his hand on Thomas as well.

Jehan the woodcarver was nearly out of food, so he had to go to market. Normally he would have done this on his own, wearing a yoke with two baskets and wearing a cloth about his face, taking care to stay as far away from others as he could; but today Delphine insisted on coming along. Which meant Thomas would go as well. The priest was half dying for want of wine, and things had gotten so bad in the quarter that Annette didn't want to be left alone. Neither did the mule, but it wasn't asked.

Annette went up to a trunk at the foot of her bed and took out a pair of pretty yellow woolen hose that had belonged to her daughter, as well as a pair of wooden pattens for tying to the bottoms of one's shoes to protect them from the mud and worse of the Parisian streets. She made a gift of these to Delphine and combed her hair out, humming the same Norman tune the girl had sung beneath their window the night before. She was smiling more than Jehan had seen her smile in months.

It was midday when they left.

The five of them kept tight to each other and walked a twisting mile through the streets, with the shop fronts shuttered, the few open windows on higher stories staring at them like dead sockets. Other groups huddled to themselves, and nobody spoke. A cart passed them, forcing them to hug up against the buildings, the driver saying, "Watch out," as mechanically as if he were talking to himself. Rats ran in the gutters and sometimes on the roofs, but otherwise things were so still that a dog barking in the distance sounded like music.

It got noisy as they drew near, however.

The market on the rue Mont-Fetard was one of the few places where people would still congregate, and, as such, was one of the most dangerous places one could go. Many of the spaces where stalls once stood were empty now, and those that remained had distanced themselves well away from their neighbors, like teeth in old gums.

Still, the market presented a rich spectacle, even in fraction.

Yellow finches fluttered and chirped in cages; an acrobat walked backward on her hands with eyes painted on her bottom and outsized gloves on her feet; a Spaniard berated two little dogs who had grown tired of spinning in circles on their hind legs while he played a horn.

People yelled and bargained as they had before the sickness; they just did it farther away from each other. Hawkers called to the group in singsong chants:

Salt from Brittany, and the Franche-Comté,
who'll save your flesh if you walk away?

Indigo, indigo, precious and blue
as the peacock's chest and his proud tail, too.

Who'll buy my musk? Who wants to make love?
The rabbit, the fox and, in his turn, the dove.

The girl, who had walked very near the group while they made their way through the dead streets, now let herself be pulled this way and that, now trailing the group, now trotting awkwardly ahead, unaccustomed as she was to wearing pattens on her shoes. She had the feeling that whatever she sought in Paris would be here, in this market, but she loved the market's éclat with the love of a child who has been quiet too long. She loved the colors and the motion of commerce, but especially the noise. The sound of foreign languages pleased her particularly, reminding her that a whole world lay beyond the horizons of Normandy and Paris: a world of varied provinces and innumerable towns and hamlets that might not all be dying.

Foreigners were in no short supply at the Mont-Fetard market; Germans hunched over stacks of iron, spraying beer through their whiskers as they called out. Spaniards sang *"Cuero, cuero, cuero de Córdoba"* over shoe leather so fine one could almost see light through it. Bohemians tapped bars of lead in rhythm and sang inscrutable songs, more to amuse themselves than to draw custom.

Delphine loved it all.

The Florentines had the biggest and most beautiful stall; they had lived in the city and had grown rich selling the bright, red wool of Florence in bolts that drew the eye from thirty paces. Now they wore plague masks that made them look like awful birds. A table sat before them with a bowl of water in which one was to place money, as it was believed this would cleanse it of bad air. These merchants had grown adept at showing their cloth by means of two sticks, and they rolled and fluttered it before Annette as she came near, though she could only come so near; little stacks of bricks marked the boundary past which customers' feet were not to step.

But where was the food?

When the priest, whose stomach was rumbling noisily, asked Jehan where the food sellers were, the woodcarver pointed up ahead, past a group of bickering men. As they approached, they saw a *sergent* with his baton of office yelling through a handkerchief at a shrugging merchant who sold tortoises and tiny owls and other exotic animals. The officer gestured at a miserable-looking monkey in a cage.

"That beast has it. You have to pitch its cage in the river, or burn it, but either way, get it out of here."

"Monkeys don't get plague. He's just tired. Who wouldn't be tired with you yelling at him?"

"Monkeys are just little men, aren't they? Foul little men who bite and throw filth. I'm telling you, he's got it."

The sergent was obliged to use reason because he had only one man with him, and the merchant, who had a Gascon accent, had several dark-skinned fellows who looked like brothers sitting within easy reach of staves and knives.

The group continued on, the ailing monkey locking eyes with the priest and staring at him with disturbing intelligence.

Now the chants of food sellers came to them; hazelnuts, apples, pork pies in crusts. One stall was wild with hanging game, some of it none too fresh; the hunter, sweating in a hat made from no less than three foxes, was using a leafy branch to swat flies away from a deflated-looking rabbit.

"Wolf pelts!" he barked at them, now gesturing at an impressive stack of hides. "Winter isn't so far away, you know. You'll want good furs for the little girl." The priest politely waved away the man's solicitation, provoking something very like a silent snarl from him.

Next were the fishmongers, their carp and sturgeons and black bass laid out on wet straw, the sellers stinking of the river, wearing aprons brown with blood and glittering with scales. Thomas went to a large carp, but Jehan pulled him away.

"Not this stall," he whispered. "They have a stall on the Right Bank as well, and whatever doesn't sell there comes here. They redden them with pig's blood."

"Let the man look!" the fishmonger hissed.

Jehan made the sound of a pig snuffling.

"That's a lie!" the man said.

"Since when is an *oink* a lie?"

"Leave it," Annette said, as the fishmonger wiped a rusty filleting knife with his apron. A look from Thomas made him put it down.

The other fish stall was ropy with eels, and neither Thomas, the priest, nor the girl wanted any part of it. The butchers were next, and there were a good many cuts of meat to be had, though the prices were ruinously high. Annette debated with Jehan about a shoulder of pork, which he haggled for and got. Soon she found a bag of onions, leeks, and garlic. Then two fistfuls of hazelnuts; Annette was happier than she had been in many weeks, and she was going to cook a proper meal for their guests.

Thomas cheerfully munched a black pudding he found for a denier, sharing pieces of it with the priest, until his attention was called by the sound of a barrel rolling. He walked over to a table full of bright, new chain mail, though this was not for sale.

"Clean your armor, my lord?" sang out a man too old for the scalloped fripperies he wore as he turned a handle that turned a barrel full of sand and vinegar. "Ten minutes in here and your hauberk will shine like God's teeth." He had the air of a squire, perhaps one whose seigneur had died. When he saw that Thomas was hooked, he said, "Two deniers to make it like new, sire. You won't find better or cheaper."

Thomas had just begun stripping off his belt and surcoat when the girl yelled "Père Matthieu! Please come!" with such urgency that he ran with one hand holding the belt closed and the other on the hilt of his sword.

The priest and Thomas arrived at the same time to find Delphine standing near a cart belonging to a seller of religious articles, a hunched, pale little man with very black hair who seemed to smile at everything, even the sight of Thomas stomping toward him.

"What in Christ's name is it?" Thomas said.

"The oil!"

"What?"

"This is the oil that the Magdalene used to wash Jesus' feet!" the girl said excitedly, bouncing a little on the balls of her own feet. She was pointing at a little clay vial stoppered with cork.

"Sure it is. And I'll bet that's the hammer that pounded in the nails," he said, gesturing at a plain wooden mallet.

"No, actually," the seller said, "it's the hammer that fixed the axle of this cart. But . . ." he continued, producing a carpenter's plane, "*This* is the plane used by the carpenter Joseph, father of Our Lord; the very one sweet Jesu learned to use as a boy. It is said that any beam planed with this is proof against fire, and no two such beams might ever be separated. Imagine! A house that would never burn and never fall!"

"Do I look as though I build houses?"

"No, my lord, you look as though you knock them down and none can stop you. But surely you will want a fine house built one day, and you may lend the carpenter this holy thing."

"I had one house. I will not have another."

"A traveler! Then look upon this . . ." he said, fishing something out of a leather sack. "A lock of Saint Christopher's hair in a reliquary of horse bone. The horse was Caesar Constantine's horse, a stallion of white so fair he made snow look like coal ash."

"You met this horse?"

"He was described to me, as I have described him to you, as it was described to him that sold it to me, and on backward to antiquity. Ride with this in your saddlebag, sir knight, and your horse will never stumble in a river, nor throw a shoe save within thirty yards of a farrier. Also, you will never lose your way again, for Saint Christopher himself will lead your horse by the nose, even to the tavern door."

Delphine had stood rapt throughout this pitch, but now the priest spoke up.

"Your stories are very pretty, but surely you see that only the child believes them. Good day to you."

Thomas had already turned his back to walk away, and the priest now reached for Delphine's hand. She withdrew it before he touched her and wove her limbs through the spokes of the cart's wheel, looking at the priest like some feral St. Catherine.

"Let's go, child," the priest said.

"No!" she all but howled, and gripped the spokes tighter. "This is why we're here! It's here!"

"Nothing is here, girl, but old tools and donkey bones. I know this man's sort. Now let's go."

"Perhaps you seek the vintner," the pale little man said, his very green eyes twinkling significantly at Père Matthieu.

"What did you say?" asked the priest.

"There's a vintner selling good wine from Auxerre just four stalls up the street. You want wine so badly you're gray from it. Your upper lip is sweating."

Thomas turned around now.

The priest opened his mouth to speak but closed it again because he had nothing to say. This man had seen right through him.

"You seem lost, brother. Perhaps you need something to point the way for you. Perhaps something very dear."

"Like what?" Thomas said.

"Something others think they have in holy shrines, but which is in this humble cart. In my keeping. The only one that's real."

"What," Thomas said, "the milk of the Virgin? The cocks of the magi?"

"Better."

"Gabriel's turd? God's piss pot?"

"Oh, much better."

So saying, he scrambled into his cart and tugged out a box of cedar with Greek letters on it. He passed his hands over it several times like a magician, then opened it to reveal a leaf-shaped shining spearhead worked with ivory, and also lettered in Greek.

"You're not saying . . ." the priest said.

"I am."

"Why is it inscribed in Greek when a Roman soldier pierced Our Lord with it?"

"It went to Alexandria for a time. Oliphants from the Afric continent gave their tusks for it."

"Why should I think this greatest of all relics should be in the care of, forgive me, a man of such . . ."

"Poverty?" the little man suggested as the priest gestured impotently in search of an inoffensive word. "Humble means?"

"Something like that."

Delphine spoke up from her wheel now, saying, "Did not Our Lord go humbly in His time? In sandals or on a donkey?"

"The child is wise," said the relic seller. "Heavenly treasures and earthly ones are not the same."

"It does look . . . quite credible," said the priest.

"Do you hear your own words?" said Thomas, stepping closer. "This is no more the holy spear than this man is Christ's wet nurse. He has bewitched you! Both of you. Let's go."

"Yes, perhaps you should go," the relic seller said, shutting the box with a loud snap and fastening the latch. He looked anxiously past the priest and hastily began to pack his goods away. Thomas saw why, and then the priest turned and saw as well. A group of agitated men was bearing down on them, pointing at the relic seller.

One of them said the word "Jew."

The *sergent* who had been arguing with the monkey seller was now being pushed along by the crowd, who seemed intent on making him do some duty or other regarding the little man and his cart.

"We have to get out of here," Thomas said. "Now."

The priest nodded, sweating now from more than want of wine, and tugged gently at the girl, who shook her head stubbornly and kept a tight grip on the wheel, shutting her eyes against the approaching group. She was frightened, too.

Thomas wasn't having any. He shoved the priest out of the way and unwound her limbs from the wheel even though his grip hurt her and made her cry out.

"Goddamn it, you'll come with me if I have to pull the whoring wheel off with you," he said, and soon had her over his shoulder even though she cried and slapped at him. The priest had already gotten clear, and now Thomas stepped out of the way as the small mob reached the cart.

The relic seller had packed away his things, if sloppily, and was now pulling at the spars of the cart to get it going. Three or four men stepped in front of him, one of them bearing a table leg as a club. He tried to ignore them and move past them, but one of them put his hand on the man's face and pushed him down. It wasn't very hard to do.

A paunchy, middle-aged fellow with a beakish nose and ginger hair took off his straw hat and faced the *sergent*.

"I am Pierre Auteuil, pardoner, and I am the licensed seller of relics in this quarter. On my oath, I affirm that this man is a known Jew. And by royal decree, there are to be no Jews in the city of Paris."

"I know him to be a Jew as well," shouted an old fellow, "I have seen him at the Hot Fair in Troyes."

The *sergent*, who saw far less harm in the little man than

he had in the sick monkey, sighed and said, "How do you know this? He wears no yellow circle."

"He was pointed out to me!"

"That's no proof."

"Ask him, then," one said.

"Yes, ask him his name," said another.

"What is your name?" said the *sergent*, not unkindly.

The perhaps-Jew said nothing.

"Tell me your name," said the *sergent*, beginning to shed his benevolence.

The man said simply, "I am a Christian."

Now the woodcarver and his wife had found Thomas, the priest, and the girl. They all stood transfixed by the scene developing on the rue Mont-Fetard, as did a number of others, many of whom forgot the danger of the plague and stood near one another to see.

"Christians have names," said the *sergent*. "What is yours?"

"Look at his cock," one said.

Now two fellows bulled to the front of the crowd and grabbed the man's arms. The pardoner yanked his trousers and underthings down and pointed at his foreskinless member.

"Stop," Delphine yelled, and was ignored.

"What more proof do we need?" said the pardoner.

"I'm a convert," pleaded the man, and he began to say a *Pater Noster* but was shoved again to the ground. Now several kicks were aimed at him, but the *sergent* and his man interposed themselves.

"This will be done right, if it's to be done. We'll pillory him and I'll send to the abbot to find out what he wants done with him."

So saying, the lawman helped him up, pulled his pants up, and took him away, directing his man to stand guard over the cart. The crowd followed behind the Jew to where a pair of pillories stood in a little square. A spice merchant who had adulterated precious sacks of peppercorns with pellets of soot and clay stood bent over in one set, with his hands and head in the stocks and a brick on a rope around his neck. The Jew was put in the other, and a lock secured through a hasp.

And there he stayed.

Delphine seemed distracted all through dinner. She chewed birdy little bites of Annette's roast pork and kept cutting her eyes toward the door.

"What has you, child?" the woodcarver's wife said.

"What will they do with the Jew?"

"If he's lucky, flog him out of the city. If he's unlucky, hang him," Jehan said.

Thomas ate wolfishly. The priest shared out his wine to the others, holding the bottle patiently while the last three drops fell into Jehan's wooden cup.

"That is," Jehan went on, "If they don't leave him out all night. God help him if they do." He crossed himself and pulled off a piece of the bread trencher he had been eating from, thumbing a stringy bit of pork on top of it and tucking it into his mouth.

Delphine looked at the door.

"Don't even think about it," Thomas said, even as she sprang out of her seat faster than seemed possible. Her little white hand was on the bolt and drawing it as Thomas shoved back the bench he shared with the priest so he could stand, spilling Père Matthieu, who, falling backward onto the packed dirt floor, held his cup of wine straight up and managed to save most of it.

The girl ran barefoot, her pattens and hose left in Annette's room, and Thomas followed behind her, yelling "Stay here!" to the rest of them. His armor was off, piled in the corner of the workshop, so he was almost light enough in his gambeson to catch her at a sprint. Almost. His fingers wisped through her bouncing hair, of which he would have grabbed a fistful to stop her, but then he began to lose speed and the gap between them grew. He growled and huffed a string of oaths behind her, causing her to call back at him, "You shouldn't swear like that."

The streets were stiller and emptier than before as they made their way to the market in the twilight; no rats ran now, and not even a dog's bark competed with the sound of Thomas's panting. At length he slowed his run to a loping walk; the girl, who had been peeking back at him at intervals, slowed to a walk as well. Even winded and angry, it occurred to him to be glad for the boots that saved him from feeling the filth of the Parisian muck between his toes, as she doubtless was.

"Where the hell do you think you're going?"

"To help the Jew," she said, peeking again to make sure he hadn't started running.

The light was failing, throwing the streets between the close buildings into yet more profound darkness.

"Help yourself. Something bad goes on here at night."

"Go back if you're scared."

"Scared?"

"You heard me."

"I should damned well turn around and let you go."

"Maybe you should."

He didn't.

They kept on all the way to the rue Mont-Fetard, the small girl before, and the large man behind, even as the last of the shutters of the living closed on the sight of them.

Thomas never noticed the smell of juniper riding over the baser scents of the gutter.

"I know you," the Jew said as he regarded the small girl before him. The pillories stood deserted in the square, not far from the relic cart, which had been completely picked over. The guard had stayed with it until as near dark as he dared, with no word back from the abbot and no orders from the *sergent*, and by the time he left for his house, nobody wanted to be burdened with the weight of the cart, which was heavier empty than it should have been full.

"How do you know me? From today?" she said.

"No."

"Then how?"

"I just do."

The spice seller was oblivious to her, tossing his head horsily against the pain of the hanging brick, until he felt its weight being lifted. She threw the brick into the muck past the platform. He opened his moist eyes and looked at her, saying, "You're not supposed to do that."

"I don't care."

Now the Jew called her over, saying, "Girl. Look at me. In the eyes."

She did.

"Is it time?" he said.

She wasn't sure why she said it, but she said, "Not yet," and the Jew nodded, closing his eyes. He looked very old just then, and very tired.

Thomas arrived.

He was so nonplussed at how calmly she was standing there, talking to the men bent over in the stocks, that he did not scoop her over his shoulder or drag her by the arm, having weighed the merits of both actions as he stomped behind her. It was almost fully dark.

"Well, little witch, what now?"

"Will you break their locks?"

"No."

"Why not?"

"I haven't got a hammer."

She looked sad.

Several streets away, the sound of knocking came.

"Get her home," the Jew said. "Now."

"Break my lock. Please," whimpered the spice seller.

Thomas reached for her, but she moved away from him, and he only grabbed the back of her shirt, which ripped, and the ribbon around her neck, which broke. The key that had been at the end of it fell onto the wooden platform with a *tink*. She bent to grab it as Thomas grabbed her hips.

He hoisted her up as she held the key in her small fist, arching her body toward the locked hasp that held the Jew.

"No!" she yelled, "Let me try it!"

"Get her home!"

Something knocked, closer now.

"Please . . ." said the spice seller.

"Please," said the girl, more softly.

"Goddamn it," Thomas said, setting her down and taking the key from her. He was about to pitch it in the muck.

"Please, *sire. Sir* Thomas," she whispered.

He spat, then shoved the key into the lock, "See? It doesn't whoring fit!"

But it did.

He turned it.

The lock opened and the Jew stood up.

A man no more than two streets away yelled, "Let go! Let me go!"

"PLEASE!" shrieked the spice seller.

The girl took the key from Thomas, who didn't try to keep it from her, and opened the other pillory. The dishonest merchant jerked straight and ran, tripping over the brick that had been around his neck and twisting his ankle. He limped off in the direction opposite the man's scream, but faraway knocking came from that way, too. The night seemed to swallow him completely.

The Jew said, "You wanted something?"

"Yes," she said. "But they got it . . . your cart."

"They got the one I showed you. Not this one."

He pulled a hemp rope from around his neck, dangling at its end a hinged wooden tube that came out of his shirt. It was about the size of a short flute case. He gave it to her. She kissed him.

Thomas hefted her and ran, even as she put the rope

around her neck.

"When?" the Jew called after her.

But she did not answer.

TWELVE

Of the Ones Who Knock by Night

When they got to the door of the woodcarver's house, Thomas had the good sense not to knock; he said, "Priest!" and then the girl said, "Annette! It's me." The bolt slid back and the door opened, the woodcarver motioning them in. The married couple and the priest were all pale with fear.

Jehan whispered into Thomas's ear, "They're here. In the quarter."

"I know," Thomas said.

"They're close."

The husband and wife stared at the shuttered windows and bolted doors, listening to the sounds of knocking, which were unmistakably drawing nearer. Thomas picked up his chain mail hauberk and began slithering into it. He put on his mail gloves as well. Annette said an *Ave Maria*, which her husband and the priest joined in, though the priest was watching the girl.

Delphine inclined near the wick in tallow, which was now a soupy graveyard for moths; moths lighted in her hair and flitted about her as she opened the tube the Jew had given her. Its hinges were tiny and delicate, but her small hands were made to open such things. The inside of the tube was cushioned with brown leather, upon which the mud-colored shaft of pitted iron was hardly visible. She took it in her hand. It was not what she expected; not leaf-bladed or triangular like a boar spear; rather, it was a thin rod that flared gently to a point at the end; more of a fire poker than a proper spear. She tested the point with her thumb and found it still sharp enough to make her gasp in a hitch of air. Had this piece of metal really been driven under one of His ribs? It seemed impossible that anything or anyone still in the world had actually touched Him. But it had. This was it. She kissed the spearhead and sealed it back in its case. The word *pilum* occurred to her, and she wondered if she had read it in her father's books, or if it simply came to her as so many words had lately.

"What is that?" Père Matthieu said.

"You know what it is."

None of them slept.

They stood around the table or sat against the wall.

Near dawn, something heavy brushed against the front of the building. Delphine held her breath, then nearly peed herself when the mule brayed next to her.

Now something scratched at the shuttered window.

"*Please God, please angels, do not leave me alone,*" she prayed.

The priest stood in front of her and put his hand on her chest. She grabbed his little finger, and felt that he was shaking. Thomas and Jehan had moved near the door, the knight with his sword behind him, ready to strike, the woodcarver holding a mallet. "Get back," Jehan whispered to his wife, but she kept her place just behind him.

Whatever was outside tapped at the window. Delphine grabbed the priest's finger so hard she would have hurt him if he had not been not too agitated to feel it. It tapped again, more urgently. Everyone but Thomas and the girl made the sign of the cross.

"*Come Saint Michael, come Saint Sebastian, do not leave us alone*," Delphine whispered, but she felt abandoned; they were going to be killed now by some wicked thing, and God would not or could not interfere.

The thing outside took two heavy steps and now banged on the door. Hard. Delphine squealed. Jehan put his free hand over his wife's mouth to stop her from whimpering, but then *he* whimpered. Delphine heard Thomas breathing in and out like a bellows, preparing to fight; she knew that for all his faults, he would die before he let harm come to her. She felt safer.

Then it banged again so hard that a flake of daub fell off the wall and the building shook, rocking the several long-headed wooden saints and Virgins in the workshop. The mule brayed madly and shuffled from side to side, restless for room to move or kick. It knocked over its water bucket, and Delphine felt the water between her toes.

The banging continued, faster and faster. It was maddening. Thomas began to reach for the door, ready to have done with it, but Jehan pushed his arm down and shook his head, wide-eyed with fear and warning.

Now everything became quiet.

It stayed quiet for some time, but Delphine knew it wasn't over. The grown-ups in the room were frozen like clockwork figures, and soon they would move again, urgently, as Hell came into the room. Waiting was so hard. The priest stroked her hair once, as he might have done to calm a dog. She heard his fast breathing and kissed his hand. His breathing slowed.

That was when they heard it.

A baby's cry.

In the street just outside the door.

"Oh sweet God," Annette said, moving toward the door.

Her husband pushed her back and shook his head, too scared to speak.

The baby cried again, bawling in terror or pain.

"We have to!" Annette shouted.

Now a woman's voice came to them through the oak door.

"Please," it begged.

Annette struggled with her husband, but he kept her back.

"Please, help us. In the name of mercy, I beg you," the woman's voice implored. "My baby . . . Help my baby."

The child cried again, more pathetically now, ending in an alarming rasp.

"I don't think you should open it," Delphine said quietly, too scared to make herself heard even by the priest. She knew she should speak louder, but she couldn't.

Thomas looked over his shoulder at the priest, who crossed himself and nodded.

"Help my baby . . ."

Delphine let go of the priest's hand and moved to grab Thomas's arm, but she was too late. She watched helplessly as the door opened.

A woman. No, a statue of a woman. With a crown. The Virgin.

Delphine's heart leapt with gladness that they were saved, and then it sank just as quickly.

And she did wet herself.

The door had opened on a six-foot statue of the Holy Virgin with a high crown, holding a scepter in one hand. But where the Holy Infant should have been cradled in the other, her stone hand held the ankle of an infant who dangled upside down with the purplish skin of a plague victim. He had been dead for some time. Flies buzzed around him. His milky eyes saw nothing. And yet he opened his swollen mouth and cried again.

"Help my baby," the statue said, its mouth moving jerkily. It ducked its crown and stepped into the room with the sound of a millstone grinding, and everyone recoiled from it. Now it flung the infant at Thomas so hard it knocked him backward. Delphine gaped at it; when it moved, it somehow seemed like a statue seen in glimpses; it moved fast, but choppily. It was impossible.

The fight was awful. It was hard to see in the near-darkness of the candlelit workshop. Delphine shook her head, trying to wake up from what couldn't be happening; the unholy Virgin had Annette by the arm. The arm broke. It bit something off her face and spat it at Jehan. It stove her head in with its scepter.

God, God, why sweet Annette?

"No!" Delphine tried to scream, but it came out like a kitten's mew.

The priest pulled Delphine behind him again, saying a *Pater Noster*, but she looked around his robes; Thomas had flipped his sword, holding it near the point, bludgeoning the living statue, making sparks and chipping it, but he could not stop it. It wanted the woodcarver now. Jehan's mallet knocked a point off the crown, but then it lowered its head like a bull and gored him against the wall, again and again, shaking the building with the force of it.

A trio of wooden Marys seemed to look on helplessly as a stone version of themselves killed their maker.

Now it was coming for the knight. Thomas, putting his back into a low swing, broke a foot off it, but it dropped to all fours and bit and gored at him, toppling wooden statues, wrecking everything around it. It swept out with the scepter, hitting his leg hard, almost spilling him. He grunted in pain, then lashed down and broke the scepter.

Get the spear.

Delphine ran to the table where the flute-shaped case held the spearhead, and she grabbed it just before the panicked mule kicked the table over, almost on top of her. She opened the case. The priest said her name; she handed him the spear and he understood.

Thomas had broken great pieces off the abomination, but still it kept after him.

Until it saw what the priest held.

It flipped over sideways like an acrobat doing an arch and righted its head, making the priest stop. It grinned at him and black ichor came out of its mouth. It grabbed the dead infant and whipped it around, trying to knock the spear out of Père Matthieu's hand.

"Touch it!" Delphine yelled now. "It doesn't want you to touch it!"

The priest stepped forward again.

Thomas swung for all he was worth and caught it square in the face with his sword's heavy hilt and quillons, breaking the nose from it.

The priest poked at it with the spear, and it scuttled backward out the door.

"I see you," it said to Delphine, though its stone eyes did not seem to see anything.

She shuddered.

"You didn't help the baby," it said, and walked backward into the night.

They had little time to mourn their hosts. The priest yelled "Fire!" as he noticed one wall of the house smoking, and licking flames spreading from a pile of wood shavings near Jehan's work desk. One of the candles had landed there when the mule kicked the table over, catching not only the wall but an apron hanging from the corner of the desk. The priest tried to swat out the apron, then tried to swat it against the walls, but only succeeded in stirring the flames to greater activity. Throwing down the apron, he took the mule by its halter and handed it to Thomas, who, with difficulty, led the terrified animal out into the street. The priest now gathered up both the spearhead and its case from the floor, and then he went to Delphine. He had to unmake her fists from where she held strands of Annette's hair to cry into, but then she allowed herself to be picked up. He took her through the kitchen and out back, put her into the cart, gave her the reliquary, and then unbolted the door that led from the tiny courtyard garden into the street; Thomas had led the beast around and now the priest hitched it up. Thomas ducked back into the house for the rest of his and the priest's things, then loped up the stairs for Delphine's sack as she yelled, "Leave it! Hurry!"

Choking, black smoke sifted up through the planks of the bedroom floor, but he found her sack and limped down the stairs, past the now-smoldering wooden figures, and through the kitchen. Coughing savagely, his eyes tearing and his face besooted, the knight lifted himself and their goods into the cart.

He patted out with his mailed hand the edge of the priest's linen robes where they glowed orange and curled, just on the verge of breaking out in flames.

Barely noticing this, Père Matthieu reined the mule, yelling, "Fire! Wake up!" several times for the benefit of any neighbors who might be left alive. They pulled away from the woodcarver's doomed house and rode into the last of the night, dazed and stinking of smoke.

They looked warily about them all the way, lest some fresh horror come at them from the blackness of an alley. Thomas coughed intermittently, the priest awkwardly slapping his back. Delphine held her spear tightly, distracting herself by singing, while crying:

Hey little Robin, Sing hey
Is it time to fly away
with your strong, young wings
as your father sings,
Is it time to fly away?

The only person they saw was a woman who dragged an old man out of her house and sat him by the door; she had trouble propping him up, but finally managed. When she saw the cart, she said, "Take him, please! I'll pay! I have radishes, you can have them! He was good to me and I want him buried. Please!"

Thomas shook his head at her.

"At least give him last rites! You're a priest, aren't you?"

Père Matthieu moaned softly in his throat but fixed his eyes forward.

"Stay in the cart," Thomas said wearily.

The priest said, "I'm sorry," too quietly for the woman to hear, and kept the cart moving, even though she followed for a few steps, imploring. The girl, who might have protested, just sang her song again and closed her eyes.

On their way out of the quarter, they passed a church whose stone walls were covered with mold and whose stained-glass windows had been broken out. Deep tracks from all directions pocked the ground around the building, which stank so badly of rot and mold that all of them gagged. The life-sized statue of the Virgin stood by the door, with a bloody, broken crown, a missing foot, and no nose. She held the broken haft of a scepter and cradled the abused form of a child dead of plague.

The priest stopped the cart.

They had to go past this church to get to the bridge.

"It's nearly dawn," said the girl. "I don't think they move in daytime."

The priest urged the mule forward, but it took its steps slowly, as though it reserved the right to stop the moment it felt inclined to.

The church was ghastly; if it had once belonged to Heaven, it did not now, and the air around it swarmed with flies. The mule swished his tail or jerked the skin of his flanks constantly against the many flies that landed on him. Flies crawled maddeningly in the priest's arm hair or landed near Thomas's mouth.

They drew closer, hugging as tightly as they could to the shops on the other side of the narrow street, but still coming uncomfortably close to the spoiled *église*.

Besides the gruesome Virgin, other statues of saints, kings, and apostles stood on their pedestals, lighter in color than the greenish-black growth quilting the walls, their limbs

161

and faces also spattered here and there with blood. Although it was hard to see in the gray of first light, the blood looked bright and fresh; they had only just returned from their hunt. Did an angel with a missing wing just shift itself? Did a gargoyle lick its forepaw as a dog might? Several of them held small forms that, as the cart drew closer, the knight, the priest, and the girl were sickened to recognize as dead children. A blood-mouthed St. Paul the apostle held his stone book in one hand and, with the other, dangled a limp boychild aloft by the head as if the saint were being fellated, the boy's arms gone entirely, his pale legs swinging gently like a hanged man's.

St. Paul turned his stone head and looked squarely at Père Matthieu. The priest felt an icy finger in his heart, and then his head exploded in pain as St. Paul assaulted him with a wordless shout:

DO YOU LIKE THIS BUGGER PRIEST WE DID THIS FOR YOU YOU FILTHY BUGGER SODOMITE DRUNK WHO THE FUCK DO YOU THINK YOU'RE FOOLING WOULD YOU LIKE TO CLIMB UP HERE WITH ME AND HOIST THOSE ROBES HOC EST ENIM VERGUM MEUM

The priest let drop the reins and put his hands over his ears, but it didn't help. At the same time, a statue of St. Martin pointed his sword at Thomas and split his head with:

COWARD HAVE YOU RAPED THE GIRL YET BECAUSE YOU WILL WE WILL MAKE YOU RAPE HER IN THE ASS BUT NOT THE CUNT BECAUSE SHE WILL BE A VIRGIN WHEN YOU CUT HER THROAT FOR YOUR MASTER AND YOU KNOW WHO THAT IS DON'T YOU

St. Anne crouched as though she might leap at the girl and thought-screamed into her head:

EVERYONE YOU LOVE WILL DIE THIS PRIEST AND THIS KNIGHT BOTH OF THEM WILL DIE BECAUSE OF YOU WE WILL KILL THEM WE DON'T KNOW WHAT YOU ARE BUT WE WILL FIND OUT EVEN IF WE HAVE TO CUT YOU OPEN AND THAT TOY WON'T HELP YOU

The cart wandered unguided as the three of them writhed under the words hurled at them. Then, beyond the buildings to the east and behind the clouds, the sun rose unseen and the voices stopped. The priest collapsed against the good weight of the knight and did something like sleeping.

Delphine, who had begun to feel nauseated and had a pain in her lower belly, comforted herself by leaning forward to stroke the priest's hair.

Thomas took his chain mail gloves off his shaking hands and took up the reins.

The only sounds as they left the Latin Quarter were the clop of the mule's hooves and, somewhere, the barking of a dog.

THIRTEEN

Of the Rain and the Figure of Death

T he rain started almost as soon as they went out the Port St. Bernard and left Paris behind, the girl thinking of the tale of Lot's wife, telling herself not to look back at the dying city and then doing it anyway. A column of smoke above Paris bade them farewell, as another column of smoke had once greeted them; this one, however, was in the city, where the fire at the woodcarver's would burn his whole block, sending the healthy into the streets, consuming the sick and the dead. The drops of cold rain that fell on Delphine's face were the vanguard of the deluge that would save the Left Bank from burning but flood the marshy land on the Right Bank all the way to the Place de Grèves. Bells tolled in the Latin Quarter; there were enough hands, at least, to pull a rope or two. Delphine tried to picture the people ringing those bells; a lone Dominican monk or a paid ringer for the convent; another priest like Père Matthieu, too scared to minister to his flock but trying to save what was left of his soul by warning them about fire. Or were the dead ringing their own bells? If statues could walk, why not them? She felt more tears coming for Annette, and also for herself; when would she feel a woman's love again? Had Annette died because Delphine had wanted to stay with her? The words of the wicked statues rang in her head again, and she looked at the men in the front of the cart.

Please don't let them die because of me, God.

And now the rain fell, and fell, and fell.

On the third day of it, and their second day without food, the priest saw a stone barn and a cottage and hoped they would be deserted. What had things come to when a man of God wished misfortune on a family because he coveted their roof?

The door to the cottage was open, but they made for the barn, as they would have more room for the mule, and none of them were in the mood to find bodies.

The barn was not deserted.

The priest walked in first and found a naked man on all fours, stuffing hay into his mouth. An abundance of hay and grasses were knotted into his white beard and hair. His ribs were showing, and he was grimed over and wet, whether with rain or the sweat of some fever was unclear. His eyes were wild, though. And he was not frail. He picked up a rusty scythe with a broken shaft from a pile of farming tools and started toward the priest.

Good God, he means to eat me.

Then Thomas and Delphine walked in, Thomas with his sword unsheathed, and the man bolted out the other door, falling when the edge of the scythe clipped the door frame and slipped from his hand, but scampering to his feet again almost instantly. He ran straight across the puddled field and kept running, his bare feet kicking up water all the way, disappearing not in the direction of the house, but toward the tree line past the field.

Thomas broke the silence that followed by saying, "So that's what the reaper looks like without his robes."

The priest laughed after a pause, but the girl just blinked rain out of her eyes and looked at them for an explanation.

"Death, girl. Death," said the priest.

Now she laughed, too, and the sound of it was good in the

barn.

They built a fire and took off as many of their clothes as decency allowed, hanging these on sticks to dry. When they had, they changed out of their underlinens and hung them now, putting the cozy, dry ones back on, glad for once not to be cold and soaked. The weather had changed, and where the days had been warm and the nights cool, now the days were cool and the nights cold. They agreed to stay in the barn until morning, then scout the fields for fruit or nut trees, or whatever they could find. In the meantime, they set out their cups and bowls, as well as Thomas's helmet and thigh armor, to catch enough water to keep their bellies full, which somewhat eased the pain of their hunger.

"I wish we had music," the priest said, poking at the glowing logs with the broken end of the scythe he was nearly killed with.

"I don't. You might be tempted to sing," Thomas said, inspecting his leg where the thing had hit him with her scepter. He suspected the bone of the shin was chipped; a truly ugly bruise had formed, and the flesh around his ankle was swollen and bruised as well. The damned thing had gotten him right where the horse had broken his leg at Crécy.

"Perhaps the girl will sing," the priest said.

"I don't feel like it," she said in a nasal little mew. She was getting sick. She had no fever, but she sniffled and complained of an ache near her hips. She had been in enough cold and wet that neither man suspected her of plague. "But what kind of music would you like to hear if you could choose?" she asked Père Matthieu.

"Oh. A lute. Most certainly a lute. And you, sir knight?"

"A lute? That's court music. That's for troubadours to make wives spread their legs when their husbands are at war."

"I find it very pretty. If the player is skillful. It takes more training to master the lute, don't you agree?"

"Than what?"

"A drum, for example. Or a cornemuse."

"That's what I'd like to hear. A drum and a cornemuse."

"Soldiers' music. That's for making husbands leave their wives behind for troubadours."

"Ha!"

As night came on, they fell to telling stories to pass the time.

The priest began, telling the story of a knight who was actually a werewolf, but a very considerate one who removed himself into the forest to change his skin. His wife, however, betrayed him by hiding his clothes so he could not change back; in this way, her husband was thought to have disappeared and she was able to marry her lover.

"Go on," Thomas said. "Finish it."

"It is finished."

"The hell it is."

"Is it not?"

"No, it is not. You only told half of it."

"It's all I know."

"What the hell kind of story is that? The adulterous wife wins out? The noble werewolf is deceived and banished?"

"Forgive me if I gave offense. Perhaps you should tell one now to instruct me in how these things are properly done."

"Imagine it's a sermon. A good story has a lesson. What's the lesson here? Whores triumph?"

"I don't know," the priest said, fidgeting. "Maybe. Something about the deceiving nature of woman."

Thomas stared intently at the priest in the firelight, and it was difficult for him to tell whether Thomas was being jocular or actually growing angry.

"That explains it, then," he said. "They tell priests stories about how bad women are so they won't fuck them."

"It's hardly working. I'm the only priest I know without an acknowledged mistress in his village."

Now Thomas laughed and the priest relaxed.

"I know how the story ends," the girl said.

"Oh?"

"Father used to tell it."

"Well, let's hear it," said Thomas.

"The knight went into the woods as a beast," Delphine said, and here she made the sound of a beast. "And one day the king and his hunting party found him. They were about to slay him, but then the big wolf bowed to the king."

"I like it better already," Thomas said, nudging the priest.

"Now the king decided to make a pet of him, and he took him home to the castle. Everyone came to marvel at the beast, who was so tame and courtly. Until one day the wife and the knight came ... wait, I forgot something."

"Are you sure you know this story?" the priest said, but Thomas nudged him again, a bit harder.

"Yes," she said gravely, looking at Père Matthieu until he held his palms up in acquiescence. She sneezed, and started again.

"When the king found the beast, the knight who had married his wife was there, and the beast growled at him."

She growled and gnashed her teeth, causing both men to laugh.

"They wanted to kill it, and that's when it went up and licked the king's hand. So, now we are back at the castle. And when the wife and the bad knight come in, the beast bites her nose ..."

Delphine trailed off and the priest knew what she was beginning to remember, so he clapped his hands twice, startling her.

"The story, the story," he said. She nodded and blinked her tears away, wiping at them with her sleeve and snuffling.

"It bites her. He bites her. The knight."

"Yes, I think we have it."

"And they want to kill it again, but the king's wise counselor says not to."

"Where do they find these wise counselors in stories?"

Thomas said, "for I've never met a king who let one speak."

"So they make the wife tell them why it bit her."

"I definitely like this version better. Whore wife bitten and tortured," Thomas said.

"And the king commands the bad knight to bring the good knight's clothes. Wait . . . he's wearing them. So he just takes them off."

"Now he's naked."

"I guess so. Yes."

"Is it cold in this castle?"

"Of course," she said, very seriously. "All castles are cold."

"Exactly how many castles have you been in?"

"I haven't been in boats, but I know they have sails."

"Ha! There's your lawyer father. I knew he'd come visit."

She sighed sharply in exasperation.

"Do you want to hear this?" she said.

"So we have a shivering knight with a shrinking *bitte*."

Both of them looked reproachfully at Thomas.

"Do you want me to finish? Because I can't when you keep interrupting me to show how clever you are."

"Ooooooh," Thomas said. "I stand rebuked. So the naked knight."

"They give him a robe."

"So the knight with the robe."

"The knight is not important now."

"So the unimportant knight."

Delphine got up and walked away, folding her arms. Both men, giggling like boys at her irritation, now implored her to come back.

"Sweet Delphine, tell us the story!"

"Don't take on so! The story, the story!"

At length she took her place again but pointed her small finger at Thomas. He put his hand over his mouth.

"So the king laid out the clothes for the beast, but it just sniffed them and sat down."

Thomas removed his hand and said, "Did it . . . ?" but she

169

cut him off with a "Ssst!" and pointed her finger again. He replaced his hand.

"The wise counselor said that the knight was ashamed to change in front of them. So they put the beast in a bedroom with the clothes. He went in on four legs and came out on two."

They both looked at her expectantly.

"What?" she said.

"Finish it," Thomas said.

"I did. He became a man again."

"What about the bastard knight and the whore wife? Were they killed?"

"If you like."

"What do you mean, 'if I like?' It happened or it didn't."

"It's just a story."

"Yes, and it has an ending."

"I told you the ending."

"But we still have loose ends."

"Fine," she said. "I'll finish it to your tastes. The knight takes his sword and cuts the heads off both of them. Blood goes everywhere. Blood, blood, blood. Then he cuts the head off the king, too. Bloody blood blood. And he puts the crown on his own head, so he's king. And the wise counselor gives him his pretty daughter to marry, even though she's only fifteen years old, and they have lots of babies, and then die and go to Heaven. How do you like that, Sir Thomas?"

He clapped his hands and hooted.

"Now that's a cunting story!" he said.

"Uh . . . I think we have a visitor," the priest said, pointing at the barn window, where a pair of eyes peeked at them below a mane of tangled, wet hair knotted with grass.

Thomas threw a log from the fire, and it hit the wall next to the window, showering sparks.

"Go on!" he shouted, reaching for his sword, but the eyes just blinked at him. He got up, and the face disappeared; they saw the naked old man run by the door, looking wildly in at them.

"This is MY BARN!" he said, outraged, and ran into the rain again.

There was no question of Thomas catching him.

The knight slept poorly.

He woke panting in darkness from a dream about riding his horse through a field of brambles, and tried to remember where he was. When he did, he noticed that the rain had stopped, and he walked outside to look up at the sky. The half moon flirted with him through gouges in slow-moving clouds that still held water, but he would not be able to look for his comet. He thought it might be out of sight now, having murdered its stellar swan, but he had no doubt that others had come; this had been a promiscuous summer for comets.

Only it wasn't summer any more. His breath plumed out in front of him. It was nearing mid-September, but it was cold like October.

He heard movement behind him, and then a sound of mild displeasure; he turned to see the priest stooping to drink from the bowl he had set out.

"It's musty," he said. "My bowl could do with a scrubbing."

Thomas looked at the sky again.

"Couldn't sleep?" the priest asked.

Thomas didn't answer.

"I know. Stupid question. Hardly worthy of William of Ockham. I should have asked if you had bad dreams. I did. Would you like to know what about?"

Thomas didn't speak.

"I was being led around the countryside by a little girl. There were horrid things in rivers and statues crawled off churches, and a great sickness had killed most everybody. I was starving, to boot."

Silence.

"My only other companion was a moody, excommunicate

knight who rarely spoke and didn't have the slightest interest in hearing about my nightmares. And, of course, a mule."

Thomas sighed.

"I liked the mule."

"What did you really dream?"

"I dreamed my brother had no legs."

"The one in Avignon? The catamite?"

"I have only one brother. He walked about with crutches, like a stilt man, but drab and sad. I fed him from my hand as if he were a bird, but he was not grateful. He hated me for my legs."

"That sounds better than the other one. Perhaps you should go back to sleep."

Now the priest looked at the sky.

"What's up there?"

"If a priest doesn't know, how should I?"

"Huh. Maybe a better priest would."

He stooped now and took rainwater from the knight's thigh-piece. Thomas took a long look at Père Matthieu.

"You haven't been defrocked or anything, have you?"

"Should have been, perhaps. But, no."

"You just don't always seem quite like a priest."

"Funny. I've felt the same way ever since the day I took orders."

"Why did you, then?"

"Like most of the others. My father sent me."

"Why didn't you follow him into his trade?"

The priest didn't say anything.

"Well?"

"He was a soldier."

"And?"

"Do I seem like a soldier to you?"

"Not even a little."

"And yet I am heroic compared with my brother."

Thomas grunted, imagining how he might look upon his son if he proved too weak for arms. He imagined himself beating it out of him and making a man of him. It occurred to him that the priest's father had probably tried.

"Our father used to say, 'Since God has sent me only daughters, I shall send the bearded ones to take orders, and the others to fetch back sons.'"

Thomas chuckled.

"Yes, I suppose it is funny," the priest said, "the first dozen times."

Thomas drank out of his helm.

Thunder rumbled in the distance.

"We're in for more of it," Thomas said.

The priest nodded.

"May I tell you?"

"What?" Thomas said.

"What I did."

"I'd rather you didn't."

"I know."

"Then why ask?"

The priest folded his arms around himself against the cold.

"I don't have anyone else to confess to."

FOURTEEN

Of the Stained Priest and the Widow's Revenge

Two months before the plague came to St. Martin-le-Preux, Père Matthieu Hanicotte was in love. His hands shook as he put on his chasuble and prepared the candles and the incense, and when he preached his sermon, his left armpit ran cold with sweat, even though the mornings were still cool that May. It seemed curious to him that only the left armpit was affected; perhaps, he thought, because the heart was supposed to sit just a little to the left. And his sin, as of this morning, was still only in his heart.

The sweat would run from the moment he approached the altar; even with his back to his flock, he thought about where the object of his affection would be standing; three or four rows back, always closest to the aisle, at the level of the stained-glass window portraying the brides with their lanterns.

He could even distinguish the young man's cough from the rest of his congregation.

On this particular day, the object was wearing his best gray cotehardie buttoned snugly up his trunk, and standing with one leg in the aisle, which the others took for rascality, but which was in fact to better display his bright red stocking and the long, well-calved leg in it.

As Père Matthieu lifted the Eucharist, he tried to keep his thoughts on the words he was pronouncing; but then he felt the cold sweat running, and knew it was making him stink. This new love-sweat hit high in the nose with a sharp note like cheese, or salt, or metal, or the miscarriage of all three. His inner cassock was so ripe with infatuation that he sweated again when he brought it to the laundresses and blushed when he gathered it back.

The boy's father was the village reeve, whose job it was to act as liaison between the farmers and their seigneur. As was often the case with reeves, Samuel Hébert was mistrusted by each side. The seigneur believed he let the villagers off too early when they worked his manor farm their customary two days per week. This was true. But many of the villagers believed Hébert was too scrupulous in counting and weighing the shares of livestock and harvests they owed their lord. In fact, this was not true; he often let the best cow stay with the inheritors after a peasant died and brought a slightly less meaty one up the river as heriot. Nonetheless, it was Samuel Hébert who took from them, and these proud Norman farmers better perceived slights than kindnesses.

And, by peasant standards, he was rich.

Michel Hébert, his second son, was going to Paris to study law. At twenty, he would be a bit older than most of his colleagues; but a tidy bribe had been administered, and a bursar from the university had met the boy and declared him good enough in Latin that something might be made of him. Soon, Père Matthieu thought, with great sadness and resignation, those red legs would not be standing in the aisle near the window. He was right, of course, but not because the boy was going to Paris.

The Great Death was coming.

It had already begun devouring Avignon, where it was said the pope heard audiences between two fires to burn off pestilential air, and nibbling at Paris, where the first afflicted households were trying to hide their sick so they would not be shunned by their neighbors.

The priest knew his congregation was hungry for news about the disease and its progress; he knew they craved some reassurance that St. Martin-le-Preux would be spared, whether for its holiness or because they had suffered enough under the hand of their greedy seigneur, but he could not summon up the words. The truth was that he knew nothing. He did not know how it was spread, what had caused it, where it would go, or what could be done for the ill. What troubled him most was his feeling that God could see into his heart and knew that his love was twisted. God would weigh his most secret thoughts and, finding them repulsive, would take an even heavier toll on the villeins of his flock. He would have thrown himself into the river, but a suicide priest might be worse in God's eyes than a would-be sodomite.

He had never felt so ignorant, useless, or doubtful in his life.

His homily addressed the sin of wrath, and how much it displeased the Lord when neighbors bickered over the placement of fences or insults spoken in the alehouse.

"What do you think will happen in the alehouse? Will you make peace there? Or will you quarrel? I tell you, a devil loves no better hiding place than a bowl of beer." He knew as soon as he said the words that he had stepped on dangerous ground; the whole village knew him for a tippler. He had more to say about alcohol making people fight, but decided to cut that short and get on to something about angels. People liked angels. But he was too late. As he cleared his throat to buy himself a moment, his most frequent sparring partner took advantage of his slip.

"If devils hide in beer, is that why you drink so much wine?" said Sylvan Bertier, the drover. Not everyone laughed, but enough of them so that he forced himself to smile rather than trying to rebuke the popular Bertier.

A drop of that awful, cold sweat ran down his left side.

"Yes. I know that I take more comfort than I should in

wine; even God's shepherds are not without sin. But which of you has seen it make me quarrelsome? Our drover here often has blacker eyes than his oxen."

He glanced at the object, who was smiling now at his skillful riposte, then cut his eyes quickly away to make it look as though he were surveying all of them. For every time he sneaked a glance at Michel Hébert, he made himself look ten more parishioners in the face.

The rest of the homily went smoothly, if blandly, until the water clock told him half an hour had gone by and he wrapped things up.

When Mass was over and he saw his congregation out, he made sure to turn his right side toward those who came to speak to him, especially Michel.

"You're a clever man," the younger Hébert said, and looked at Père Matthieu just long enough for him to notice the boy had a sort of black freckle in the hazel of his eye. His left eye.

"There are greater virtues," the priest said, wishing Michel would clasp hands with him before he turned and left. He did not. Rather, he hurried on his pretty red legs to walk beside Mélisande Arnaut, a plump girl whose pretty face, just the color of cream, turned the heads of even those who liked their women lean.

He knew from the confessional that Michel had already fornicated with several girls, including his own half-sister, and fully expected Mélisande to be inventoried soon. He had also lately confessed to having impure thoughts about men. Whatever demon oversaw libido had his hooks deep in Michel Hébert and used him now to ensnare others.

If there were demons at all.

If that boy is Satan's instrument, God, show me some sign. Let him look back at me.

But he wanted that backward glance so much that he couldn't bear to attach wickedness to it, so he confounded himself.

Rather, let him look back at me if there are no devils in him.

The boy did look back over his shoulder at him. Just once, and only for an instant, but it was enough.

He would always think of it as having started that day.

Each night became a battle for Matthieu Hanicotte. He was in danger of losing his belief, if not his soul. Were there souls at all? Was there really a naked, invisible little version of himself hiding under his skin, so valuable to Heaven and Hell that each would send emissaries down to fight for it?

He started by telling himself he would not drink more than one cup of wine, then two, and then three, lest he should become drunk and give himself up to thinking about those red legs. In the end his head was reeling, he was spent, dry-mouthed from spitting in his hand, and he lay in his shame and guilt until the small hours of the morning.

The days were better; even though his parishioners began to ask after his health because he had lost weight and had bags under his eyes, he was far less miserable ministering to them than lying alone with his thoughts. It was better to counsel fat, bearded Sanson Bertier to apologize to his wife for menacing her with his billhook, and to smell the farts Bertier would gravely fan away with his straw hat; it was better to walk with his box of holies out to give last rites to Clement Fougière three times in one week only to have him get well; it was even better to be bitten by Fougière's dog on the last visit and hear the old man laugh from his sickbed.

One night near the end of May, he went down to the river and walked along its banks, enjoying the pleasantly cool air and getting lost in the beauty of the sky, where the moon was veiling herself with gauzy, fast-moving clouds. She was not full, but she was bright enough to illuminate the river, sending cloud shadows racing over the water and the willows near this part of the bank.

It was near one of these willows that a bright swath of

moonlight dragged itself over a set of cast-aside clothes. Père Matthieu could not resist peeking at the river, where he was sure he would spy a bather. He was not disappointed. In fact, there were two of them, and much closer than the clothes.

Seeing him, a girl inexpertly stifled a squeal, then thrashed out of the water, covering her breasts and running for her homespun dress. She was plump and pale. God help him, it was Mélisande.

He knew who was in the river.

The girl picked up her clothes and ran to where the trees got thicker before dressing and loping home. The other made no effort to run; he did not even leave the river; rather, he just crouched to hide all but his head and languidly oared the water around him with his arms.

He was looking directly at the priest, who stood there for a long moment, torn between turning and walking home and trying to find something to say. Nothing occurred to him. He could not see the freckle in the boy's eye, but he imagined it. He imagined more than that. Cloud shadows moved across the water, now darkening the lad's head, now letting the moon paint it silver.

"Come in," the boy said, so quietly that Père Matthieu convinced himself he had not heard it. He just opened his mouth and closed it again, like a landed fish trying to breathe.

"Come in," the object of his affection said again.

"I can't."

"Père Matthieu can't."

"No."

"So shed him with your clothes, and put him back on when you leave."

"No."

"That's the beauty of being nude in a river; you're nobody. You're anybody you want to be. It's just a dream."

You used the same words to get the girl in there.

The priest opened and closed his mouth.

"Come in," the boy said again.

And he did.

The Great Death got close in June, and the bridge leading to Paris was burned on the seigneur's command. Little groups of armed farmers hid in the woods and frightened off those coming overland from the other side; they soon found that the days off from farm labor were to their liking. They also found that, with no wives to nag them, they could drink all the beer and cider they cared to. They fashioned masks of river reeds and clay, raven's feathers, and the teeth of foxes to make themselves terrifying, and also to remind them not to look anyone in the eyes—it was widely believed that the plague leapt from one man to another by means of a deadly beam from the eyes. They called themselves the Brotherhood of St. Martin's Arse. They drank themselves into such a state of belligerence that even groups of strangers who agreed to turn around found themselves cudgeled so they would remember not to try again.

It was not long before they carried their antics back with them into town; Élise Planchette, the widow who ran the alehouse, soon learned to hate the hooting and boasts that announced the brotherhood's return from patrol. Shutting the door was no good—they would keep at her until she opened it, then expect their drinks for free for their solemn work guarding the town from pestilence. Nearly every day they could be seen at the widow's tables, dicing and carousing with their masks tipped back; those who watched by day came in the evening. Those who watched in the evening came by day. Their farms suffered as their wives and fathers took up the manuring and the weeding and the harrowing, but the men of the brotherhood had grown so fond of their newfound status as militiamen that there was no reasoning with them. The reeve could not make them work. The priest could not turn them away from their folly. Their number did shrink as some men, like Sanson Bertier, dropped out; but it grew again as bullies saw a way out of work.

When one of them stole wood from the widow's house, saying his duties left him no time for chopping, she tried to block his way out but found herself pushed down on her backside. She complained to the herald. This herald promised to take the matter before their lord, but nothing was done. The seigneur, terrified of plague, had suspended court sessions and shut himself away with his retinue. Only the herald was seen, arching his painted eyebrows and reading unenforceable proclamations from the back of his palfrey. Men-at-arms could be seen walking the parapet of the keep, their armor winking in the early summer light; but they never came down anymore. The Brotherhood of St. Martin's Arse was all the justice there was in St. Martin-le-Preux.

One night, when there was enough moon, several of the day watch went drunkenly to the river to gather reeds for new members to make masks with. Steering for a growth of reeds near the charred and collapsed timber of the bridge, one of them noticed a pair of red stockings balled up on the shore. Other clothes were concealed nearby.

"Look here, boys," he whispered, "we've got some June frolics in the river!"

"Ho," one of them cried, slapping the water with his staff. "Come out, little fishes. One of you can show us her gills!"

They guffawed at that and began whistling, but no head broke the water.

"Under there," one said, pointing at where the western ruin of the bridge still stood. They waded in the mud and looked underneath. There, hiding by the pilings, shivered a very pale and naked priest holding the hands of the reeve's son, who was also in the state of Adam. Both of them were slicked with mud halfway up their shins.

"I don't believe my whoring eyes," one man said.

Now the boy panicked and sloshed out toward the other side of the bridge, running when he got to the bank. Père Matthieu nearly followed him, but then lost all hope. He turned his back to the men, held his face in his hands and cried.

He was sure they would kill him.

None of them moved for a long moment. Then one of them spat on him. Then another. When all of them had done so, they turned, laughing, and walked back up the river and into town to spread the news.

So it was that when the plague came, only a dozen souls were coming to Mass. Père Matthieu's assistant and bell ringer, a stocky, busy, black-haired child everyone called Bourdon, performed his duties without his former energy. Hardly any received the priest when he came to anoint their loved ones in death. Only a handful sought confession. Soon the reeve's son died, and the reeve, and nearly the whole village. Heartbroken yet afraid for his life, the priest stopped going to church at all, shutting himself up in his house with his wine. It was not until the monster moved into the river that the villagers sought their shepherd out and shamed him into helping them. There was no one else they could go to. So he tried. He went house to house seeking men who could use a weapon. When he saw how strong the thing was and knew he did not have enough healthy men to fight it, he took up the place where the brotherhood used to wait, and sat with his lantern, praying for soldiers to come down the road.

As it turned out, one did.

As for the Brotherhood of St. Martin's Arse, they were already gone. They were, in fact, among the first victims. The widow fell ill, having caught it from the farmer's child who helped her clear up, and the surgeon had refused to see her. Trying to do for herself what she believed he would have done for her, she bled herself into a wooden bowl, though this only made her weaker. The lump in her groin was so painful that it was all she could do to drag herself down the stairs and to the alehouse door when, after one of her bleedings, the brotherhood pounded at it. They wore their masks. They stank of drink and were demanding more.

She told them to go away because she was tired.

They insisted.

She told them to go away, for the love of God.

They said they had none.

So she served them.

If they tasted the blood mixed into their beer, they never said a word about it.

FIFTEEN

Of the Visitation in the Barn

"**S**o I damned half my village. My weakness made them hate me, so they stayed away from Mass. They were cut off from the sacraments."

Thomas furrowed his brow at the priest.

"But it doesn't make sense. As you said yourself, most priests have a mistress. Why would they hate you so for dallying with the girl?"

The priest shook his head and looked at the sky.

"Why would the boy run off and leave the girl in the river with you? And why would she want a knobby old priest twice her age when she could have a handsome lad who was going to be a lawyer?"

"The mysteries of the heart are unknowable."

"And the way you described his legs. It was the boy, wasn't it? You kept saying 'the object of my affection' because you plumbed the boy."

"No," the priest lied.

"What good is confession if you lie?"

"Everyone lies at confession. Around the edges, at least. A man who fornicates with his brother's wife will say it was a whore. A woman will say she was glad in her heart that her blind and deaf baby died, when what she means is that she drowned it. But I wasn't lying. Because a man of war like you cannot travel with a known sodomite."

"You're goddamned right," Thomas said.

"You need the object of my affection to have been the girl."

"Yes."

"So it was the girl."

"Good. I hope you fucked her right in half."

The priest smiled sadly and kept looking at the sky, though the moon was gone again, covered over with clouds. Thomas drank another swig of rainwater and went inside, mildly fuming.

"I wouldn't leave you," a small voice said. The priest looked down and saw that Delphine had come from the barn. "If it was the boy," she continued. "I wouldn't leave."

He smiled at her and wiped at his eye with the back of his hand.

Then the rain came again and they all tried to sleep.

In the loft above the barn, a mouse had just peeled herself away from nursing her litter. She left them in the nest and went through a tunnel in the rotten hay, sensing that the rain had driven hosts of little bugs from the sodden ground and into the structure. It was the perfect time to hunt; ants or grubs would make better milk than grain, and there hadn't been grain in this barn since before she birthed. As she got to the end of the tunnel, she stopped before she crossed the plain of planks that led to the beam she would skitter down to forage in the barn. She poked her nose into the air and sniffed. This was where an owl could most easily kill her, as one had had taken her mate on the path between the barn and the house. She smelled something, but it was no owl.

Something landed wetly on the roof; no heavier than a branch full of wet leaves, but that wasn't what it was.

She looked up, then froze.

It came through the straw thatching on the roof, forcing

its way between the fibers, at once liquid and not liquid. She had never seen tentacles, but that was what it was: a mass of tentacles that knotted on itself again and again to move. It had no head at all; to her, it looked like a nest of snakes' tails.

She was too afraid to move back into the tunnel, even when it dropped onto the planks not two yards from her.

It writhed nearer, rearing up several of its tail-arms to regard her, but then, thankfully, decided she was not what it was looking for. It collapsed on itself and went liquid again, blacker than blood, so black it was less like a stain and more like the most profound absence of light. It oozed through the spaces between the planks and disappeared.

She had never given any thought to the people sleeping below her, but she knew this not-owl, this snake-knot was after them.

She went back into the tunnel and burrowed in with her blind young ones, shivering so hard they moved away from her.

Thomas dreamed.

He was walking across a burning landscape of dry grass and nettles, and sand that shifted in the hot wind and stung his eyes. He was wearing armor. The sun seemed to hang closer to the earth than it should have; it seemed to press on his armor as if it had hands, heating the links of his mail unbearably. Smoke began to fill the air; fires at the horizon line twinkled as figures moved near them, fanning the flames.

He had heard that the infidels under Saladin had burned the grass at the Horns of Hattin to drive the crusaders mad with thirst before he crushed them in battle, driving them out of the Holy Land, and Thomas thought that was where he was. Near Jerusalem, in the Levant. The figures working the fires didn't look like people, though, not even Moslems.

"Goddamn it, stop that!" he tried to shout, but the words caught in his throat as if they had hooks. His throat was unbearably dry, and he knew he might die of thirst. It was the figures who were doing this to him; if he could reach them and kill them, it would stop. But they were so very far away, and his sword was so rusted it looked as though it would break if it struck anything hard. He clenched his teeth and moved forward, but then one of his teeth broke; he pulled a mailed glove off and pulled the tooth out. The action of doing this dislodged another one so it wobbled in his gums, then another; soon his whole mouth was full of loose teeth as dry and fragile as kindling. He opened his mouth to try to get some air in it, but then he realized that was a mistake. Almost as soon as the idea came to him that the sun was so hot it might light his teeth on fire, it did exactly that. They smoldered painfully in his gums, even after he shut his mouth, and he looked around for anything at all that might give him relief.

That was when he saw the thorn bush.

It was about as high as his ribs, with long, wicked thorns. The whole bush seemed to bend around something at its center: a pear. But not just any pear. This was the fattest, sweetest-looking pear he had ever seen, with a leaf on its stem of impossible greenness. He knew that it was so full of watery nectar that one bite would not just ease his pain, but strengthen his limbs so he could set about the business of killing the shadowy fire makers on the horizon.

He put his glove back on against the thorns and knelt down before the bush, picking gently at the needled twigs encasing the fruit. How like ribs around a heart they were. He had to be delicate so he didn't rupture the pear, but this was hard. The thorns were so long and slender they slid deeply into his fingers even through the links of his mail. He had to make the thorn bush want to yield the pear, so he tried to say *Please*, but all that came through his ruined mouth was a grunt. Smoke came from his nose. The arrowhead was lodged in his tongue again. He couldn't speak; he would never speak. He would never be understood by anyone or anything again. He jerked more roughly at the branches, but they pulled back.

Rip it open. Use your strength. Destroy it and eat the pulp. You can't know how sweet it is!

Lies.

He was being lied to.

He understood at once that this pear was cousin to the fruit that ruined man in the Garden of Eden, and it would ruin him, too. If he ate it, he would march to the horizon, but he would not fight the fire makers. He would become one of them. Forever. He had to pull himself away from it and then move toward the horizon.

He had to fight them.

It was impossibly hard to leave that sweetness behind, but he did.

He got up on his leaden legs and marched toward the fire.

He coughed a huge gout of stinging smoke from his mouth and nostrils into his eyes, sending him to his knees.

That was when he sneezed a horrific sneeze that ejected smoke, snot, and blood all at once. He even thought some of his brain came out of his nose. Something definitely came out of his nose, and maybe his ears as well.

And then he realized he was kneeling not in a hot and dry grassland, but somewhere cold, dark, and damp.

The barn.

With the rain on the roof and thunder growling outside.

Something ran across his lap, something oily and dark,

die with her then you limp weak prick

and it rained itself upward somehow through the planks of the loft above them.

It had left smears on his white thighs.

Or was that blood?

His breeches were down and his *verge* was half erect.

Delphine was in front of him, and he was holding her arms so tightly he must have been close to breaking her delicate bones. He loosened his grip but still held her, trying to understand.

She was naked.

"Oh Christ, Christ, no," he moaned helplessly.

She shook her head.

"You didn't," she said. "You stopped. It tried to make you, and you could have, but you stopped."

He blinked dumbly at her dark outline with the sound of the rain dripping.

The priest snored.

She managed to smile through her quiet sobbing.

He let her arms go and she put her gown back on.

He pulled his breeches up, still staring at her, peripherally aware that his hands hurt.

When they were both clothed again, she hugged him and cried warm tears onto his neck. He patted her sides and shoulders awkwardly.

"You beat it," she said, her lean body hitching with sobs. "You won."

He saw that her gown was bloody, but then realized it was his blood. His hands were bleeding freely where they had been stuck with thorns.

In the morning, Delphine woke again to find that not all the blood on her gown was from Thomas's hands, which she knew had been injured.

Thomas was at the other end of the barn, with the mule's leg between his, scraping mud and rocks from its shoe. How like him, to defy his pain by doing something to make it worse.

Her belly hurt, and her thighs were slick with blood. At first she feared that she might have been wrong and that he might have violated her in the night, but this was only for an instant.

The dream had seemed like other true dreams. She had dreamed that Thomas had a black crab in his head that was driving him as a man drives a cart, and this crab wanted him to hurt her. She had awakened in the darkness to find him undressing her, delicately at first, but then roughly, his eyes far away. But as she tried to pull away from him, he sneezed violently and something came out of him. He had pushed it out of him. Besides, the pain was in her belly, not where it would have been had she been taken.

No, the blood was not from the loss of her maidenhead.

Sometime in the night, she had become a woman.

She would have liked to speak to her mother about this, or to Annette. As soon as she remembered these two vacancies in her heart, she braced herself for sadness to overwhelm her. Instead, she imagined Père Matthieu trying to advise her on these matters, and the thought struck her so funny that she giggled. Her giggling turned to laughter, and even though she cupped her hand over her mouth, she woke the priest.

"My, but you're in a good mood this morning," he said; but then he caught sight of the blood and turned the corners of his mouth down, saying "Sweet heavens," which seemed such a ridiculous oath to attach to the mess in her lap that she laughed even harder.

"What's so funny?" Thomas said, still scraping. The mule looked over, too.

The priest went and washed his hands in rainwater even though he had not touched her, stammering a moment before he found his voice.

"Well, er ... it ... it seems our kitten is a cat."

SIXTEEN

Of the Maple Tree

Delphine was too restless to sit in the cart, so she walked alongside while the two older men rode. The cloths she had bundled around her middle were coarse and chafed her, but she was glad to have found them in the farmhouse; the mother of the dead family inside had been halfway through sewing a dress for herself when the disease came and made her lay her needle aside. She had been found leaning out the window, dead a good month so she was mostly bone, the wattle under her dark as though she had melted into the wall. Delphine thought the woman's fever might have made her want air at the end of it. She guessed, too, that the whole family had sickened at once; one small corpse hugged another in the corner opposite, the smaller of them clutching a cloth poppet with eyes of snail shell. The mother was already too weak to bury them when they died. And where was the man of the house? Was it the old man in the barn? Or was he the woman's father? She guessed it was the father, and that he had been mad before and they kept him in the barn; but then it occurred to her that he might have hidden himself there to save his life, perhaps warning others away with that rusty scythe, and there lost his mind. And the husband? Was he dead before the plague came, in the war perhaps, or

CHRISTOPHER BUEHLMAN

had he run off to save himself? She knew many such stories of betrayal and selfishness from her village, though she also knew stories of great faithfulness and courage. This pestilence cooked away pretense and showed people's souls, as surely as it eventually showed their bones.

"What are you thinking about over there?" Thomas said. Ever since the incident in the barn, he had been kinder to her. She wondered how long it would last.

"Death," she said.

"That's cheerful. Perhaps you'd like to sing us a song about it?"

She ignored this.

"No singing? Maybe you'll dance us a merry brawl, then? The priest and I grow bored with watching this mule's ass."

She wrinkled her mouth, trying not to encourage his vulgarity by smiling at it. Instead she bent down for a mud clot and threw it, though it sailed well behind and landed in the cart.

"Ha!" he laughed at her. "Now that you're a woman, you can't do things boys can do, can you? A boy would have pelted me right between the eyes."

She snarled at him and walked faster, cutting in front of the mule.

"Now I will watch the mule's ass and he will watch yours, is that your remedy?"

She walked faster, letting herself smile now that the coarse knight would not have the satisfaction of seeing it.

The priest knew something had transpired between the knight and the girl, but the nature of the change puzzled him. If Thomas had forced himself upon her, would she still go with them? To keep herself alive, perhaps, but surely she would not jest and smile so much. What if she had allowed him? Or had gone to him? She was the right age to start thinking of such things, after all, now that she bore the mark of Eve. If that were the case, surely he would see it in a thoughtless caress or in a too-long glance; they did look at each other more, but almost as a father and daughter might where the father had picked the child as his favorite and teased her playfully. It did not seem carnal; he had taught himself to divine when his parishioners were fornicating so he could better coax them to lighten their souls with confession.

But who was he to judge anyone, or propose any remedy for sin?

He was such a profound sinner that he had considered leaving off his robes and stopping the pretense. He was just an old bugger who would sell his last possession for a barrel of good wine. Or any wine.

And he was lonely.

The most puzzling thing for him was his own reaction to the newfound, though seemingly platonic intimacy between his companions; Père Matthieu was jealous.

On their fifth day since Paris, they camped near a swollen stream, up on a rocky bank that gave them a decent view of the country around them. Thomas and the priest sharpened long sticks to use as spears and spent the last hours of daylight trying to gig fish in the river. They got only one, and a small one. The frogs they had hunted eluded them easily, sheltering between rocks or hopping into thick river grass, and now mocked them with their buzzing evensong farther down the stream. The girl went to forage in the woods; she returned at twilight with a rusty, hole-ridden pot in which she carried two handfuls of acorns, several walnuts, and a broken horseshoe.

"Goddamn it," Thomas said, gazing at her small cache.

"Maybe God would be more generous if you swore less."

"God starves babies sometimes, and they don't swear at all."

Having no answer for that, Delphine found a tree stump and began pounding acorns with the horseshoe. They would make an awful, mouth-puckering companion to the two mouthfuls of trout they could each look forward to, but it would be marginally better than nothing.

"Babies go straight to Heaven," she said now.

Thomas didn't look up from his work setting river stones to make a fire. "Bad ones don't," he said.

"There are no bad babies," she said. "They don't know any better."

"Sounds like you've never met a baby. Many of them are awful. I knew one in Picardy who stole his father's money and crawled down the road to the whorehouse. "

"It was you," she said. "The only bad baby ever was you."

The priest sighed and went off to gather more sticks for the fire.

They ate their awful dinner, sucking each slender bone and washing the bitter acorn meal down with water. The walnuts were last, least and best. Stomachs still rumbling, they each settled down, the men near the cart, the girl with her head against the tree stump. The only sounds were the stream, the frogs, and the mule munching his fill of grass.

In the morning, as the men stirred, Delphine woke up at dawn, but the exhausted men slept later. She amused herself first by collecting river pebbles in her gathered gown front, and then sowing them as a farmer would with an apron full of seeds. When she was out of pebbles, she took up one of the fishing spears and, holding it butt end down, pretended to stir the rusty pot. The priest sat up, stiff from his night on the rocky ground, and noticed her at her game.

"What are you cooking for us, daughter?" he said.

"A stew!"

"Christ, don't start that," Thomas said.

"What kind of stew?" the priest asked, secretly happy to needle the knight's hunger.

"Cabbages and pepper."

"Real pepper?" the priest said. "Will the king be joining

us?"

"Yes," she said, "and all his ministers. But I wasn't done with the stew."

"Christ drowning in shit," Thomas said, putting his straw hat over his face.

"Mushrooms and turnips and even pork belly."

"And shit," Thomas grumbled from his hat. "Don't forget the shit."

"What a lovely meal," the priest said. "May I have some?"

Delphine nodded gravely, still stirring. The priest got up and held his wooden bowl out so she could pretend to fill it with her stick-ladle. He slurped air from a pretend spoon and said, "My compliments. It's perfect."

Thomas peeked from under the hat to confirm what he thought he was hearing. Then he replaced the hat, saying, "Jesus wept."

Just before they left their camp, the priest found another walnut, which had escaped through a hole in the girl's gathering pot. He found the broken horseshoe and looked around for the stump but couldn't find it. Thinking nothing of it, he opened the nut against the cart and brought it to Delphine, who did her best to take exactly one third of it. He shared the rest with Thomas, who said, "How can you stuff yourself so? Aren't you full of shit and cabbage stew?"

They climbed wearily into the cart and left.

None of them noticed that the maple stump against which Delphine had slept had grown into a tree.

SEVENTEEN

Of St. Lazarus and the Rotten Fruit

T he soldiers passed them near the town of Nemours, just as deep, cold woods gave way to overgrown and deserted farms. They had just broken camp, and their hunger gnawed at them. They had begun to discuss the possibility of eating their mule. Rather, Thomas had started discussing it, provoking fierce resistance from Delphine and causing the priest to say, "I would rather starve than walk."

"We can all see our ribs. It isn't right. We could smoke this bastard and eat like kings for a week."

"Did you see his ear twitch?" Delphine said. "He heard you."

"I don't care if he did."

"You can't really want to eat our friend? He's been so faithful."

"I have to eat something. I'm losing my whoring mind."

"*Not* the mule," she said, and that put an end to it.

The soldiers came then, just at first light. No fewer than six knights and another twenty men-at-arms rode up on them, the horses' hooves shaking the road. A voice shouted, "Get that cart out of the way," barely leaving them enough time to do so, startling Père Matthieu so that he reined the mule hard, taking one wheel off the road and causing them all to be buffeted by low branches. One of the knights called "Hoooa," slowing his horse to a stop and obliging the rest to stop as well.

"I know that man," the knight said, wheeling his horse around to get another look at Thomas. Thomas recognized him, too, though he could not retrieve his name or title; his surcoat bore a red chevron bisecting a silver griffin rampant on a field of blue.

"That man fought at Crécy, and bravely, too."

Thomas squirmed with shame at his shoddy armor and his mule cart, and wished the troop would ride on.

"Am I right? You were beside the Comte de Givras when he fell."

"I was."

"Where is your coat of arms?"

"I lost it at dice."

The man stared at him for a moment while he decided whether Thomas's comment was a joke or an insult. He decided it was a joke.

"*Ha!*" he barked. "What are you doing in that cart, man?"

"We're going to the Holy Land to fetch back the True Cross."

"*Ha!* This is a man of levity. He might lighten our journey with his japes if he were of a mind to come with us."

"Never mind him," said a youthful knight with golden locks. "Can't you see he's fallen? This man is a brigand."

Thomas chafed, but Delphine put her hand on his before he could rest it on the hilt of his sword.

"What is a brigand in these days? Which of you does not charge tolls on travelers? And woe to those who do not pay their due, eh? Besot me, I'll not have you insult a man who rode up that hill while you dandled dolls in Évry."

The blond knight grimaced but did not respond.

"What say, man? We've got a spare horse. It's yours if you'll ride with us."

Delphine's hand gripped Thomas's harder, but he pulled away from her.

"Where are you bound?"

"Avignon. His Holiness has summoned certain knights to him. There's talk of a new crusade."

"Jerusalem?"

"Aye. So it is whispered. He will not issue a bull until the English have declared they will join us, though it is said their king already gave his word."

Thomas considered this.

"We are also bound for Avignon."

"Then it is decided! Bring up the bay."

An acneous squire in saffron yellow rode up now, holding the reins of a handsome bay stallion.

"Where may my companions ride?"

The knight leaned closer, looking the priest and the girl over.

"In the cart, of course, as befits their station. We will be in Avignon before a fortnight. This cart will still be clopping about at Christmastime. On your horse, man, and let them meet you there."

"I . . ."

"I, I, I. This is not the time for speeches, sir. On your horse and piss standing up, or in your cart and squat for it."

"Go your ways," Thomas said coolly, "and I will go mine."

Did that knight's nose just wrinkle like a lion's?

His surcoat was different now; behind the chevron, a lion rampant tore an old man in an arena.

Monkeys eating a wild-eyed horse.

The dead woman's moley back in the pit.

"Who is the girl?" the knight said.

"Just an orphan."

"Who is she *really*?"

"Ask your mother."

"Ha."

Thomas's hand drifted for the handle again, and again Delphine steered it away, saying under her breath, *"It's what they want. These are only shades, but your anger is feeding them. Get rid of it.*"

"Ha," Thomas said. Then he imagined the knight's nose was the tail of a horse. He pictured it lifting and a pile of road apples falling out of the knight's mouth. His defiant "Ha" turned into an actual laugh, and he let himself laugh freely.

The knight's face reddened.

He showed his teeth for just an instant.

Thomas laughed harder.

The knight gathered himself enough to speak again, his voice trembling.

"Would that we had more time. I would like to discuss this further with you. But we are stayed for. Perhaps our paths will cross again, when we may linger in knightly fellowship."

"Good luck on your crusade," the priest offered.

"Go to Hell," the squire in yellow said, unconsciously fingering one of his pimples.

They turned their horses and thundered down the road leading to Nemours, tramping autumn's first golden leaves into the black mud beneath them.

They were not out of sight the length of a troubadour's verse before the sun peeked between the trees.

Nemours would not let the three of them in. The gates were barred, and the very skinny man at the parapet told them they would be shot if they rode closer.

"Where may we ford the river, then? If we may not use your bridge?"

"I don't know."

"Where may we find food?"

"Wait till one of you starves," he advised. "Then eat that one. That's how we're managing. We call it *Gigot de Nemours*. But no one comes in, and by God no one goes out."

On the other side of the town, near the banks of the Loing, they came across an encampment of twenty or so men and women hauling in nets and working little patches of field. It was unusual to see such industry now. Something was cooking in a large stew pot, and it smelled like hot, greasy heaven. The priest pulled the cart up to the rough-hewn new-wood fence.

A woman with very red cheeks and a veiny nose motioned two men over. They had been working a two-man saw, but now they put that down and hefted wood axes, holding them casually over their shoulders, standing near the woman.

The trio walked uncommonly close to the cart—people just didn't walk up to strangers like this anymore. The priest unconsciously leaned back from them.

"Are you healthy?" the priest asked.

"I don't give a shit if they aren't," Thomas said, "We're asking them for food if I have to eat it from a leper's hands."

"We're healthy now," the woman said.

"If you don't mind my asking, what does that mean?"

"It means we've already had it here."

"And it's gone?"

"It's never gone. I mean we've all had it. And lived. Nobody gets it twice. We call our town Saint Lazarus; the bastards behind the walls wouldn't let my husband and me in. He died. I didn't, and neither did my boys. The girls died, though. Four of them. Others came. Now Nemours is full of scarecrows and cannibals and we get survivors every week or so. We'll let you move in if you're willing to spend the first night in a sick-blanket. Have any of you had it?"

"Just him," the priest said, indicating Thomas.

"Yep. He looks strong, though you can't always tell by that. We think it's one in five gets through, as long as it's the swelling kind. The blood coughers all die. The ones who turn black die, too. And quick."

"We didn't have any of those in my town."

"Lucky you."

"We're starving. Can you help us?"

The woman scratched her chin, looking them over.

"Will you work for it?"

200

"God, yes."

"What can you do?"

"He kills people. I read Latin. The little girl asks questions. And also reads Latin."

"All right. The big one helps build the fence. You, too. And the girl mends nets. You give us a half day of work and we'll feed you tonight. But then you're on your way tomorrow. We don't want to start liking you and have you up and die on us."

"You've got a deal. Would you like me to say a Mass for you in the morning?"

"What, God-in-Heaven? The only thing I say to God is my daughters' names. And it's not a prayer. It's a rebuke. We'll thank you not to say any blessings at dinner."

The work was hard, but good. Delphine learned the fine points of net mending from a little boy whose parents had died, and whose father, mad with fever, had tried to blind him with a hot poker so the boy wouldn't catch the illness through his eyes. He managed to snuff only one eye before the boy, who was already infected, ran to his uncle's house and carried it there. He awoke from his fevers to find himself alone in a dead-house. Nobody else would take him in, so he walked to Nemours. And then St. Lazarus.

The woman ate first, with her sons. Then they served the rest, measuring it out to the drop so all got the same portion.

"This is exceptional stew," the priest said. "What's in it?"

The woman told him.

Cabbage. Turnips. Mushrooms. Pork belly. And a few pinches of real pepper.

And at precisely that moment a sparrow in the tree above Thomas shat in his.

They slept in a threshing room that still smelled like last year's barley, and in the morning they got back into the cart. The woman gave them a sack of blueberries and a squash to take with them, and told them there was a town three miles downriver with a wooden bridge still standing.

"What's it's name?" the priest asked.

"Doesn't matter. Everyone's dead. It'll be all weeds in a year, except for the steeple. Oh, and if you see any yellow fruit in the trees, don't eat it. It's rotten."

She laughed inscrutably at this, then slapped the mule's ass to get it moving, showing them the callused palm of her hand in farewell as they clopped away.

The woods got thick again, and beneath the limbs of a very old oak tree they saw a flash of yellow. As they got closer, they saw that it was a cotehardie, saffron yellow, adorning the week-old, grinning corpse of a hanged squire; they all knew that cotehardie, and knew that its owner had once had pimples. There was a sign around his neck.

The priest shivered and crossed himself.

rapist

EIGHTEEN

Of the Penitents, and of Auxerre

T he first sign of the group they were following was their tracks. They had pocked the damp ground of the road with their footprints, as any large group walking would have; but every hundred yards or so they left an imprint where it seemed as though they had all fallen and pressed their bodies into the mud. Also, Thomas had noticed the white stumps of freshly snapped branches on trees near the road, with tracks leading up to those trees. When they got to the town of Ponchelvert, a strange sight greeted them.

Someone had crucified a dwarf.

He was still very much alive, however.

As the cart drew closer, they saw that he had been tied in place rather than nailed there, and his feet rested on a little platform, although he was wearing a crown of very real thorns. A ladder lay in the grass near him, as well as a bucket of water with a sponge on a long stick.

He did not speak to them as they approached, though he watched them the whole way. Père Matthieu stopped the mule and they all looked at him, dumbstruck.

He nodded at the bucket.

Delphine clambered out of the cart and soaked the sponge, which she then held up to his mouth. He lipped at the sponge in a way that made her think of a sheep.

"Do you want to come down?" she said.

He shook his head.

"Are you sworn to silence?"

"No," he said. "They didn't say anything about that."

"They who?" said Thomas.

"The Penitents."

"Who?"

"Never mind."

He closed his eyes now, moving his lips silently in prayer.

"Pardon me," Delphine said.

"What?"

"You should come down," she said. "That can't be good for you."

"I have two days to go. I'm only on my first day, and each town is to crucify someone for three days. Don't you know?"

"No," she said.

"It's the only way."

"The only way for what?"

"If you're going to make me talk, give me more water. My throat hurts."

She dipped the sponge again and held it aloft for him.

"The only way to appease God. So He'll take the pestilence away."

"Oh," she said.

"Very wicked towns are to crucify three people. But we were no better or worse than most."

"Who decides how wicked your town is?" said Père Matthieu, fascinated.

"They do."

"Were you out in the rain?" Delphine asked.

"They came after the rain. They came yesterday."

"Do you have to stay out all night?" she said.

He tried to ignore her and return to his prayers, but she repeated her question.

"They come and take me down at night."

"The Penitents?"

"No. The town. The Penitents are heading for Auxerre to perform a great miracle."

"Come down," she said.

He shook his head.

"Why you?"

"What?" he said again, clearly annoyed.

"Why did they pick you? Did you volunteer?"

"The town picks. They vote. It's a big honor."

Thomas laughed, and the dwarf gave him a dirty look.

"Are you sure they're coming back for you?" Thomas said, still amused.

The dwarf went back to his prayers.

"Deus meus, ex toto corde poenitet me omnium meorum peccatorum, eaque detestor, quia peccando, non solum poenas . . ."

"Because if it were me up there, I'd start thinking maybe the good people would leave me on the cross to make sure God was happy. Did you think of that?"

". . . non solum poenas a Te iuste statutas promeritus sum, sed praesertim quia offendi . . ."

The girl looked at Thomas.

"I think you should take him down."

"He clearly wants to stay there," the priest said.

Thomas smiled. He knew the girl wanted to keep the man from harm; Thomas liked the idea less for that reason and more because he knew the dwarf would fuss about it, and he was glad to do something good that was also entertaining.

He didn't expect the fight he got, though. As soon as he untied the dwarf's feet, the man started kicking at Thomas so hard he made the cross rock; it was all Thomas could do to keep the ladder upright, especially since he was laughing the whole time. Delphine furrowed her brow at Thomas's attitude, and the priest paced restlessly, afraid one of them would be hurt.

Thomas had the dwarf over his shoulder and nearly down the ladder when his burden kicked against the side of the cross and tipped the ladder, spilling them both into the soggy grass.

"You little *bastard*," Thomas said, angry now.

The little man fumed at him from where he sat in the high grass. The priest thought of a surly rabbit and laughed into his hand despite his best intentions.

The dwarf righted the ladder against the cross and started to climb, but Thomas grabbed him by the britches and hauled him down again.

"I want to save my town!" the dwarf screamed, with tears of frustration in his eyes, and the game lost its humor even for Thomas.

"Do you really want to go back up there?" Thomas asked.

The man sat down in the grass and looked bewildered.

"I don't know," he said. "But don't you see? This is the one thing I can do as well as anyone else. I can't plow. I can't build. But I *can* suffer. God wants suffering now."

The priest opened his mouth to contradict the man, but nothing came out.

"Shit," Thomas said.

And then he helped the dwarf back up the ladder and tied him fast to the cross.

Emma LaTour looked out from the darkness of her house, stunned by the beauty of the day; except for visits to the well, she had not left her home since her Richard had been racked with pains by the fence and died there. At the end, he had been grabbing his knees, and now his joints had locked him in a parody of childbirth, bloated like a dead dog or sheep. How was she to believe man was anything special when he looked so much like any other animal in death? He was just a rained-on, ruined carcass, as if he had never kissed her, as if he had never danced. The beautiful blue sky seemed to mock him, as did the bulk of the St. Etienne cathedral and the spire of the abbey, both of these stabbing upward from the high ground across the river in Auxerre. Nothing but false promises lay across the river, or up in the sky.

Her carrots were nearly gone, and she was sick to death of them; they hurt her few teeth and she checked the skin of her arms constantly because she had the idea the carrots would turn her yellow. She needed to cross the bridge into town, though the thought made her shiver with fear. If only her sons would come; but they had their own children to think of, and she had not seen any of them in a week or more. Her little cottage had been forgotten.

Now she was looking out her window, staying well back from the light so it wouldn't illuminate her yellow skin; she heard a voice coming across the fields.

And it was beautiful.

It belonged to an angel.

She saw him (or her?) sprinting down the weedy path, wearing a white skirt of sorts ruched up to the belt for running, bare of chest and foot. It was a boy. Nimble as a fox, and so lovely to watch, with his tangled blond hair bouncing. The child-angel leapt upon her fence of uneven branches and balanced along its length, calling to the window in a beautiful, heavily accented singsong, as if he could see her where she cowered in shadow.

> And der angel open das seal, and all of Auxerre behold
> For they are afraid, but now the holy men are come
> So holy from *Gott* in Heaven, to make miracles on dem square,
> Come and see!
> In front of dee church,
> but not in it,
> for thrown down are the priests
> and dead are dee bishops.
> Come and see! Come and see!
> People of Auxerre, come and see!

He leapt off the fence and over the birthing corpse of her husband and ran through the field, which was spotted purple with new growths of thistles; Emma had a mother's instinct to yell at him not to stick his feet on their evil little crowns of spines, but he ran through them as if on purpose, then dove and *actually rolled through the thickest patch of them*, laughing and shouting "*Iesu! Iesu! Iesu!*"

The Penitents had come to Auxerre.

The threescore farmers, carpenters, drapers, vintners, wives, and daughters who stood in cool sunlight near the St. Etienne cathedral had all been summoned by the beautiful boy. He gathered them with his songs and gambols, but especially with his promises of miracles against the plague. Hucksters of every stripe had tried to profit from the disease, especially in the early days, before they, too, sickened or grew afraid; so many relic sellers and apothecaries had come that soon any stranger with a case and a gleam in his eye was in danger of being beaten and flung into the Yonne, along with his sweetly herbed potions, deer bones, magic feathers, Galen cakes, or sap from the Cedars of Lebanon.

When the disease bore down and the die-off began, the town was left alone, although her gates stood open. The bishop had said, when asked for his counsel on whether to impose a quarantine, "the fox already makes his bed among the hens," which was very close in spirit to the seigneur's observation that "closing those gates would be leading hens to piss." Auxerre, thus, dutifully flew the black banner announcing the presence of the Great Death but remained open to whoever cared to brave it, be they pilgrims, refugees, or men with pretty lies to tell.

But now the boy had come, and he was different.

He was quite credible as the herald to a prophet, with his eyes of northern ocean blue and his dimpled smile. Even his German accent, normally a hindrance in these xenophobic times, lent him an air of exoticism; after all, if some holy cure were to come to Auxerre, it would not come from Burgundy. Why not the piney forests of the north?

But this boy sold no cures.

He never mentioned money at all.

"Wait!" he said, capturing his audience with an up-pointed finger and a theatrical tilt to his head. "I believes I hear them. But perhaps you will hear them, too, if you make *der* Alleluia."

Nobody spoke.

"Children of Gott, make *der* ALLELUIA!"

"ALLELUIA!" they cried, and a drum began to beat a simple march.

The sound came up through the narrow streets that led down and to the river and echoed on the shuttered shop fronts and timbered houses that bordered the square. A line of ecstatic men and women entered the Place St. Etienne, shuffling slowly in something like a drugged march, striking themselves in time to the drumbeats with leather thongs fitted with iron hooks or spikes. They were naked from the waist up, like the boy, all wearing simple skirts that had once been white but had been marched in and bled on until they were the color of earth and as stiff as leather. The crowd gasped at the sight of them; the women's bare breasts, the old blood drying, the new blood trickling, the white caps they wore with red crosses on the front and back. Some of the Auxerrois even fell to their knees wailing, thinking Judgment Day had come, here, now, and soon Christ himself would split the sky and part the damned from the saved.

Now four women called out and four men answered:

Iesu will you die for us?
—Yes love yes love!
Do you fear the Roman whip?
—No love no!

And then the men called and the women answered:

Sinners, will you bleed for me?
—Yes love yes love!
Do you fear the pestilence?
—No love no!

Then, all together:

Who will come and walk with us
In His steps?
To show Him that our love is true
Thirty days!

Behind these eight and the drummer trailed a score or so who had clearly been recruited from other towns, all stripped to the waist, though less uniform in appearance. Some of them whipped themselves with tree branches; a girl walked behind bearing a bundle of sticks on her back to replace those that split.

Now the drummer beat three beats and they all stopped. They shouted "*Iesu!*" and flung themselves facedown into the street, arms out, cruciform, eliciting a gasp from the crowd. The ones at the rear then stood and came forward, giving a stroke of the whip or the branch to each prone figure they passed, until they reached the front and flung themselves down again. In this way, like some horrible caterpillar, the entire line worked its way toward the square in front of St. Etienne and the astonished crowd of onlookers, then collapsed all at once.

All but the man beating the drum.

He set this aside now and looked at the crowd.

"I am Rutger the Fair," he said, drawing himself up to his full height. *Fair* might have been a name from his youth; it seemed a better word to hang on an urbane womanizer than on this handsome but shocking man of thirty or so, graced with the broad, muscular chest of a woodcutter or a swordsman, brutally scarred from months of flagellation. His carelessly shaven (or intentionally cut) scalp would have sat well on a madman, but his deep-set eyes shone with intelligence, even wisdom. A goatish beard of blond and gray erupted from his chin. He seemed less a cleric than the antidote to clericism. If Christ had been German as well as a carpenter, and if He had survived His scourging, and if He had shorn His head with a broken bottle, He might well have looked like this man.

"I come to you, Auxerre, from the land of Saxony, where the plague is not yet come, and shall never come; I stand before you to offer you either the cup or the sword. The cup is that of forgiveness, and the sword is that of wrath."

Now the boy came up from behind the crowd, bearing a pewter goblet and a small sword. He stood by the man, stomping his feet twice.

"God demands a tithe. If one in ten of you turn from your lives of false comfort and walk with us for thirty days, your town will be spared. Or if three of you will sit the cross for three days, your town will also be spared. But if you stay here and do not show the Lord your love, you will all die the death of the stone under the arm, or the stone in the crotch, or the death of the spitting of the blood. I see by your faces you know these deaths, *ja*? Well, you have now the chance to turn the face of death away from you. Shall I speak further on God's offer, or will you harden your hearts and go to your houses to die in sin?"

"Speak on!" someone yelled.

Another repeated it.

"*Hup!*" Rutger said, and the cruciform Penitents behind him stood, arms out, faces lifted to the sky.

Some of them were sobbing.

He spoke.

Emma watched amazed as the butcher and a vintner named Jules, who had once courted her sister, came bearing a two-wheeled cart. They put her poor, stiff husband in it, revolted by his decomposition but seemingly unafraid of his disease. Why were they not calling out to her? Because she sat in shadow and they thought she was dead, too, like almost everyone on this side of the Yonne. Or they thought that she had run away.

"Where are you taking him?" she asked, letting a little sunlight fall on her face so they could see her. She winced as much from the sunlight as from her fear of their reaction to her color, but she did not startle them. If they thought she was yellow, they were very polite about it.

"The cathedral," Jules said. "You'll want to see this, Emma."

"Are you burying him?"

"No, Emma. Come to Saint Etienne."

So saying, they carted her Richard away, his knees still locked against his chest, the little blond boy now visible, skipping before them through the thistles and singing a song in German.

The sun was lowering when the three dead Auxerrois were brought before the cathedral of St. Etienne. Richard was the worst of them, having been dead a week, but two others had been chosen. A beautiful young maid who had broken hearts in the wine shop by the front gate was only one day gone, though her beauty had already been cast down; she had been healthy at daybreak, but by Nones, the plague had turned her the color of an eggplant and killed her outright.

The third was Yvette Michonneau, the bishop's acknowledged mistress, who died after fighting grimly through an unheard-of ten days of lancings and bleedings, leaving behind three of the bishop of Auxerre's chubby, dark-eyed bastards. She had been wrapped in a shroud and buried, but the German boy commanded her to be retrieved. Yvette's mother, also a fighter, had brawled in the churchyard to keep her daughter's hard-won Christian burial from being upset, grabbing away the sexton's shovel and breaking one Penitent's nose with it before being wrestled down and hustled off by her neighbors.

Auxerre had tried to please God with Christian burials, but clearly something more was required.

The cart was drawing near Auxerre; the square tower of the cathedral beckoned them as they topped a hill near Perigny, but, with only an hour of sun left, they decided to make camp near the wall of an old convent, long abandoned and swarmed with ivy now blushing mostly red. All the ivy in the abandoned village of Perigny crawled toward Auxerre, as if reaching for it with delicate fingers.

The girl slept hard and neither man wanted to rouse her from her sleep. Thomas covered her with their horse blanket, and then he and the priest left her and went into the damp woods bordering the field looking for sticks dry enough to burn.

Delphine woke alone in the cart, her heart racing from a dream that a devil was in Auxerre turning people into poppets. In the dream, she was able to stop it, but the devil, who had too many eyes, was very angry, and it chased her. That was when she awoke. She knew the dream was true, but she was very frightened and pulled the blanket over her head. Then she thought of her father and mother, and of how she would have felt to see either of them turned into a devil's plaything. She gathered her blanket around her, meaning to set off down the road, knowing she didn't have much daylight in which to walk the last few miles.

An angel was sitting on the back of the mule, facing her and wringing its hands. It was the same one she had seen in Paris and back home in Normandy; it was the saddest she had ever seen an angel look. It told her to stay in the cart, speaking as if every word hurt it.

"Why?" she said.

She would only make things worse, it said, however noble her desire was. Getting to Avignon was all that mattered.

"Is a devil going to Auxerre?"

Yes. A very strong one is already there. And another is coming.

"Who will help the people in the town? Will you?"

It hung its head. It was a minor angel, made better at messages than war. The strong ones were fighting in Heaven.

Delphine thought, from the way the angel spoke, that this fight must not be going well.

She wanted to cry.

What would happen to the souls in Heaven if the angels lost? Would they have to go back to their bodies? Now she imagined her mother and father at the end of a stick, jerking beneath a devil's hand in a parody of a dance.

Stay in the cart.

She could not bear to say no to the angel, so she shook her head, though so gently a person might not have noticed.

She looked around to make sure the priest and the knight didn't see her, because they would stop her, or follow her and put themselves in danger. She bent to muddy her finger and wrote on the side of the cart. Then she patted the mule's side, as much to comfort herself as him, and started off down the road barefoot.

Please, the angel said behind her, and she stopped for a heartbeat and then kept going. She was afraid she might lose heart, so she made herself count ten steps before she looked behind her.

The angel was gone.

Thomas found the cart empty, with writing on its side. He put his meager bundle of sticks and chestnuts on the ground and called the priest over.

stay here

Fully one hundred people had gathered to see the Penitents perform their miracle in the square before Auxerre's cathedral. A light breeze blew, but it was not so cold since the rains stopped. Rutger's followers held candles, the last candles the remaining Benedictine monks at the abbey of St. Germain had. They wanted no part of the Penitents' display, but the Auxerrois had told them plainly that they would have no more food brought to them unless they gave over their tapers; the brothers had already killed their last hog and chickens, and their measly garden could not get them though the winter. They had reminded the crowd that starving out monks was not high on the list of deeds that would get one into Heaven; further, the abbey was dedicated to St. Germanus, who had taught St. Patrick and argued against the Pelagian heresy, and these brothers were the keepers of his holy bones.

When Giles the armorer suggested that these bones might be put into broth, the monks knew they would get nowhere appealing to the better natures of the Auxerrois, and the candles were surrendered.

Rutger beat his drum, slowly at first, then faster and faster.

The Penitents, having handed their candles off to the people, bloodied themselves with their whips and branches in time to the rhythm, ending in an orgiastic frenzy that actually sprayed droplets into the crowd. The madness spread from the flagellants to their audience; many cried out or swayed, and some were moved to begin striking themselves or one another.

"More!" shouted Rutger, and the blond boy echoed him, crying *"More!"* His openmouthed grin might have been the same if he were sledding down a steep hill.

Some in the crowd punched each other.

Then the biting began, and the scratching.

One who held a candle held it to his face, lighting his beard, then slapping it out with a hoarse scream.

At the crescendo, Jules cut his little finger off with his own knife, shocking Emma, who stood near him openmouthed.

Rutger saw this and smiled for the first time, showing his crooked teeth.

"Yes!" Rutger said. "*Und* zo! It is enough!"

He beat the drum one time hard.

The crowd's violence ebbed, and they edged closer.

Now he pointed at his acolytes, the four men and women who had given the call and response.

They took their evil, hooked whips and stood near the dead.

Rutger banged the drum.

"*Death, where is your power?*" he asked.

"*Gone!*" responded the eight, whipping the dead ones.

With each question, he banged the drum.

With each response, the dead were scourged.

Death, where are your teeth?
—Broken!
Death, where are your wings?
—Gone!
Death, where is your staff?
—Broken!
Death, where is your glass?
—Gone!

With this last stroke, the body of Yvette Michonneau jerked.

The crowd gasped.

Death, whom do you serve?
—The Lord!
Death, will you obey?
—Yes, love!
Death, will you relent?
—Yes, love!

Now all of the dead spasmed when struck. Some at the edges of the crowd ran away, but others leaned in, eyes wide.

The last slice of sun dipped below the horizon, leaving the sky lavender and pink.

Death, will you release this woman?
—YES!

Yvette stood in her shroud. A stain spread from where her mouth was. A woman screamed while a few men cheered, and more ran.

Death, will you release this girl?
—YES!

The once-pretty barmaid stood, her blackened face searching the crowd, bewildered.

Death, will you release this man?
—YES, LOVE, YES!

After three savage whip blows, Richard unbent his legs and rolled over on his stomach. He lacked the strength in his limbs to stand unaided, so the acolytes helped him. He swayed there, his simple cap still tied below his chin, moving his ruined jaw as if to speak, but nothing came out. Another half dozen broke and ran, including two shirtless Penitents who had come from the last town.

"When these sisters and this brother are strong enough, I will send them to find the unbelievers who ran from this holy place. They are very good at finding. And all of you who march with me shall be proof against the plague; for if you die, I will make you live again, as you have seen with your own eyes."

Emma, who had been watching all of this as if in a dream, moved forward shouting, "No!"

Rutger saw her, and said, "This woman fears her husband,

even as Lazarus was feared. But her man will heal, and he will love her once more. All these departed shall be restored to health. If you believe."

"This is wrong!" Emma shouted, pointing her cane. And then, pathetically, "Leave him alone."

"Wrong? How can this be wrong when it comes from the Lord?"

"It is only for Christ to raise the dead. And I do not think you are Him."

"Are you sure? There is no middle place, you know. You had better be sure."

"If you're a man of God," Emma said, "pray the *Pater Noster*."

Rutger smiled and wagged his finger at her, as if she were a naughty child.

"Lord," Rutger said, "if this woman's disbelief displeases you, show us some sign."

The boy threw the stub of a carrot at her, hitting her dress.

The crowd gasped.

Everyone was looking at her, many with their mouths open in disbelief.

She looked at her arms and saw why.

She had turned yellow.

Now a voice from the crowd spoke up.

"Stop it!"

A young girl in a dirty gown stood near the front of the crowd, holding a blanket around her.

"*Stop it!*" she shrieked. The people of Auxerre parted to let her through. All of the Penitents, even Rutger, were dumbstruck at the sight of her, and nobody stopped her as she went to poor old Richard and kissed his hand.

As soon as she did, he collapsed and returned to death.

"*No!*" Rutger shouted.

The boy ran over to her, shouting madly, "*Was tust du?!*

Was tust du?" She ignored his words and shouldered him aside, now kissing the hand of the wine maiden, who also gratefully crumbled.

Now the boy pushed her from behind, but instead of falling, she let the momentum carry her forward toward Yvette, whose hands were still bound in the shroud. The girl knelt and kissed one of her bare feet, causing her, too, to fall.

The boy spun the girl around.

"WAS TUST DU, HEXE!?"

"I'm sorry," she said, looking at him, even through him, with her sad, luminous gray eyes, "It's not your fault. But you're dead, too."

She kissed the beautiful boy on the cheek and he exhaled in a long rasp, and did not inhale again. Rather, he turned back to the plague-spotted dead boy he had been when Rutger found him, and fell as if exhausted into Delphine's arms. She laid him down and gently closed his eyes.

Now two of the Penitents grabbed Delphine's arms brutally, shouting "Witch! Witch!"

"Let go of her!" shouted a woman.

"No! She *is* a witch!" a man screamed, and soon the crowd was pushing and tearing at itself, some trying to get at the girl, some trying to protect her. She was slapped sharply, and her hair was yanked so hard it hurt her neck. The acolytes who held her pulled her back, looking at Rutger for leadership, but he was oblivious to them, staring at the girl as if he might stare through her skin and see what she was.

The crowd had become a mob.

Those who saw the girl as wicked had overpowered the others and now surged toward the acolytes, who threw her to them and ran.

The crowd grabbed her roughly, tearing her blanket from her and using it to bind her arms to her sides. She knew she was too weak to fight them; she wished Thomas were here, then blinked that wish away, knowing he would die for her and still the mob would have her.

They lifted her up above them, and she was sure they would dash her head against some wall; it seemed they were all shouting at once. She let her body go limp, trying to see it from outside herself. If she must die, she would neither cry nor cry out—it was all she could do, so she focused on that. She would die bravely.

Rutger was walking closer, still staring at her.

What are you?

"Throw her in the Yonne!" one shouted.

"Yes! And with a stone around her neck!"

They had started moving in that direction, toward one of the dark little streets that led steeply downhill and to the river, but they did not leave the square with her.

A woman who was holding Delphine's leg screamed.

Then another.

Delphine was dropped, but thankfully landed on her feet.

She worked her arms free from the hastily bound blanket as a man yelled, "I'm blind!"

"Me, too!" said another.

"God help us!"

Rutger pulled the tongue from the one who said that and flung it to the ground, now looking around madly for whatever or whoever had struck the people blind.

All of the townsfolk and acolytes near the girl had lost their sight, falling on all fours, groping their way toward the walls of the church or the buildings nearby, moaning or sobbing or praying. She took a thumb in the eye from one of them, got kicked in the back, and scampered between the legs of another. It was chaos.

A knight with a face somewhere between a man's and a lion's had entered the square from the direction of the river. His armor was bloody, as was the axe he carried head down in his left hand. He was riding a grayish horse with human mouths where its eyes should be and hands instead of hooves.

Rutger, who was a head taller than he had been, started moving toward Delphine, flinging the blind out of his way;

his eyes seemed to be multiplying, now four, now eight. The ghastly horse at the far end of the square reared, the hands at the ends of its forelegs grasping at the air.

Now Delphine saw the angel; it stood in an alley, unseen by the devils in the square, more purely itself than it had been upon the mule. Its beauty crushed something inside Delphine and made nectar of it.

It looked right at her.

Then, with what seemed very little effort, it pushed over the glover's shop it stood next to, a woman screaming from the top floor; the building fell heavily between Delphine and the devils, shielding her from their view.

The angel said only one word.

It said

Run.

NINETEEN

Of the War Drawing Near

The wind picked up, now rushing north, then turning hard south as though something massive were sucking air in and blowing it out again. Thomas and the priest looked at one another, the sound of the rustling leaves thick around them and the sky seeming to glow faintly green, though the sun was well down.

The glowing coals of their fire went out entirely.

"The girl," Thomas said.

The priest licked his lips and looked at the sky.

A tar-black cloud of sorts bled up from Auxerre, tapered from the ground like a snake's tail, spinning. He had heard of such a thing before; a sailor had told him of spouts that came down from the clouds and played on the face of the sea. But this one did not dip down from clouds; it rose from the ground and spread, *making* clouds where there had been none, blackening the faint green of the sky like ink polluting water. The tapered cloud, spinning ever faster, swayed now like a seductress at her dance, kicking up debris at its base.

The two men thought they heard the sound of screaming, but it was impossible to tell if it was coming from Auxerre or the awful wind, which blew harder now, sucking in, blowing out.

"Mary, Mother of God," the priest said, wiping his lips with the back of his hand.

"We have to find her!" Thomas said, pulling the priest into the cart, but neither one of them could make the mule move. So they went on foot, at something between a walk and a run, Thomas still limping on his hurt leg.

Now the ground shook, as though something impossibly heavy had fallen. One corner of a stone farmhouse to their right collapsed, and the wind blew harder yet, slowing the men to the speed of a steep uphill walk. Stinging twigs and other small missiles pelted them, and then a branch tumbled from the sky, catching the priest on the crown of his head, knocking him down. Thomas took his hand and yanked him up; they trudged on, coming to a higher place on the road. Shielding their faces with their arms as best they could, they saw that a second spinning cloud had joined the first, both of them tearing trees from the ground and sucking them upward. A man's shout rose from a farmhouse nearby, and the men saw why; the two clouds had broken contact with the ground. Their tapered bottoms became tails, and their thicker tops seemed to become wings. One of the clouds grew two great black wings, and the other grew six that seemed to fold in on one another

Seraph good sweet Lord a fallen seraph

and, just like that, both of them bled themselves up into the larger cloud that now covered most of the sky.

The exhausted priest stopped running and fell to his knees.

God God God

"Where are you?" the priest yelled.

"Here!" Thomas said, but the priest was looking at the sky.

"*Where are you?*" the priest screamed again, gnashing his teeth.

Thomas yanked him up, but he pulled away, shaking his head. Finally he collapsed against a tree and wrapped his arms around it, refusing to move farther.

Thomas left him and trudged on for Auxerre, where the bells of the cathedral were ringing with great urgency.

The cloud had become a proper thunderhead now, its tops chaining with jags of lightning.

Everything about the sky was wrong.

It was a sky of Revelation.

The ground shook again, harder than before, raising a chorus of shouts from the town.

The bell stopped ringing.

Thomas stopped walking now, transfixed by the spectacle taking place in the sky.

And then he saw it.

A great blackness against the sky.

It circled twice, then stopped. How unlike a bird it was, though it had wings, or at least explained itself with them; no bird could just hang in the sky like a still image of itself. It peered down into the fields, its face almost feline, but wrong, its teeth black in a sickly glowing mouth. It roared, and its roar was familiar, that lion's roar in grotesque.

An angel of wrath

A lion tearing an old man in an arena

It saw something that interested it; a great black limb, now an arm, now a sort of paw, reached down impossibly far and picked something up.

A girl.

Christ, no, no, not her.

But it was not her.

This girl was older and wore a dark dress, though her hair was the same length and color. She hung limply, doll-sized. The lion-devil's two hot eyes regarded her, and then it huffed in disappointment, bit the legs from her, and flung her so she spun end over end into the greenish night.

It was closer now, and a great stink came down from the sky, at once sour and burned. Still it looked down in the fields, pulling the roofs from houses, knocking carts over to look beneath them.

A flung cart hit the road near Thomas, its wheel flying off and striking the knight above the eye, knocking him to all fours.

It was coming closer.

It searched the road, the field.

Thomas crawled into a gully and pulled branches over himself.

But it was not looking for him.

It wanted Delphine.

Pére Matthieu hugged his tree and shuddered, too afraid to move again, and too angry that God had abandoned them to these horrors. "Where are you, where are you," he said at intervals, but it was not until the wind calmed down that he heard a voice above.

"Here," it said.

It was small and scared.

Delphine.

She was up a tree.

Of course.

She had run to the same strong old oak tree that had attracted him.

With her to protect, some small strength came back to him. He let go of the trunk and reached up to her.

"Come down," he said.

"No. You come up."

"I'm old. I can't climb a tree."

"If you don't, I think he will find you."

"Who?"

"The fallen angel. The bad one. It's coming."

Père Matthieu Hanicotte climbed the tree.

The wind picked up again.

The priest prayed silently, forming his mouth around the unvoiced Latin but giving no thought to the words; his mind was on the sky above them and he listened, as she did, to the awful noise battering them from above. Growing closer. The stink pouring down on them was as bad as the noise, and he fought hard not to retch, for fear that if he started he wouldn't stop until he had fallen from the limb he clung to. The noise grew louder and closer yet, banging like fists inside his skull. He squared his mouth to scream, but Delphine's small hand stoppered it. He looked up at her where she perched on the small branch above his. She pulsed her hand and shook her head no. Tears wet her cheeks, and her mouth, too, was a rictus, but she did not cry out.

Don't, her eyes said.

Please.

He choked back the sound in his throat and clung tighter to the rough branch that swayed wildly in his arms and between his knees. The wind raged, needling his face and hands with small debris. He was becoming dizzy. Squinting, he glanced up to make sure the girl was still holding on, too.

She was.

But it was over them now.

Its round mouth of fire hot behind backlit leaves.

The idiot scream in his head formed into words.

WHERE ARE YOU LITTLE WHORE WE'LL FIND YOU IF WE HAVE TO PRY UP EVERY ROOF FROM HERE TO THE SEA AND YANK UP EVERY TREE THAT'S IT ISN'T IT YOU'RE IN A TREE WE SMELL YOUR FEAR CLOSE YOUR THOUGHTS OF HOW YOUR DEATH WILL BE BUT IT WILL BE WORSE AND DEATH ISN'T THE END OF IT YES! HERE! We see you.

Now a white hand

A fucking hand!

the size of a pony snaked down from the sky on the end of an arm with far too many joints. It pulled branches from their tree. Now the priest did scream. As did Delphine. More hands. Five? Six?

They grabbed the tree now and heaved and shuddered it up from the earth. It turned upside down, turning around Père

Matthieu as he fell, buffeting him with branches and what leaves remained, but slowing his fall so when the earth rose and whacked his side and head and banged his knees together, he lost the wind from his lungs but broke nothing.

He watched the tree recede above him, her face white in the foliage, her legs padlocked on her branch.

NO! he tried to scream, but his flat lungs allowed only a croak.

The thing above him held the tree like a toy.

It was an abomination.

Six wings.

Six arms.

Pulling the tree apart now.

Why must you hurt her she's so small

Twelve eyes glowing and a round mouth of fire.

Père Matthieu clasped his hands together in prayer, unable to form words but imagining an angel of God coming down.

Then he saw it.

It came.

A small moon, newly risen, amber behind the clouds, moving fast.

One of the thing's twelve eyes cocked that way, but the rest stayed fixed on its task. It shook the tree.

Something fell.

One of those white hands just missed it.

The girl.

The priest stumbled to his feet, tried to get beneath her, but he was too far away. Too old. Too slow.

Still he ran.

He had some air in him now, and he cried out.

"God, please!"

The light from the cloud dove as a falcon would, one of the smallest and fastest of them for which kings pay the price of towns, and it caught her.

And was itself caught.

A hand jerked its beautiful ankle.

More tore at its wings.

The forgotten tree tumbled, slowly, as if in a dream.

The angel, yanked backward, lost its grip on the girl, and she fell again; something from the other (a tail?) grabbed for her and missed.

A sword of pure moonlight flashed in the angel's hand.

The two fought viciously as another dark shape closed in.

The girl fell.

Closer to the ground now.

Close to the priest.

He ran under her.

Her form grew bigger swiftly, coming at him.

Please, God.

He caught her, mostly.

His nose bloodied, his eye shut, his mouth full of grit.

They rolled.

She smelled of juniper.

Somehow he picked her up and ran.

Thomas lay in his gully, covered in sticks, struggling to stay conscious—the wheel from the dropped cart had hurt him.

He had to watch for the girl, but he could not tear his eyes from the fight.

An angel and two devils.

The end of the world.

The battle pitched through the sky, careening over Auxerre, then back over the fields. Now a light, golden-orange and lovely, just the sort the sun casts through clouds before it sinks, broke and lit up the river and the eastern part of town. Then everything went black, and the light shone only in flashes, painting scenes that formed in instants and dissolved into darkness again. Now a mass of black tentacles roped around the source of the light; now a beautiful arm glowing with pale light flashed down with a sword, cutting some of these, and causing the firmament to shudder like a ripple going through a pan of water. Thomas knew somehow that what he was seeing was not precisely true, but a translation; he had no way to understand what he was seeing, so his mind painted its own pictures. Now one black, winged thing tore at the beautiful winged thing with a mouth like a lion's mouth, over which its two eyes blazed with insanity and rage. Now the six-winged darkness wheeled down and fire from its round mouth spouted against the beautiful one, in a huge gout that impacted against its target and was deflected, flowering and raining down all over the fields, lighting up the countryside here and there in a multitude of small fires. Everything went black again until the three figures locked together, the black ones driving the illuminated one down and down, into a field of barley not far from the river. A screaming sound that was at once animalistic and mechanical shocked Thomas's ears and raised all the small hairs on his body.

The shock of their fall dug a deep trench, knocked trees down in a circle, their tops pointed away.

In the barley field, great beings, beings the size of wind-mills, thrashed and rolled and gouged the earth. Two of them were as black as though holes had been cut in the fabric of the world; one shone like the full moon, just that heartbreak-ing in its beauty, casting mad shadows through the grain and the trees and along the hills as it moved. Now its light grew fainter as the six-winged one pinned it down and smothered it. Thomas stood up to see the two-winged one rise up, filling the air with a lion's roar that was at once tortured and tri-umphant; its great arms whipped down and thrust a spear at the source of the light, which sputtered and quit. The ground shuddered so hard that Thomas was knocked from his feet.

At just that moment, every bird in the forest and fields cried out in a great cacophony, even those that sing only by day, so loud and crazed that it even drowned out the roaring wind.

Thomas realized that he was shouting, but, even realizing

it, he couldn't stop. A warm rain began to fall, but what fell was thicker than water, smearing on the knight's face, even into his mouth, affronting it with the coppery, salty taste of blood.

He covered his eyes with his hands and curled his knees up to his chin, still shouting hoarsely, at the edge of his sanity.

He passed from consciousness and, mercifully, dreamed nothing.

PART III

For they had been so long alone in the lower depths, the fallen had made their own kingdom there and declared themselves lords of that place. From the first days of their captivity, they had ignited false stars on the roof of Hell to make a mockery of what was above. They had dug dead rivers and gouged seas that smoked and blistered; they had raised cruel hills; they had set forests of iron beneath an igneous moon.

This was allowed them in their exile, but one thing was forbidden.

To engender life had been reserved unto the Lord of Hosts, and the numbers of the alchemy of life had been hidden from the angels.

Yet on the eve of the New War, the fallen under Lucifer had set their hands to the task of creation, and tried to bring forth fresh invention; but so far below the Lord were they that they could not quicken any new thing, but only the dead; and they wedded dead flesh together with the souls of the damned and made both live again; and they took the fishes of the sea and river and the creatures of the mountain and woods and corrupted them, made them monstrous in size and quick to do harm; because none of these could propagate, save by killing, the devils set their hands to each one, working in secret until they made an arsenal of unclean flesh against the day they might release their bestiary into the world of men.

That day had come.

The vaults of the seas opened in the dark that was blacker than ink, and the devils' children snaked up into the rivers that veined between the cities of men; and the vaults of the mountains opened, and heinous things walked down the roads that bound the towns to one another; and great was the suffering of the seed of Adam.

And the Lord made no answer.

And still the war in Heaven persisted, and neither could the wicked angels break through, nor those of God drive them down.

So one of the fallen, whose name was Baal-Zebuth, said, "Let us wear their greatest men like skins, and when they speak, they will speak our words; they will speak of wars and purgings, and of dashing the babe's head. We will turn their understanding so they make their Christ a god of war, and we will cause them to set navies to the seas and armies under the moon with generals whose eyes glow like brands, and we will stir Turk and Christian alike to madness by our own deeds, and by our own hands will we hasten the death of men."

And great was the noise of flies around him as he walked the earth.

And Ra'um walked with him with his twelve eyes blazing.

And Bel-phegor shook off his mane and walked in armor, received at the tables of wrathful men, who knew him not.

And the damned who had deceived men as false prophets rose again, and again lied.

And the Lord made no answer.

TWENTY

Of the Monk in White

"We have to build a raft."

"What?"

"A raft. Build one or find one."

Thomas looked at the girl.

A brisk wind had just blown a shower of brown leaves on them, and one perfectly shaped maple leaf, stippled red on its points, perched in Delphine's hair. Thomas removed it and chewed on the stem, trying to keep his balance in the pitching cart; the road, if it could be called that after the rains had furrowed it, was quite rough here. He had found them near dawn. They had gone to town together, but now they were in the cart again and moving south and east. His head throbbed from the blow it had sustained last night; he touched the egg above his eye, remembering how gently the girl had wiped the dried blood from it. He was drunk. The priest, bearing two black eyes from catching the girl, was worse. And the girl was not sober.

Their tour through the ruins of Auxerre had yielded a cask of good wine; it had been the priest who spied it among the timbers and wattle of a fallen wine shop. It had not seemed wrong to him to take it, nor to ask the girl to help him roll it past the fallen buildings, past the dead Penitents (all of them, it seemed—none of those zealots moved among the injured and dazed, though he saw one hand clutching a hooked whip, its owner obscured beneath stones). He had said Mass again for the first time in months, given last rites, issued wafer, issued wine. The remaining Auxerrois had even helped hoist the barrel into his cart; they had seen the angel, too. Even though catastrophe had visited them, the long months of death and suffering at last seemed to mean something; Good was fighting back. They knew the girl was blessed. As the cart pulled away, a woman had touched Delphine's sleeve with a hand as yellow as an onion's skin, and its proper color had been restored, though Delphine had been unaware of this.

And now this talk of a raft.

"Did you dream this, daughter?" the priest said, belching terribly at the end of it. His teeth were darker than his skin.

"No. I thought about it. The devil on the road said we would still be clip-clopping around at Christmas. I thought, too, about the wine. It's very good wine."

"It is," both men agreed.

"But what about the wine?" Thomas asked.

"Oh. Yes. They ship it on the river. It would take too long on a cart. Rivers are fast."

"Some rivers are fast."

"They're all faster than a mule because they don't rest."

The priest nodded, impressed.

"Agreed. But the Yonne doesn't go to Avignon," Thomas said, spitting out his leaf.

"The Rhône does," said the priest.

The girl filled her bowl again, drinking while the men spoke. Thomas took the spoon of ram's horn from his hat and chewed it, punctuating his words by poking its gently gnawed end at Père Matthieu.

"What's the closest city on the Rhône?"

"Lyon."

"That's far."

"A river feeds it, though. I can't remember the name."

"The name doesn't matter. What near town sits on it?"

"I'm not sure."

"You know wine. What wine comes from Burgundy?"

"Burgundy," the priest said, blinking his bloodshot eyes.

"Don't be funny. Think."

"I'm too drunk to think."

"Then just say something. A wine town. Burgundy. Quick!"

"Auxerre."

Thomas winced, thinking about their exit across the Pont Roi Louis, where many of those fleeing the town had been hacked apart by something stronger than a man.

"We're drinking the last from Auxerre. Name another."

"Arbois? No, that's Franche-Comté. And it's straw-colored."

"The river?"

"No. The wine. From Arbois."

"What's its river?"

"I don't know."

Thomas grunted. "Name another."

"Beaune."

"That's Burgundy, all right. But what's the river?"

"I don't know."

The conversation continued like that until the girl fell asleep, the priest got too drunk to guide the mule, and Thomas took the reins. Soon the road forked, and a sign stood by the right fork, which led into very pretty woods whose leaves were going soft yellow and startling red.

vézelay mortis est

The priest was puking over the side, oblivious, trying vainly not to get any on his robes. Thomas had enough Latin for this one, though.

vézelay is dead

"We won't be going to Vézelay," Thomas said, though only

the mule, who twitched an ear in his direction, seemed to hear him. "Hope you weren't counting on finding a nice jenny-ass there, you grass-eating bastard."

The mule made no reply.

"I hope you don't take this personally, but if we build a raft, you're not coming aboard. Except in our bellies."

"Not the mule," the girl slurred, half asleep, halfheartedly striking Thomas with the back of her hand.

"The Saône," she said.

"What?"

"The Saône feeds the Rhône," she said dreamily. "This road goes to Beaune. Another road goes to Chalon-sur-Saône. *Beaune-Saône-Rhône.*"

"Beaune-Saône-Rhône," Thomas repeated. "Even I can remember that."

"But we'll steer around Beaune."

"Why?"

"Monsters there," she said, drawing her blanket around her head against the chill.

And she slept.

Père Matthieu woke in the abandoned grain loft he shared with Thomas and the girl, putting his hands immediately to his head, which was splitting. Thomas's snore, a deep, bullish noise, shook the priest to his bones, and his mouth was so dry he thought it was full of nettles.

The night was dark and cold.

A stream. This loft was near a stream.

He got to his feet, stepped over the knight, and eased himself past Delphine, who was also snoring, and louder than such a small creature should have been able to. He descended the rickety ladder. He pulled his robes aside, meaning to piss against a fence of sticks, but only groaned, unable to start.

"God forgive me my excess," he whispered, "and I will try never to drink so very much again."

"*Try* is the word that trips you, brother."

The priest fumbled his robes closed and looked for the source of the voice. A monk in Cistercian white stood near him, a silver-white ring of hair around his bald crown.

"I know," the priest said. "You are right to point out my evasion."

"God has no love for half measures. I believe you need water. Come with me."

The priest stumbled through the brush behind this man, who seemed to radiate a calm strength he found irresistible. He wanted to cry. They came to the stream, and both of them bent and sipped water from their cupped hands.

"Are you with an abbey here?" Père Matthieu asked when both of them had slurped their fill.

"I have come home."

"Did your abbey succumb?"

"All I served with are gone to their reward. And you? I do not think you are Burgundian."

"No. Norman."

"You follow a girl."

"Yes."

"A girl who is not what she seems."

The priest chuckled fondly. "Quite so."

"She seems to be from God."

Père Matthieu lost his smile at the other man's implication.

"She *is* from God. I would stake my soul on it."

"And so you have."

The priest stared at the old monk.

"Who are you?" he said after a long moment.

The monk put his hand over the priest's eyes and closed them, as one might close a dead man's eyes. At that moment, his headache left him and a great sense of ease filled him.

The old man turned and walked away.

Père Matthieu followed.

When next the old man stopped, he sat down on the side of a hill, the grass and wildflowers of which rippled in the cold breeze. The priest sat next to him, and they both looked out across the dark countryside. One house on the side of a hill opposite had a fire in the hearth. Everywhere else was dark, save above them, where the stars blazed with a sad, desperate light that seemed to Matthieu Hanicotte like the gaze of a mother watching her child wrestle with a killing fever. A comet with a long, greenish tail chased two more near the constellation of the Cart.

"What do you have against the girl?" asked the priest.

"You should rather ask why you trust her."

"She has given me every reason to do so, and none to doubt her."

"Who was her father?"

"A country lawyer."

"Or a heretic who fled justice in Langue d'Oc."

Père Matthieu rubbed his temples, even though they had long since stopped hurting.

"She stopped devils in Auxerre."

"Or brought them there."

The priest shook his head and opened his mouth, closing it again.

The weight of the old monk's stare yoked him, and he rubbed his neck. At length he said, "She is good. We travel with a knight . . ."

"A thief."

"A knight who has sinned."

"A knight who has been spat out by the church. A knight no longer."

"My point was . . ."

"What was your point, brother?"

"She is good. She . . . loves."

"As Salomé loved Herod."

"She always counsels peace."

"When the wicked are near, for she protects them. She will tell the thief to kill when it suits her. But we are wasting time."

"Who are you?"

The old man got up and walked down the hill. He never looked back to see if the priest was following, and the priest almost did not follow him. Then he realized he was about to lose sight of him in the very dark night, and he would never find him again. So he got up and hurried after him.

The old monk walked quickly now, so much so that the priest had to skip every third step to keep up. They crossed a low stone wall and walked past a living calf, something the priest had not seen for a long while. It was a white Charolais, and it moved away casually, unconcerned with them. Its mother lowed nearby, as faint in the night as a diurnal moon, and it went to her. He stared after the wondrous creature so long he nearly lost his guide.

Who are you

Who are you

Who

"Are you?" the old Cistercian said as the priest drew near him.

"Pardon me?"

"Are you prepared to see what God wants from you?"

The priest did not answer but still followed him, uphill now, across another wall and around a hedge. Now the window that shone across the hill glowed warm before them and they approached a door. The old monk knocked and a woman opened; she was plain and modest, more handsome than pretty, her hair bound in a clean wimple, her apron stained with sauce. The smell of wine-stewed beef rose up and made the priest's stomach rumble; he had put nothing in it since he had vacated his wine over the side of the cart that afternoon.

"Come in," she said, looking intimately upon the priest and taking his hand. "Papa!" a girl at the table said, bouncing excitedly on her bench; she was long-headed like him, like his brother. "Papa," an even younger girl echoed, both of them ecstatic at the sight of him. "Mama said you weren't coming!"

They were not saying *papa* as in priest, but *papa* as in father.

It was like a bad joke.

The priest looked for the monk, but he was gone.

The woman took his chasuble and robe off, throwing them in the fire.

"Wait," he said. "You can't . . ."

The woman put her finger to her lips to silence him.

She brought him a coarse wool overshirt and helped him on with it. He had decided this was a dream and was now content to see where it led him. It was not unpleasant.

Except that . . .

"Mama said you almost went to Hell because you were a bugger. And that you were following a wicked little girl to commit murder. Is that true, Papa?"

"Yes, dear," he said, smiling at her.

"Well, I'm glad you're home," the other one said, smiling and showing the gap where a baby tooth had fallen out.

"I am too," the mother-wife-woman said, ladling out a rich spoonful of beef and onions and mushrooms on Matthieu's trencher.

They all watched him.

He ate.

Then they ate as well.

A ripple of gooseflesh went down his arm; nothing had ever tasted so good.

Now his wife brought wine.

At first his stomach quivered at the thought of it, but then a sense of peace came over him. He was about to reach for it, but then the older girl spoke up.

"Papa?" she said.

His hand hovered near the cup.

"Yes?"

"I want to live."

"Of course you do. We all do."

"But I can't."

"Why not?"

"I can't be born unless you renounce your love of men."

"No . . . I suppose not. You're a very smart child."

"And quit being a priest."

"I was never a very good priest."

"And stop that girl."

The room got just a little darker as smoke from his robes obscured the fire. He could smell them burning.

"Excuse me?" he said.

"Delphine. She calls herself Delphine. But that's not her name."

"Did you say . . . stop her?"

Both girls nodded now, and the elder spoke.

"Stop her with a rusty old sword between her eyes. Or hold her head under water. Or dash her brains out with a big stick."

The younger one hit the table three times with her fist for emphasis, making the serving vessels rattle, then smiled.

"Because she's wicked, Papa. Her father was a Cathar and she serves the devil. And she's going to commit murder."

He looked down and reached for the wine, his brow furrowed.

The old monk, who had reappeared at his side, grabbed his wrist before he took the cup and hauled him standing, hurting his shoulder. The monk slapped him hard.

The children started crying, but the monk made the same gesture in the air that he had made on the priest's eyes to banish his hangover. The girls stopped crying and sucked their thumbs like placid infants. The wife did as well.

He hissed his next words at Matthieu Hanicotte.

"Will you drink your wine before you agree to what is asked of you? God should be your comfort, but you have made comfort your god. What have you ever given up in His name, except the promise of a wife and family you never wanted?"

"How can you ask me to kill a girl?"

"Killing in God's name is a holy thing."

The room seemed to spin.

"Pick up that sword."

"What sword?"

The room and the hearth winked out into darkness, and when Père Matthieu's eyes adjusted, he was standing near the stream, struggling to start pissing.

He managed.

As relief came to him, he saw a sword, badly rusted, stuck in the bank of the stream. He finished, tucked himself away, and looked again at the sword. It repulsed him.

"Pick it up, sweet Matthieu," a voice behind him said. A gentle voice. A beautiful voice. "And take it up the ladder."

He turned now to see Michel Hébert standing nude and glorious before him, his feet in the stream, mud up to his shins as when Matthieu last saw him nude under the burned bridge. The priest walked through the stream to him and put his face quite close to the boy's, trying to see if the freckle was still in his eye.

The left eye.

"Go up the ladder and do what you have to."

He could smell Michel's breath, somewhere between a young dog's breath and cloves. He could never get enough of that breath in his face.

"But . . ."

"The knight will sleep through it."

"Michel . . . I . . ."

He tried to kiss the boy, but the boy smiled and moved his mouth away.

"Do it. We'll kiss, and more, when you get back."

The priest took the sword out of the bank. He felt the end of it, and it was sharp. He took it to the base of the ladder. If this was a dream, he might do what was asked for in the dream and dream a kiss from the only being for whom he had ever known carnal love.

He was owed at least that.

And perhaps more.

He took the first step.

And the second.

At the third, his testicles turned to ice.

The knight will kill me.

THE FUCKING THIEF WILL FUCKING SLEEP NOW DO IT

He took another rung. And another. And he stood in the loft, looking down at the girl.

None of this is real

He held the sword by the hilt, point down, one hand over the other, his knees bent like a man about to drive a stake into the ground.

Quick so it doesn't hurt

How can it hurt if it's not real

Should have wiped the mud off the end at least

The girl hiccupped in her sleep.

He smiled despite himself even as tears ran down his cheeks.

The light was growing less faint.

He saw one of his tears run down the runnel in the blade and perch at the point swaying back and forth, threatening to drop on the child's nose.

He lifted the point carefully, taking care to lift the drop, until the sword pointed up and the drop ran back toward the hilt.

He exhaled and came to himself.

Good Lord what am I doing

MISERABLE EUNUCH DO IT NOW OR DIE WITH THEM

He went back down the ladder.

The boy was gone.

The monk had returned, but there was something wrong with him.

His eyes were mouths.

They spoke in unison while the mouth below his nose

grinned like that of a father about to spank a richly deserving child.

"Too weak, were you? You'll have to give your gifts back."

He took the sword from the priest's hand and threw it so it spun end over end out of sight.

I'll never hold a sword again.

Then he grabbed the priest's face with a hand as cold and hard as a horseshoe and forced the first two fingers of the other hand into the priest's mouth and down his throat, making him gag.

"I thought you liked this. Being penetrated."

The fingers jammed in hard.

Matthieu vomited the stew he had eaten.

It came out his nose as well as his mouth and burned.

And the monk was gone.

Breathing hard, he went to rest his head on the mule's side, then climbed into the back of the cart.

Before sleep took him, he saw the girl's eyes as she peered over the side of the cart at him. Her bare feet must have been on the hub of the wheel.

"What do you want?" he asked.

"I had a bad dream," she said.

"Me too. What was yours about?"

"Saint Bernard."

"Of Clairvaux?"

She nodded, saying "His abbey was in Clairvaux. But he's from here. Near here."

She waited for him to ask.

"What happened in your dream, daughter?"

"He made you kill me."

The priest shuddered.

Despite the cold air, he broke into a sweat.

"Why would he do that? I heard he was a very good man."

"My father said he condemned Abelard. He argued against the Cathars. He founded the order of the Templars and told men God wanted them to kill for him."

The priest's testicles, which had only just warmed up, went cold again.

"But, surely a saint . . ."

"He's not really a saint."

"No?"

She shook her head.

"Men made him a saint. Not God."

The priest said nothing.

"He's in Hell."

"Oh," the priest said.

"Or he was."

The girl blinked a couple of times, still looking at the priest.

"He would hurt me if he could. You wouldn't let him do that, would you? Hurt me?"

"Not for all the world."

He could tell by the way her eyes turned up that she was smiling.

"Not even for wine?"

He smiled, too.

"Not even for wine."

He looked down and noticed that his robes were still on; they had not burned. Though they did smell like a hearth fire.

A rooster crowed, and Delphine went back up the ladder, looking just a little less like a child.

TWENTY-ONE

Of Monsters, and of Blessings

Despite the wide berth they gave the city of Beaune, they did see evidence of Delphine's monsters in the farmlands just south of the town; a tree in the middle of a field had all the leaves stripped from it, and now its branches hung with people and animals, all still as herrings. A fire twinkled at the base of the tree. They were being smoked. A heap of clothes lay nearby, as well as a separate pile of logs to feed the fire. A large, recently dug hole gaped in the side of a hillock not far from the tree; the darkness of this hole was preternatural, seeming to push back against the daylight. It was big enough for a man on stilts to have entered without ducking. At the entrance to the hole was a scattering of feet. Whatever it was, it didn't like feet. Something moved in the darkness of the hole, and then they heard a sound that was somewhere between a rattling groan and an insect's buzz. The mule sped up his trot with no encouragement from his driver.

That night and the next day brought them tremendous luck.

The town of Chagny had not admitted them, but three miles on they were able to find a functioning inn that was actually willing to rent them a room, and use of a dry stable. The man who ran the inn was a former Franciscan monk who had left orders and taken a wife, the very same who now served them watery radish soup with some bitter green in it. Outside, near the well, a statue of the saint, covered in little stone birds and well shat on by living ones, looked toward the gate; it was the innkeeper's avowed belief that the saint himself protected his house from plague, as well as from the things that had hammered their way into Beaune, and sometimes ranged as far south as Chagny.

"Have you seen them?" Thomas asked him.

"Yes," he said in a very final way, looking down. He said no more about them.

One other guest shared the inn that night: a young merchant from Tuscany who was on his way home from Paris on foot. His French was terrible, but the priest figured out from his badly grafted snatches of Franco-Italian that his wife had gotten a letter to him saying she was still alive. He took it out and cried over it, and asked the priest to kiss it, and to touch it with a rosary. He did.

His translation of news from home gave them a taste of Florentine dark humor; the mass graves, with their layers of bodies, lime, and dirt, had inspired less reverential Tuscans to say the dead had "gone to the lasagna."

Rinaldo Carbonelli had thick, well-shaped eyebrows over his almond eyes, and Delphine found herself wishing she were the wife who had sent him his letter, alive in Italy with a handsome man walking home to her. She found herself looking at his hands as he spoke, and wondering what those hands would feel like touching her hair; in her innocence, she imagined him petting her hair as if she were a kitten; she knew there was more after that, but she contented herself with letting her thoughts run to the edge of that cliff without looking over. Suffice it to say that she would have very much liked for the Italian to pet her hair.

Her gaze was so intense that the Tuscan caught her looking, and smiled, indicating her to the others with a nod and a flick of his expressive eyes.

"*Ragazza*," he said, as if that explained everything, eliciting a chuckle from Thomas.

"You could come with us," the priest said at one point. "As far as Avignon, at least." The Italian understood, and nodded slowly, considering.

The sparrow was fluttering in Delphine's chest now; she was enjoying herself so much mooning over her new infatuation that she wished it would go away, but it fluttered harder and harder until she spoke.

"Please don't come with us."

The Italian understood that.

"Why . . . why you say this thing?"

She just stared at him.

He laughed.

"What, you no like my face?"

She answered him in rapid, perfect, Florentine Italian.

Nobody else at the table could follow what the girl said, but his face went white, and he excused himself and went to bed.

"What did you tell him?" the innkeeper asked, crossing himself.

She looked into her empty soup bowl.

"I don't know."

The Italian came with them as far as Chalon-sur-Saône, walking beside the cart on his nimble young legs. He carried a bow and had six arrows left in his quiver, and, soon after their departure, agreed to accompany Thomas into a patch of woods to hunt. Thomas, stripping out of his armor near the cart, guessed from Rinaldo's gestures that he intended to shoot one arrow, and that he would not shoot a second for any reason whatever. If that was what he said, he proved himself a liar.

They moved as silently as they could in the brown leaves, following a sort of path in the undergrowth that less experienced hunters than the Italian might have missed. To his eye, the broken twigs, missing leaves and bent grass were as plain as a Roman highway; the trail led to a lush dip in the land where crabapple trees had been savaged for their fruit. He pointed and winked at Thomas, splaying his fingers over his head to suggest horns. As if this gesture summoned them, antler marks appeared on the bark of a chestnut tree, with little bits of velvet adhering.

This would be a good place.

The men crouched upwind, Thomas's straw hat covered in branches, both of their faces darkened with mud; Thomas, having no bow, held his sword over his shoulders, knowing that his limited role encompassed only protecting Rinaldo, and, if they were lucky, hauling back their prize.

They were just about to give up, having been out for two hours or more, their fear of being caught at night too close to Beaune and Chagny finally overcoming their hunger, when they saw the stag. It entered the woods before them at a kingly, slow walk, its coat the same reddish brown as the carpet of leaves below it. Its antlers were magnificent, a trophy Thomas would have loved to set on his hearth in Picardy, though he knew he could never take such a prize, as feeble as he was with the bow. Rinaldo drew his breath in and drew the fletching of the arrow halfway to his cheek; he would pull it all the way and release in the same motion as soon as the deer turned its side or back to them. He never got the chance, though.

The deer heard something moving in the brush nearer to the two men and raised its head. Ten steps closer and Rinaldo would have loosed at its exposed chest, but at this distance he would have to shoot higher to account for the drop, and he didn't want to strike its head or clip its nose, wounding the magnificent thing for no reason.

The noise came again, a crackling of leaves, louder this time. The deer left, not at a run, but too quickly for the Italian to adjust for both its motion and the saplings it crossed behind. He grimaced with his mouth open, his breath steaming out between his clenched teeth, still tracking the stag in case it turned, but it did not seem likely to do so.

He felt Thomas's hand on his shoulder and reluctantly turned his head away from the disappearing red deer. Thomas was looking at him as if to say, *Can you believe this?*

In a time of famine, when poaching laws were forgotten and men had all but emptied the woods of game, one magnificent trophy animal had been saved by a second.

A wild boar snuffled in the brush, as yet unaware of the hunters.

"*Porca troia,*" Rinaldo whispered, drawing the bow again and loosing.

His arrow sank into the cheek of the wild boar, causing it to squeal and lash out in all directions with its tusked snout. He drew a second arrow, and that was when it locked its black little eyes on him and identified him as the source of its pain.

It charged.

He was now glad for the broad-shouldered Frenchman beside him, whom he had regarded as something of a hindrance on a deer hunt.

This was a goddamned big boar.

Rinaldo knew Thomas had stood up to a crouch and cocked his sword for a two-handed thrust, but he was too busy loosing his second arrow to see that Thomas was smiling like a little boy.

And so it was that the four of them approached Chalon-sur-Saône with their bellies full, a blanket full of cooked meat in the cart and in possession of the boar skin that would keep Rinaldo Carbonelli warm on his long trek over the mountains, since the girl had told him he would surely die if he came with them to the river.

He might have dismissed this warning had she not also told him that his wife, Caterina, prayed for him each night, looking out the window that gave on the Arno; that when she prayed, she held between her clasped hands the little figurine of an angel he had carved for her from the bones of the stag he brought her father on the day he asked to marry her.

Although Rinaldo would never see the priest, the girl, or the knight again in this world—he would bid them farewell on the banks of the Saône as they embarked in the company of dangerous men—his hard-won reunion with his Caterina would be celebrated in a public feast for which half the town would gather; the couple's embraces would inspire a local sculptor to carve an Apollo and Daphne so beautiful that Apollo's fingers would be worn away with two centuries of women's kisses.

TWENTY-TWO

Of the Fishers of Men

"**I** told you to go to sleep," Thomas whispered to the priest.

They stood in the front of the raft, watching the fat orange sun sink on their right.

"I can't sleep. I'm too ... agitated."

"How are you going to keep watch tonight?"

"I don't know."

"For Christ's love, Father..."

"Perhaps *you* should sleep now and keep watch later."

"I should be awake when they are."

Both men turned to look at the men on the rudders, who were moving them back and forth with their strong, brown arms to add a little speed. The younger of the two was missing an ear.

A thief.

The captain sat atop the cabin, eating salted herring and drinking beer from a goatskin. He was a lanky, untrustworthy, but highly intelligent fellow with perhaps the most decisively separated walleyes Thomas had ever seen. While negotiating the outrageous price of passage with these river men, who were clearly more pirates than raftsmen, it had been difficult to figure out where the captain was resting his gaze. He had undoubtedly used this to his advantage in business as well as war, though he was clearly not half the warrior his first mate was.

The fourth man, the strong one, bent and cocked two more crossbows, his arms getting even thicker as he used his muscles to work the windlass. He had the look of a wrestler, the kind who fought for small purses at fairs. And won them. Once he had fitted the deadly, iron-tipped bolts into their grooves and propped the bows against the cabin, he removed the bolts from the cocked ones and discharged them.

"Resting the crosspiece," Thomas said. The man knew his weapons.

"Some of them will have to sleep."

"Yes, probably two while the others steer. I can watch all four of them at once. Can you?"

"Better than I can at night. I don't see as well at night as I used to."

Thomas threw up his hands and stepped over Delphine, who was sleeping soundly at their feet, using Thomas's leather satchel as a pillow. She had made it her practice to sleep or sit on the satchel whenever possible, as it contained their remaining gold and silver coins, as well as a handful of rings and necklaces left over from the spoils of Thomas's brigandage. The three of them would be in mortal danger if their hosts got a look in that bag, or if the men seemed to be guarding it.

The captain came up to the front now, leaning on his pole. He spoke to them for the first time since they came to terms at the docks.

"Tournus," he said, pointing his long spear at a cluster of houses over which the two towers of a church peered. Two men with cloths around their noses unloaded three women and a dead Benedictine monk into the water. One of these used a pole to push them out into the current.

"Greetings, friends!" the captain shouted at them. "Is it not a merry day to feed the fish? Merrier still, for you feed them a fisher of men!"

The carters looked up, one of them twitching his arm as though he thought to make a rude gesture but reconsidered when he saw the blue fish on red strung over the cabin; this was the sigil of the Guild of Simon Peter, the disarming name used by the ring of pirates that controlled the Saône all the way to Lyon.

"Merry enough," one shouted back submissively, and they turned their backs and wheeled their cart away. The bodies floated near the raft for a short way, as though trying to keep up.

"Sad bastard dolphins we have to play in our wake," the captain said, spittle flying from his lips. He turned to face his guests. "Have you been to the sea?"

As it was not possible to tell which one he was looking at, both men said, "No."

"Too bad," he said. "You may have missed your chance. There's talk of the sea turning to gravel soon. Or was it glass? Or maybe it will just roll out and keep rolling and never come back. But that's not all bad. I'd like to have a look at what's on the bottom. Maybe come back with a mermaid's ribs for a hat. Eh?"

Neither man responded.

"Eh?" he said again, more forcefully.

"As you say," said the priest.

He nodded happily, satisfied. There was something weak in this man, Thomas thought. Something that needed to be told he was in charge, where stronger men just knew it. The one with the hammy arms would be captain soon, if he wanted it. Maybe he was more like Thomas had been, though. Happy to fight and take his share. Until he was given the wrong order.

"Captain," one of the oarsmen said, "that plaguey geezer's about to bump us."

The captain turned his attention to where the monk floated on his back, as if at leisure, with his arms trailing beside him. His face, though waxy from the sickness, looked beautiful in the rippled orange water. The captain used his spear to push the dead man farther off.

"You would have liked to float with your arms out-stretched like Our Lord, would you not? Float to glory like Our Lord? Maybe you weren't such a good monk as you thought. Go and ask Saint Philibert, sad dolphin." Now he called back at the oarsman, "It is Saint Philibert, that abbey?"

"It is," the oarsman said.

"It's important to know the names of things," he said, as if to himself.

Thomas woke to the girl's fingers pinching his nose. He slapped her hand away and reached for the hilt of his sword, but she held a finger to her lips, then pointed. It was just dawn. The river seemed a mirror of itself from the night before, just the same rose-orange light in the sky and reflected on the water, only now the red ball of the sun was on their left.

The river men were arming themselves.

Thomas kicked the priest, who sat up quickly with fish scales on his cheek, so startled he broke wind.

The raft was closing in on a larger vessel, a barge, riding low in the water with its cargo of stone from the quarries near Tournus. A half dozen stout fellows stood watching the raft approach; it was clear to Thomas that they didn't know whether they should arm themselves and provoke a fight, or allow themselves to be boarded. Their inaction made the decision for them.

The captain came over to Thomas now, assaulting him with the oniony smell of his recently dyed yellow shirt, saying, "You'll help us. I doubt it will come to blows, but stand with your sword ready as if you're one of us."

Thomas stood, giving his friends a reassuring look. He didn't believe the bargemen had the stomach for a fight. Still, he traded his straw hat for his chain hood and helmet.

"You know who we are?" the captain shouted.

"Simon Peter's Guild," the captain of the other boat said. "Where's your banner?"

The bargeman said nothing.

"How am I to know you've paid tribute if you don't fly the proper banner?"

"I haven't paid."

"No worries, friend. You can pay now."

So saying, he grabbed up a pole-hook from the bow and pulled the raft snug up against the barge. The two oarsmen held crossbows now, and the captain, big-arms, and Thomas all stepped onto the other ship. The men suffered their boat to be completely looted, losing all their food, a cask of wine, and a small box of coins that the crew would later make impressed noises over, even though it was slightly less than Thomas and the priest together carried.

All the while, Thomas stood at the ready, though he was embarrassed enough to be back at his old vocation that he didn't return the hateful glare of one of the young bargemen, who seemed to be working himself up to act foolishly.

Instead, the massive armored man with the scarred cheek and broken nose looked mildly at the boy and said, "Don't."

The boy didn't.

"Do we at least get our whoring banner so we don't get robbed by the next lot?"

The raft captain, taking up his long spear, said, "But you haven't sold your stone yet! This was only half the necessary amount. You'll have to settle accounts with the next boat. But, as a personal favor, I will allow you to keep your cargo."

"You sure, captain?" one of the oarsmen said, chuckling a bully's chuckle. "That's some really nice granite. I could build a hell of a bridge with granite like that."

"No, Thierry. Fair is fair. Let them keep it."

"Thanks," the barge captain said. "You're a real friend."

The captain lost his wagging-dog look and his voice shed

its false good humor.

"I'm a better friend than you know, you fat, whoring slug. You've been very lucky today, and only because of my Christian spirit. If you'd like to remember me at Mass, my name is Carolus."

So saying, the walleyed pirate pushed off with the spear, leaving the granite barge to drift.

The raft moved down the river without incident over the next days. The girl slept on the knight's satchel by day and watched over Thomas and the priest when their sleeping hours overlapped, all the way to Lyon, where the Saône married the glacier-cooled Rhône and took its name. This was the biggest town on the river until Avignon, and the captain and both oarsmen were willing to take their chances with the plague to sample her remaining pleasures. Big-arms stayed on the raft.

"You roll dice?" the pirate asked Thomas.

"Every day I wake up in this world, the same as you."

Big-arms liked that, and took that as a yes, producing pig-knuckle dice.

The two soldiers gambled for small coins, big-arms winning more often. When the others came they bore bad news about the whores but good news about the alehouse; they shared out generous bowlfuls of beer for everyone and joined in the dicing. The captain remarked, "I like your priest. He doesn't waste his breath telling us what Christ would and wouldn't like."

The priest looked down at his hands.

Later, when the captain and the younger oarsman pissed over the side and the other oarsman went to fetch an instrument, big-arms leaned very close to Thomas.

"You were there, weren't you?" he said.

"Where?"

The man pointed at the pit in Thomas's cheek.

He nodded.

"I was there," big-arms said, "French crossbowmen mixed in with the Salamis. I've got one of those too," he said, pointing at the scar again, "but I won't show you where."

Thomas laughed. They looked at each other for two heartbeats, then looked away. It occurred to Thomas that big-arms hadn't brought up Crécy while the others were ashore because he hadn't wanted to linger on that field too long. The man slapped Thomas on the back. There was nothing else to say about it.

Now the older of the two oarsmen returned with his cornemuse and began to play it with some skill. The captain took off his leather shoes and beat time on the raft's dirty floor, and soon the other oarsman and big-arms started dancing. Thomas joined them, imitating their raftsman's dance, which involved a lot of heel stamping and sliding of the feet on the gritty boards, all done with the hands on the hips or linking arms.

They called for the priest to join them.

"We're only supposed to dance at Christmas. And the feasts of Saints Nicholas and Catherine."

Père Matthieu did sing, though, when the piper left his raftsman's dances and played a Norman harvest song. The girl sang, too, joining in on the second verse.

For soon the winter's breath shall breathe
the summer's greens away-O
but what care we with bread enough
and instruments to play-O

Jean will cut us sheaves of wheat
and his two sons will bind them
while his daughters hide away
where none of us can find them

Swing-ho, swing your scythe
For God is in His Heaven

And if we do not work He will
not give us bread to leaven

Swing-ho, swing your scythe,
For Mother Mary loves you
And as you sing your working song
She sings along above you.

For the first time, Thomas allowed himself to think they might just get to Avignon, and that whatever the girl had come to do might just get done.

The raftsmen boarded two more vessels in the next three days: one a fishing boat manned by two frightened teenagers, both missing fingers, and their one-handed father, who surrendered their astonishing catch of pike without incident. The other was a shallow-hulled sailing boat that tried to run. Big-arms cranked the windlass while the younger oarsman and the captain shot bolt after bolt into the ship; a man with a parti-colored cowl took a quarrel in the hip, and he howled lamentably while the other two fought over the limited shelter provided by a wooden chest aft, one getting his scalp grazed so he bled awfully, though the wound was not serious. Neither bothered about the rudder, and the quick little boat ran aground at a bend in the river just as the distance was getting too great for real accuracy.

Big-arms and the younger oarsman searched the boat, the latter pitching the man with the hip wound into the shallows to stop his caterwauling; he managed to scramble onto the bank and limp away in great, loping spasms that made the captain laugh girlishly from where he sat his supervisory post cross-legged atop the cabin. He laughed harder yet when the man collapsed in a field of rotten squash.

The take was unimpressive.

A few coins, a small drum, some extra clothes, and three

finches in wooden cages; the oarsman put his foot exactly next to the foot of the wounded man and then made him remove his leather boots.

"You idiots fled to save this shit?" he said, trading shoes, handing the hurt man his worn-out slippers.

The other man, a paunchy youth with soft hands, said, "We did not wish to be harmed for our poverty. We were going to Avignon to seek work at the court of His Holiness—the man you pitched over is a great jester."

"Well, he sure runs funny."

The oarsman presented the cages to the captain, who had leapt down from the cabin.

He reached inside a cage, caught the panicked bird with some difficulty and wrung its neck, throwing it at soft-hands. He was reaching for another cage when Delphine ran forward, just escaping the grasp of the priest, who tried to stop her. She wrapped her arms around the cage and sat down, putting her hand over the door. The oarsman tried to yank the cage away, but she held tight, letting him jerk her halfway to her feet. The captain instinctively drew back to strike her, but checked himself, sensing that Thomas had taken a step in his direction, also having noted that big-arms was still on the other boat.

He changed what would have been a vicious backhand into a tousling of her hair, at which she grimaced, clutching the cage more tightly.

"Let her have the birds," the walleyed man said, proud of his spontaneous magnanimity. "Her papa has been useful."

"We thank you," the priest said, as Delphine set the cages down and opened their doors, taking one docile bird and then the other into her hands. She kissed them both, then released them. One flew up into the sky; the other went toward the bank.

The captain turned his head toward Thomas.

"Happy?" he said.

Thomas pulled Delphine behind him.

"So happy I could shit," he said, sheathing his sword.

Big-arms got back on the raft. The uninjured man tended his friend's scalp.

Nobody saw the second finch fly into the squash field, where it stayed for a moment before flying up again and into the clouds.

Neither did they see the jester now get to his feet and run toward a farmhouse in the distance, no longer limping.

Big-arms, whose Christian name was Guillaume, had argued against it, but now it was happening.

The captain, seeing that the foolish priest was sleepy, had given him unwatered wine to put him under so he might peek at what their passengers were carrying. Once the priest was asleep, the captain had looked into the knight's satchel even as the girl slept on it, and the sight of gold had maddened him. He took a chain and a few coins without waking her, but more lurked under her head. He called the others to the rear of the raft and told them the time had come to bid their passengers farewell.

Guillaume and the older oarsman wanted none of it; the oarsman was fine with piracy but felt that harming paying passengers was a kind of oath-breaking.

Guillaume, for his part, felt a deeper loyalty to the knight who had also faced the English at Crécy-en-Ponthieu than he now did to this captain, whose arrogance and madness were worsening by the day. He said it went against his conscience to rob their guests, who had been good and useful companions.

The captain had said, "The guild knows its own, and has no loyalty to any other. It also saw fit to make me captain of this raft, and master of you, even unto your life. We send them from this wicked world, and take upon ourselves the guilt of their wealth. That is my command."

Guillaume nodded his assent but asked that the girl should be spared and brought to Avignon, if she would go with them after.

The captain had agreed, but Guillaume knew he was lying. And now it had begun.

The oarsmen had their daggers out and were creeping toward Thomas as if toward a sleeping bear. The captain, holding a brutal, rusty falchion, was on his way to dispatch the priest where he snored sitting up near his empty wine bowl. The stars were very bright above them and the Rhône was creeping slowly, lulling with its mutter, leaving the raft a steady platform for murder. Guillaume had his crossbow at the ready, and two others at his feet. If the knight stirred, he was to shoot him.

The oarsman's knife was almost at the knight's throat.

Guillaume only knew he was going to do it a heartbeat before he did; the thought came to him and seemed so clear and correct that his fingers squeezed the lever almost on their own.

He shot the oarsman.

The man made a small gagging sound and jerked, reaching for the quarrel in his back.

He dropped his dagger pommel first, and the sound woke Thomas.

The younger oarsman looked back at Guillaume with wide, betrayed eyes, and at that moment Guillaume's sight went black as the captain's falchion struck him on the crown and he fell.

Thomas had been dreaming of his wife; she was crying, pounding the heel of her hand against the table and shaking with something between remorse and outrage. It seemed wrong that her small hand had made such a loud noise on the table, a noise like dropped metal, and Thomas opened his eyes to see two men standing over him, one of them twisting, grabbing at his own back, the other turning now to look behind him. Farther down the raft, big-arms went to his knees and the figure that had struck him moved toward Thomas.

He scooted forward on his butt and kicked the feet out from under the confused oarsman while the wounded one managed to touch the feathered part of the quarrel in him, the pain making him vomit all over himself. He fell suddenly, and then lay still.

Thomas just had time to get to his feet, taking a slash from the falchion that numbed his mailed forearm, and then he kicked the captain in the hip to push him back. He used his still-sheathed sword to slap the younger oarsman across the head, knocking him down, and then he drew his weapon.

The girl was awake now, howling, "Stop! Stop!" at the brawling men, shaking the priest to wake him.

The captain sprang back, sheathed his falchion, and grabbed up his long spear.

"Don't kill him!" the girl yelled.

"I won't if he jumps over!" Thomas answered.

Guillaume fell on his stomach, but then struggled up on all fours, panting like a dog, trying to make sense of the chaos around him, and of the blood pooling under his face.

The younger oarsman, also stunned, shook his head clear and dashed between Thomas and the captain. He grabbed the girl by her hair now and exposed her throat. The priest tried to grab his arm but was viciously elbowed in the nose and fell backward.

"Drop the sword or I'll open her!" the oarsman said.

"Don't kill them, *please!*" the girl yelled, as if she were not the one closest to death. Her hands were on the man's knife arm, but they were little more use than a cat's paws would have been.

Then she shut her eyes because she felt the oarsman's arms tense and knew he was about to cut her throat.

Except that he didn't.

Big-armed Guillaume, blinking blood out of his eyes, had crawled over and now held the oarsman's arms from the outside, pulling them apart as slowly and irresistibly as a starfish opening a clam, clutching as hard as he could and hoping his blood-slick hands kept their grip; if he slipped, the other man's knife would all but cut the girl's head off.

"*Don't!*" she yelled again now, still at Thomas, who was coming at the captain, ducking his spear slashes laterally, but unable to get inside because the other man circled so quickly.

Guillaume had the oarsman spread-armed now, and the priest hit him in the face with his wooden bowl so hard he broke the bowl; the oarsman dropped his knife. Guillaume let the man's arms go, then heaved him over the side, passing out as he did so that one arm trailed in the cold water.

The girl got to her feet, as did the priest, and she stood behind him, wanting to jump between Thomas and the captain, but knowing the captain would kill her.

"Drop that whoring thing and jump if you want to live," Thomas said to the walleyed man.

"I don't need to live," the captain said, "I've already seen the sea!" and, keeping his gaze deceptively on Thomas, he lashed out sideways with his spear, just missing the priest, whom he would have impaled.

The girl cried out in a startled squeak.

Thomas attacked the spear rather than the man now, driving it down with his sword and stepping through it, breaking off the first third. The captain, not missing a beat, whipped the remaining part of his shaft around and caught Thomas a glancing blow on the shoulder that also struck his head, rattling him even through his chain hood.

It wasn't enough.

Thomas cut the man's arm off just below the elbow.

He looked stupidly at it where it lay, and bent to pick it up with the remaining one.

"Thomas!" the girl yelled at him. "Thomas!"

She meant to make him spare the beaten man, if his life could still be saved at all, but her words had the opposite effect; the captain's jab at the priest had clipped her below the mouth; not much, but enough to beard her chin in blood.

When Thomas saw that the girl was cut, he breathed out

like a bull, grabbed the dazed captain's hair, yanked his head back and cut his throat with the long, notched blade. He took his time about it.

The girl screamed, "Noooo!" and then she just said, "No," and she let the priest take her in his arms even though the tears she thought herself about to shed didn't come.

The captain fell so his head lolled back and his open throat bled into the river. Thomas watched this for a moment, then wiped his sword.

"I told you not to," the girl said, but her face betrayed her relief that the hurtful man was gone.

"We're going to pay for that," she said.

"I'm ready," said Thomas.

"I'm not," she said, clutching the priest's arm, and looked at the water. Thomas rolled the captain's limp body off the raft, and it sank as if pulled down.

A fucking hand!

The raft drifted sideways and into the darkness.

When the sky got light enough for the work that had to be done, Guillaume bowed his head and let Thomas stitch him. Thomas had sat with Guillaume through the last hours of darkness, holding the captain's extra shirt to the wound as the big man shivered and swore. The bone needle and twine had also come from the captain's trunk.

Guillaume was strong, and he lived.

For a time.

TWENTY-THREE

Of the Island of the Dead

At first it was not easy for the knight and priest to control the raft, but the soldier told them what to do until he was strong enough to take an oar himself. On the second day after the fight, he and Thomas were bending their bodies into the effort of wagging the oars of the raft behind it, pushing it forward just that little bit faster than the current, telling stories and sharing jokes.

"What will you do with yourself?" Thomas asked.

"I'll keep on for Avignon. I'll sign on for the new crusade."

Thomas's face soured at the memory of the knight and his retinue that passed them close to Auxerre.

A devil and a host of the dead

"Some face you pull. Do you not love the thought of Jerusalem in Christian hands again? It might be just the thing to quench God's wrath at us."

"About that," Thomas said, "What have we done to make God so mad at us? What have we done that our fathers and their fathers did not do?"

"They were punished, too. The year I was born, the famine near made my mother's milk dry."

"It can't have been that bad; look at the size of you."

But it was that bad, and Thomas remembered it well; for

nearly five years, when he was first a page and then a squire, the crops drowned in the rain and murrains killed the beasts; a hanged man had disappeared from the gibbet, and everyone knew the farmers on the edge of town had eaten him. Only the kindness of Thomas's seigneur had kept his family from taking such desperate measures.

Père Matthieu drew closer, waiting for his chance to join the conversation. The girl ate a salted fish and stared at the water.

"We have famine, too," Thomas rejoined, "on top of war and pestilence. How are we so wicked as to deserve all of this?"

"Well, you may not be wicked, but I'm wicked enough for both of us."

"If you were wicked, I'd be in that river. All three of us would. You're a good man, Guillaume."

"That wasn't goodness. That was fellowship."

"Martial camaraderie," said the priest.

"Fellowship will do," said Guillaume, nodding his head at the priest as if to say, *Can you believe him?* Then Thomas was struck funny and laughed, looking not at the priest but at Guillaume.

The priest laughed, too.

"What?" the big-armed man asked.

Thomas said, "I should trim that last stitch. When you jerked your head it stuck straight up. You look like a sour apple with a little stem."

His face flushed red, though he was smiling.

"And you look like . . ."

"What?" Thomas dared him.

"The ass of . . ."

"The ass of what?"

The soldier thought for a moment.

"Something I wouldn't want to walk behind."

Even the girl laughed at that.

"Even if we are wicked . . . " Thomas said, but the soldier cut him off.

"*Everyone* is wicked."

"What about her?" Thomas said, pointing a thumb at Delphine.

"Well, I don't know her, do I? She doesn't look rotten, but she could be. Or maybe she will be later. Everyone sins. Isn't that right, Father?"

"Undoubtedly," Père Matthieu said, with some enthusiasm, glad the men had moved from martial stories about camp and training (though never Crécy) to something he knew how to talk about. "Man is born into sin. All because of Adam."

Guillaume said, "Mostly Eve, my priest told us."

Delphine looked up from the water now.

"That's not fair."

"How's that?" said Guillaume.

"She was tempted by something stronger than her. Adam was tempted by a weaker creature. Or so we are told. If Eve was his inferior, his sin was greater. You can't have it both ways."

"Huh," the priest said, trying to knock the rust off his rhetoric, but failing to find the proper argument.

"I told you everyone was wicked," said the soldier. "Her sin is that she goes against the teachings of the church."

The priest said, "May not a man be tempted by a sinful child?"

"As we are now," laughed the soldier.

The girl thought, and said, "Yes. But what of a child tempted by a sinful man?"

"As Guillaume was, in the field, by an uncle. Two uncles," Thomas said.

"Don't be crude," she said. "This is important. Is the child misled by the man more sinful than the man misled by a child?"

"I should have warned you her father was a lawyer," said Thomas.

"Are you not her father?"

"Christ, no. I'd have shaken that out of her."

"It's never too late," said Guillaume.

"Oh, I fear it is."

"You haven't answered the question," Delphine said.

"I'm just going to pull my whoring oar," said the man.

"Me too," said the knight.

"Are men who swear foul oaths during a conversation about God fit to point out sin in someone else?" said the girl. And she ate her fish right down to the tail, looking more than a little proud of herself.

At the end the third day after the fight, just at dusk, they came to a dam in the river. At first it seemed to be something men had made with logs, but as they grew closer, it became clear that the obstruction was composed mostly of dead cows, sheep, and the bodies of men and women. Dead fish, heaps of them, also glittered in the last of the sunlight.

"How the Christ are we to get around *that*?" Thomas said.

Guillaume shook his head.

"Shit, what is it? You know this river."

The big-armed man shrugged his shoulders.

The raft drew closer.

One of the cows moved now, but not of its own power—something under it had shifted, causing it to lurch in the water and bump against the other flotsam.

"I think we should pull to the shore," the soldier said, and the priest said, "Yes. Yes, please."

They turned the oars, and the raft turned a little but just kept heading for the island of dead things; they wrenched the oars with all their strength now, leaning back, but still the raft moved downriver, though it faced diagonally.

Something was pulling it.

The girl whimpered and took up the flute-shaped box around her neck, opening the tiny hinges. The priest crossed himself and looked over the side; something white bobbed in the water not far below the surface, and it seemed as though something viscous and opaque had formed itself into long ropes. That was what had the raft; that was what reeled it in.

Other white things bobbed as well; one of them now rushed past the vessel, and the priest saw it was a sheep's head —but the head was encased in a kind of gelatinous creature the size and shape of a large basket; it pulsed itself to move, opening and closing itself like a flower, its rim fringed with reddish purple tendrils that trailed behind it.

"God preserve us, please, please," Père Matthieu said. The men at the oars stopped trying to use them to move the boat and came to look at what the priest was gaping at.

Now several of the jellied things pulsed underwater around the raft, seeming to glow with their own faint light; at the center of each of them was the head of a man, woman, beast, or child.

The raft lurched against the dam of bodies, none of which had heads attached. Thomas looked at the nearer shore and removed his helm and chain hood. Guillaume, seeing his intention, began to help him off with his surcoat, but it was too late.

One of the things flopped onto the raft.

The head in the middle of this one was decomposed, but not so much they could not tell its filmy eyes were set too far apart and looking in different directions. It pulsed and slithered forward, its frill of tentacles waving in the air now. Thomas lashed at it with his sword, but it parted around his blade and did not suffer. The girl tried to touch it with her spear, but it twitched away from her, one of its frills brushing her wrist in riposte.

It stung her.

She cried out in pain and nearly dropped the spear; that brief caress had burned like touching a hot coal. The priest pulled her back.

Now another one, with an old woman's head at the middle of it, flowed up from the river onto the raft.

Yellowish tentacles, presumably from a much larger cousin of theirs, began to rise up from below and wrap themselves around the raft, causing a corner of it to dip under water. Desperate, Thomas writhed out of his surcoat, but the chain hauberk was still on him, threatening to pull him down like so many bricks if he went over.

He had no time.

The tendrils yanked harder, pulling the raft at a sharper angle, causing some of their cargo to slide forward. A case of weapons slid into the water; now the wrapped salt cases were moving, too.

Salt!

The priest ran for the salt and began working at the twine that kept the oiled cover on it.

Delphine backed up, lashed at the first horrid thing with her spear, though she missed and was stung every time; her wrist had swollen and she could barely feel her hand.

Worse than its stings were its words; it spoke to her, and even though the mouth of the captain's head moved in its viscous host, she wasn't sure if the voice was only in her thoughts or not:

I AM CAROLUS THAT WAS A GIFT FROM CAROLUS CAROLUS AND WHAT IS YOUR NAME YOU'LL TELL ME WHEN I TAKE YOUR HEAD UNDER WITH ME TO THE BEAUTIFUL THE LIGHTLESS BOTTOM OF THE SEA WHERE THE DROWNED WILL MARRY US

Guillaume grabbed an axe and hacked at the jaundiced ropes hauling the raft under, but some of these lashed about and stung him, too. Thomas sidestepped the second of the jellied things, which were not graceful out of water, and saw what the priest was doing. He stepped over and cut the twine. The priest opened a sack and flung it now, hoping he was right about its properties.

The properties of salt.

He was.

The one he salted twitched and recoiled at the first grains of the desiccant, and, when showered with a proper fistful, browned and died, melting from around the stinking head of the woman, which now lay still and dead.

Thomas sheathed his sword and opened two sacks, grabbing one in each fist; he hurled these at the monster that was hurting Delphine and it, too, hissed and died its second death, leaving the captain's head openmouthed in a rictus of betrayal and pain.

The sun was long gone now, and the gloaming was upon them.

The water shone with phosphorescence; it would have been impossible to count the number of them moving about in the river.

"Salt!" Thomas yelled to Guillaume. "Salt the bastard that's sinking us!"

He turned now and ran for the sacks, as Thomas also went to grab more, but a fresh bloom of tentacles rose from the river and lashed the fore of the raft, pulling it so sharply that the salt, the weapons, the fish, the men, and the girl all went into the cold water.

They plunged into the river, which was mercifully shallow here, having flattened out to flow around the dam as best it could, perhaps thirty yards from the shore. At once, the priest grabbed for Delphine and made for the bank, half swimming and half stumbling on the bottom.

At the same time, Guillaume put himself under Thomas and hoisted him to help keep his head above water.

They got ten yards before the things realized where they were.

And the stinging began again.

The large one, visible now that night had come, shone dimly as a sort of luminous, grayish-white sail in the middle of the dead island; it could not move from the deeper middle of the Rhône, but it sent out long strands of its underside, trying to wrap them around the fleeing men and the fleeing child, which it wanted most. Its tendrils smoked and broke when she touched them with her stinger, but the smaller swimmers were stinging them dead.

Thomas lived because his armor and surcoat protected him from the worst of the stings. Delphine lived because the priest used his body to shield her.

Guillaume was taken.

He had been pushing Thomas forward, but the things had stung his submerged groin and legs countless times, and he fell behind, jerking now with every sting.

Three or four of them crowded around him now and brushed him all over with their frills.

The poison in him stopped his heart.

He went still and sank.

The tentacles from the big one webbed him now; they pulled his head from him and reeled it back into itself, where a new swimmer would be made. Guillaume's body was pulled into the island.

Thomas, unaware of Guillaume's fate and mad to get out of the river, strode through the shallower water now, bulling forward so as not to slip under; he caught up with the envenomed priest, who was barely moving, his remaining force going to his arms, which held the girl up and out of the water.

She had passed out.

She was dead weight.

And yet he held her.

The knight would never forget the image of the faltering priest holding the girl up; how like the raising of the Eucharist it looked.

Thomas, kicking one of the swimmers out of the way, grabbed the priest's belt, hauling him the last yards to the shore. The priest wanted to fall, but Thomas would not let him; not until they reached a small road by the river, crossed that, and made their way to a field gone fallow and wild with lavender bushes past their flowering.

They were almost in Provence.

When the men and the girl were clear of the water, the tentacles from the thing in the island whipped around furiously, making a small rain fall around it, and, from below, a ghastly moaning came from the submerged and captive mouths of the dead.

It was supposed to take the girl.

It would be punished.

The island bobbed and shifted and moved south as the abomination in its middle dragged its prizes down the Rhône and to the sea.

TWENTY-FOUR

Of the Cottage, and of the Song

T homas took the girl from Père Matthieu, hoisting her over his shoulder in the same way that Jacquot had so long ago on that rainy afternoon in Normandy. The knight pulled the priest along by the arm for as far as the cleric could walk, which was not far; he was struggling to breathe, and his face had swollen so badly his eyes had shut. He looked dead already. He collapsed in a field not far from a house where the light of a hearth fire danced behind closed shutters.

Thomas, dripping and cold in his armor, laid the girl down next to the priest. He knew they would both need warmth— he must go to the house, and he must hurry—but the priest sounded as if he were choking even now. Thomas stripped down to his shirt and breeches and propped Père Matthieu's head up as best he could with the soaked gambeson he wore beneath his chain mail, and that seemed to help.

The priest pawed the air blindly with one shaking hand, and Thomas squeezed it.

"Don't die, bugger," he said, now picking up the girl and sloshing through the high grass and wildflowers toward the cottage.

Dogs barked at him from inside, and he heard a goat bleat as well. A shadow blocked the firelit gaps in the shutters as someone inside peeked at him. He held the girl out as if she were his bond of peace.

"I am unarmed. I need help."

"Are you sick?" an old man said.

"No."

"Well, I am. I buried my last son yesterday and today I can't stop sneezing. I know what that means."

"I'm not afraid."

"Neither am I."

"Our ship sank in the river. My daughter will die without warmth."

"She'll die if she comes in here, like as not. There's a horse blanket in the stable, if nobody's taken it."

"I want to bring her near the fire. Please."

"Your choice," he said, and drew the bolt, letting the door swing wide.

The goat ran out but stayed near the house.

The dogs whimpered and barked uncertainly until their master kicked them, which was what he always did to show them a visitor was safe, so they stopped and settled near the fire, one of them halfheartedly wagging her tail. They were kicked again to clear a spot for the girl, who was waking up now.

She whimpered.

"What happened to your faces?" the old man said.

"River. Something in it stung us."

He looked at the old man now, with his fine white hair plastered to his head, and saw the sorrow in his eyes, and the sag of the skin around them. The man looked gray. The man looked sick.

"Stung you? I've fished that river fifty years and nothing ever stung me."

"I'll talk later. Our priest dies tonight, but not in a field."

The old man looked Thomas over but then sighed, concluding that he had nothing to lose by trusting him; death at this giant's hands would be kinder than what would come in a day or two.

And it would be nice to see a priest.

"Bring him, then."

The old man sneezed three times in a row and crossed himself as Thomas limped off into the darkness beyond the door.

The female dog licked the priest's face.

Thomas went to push it away, but Delphine pointed at the priest's mouth, which bore a hint of a smile, so Thomas acceded. He wondered how long the man had left—he had thrown up violently and now he couldn't stop shaking; worse, he fought for every breath.

But he did not cry out.

"You might not have been a soldier, bugger, but you're tough."

"Stop calling him that," said the girl.

Thomas turned an angry glance at her but softened it immediately.

"Yes."

He put his hand on the priest's chest.

The priest fought one of his slitted eyes open and looked at the knight. Then he looked up and past him, pointing at something on the wall.

A lute hung diagonally, covered in dust, near several upside-down bouquets of dried flowers.

Thomas turned now to the old man and said, "Do you play?"

"I did," he said, holding up two hands with gnarled fingers. "I thought I wanted to be a troubadour, but then I married."

"Can you play at all?"

"Maybe a little."

The old man clambered onto a stump and pulled the instrument down from its pegs, blowing a plume of dust off it. He tried to tune it, but couldn't manage with his wrecked fingers; he plucked a few sour strings and limped through half a Provençal love song, singing in his croaking voice; then he couldn't stand the sound of himself anymore, and he stopped.

He sneezed, wincing, putting his finger to his neck and feeling for the first time the exquisitely painful, acorn-sized lump there.

"And so," he said, letting the lute dangle from his hand.

He looked at the man dying by the fire, and at the sadness in the knight's face, and he thought about the shallow graves near the lavender. All he could do was to chuckle without humor, coughing as he did, shaking his head at the lies he'd believed in his youth about God's love and mercy.

At least there might be someone to bury him now, in the lavender, near all that he had loved.

The girl held out her hand for the lute.

He narrowed his eyes; she seemed half asleep, and he knew no young girls who played.

Yet, when he handed it to her, she tuned it expertly.

"I had no idea," Thomas said, but she ignored him and he was silent.

She played.

She sang.

It was a song Thomas dimly remembered from his wedding feast, when his wife's eyes looked so kindly upon him; he had thrown a handful of sweetened nuts into his mouth, and his new, heavy ring had hit his tooth, making him swear, making her laugh. The whole table had laughed.

From that day forward, three taps of her ring on anything meant, *Do you remember our wedding day?* and three taps on his part meant, *God, yes.*

He recalled it all quite sharply: the smell of bergamot in her hair, the whiteness of her neck, her eyes pear-green, how sweet the marriage bed had been. How, even after years of amorous tusslings with camp women and kitchen girls, he had stood nervously while the old women took the ribbons off his *verge*, looking at this beauty whose pale, lovely belly was his to put children in and whose mouth was his to kiss for as long as she lived.

Or, as it turned out, until he left for war.

The old man knew this song, too; it was the one he had learned in Valence his seventeenth year, in the music teacher's studio above a candle shop, where those gorgeous sounds had married themselves to the smell of tallow such that even fifty years later he could not smell candles in church without being transported. It was this song, more than any other, that made him want to travel with his lute; it was this one he played to seduce the chestnut-haired girl whose pregnancy anchored him on this little patch of land forever.

The priest also remembered the song. He had heard it just before he went to take orders, when the bishop's personal musician came to the lord's castle and hushed the room with it, making it seem possible to Matthieu that a greater world lay beyond the disappointment of his father and the vanity of his brother; a world where God's love was unfiltered by priests or texts and could be had freely by looking up at the sky. Or hearing a man sing. It was a promise of joy he would not feel again until the May before the Great Death came, a joy made even brighter by how swiftly it was seized back again, how much it cost him.

It had never occurred to him that a female voice might animate those fondly remembered lyrics even more sweetly than that long-ago minstrel in the bishop's train, but now it did.

The next two days would be hard.

Thomas would dig Père Matthieu's grave as their host burned with fever and lost his reason; he would pull Matthieu from under the arms while his feet dragged and the girl cried and he got a last noseful of the priest's woolly, winey, lonely smell. The following day Thomas would dig another grave and lay the old man in it without ever learning his name, though he knew the name of the wife, because it was to her the old man addressed his last words. On the third day, he and the girl would make for Avignon, pulling the little goat on a rope, trying to call the dogs to follow them; but the male would stay whimpering in his master's house and the female would lie on his grave, wagging her tail at them until their forward motion eclipsed her behind a stand of goldenrod.

That would be tomorrow.

For this moment, all three men remembered the best hours of their lives.

When the song finished, the priest spoke.

"The river," he said, and Thomas thought he meant the Rhône, the one that had killed him.

"River froze last winter . . . saw you on skates of horse's shinbones . . . and now . . . so white . . . your legs . . . not red at all."

Thomas understood now.

"moon's light . . . on you . . ."

He wanted to turn his gaze away at this talk of love between men, but couldn't; he knew it was the last he would see of this flawed priest who had become so dear to him so quickly. This was harder than the comte's death. For all his goodness, the comte was not gentle; he was of this world, and of the brutality of the world. This man, Matthieu Hanicotte, seemed to have been misplaced here.

He hoped there was wine in his Heaven.

Could a sodomite attain to Heaven? He remembered the priest holding the girl up out of the water as the abominations stung the life from him.

Hoc est corpus meum.

If that was not good enough, nothing would be.

"Robert . . ." he said now, grabbing Thomas's hand.

"Thomas," the knight said in the husky voice of one fighting with tears, "I am Thomas."

"No ... find Robert ... tell him ..."

"Who's Robert?"

"My brother ... tell him ..."

"Tell him what?"

The priest worked one eye open again and looked at Thomas, breathing with great difficulty.

"What do you want me to tell him?"

The priest smiled.

"I don't know," he said.

He breathed three more hard breaths, each one longer in coming, and then he stopped.

Thomas had seen so many die that his hand moved with the reflex to close the priest's eyes, but they were already glued shut for good.

"Play another song, would you?" the old man said.

Delphine looked up at him, surprised he was looking at her.

He repeated himself, and she looked down at the instrument in her lap as though it had just appeared there. Her tears fell on its face.

"Play us something sad and sweet."

"Go on," the knight said. "I don't think his soul's so far above us yet."

She gave them a look and a sad smile that puzzled the old man, but Thomas had seen enough from her to understand.

She doesn't know how.

It wasn't her that played.

Later that night, while the old man and Thomas stole a few hour's sleep, Delphine went to Matthieu's cold body. She put her finger below his nose and felt nothing. She sensed herself on the verge of some great blasphemy but felt so angered at the sweet priest's death that she didn't care if she made God angry now.

It would serve Him right.

I can't think like that.

She prayed.

"Let me do this, please, work through me."

She pried open the priest's waxy mouth and breathed into it, as if she were God Himself breathing life into Adam's dead clay.

Nothing.

She tried to conjure the feeling of the sparrow fluttering in her chest, and she thought she did, but wasn't sure. She sensed that she could almost do this, that with just a little help . . .

Is this a sin?

Delphine breathed into his mouth again.

His big, cool hand, into which she had slipped her fingers, squeezed hers gently.

Her heart beat like a rabbit's in her chest.

She almost laughed with joy.

And then the hand relaxed.

No!

She breathed into his mouth again.

Nothing.

PLEASE! she thought, *He's so good I need him please I love him.*

Now the fluttering, different than her racing heart.

Now her answer.

Leave him with us, little moon.

You're not strong enough for that.

Not yet.

She shook her head against this denial.

She blew into the dead man's mouth a dozen more times, but his fingers never moved again, and, when she began to have the feeling she was troubling him, she went to a corner and sobbed until she washed the whites out of her eyes.

TWENTY-FIVE

Of Delphine, and of the Scarecrow

D elphine traced her fingers on the sleeping knight's face.

ThomasThomasThomasThomas.

She touched him lightly enough that she knew he would not stir; he slept like a soldier, always set to spring awake at a strange sound, but he seemed to know it was her hand upon his face, and that she was no threat to him.

But I am.

The land was drier now, rockier. Warmer. The sky blazoned its unquenchable Provençal blue over plane trees with yellow-green leaves and bark like linen. It had not rained since they left the old man's house, and the vines were still green here. They had stopped in a shallow cave near a stream, exhausted after two days on foot. They had sold the goat to a Provençal family the day before, Thomas gesturing his way through much of the exchange, getting in return a hot meal and a small pouch of silver that wouldn't get them far.

Thomas had told her flatly that he intended to steal the first horse they saw, but they saw horses only when troops of men, sometimes soldiers, sometimes laborers, headed south and past them. It had not seemed plausible that any of these groups would turn their horses over to one man, no matter how big and dangerous he looked, so Thomas stole nothing.

It wasn't going to work like this.

She had been thinking about it for both days as they walked.

She had prayed, and prayed hard, for a dream to tell her what to do. In the dream, she saw the city of Avignon lying before her, a little below her as if she were a bird; and then the city filled with birds that flew about and ate a multitude of flies. She did not see herself or Thomas, nor did she have any sense of what she was supposed to do there.

It made her angry.

She tried to imagine what her father would do, but she already knew, and it scared her. Her father would not want to bring harm to another. How many were gone now because of her? Annette and her husband, the soldier on the raft.

And now funny, sad-eyed Père Matthieu.

Even an angel of God.

This was not counting the three men Thomas had slain.

Her father would not bring this knight any farther to kill or, worse, get killed himself. And what was she becoming now, to think it better if Thomas killed another than that any harm should come to him? That was the way everyone thought, protecting the beloved at the cost of the stranger.

She would go on alone.

Her fingers lingered just below his nostrils, and the feel of his living breath pleased and thrilled her.

If God wanted her in Avignon, He would have to get her there safely without using Thomas and then casting him away when he was no longer needed.

Am I tempting God or doing His will?

Mother Mary, help me.

She climbed to the top of a rocky outjut full of ocher and crowned with thorny bushes and bushes whose leaves flashed silver undersides when the wind blew. And the wind did blow here, not quite cool, but neither warm. Just hard. She gathered her new horse blanket, the one from the old man's stable, around her shoulders. A mountain rose to the south, slightly blurred with haze, protected by a pack of smaller, sharp mountains that seemed ready to intercept anyone who tried to approach the large one. She saw the Rhône snaking south to her right, deceptively blue.

Come get your raft dear

Follow me to the city of your dying

She wanted to cry but pushed that down and lifted her chin.

Her shoes were nearly worn through. The road that had been punishing her feet lay close to the river.

Romans made that road.

How do I know this?

I'm becoming something.

She turned now and looked for Thomas, conflicted about whether she hoped to see him. She knew he would be following her—there was no mystery about where she was going—but she was sure she had a long head start. Her heart sank just a little to see that the road behind her was empty.

She wanted to play her bird flute, but it had fallen out of her pouch in the river. Her mother's comb had not, and she put it to her lips now, blowing through its teeth, but unable to get anything like music out of it.

She walked on.

As late afternoon came on, she found a pretty little farmhouse roofed with the lazy U-shaped tiles they used here. Whoever had been here must have left; she found nothing in the house but furniture and tools. She went to the well in the back, her throat parched, and started lowering the bucket. She stopped, though, when she first smelled, then saw how rancid the well was.

Very little water pooled in that well, not at all enough to

cover a man's mostly skeletal remains bunched at the bottom, his back twisted so his skull and torso faced the wrong way, the eye sockets drilling up at her.

An accident? Did people still die of those?

Then she saw the child's skull, just the top and one eye visible, one small foot perched on a rock.

No. He threw the body in and jumped.

May God forgive him, since he couldn't forgive God.

Can I?

She crossed herself.

Did the child's skull move?

Were two eye-pits now visible?

Join us! Tell us stories about the world where the sun shines all day!

She went back toward the road.

The bucket's rope creaked.

Her hand went to the flute-shaped box around her neck.

She walked faster.

She couldn't find any water near the road or in the several houses she visited. She did, however, spend nearly an hour crouching in a vineyard where the dark little grapes had missed their harvest time, some of them beginning to pucker at the stem. She stuffed her mouth with them almost to the peril of her fingers until she vomited, then slowed down, eating a little more and napping under an iron-wheeled cart; she got her strength back, but after another hour on the road her thirst returned.

Still no Thomas.

She chided herself for looking.

One house was occupied, its shutters flung wide, but two men quarreled there; she saw their shapes move in the darkness of the house, their angry, bearded faces illuminated in flashes as they circled each other and took turns passing through a swath of sunlight where roof tiles were missing.

Likewise, she could understand only flashes of their southern language, which was like French but not French:

"Hate you . . . your . . . kill you . . . No, no, You . . . MINE . . . CHRIST . . . last time. . . ."

She hugged the limestone wall near the house and kept on, tempted by their well but not wanting to risk being seen. A skinny pig in an enclosure of twined-together branches saw her and snuffed the air at her, but then rolled in the little bit of mud near its trough. She leaned over and stole a palmful of water from that trough, and then scurried on, her thirst worsened.

It was only when she was out of earshot that her fear gave way to pain and her limp returned.

She went to the Rhône an hour before sunset—she would want to be away from it before the sun slipped behind the hills.

No bodies floated there, and no monsters shouldered up from the river's middle. She saw nothing but weeds on the sandy bottom near the shore; half of a wrecked fishing boat mudded in the shallows looked to have been there a long time, perhaps since before the world and Hell began to couple.

The wind stung her with grit and chopped the surface of the river, but she knelt in the shallows, happy for the cool water lapping at her knees. She cupped her hands to her mouth and slurped, her lips stinging insignificantly just before she swallowed and her cooled, slaked throat became the glad center of her awareness.

She took off her stiff, almost formless shoes, delicately so as not to snap what was left of the thong that wrapped around her ankles, and put her feet in the water.

It was good.

She felt herself smiling for the first time since Père Matthieu died.

Delphine started awake with the feeling that someone was

watching her. She opened her eyes, but the night was so dark they may as well have been shut.

Where am I?

Think!

The old man's house?

No.

She remembered now; the priest was dead and she had left Thomas—she was alone. But where?

The convent.

The wind whipped outside, moaning in little nooks of the stone building. She panted, scared of the dark, scared of her solitude.

But someone *was* watching her—she was sure of it.

Who or what could see in this pitch?

"I hear you breathing, child."

A woman's voice. Not unfriendly.

But all the nuns in this little grotto convent were dead; she had seen them arranged in the garden, their faces wrapped tightly in cloths, nearly skeletal arms clasped as if in prayer and wound with wooden rosaries. She remembered that several of these cadavers had no arms on them, but she had seen the human body so abused in so many ways in the last three months that she gave it no further thought.

Despite the sadness in the garden, the building itself had been empty and had offered protection from the wind. She liked the stone cross over the chapel.

But now.

Who was in the room with her?

"You needn't breathe like a hunted thing. You rest in the arms of the Lord tonight."

She was in the chapel. She remembered now, an old stone dome near rows of lavender past its blooming time, and a palm tree! She had never seen a palm tree before. The wind made its leaves rattle, and it was browner than she thought a healthy one should be, though not from thirst, surely? It inclined gently toward a statue of Mary with neither crown nor scepter nor babe.

"Who are you?" the girl asked.

"A sister. Sister Broom, if you like. I clean up here."

"Will you light a lamp, Sister?"

"I haven't one. I see quite well in the dark. The older sisters who did not see so well have no need of lamps now."

Delphine forced herself to breathe more easily.

"That's better," the other said.

She felt a hand on her chest, patting her as if in reassurance, but it seemed to be feeling its way toward what she carried around her neck. She shifted away from the hand. The hand was withdrawn.

"My, but you're a nervous little thing."

"Forgive me. I am ... Forgive me."

"What is it that you're so worried about?"

"A gift. My father gave it to me."

"I love gifts. What kind of gift is it?"

She struggled to see but could make nothing out.

"A ... an instrument."

"Of song?"

"... Yes."

"May I see it?"

Delphine swallowed hard, trying to think of a response, but she couldn't. Then she remembered not to think at all, but just to speak and see what came out.

"My father told me not to let anyone touch it."

"That's too bad. Well, I shouldn't be selfish. All the things of the convent are mine to amuse myself with now."

Delphine heard what sounded like a sack being dragged closer, and then the sound of someone fishing around in that sack.

"Here," the woman's voice said, "what do you imagine this is?"

An object was placed in Delphine's hand. It was round and thin and made of metal.

"A bracelet?"

"Yes. The Mother Superior bought it with money from the convent treasury. She wore it over her elbow where the others could not see it, and looked at herself nude in a glass, imagining she was Salomé. Can you imagine? It's silver with little grape vines and jeweled grapes on it. It was from the time when this place was called Gaul. I do wish I had a lamp. Can you feel the vines in the metal? They're exquisite, aren't they?"

Delphine grew afraid again and panted, but she managed to nod, not thinking about the darkness.

She was seen.

"Clever thing," Sister Broom said.

The hand was on her chest again, but she twisted away.

The hand was withdrawn.

"But what is in that case?"

"I want to go outside."

Silence.

Delphine started to get to her feet.

The woman's voice spoke before she stood.

"I'll be angry if you stand up."

She stayed sitting on her heels, sweating and trying not to pass out from fear, wishing she could see well enough to run somewhere. Wasn't there a window in this place? Yes, past the altar. She should at least be able to make out a window by the stars, unless clouds had come. Was the other in front of it?

"I don't want to make you angry."

"And I don't want to *be* angry. We're friends, aren't we?"

"As you say."

A hand moved again in the sack. Now a cold, round object went into Delphine's hand, the hand that placed it there brushing hers, dry and cool.

"What is that, do you think?"

She struggled to control her breathing.

"A coin."

"Good! A piece of silver. One of thirty Judas received for the betrayal of the Nazarene. This convent kept it in a box of cedar, but the Mother Superior broke it and took it out, took it for herself. How selfish she was! Can you imagine what they'd pay for it in Avignon? Would you like to keep it? I'll give it to you for what's around your neck."

"No . . ." she managed to mew. "The coin belongs to you now."

The cold, dry hand took the coin back, and a sound like very dry hissing or rattling came from the other in the room.

"May I please go outside now?"

"Not unless you wish to end our friendship. Is that what you want?"

"No."

"I agree. Let us be loving with each other. There's so little love anywhere."

Now another object was removed from the sack.

She heard the sound of sawing near her.

She smelled the dust of very old wood.

Now the saw was placed in her hand.

"I know you know what that is, but can you guess its significance?"

"Something . . . something to do with the Mother Superior?"

"Of course! She used this to build something very special before she left this place. Her lord told her to. Her new lord."

"Where is she? Now? Are you . . ."

"No, child, you flatter me! I am not the Mother Superior! She went to Avignon. Or, that's where she thought she was going. But as she packed her sack, what she made came to life. It had orders of its own to follow. She is still here now, part of her at least, and that part is past vanity and greed."

Delphine shivered now and could not stop.

This thing was going to kill her.

She reached for the case and began to open its tiny latches.

"If you open that case, I'll bite your fucking thumbs off."

She withdrew her hands.

"Now give it to me."

Something occurred to Delphine.

Her breathing calmed.

"Why don't you take it?" she said, her voice trembling.

Silence.

"You wouldn't like that very much."

"Well, I don't like being threatened very much, either. I repeat my question. If you're capable of hurting me, why do you ask me for what you want? Why not just take it?"

"Because that wouldn't be friendly."

Delphine took a deep breath. When she spoke again, her voice was steady.

"Friends don't terrorize one another. If you're really my friend, leave me in peace."

The rattling hiss came.

The thing in the room dropped the pretense of human voice.

Give me that fucking case.

"I refuse."

Something bit in front of her face, the smell of mold and dust and stale death washing over her.

Delphine stood up now. Hands groped and clutched at her, *more than two hands*, but she pushed them off and stood up anyway. Now she opened the case and took the spearhead out. The thing scuttled back with a dry, scratching sound.

"I believe you are only able to do to me what I permit. I forbid you to touch me again."

The room now exploded in a fury of flung objects as something moved around the room, banging on the altar, punching what glass was left out of the windows, and a dry scream bounced off the walls, hurting Delphine's ears.

She felt her way to the door and stepped out into the wind; the stars were out, and she could see well enough to walk toward a tree. She climbed it, the spear in her teeth, and found a branch she could sleep on.

It followed her outside and to the base of the tree, but it had drawn around itself her blanket, which she had forgotten inside, and she could not see what it was; she thought she saw a blackened face and a wisp of hair.

You stupid Norman cunt you'll die in your sleep tonight and fall from that tree like rotten fruit

"I will not fall. And you will not be here in the morning. There are wicked things strong enough to harm me, but you are not one of them. You're a scarecrow. You are made of lies, and you are not made well. I feared you, but now I pity your suffering. Good night."

The only sound that answered Delphine was the wind in the leaves around her.

By and by she slept.

In the morning, she saw her blanket at the bottom of the tree. A profanity of sorts lay atop it, but a very sad one, made from a broom, three cross-sticks, and the missing arms from the nuns in the garden. A skull crowned with reddish-gray hair sat atop the broom. She dragged the blanket over to the garden, then took the thing apart, using the saw she found in the chapel to cut the twine that bound it together. She put the human remains in the garden and said an *Ave Maria* over them. She used the broom to sweep the chapel out and then leaned it against the chapel door.

Delphine shook out her blanket and put it around her shoulders, walking down the road that led to Orange and then to the city of the pope.

TWENTY-SIX

Of Thomas, and of an Oath Long Overdue

T he girl was gone.

The knight looked around their camp for signs that she had been taken, but found nothing.

He was sure she had left.

She had barely spoken since the priest's death, and he believed she blamed him for it.

"We'll pay for that," she had said when he cut the raftsman's throat, and he was sure she had decided the priest's death was ordained from the moment Thomas broke her commandment not to kill.

He wasn't sure she was wrong.

Yet he could not bring himself to regret finishing that wretched, murderous walleye.

"Goddamn it," he said, feeling truly lost for the first time since this had all begun. Who was he now, without his pack of brigands, without that girl and her visions, without a coat of arms on his chest or a horse or the first whoring idea what he might do if he never saw her again?

"Goddamn it."

Thomas called for her for a dozen times or more, but then his voice went hoarse fighting the dry wind, and he set off down the road heading south.

If he took big steps, he just might pass her.

When the big, dirty soldier saw anyone at all, he asked "Have you seen a girl?" The first response he got, other than a shrug, or a quick flight up a hill or into the shadows of a thicket, was from a Provençal with a deeply lined face. The man nodded, slowly got up from the shadow of his house, and went inside, fetching out a homely teenager who pouted her lips at Thomas despite the fact that she was nursing a large infant.

There was no fixing the misunderstanding.

From then on, Thomas said, "I'm looking for my daughter —have you seen a young blond girl?" but those were too many words for the others he caught sight of. They either cupped a hand to an ear and shook their heads, or else they fired their own language back at him, causing him to cup *his* hand and shake *his* head.

He passed a large ocher rock covered in scrub, and then a small village. Two bearded men sat on the ground outside a house with missing roof tiles, one of them whittling a stick with a knife, the other sitting far away from him, holding a bloody cloth to his face and glaring at Thomas as he passed. A pig slept in the sun nearby.

He kept walking into the evening, past a convent with a garden full of long-dead nuns and then to a gully, where he lay down and slept until just before sunrise.

The castle on the hill near Mornas flew the cross-key ensign that announced it belonged to the pope. When he tried to approach the walled city, he was shouted away without even the chance to ask about the girl.

"Goddamn it."

As he turned his back on Mornas, he heard bells ringing in the south.

He found out why within the hour.

His first thought, upon seeing the crowd gathered in the street of the next village he came to, was that the plague must be over here. Although he had seen a great many desiccated cadavers in Provence, he had not seen a fresh body in some time, and these people were standing near one another with no apparent concern for contagion. As he drew closer, he saw that there were, in fact, fresh bodies here: a dozen or so of them laid out in front of the church. These were not plague victims, though. They bled. A priest bent over one on the end, removing an arrow that looked to have stuck the young man's liver.

A very long arrow.

Several of the mourners saw Thomas now, and began to shout and point.

This was not just a group of villagers.

It was a group of furious villagers.

It was a mob.

"Oh, whore," he said.

There were too many to fight and he was too encumbered to run.

Mostly women and old men, too.

This would be a hell of a way to die.

He showed them his hands.

An old man grabbed one of these and jerked him toward the bodies. He pulled away, but then several sets of hands grabbed him, and he allowed himself to be pulled and pushed along. A woman whose eyes blazed wide with grief and hate dipped her hand in a young corpse's wound and rubbed blood on Thomas's face.

"Wait! I haven't done anything!" he said, though he wasn't sure they could hear him through the shouts.

"I did not kill these men!"

He was hit several times, once with the end of a rake, and a remarkably quick little boy took Thomas's sword from his sheath, running away with it, its edge making sparks on the ground.

Another man now shouted at the crowd and moved his hands in a gesture to suggest calm, although he still held in one hand the arrow he had just pulled from a dead man.

It was their priest.

Despite his predicament, Thomas suddenly missed Père Matthieu so badly he almost sobbed.

The crowd stopped its jeering.

"You are . . . from France?" the cleric said.

"Yes."

"Not English?"

"No! Picardy. I'm from Picardy," he said, careful to enunciate every syllable, pointing back up the road that led north.

"You are come for crusade?"

"I . . . am looking for my daughter. Have you seen a strange girl? A blond girl?"

The priest's eyes narrowed, and he shook his head, suspicious of distraction.

"You are not with these English *routiers*?" he said now, showing Thomas the bloody arrow. Priest or not, he looked capable of shoving it into Thomas's eye.

"No," Thomas said solemnly. "I swear it."

An old man, his cheeks soaked with tears, said something to the priest and pointed at the church. The priest nodded.

"You make your oath in church."

Thomas knelt. The priest stood before him.

"Are you a knight of France?"

"I am."

"Swear it."

"Yes. I do so swear."

"By Saint Michael and Saint Denis?"

"By Saint Michael and Saint Denis, I swear that I am a knight."

"Are you a knight turned *routier*? Brigand?"

"No."

"Swear it."

"I swear I am no brigand, nor taker of men's goods, nor of their lives. I swear that I am a loyal knight of France, servant to God and to the king, and a friend to Provence."

"These men who come . . . with the long bows. *They* are *routiers*. If you see them, and you are able, you give them God's justice? You will find others and give them justice?"

"Yes. I swear it."

The priest motioned for Thomas to stand, and he did so.

Now the holy man made an announcement to the crowd.

Many nodded, and some stepped forward to clap the knight's shoulder.

The boy brought his sword back, his father at his arm, the point well off the ground.

Thomas wiped it with the tail of his gambeson and sheathed it.

Before he left, women sat him down and pulled off his boots. His feet and face were washed for him. He was offered a pot of lukewarm chicken stew, redolent with garlic and leeks, and so thick the wooden spoon stuck straight up out of it.

He ate it all.

He stood tall as he walked toward the town of Orange. Even in his all-but-ruined chain mail, even with his tattered boots and his sweat and rust-stained gambeson, his bearing made him look more like a knight than he had in years.

A hare crossed the road in front of him.

He laughed.

TWENTY-SEVEN

Of the Routiers

The city of Orange sat behind a big Roman arch that seemed to guard the road it straddled, the road leading up to the gates. Shops and houses that had sprung up outside the city walls leaned against those walls, or against one another, but a reverential space had been left around the arch. It was as if the emperor or general who had commanded it to be raised were still held in such awe that his arch was left unmarred, even when men seeking stone for houses poached freely from the amphitheater against the hill.

The bathhouse sat closer to the arch than any other building, and the girls who worked there loved the old monument. They pulled vines from it and pulled up young trees whose roots might one day have harmed its foundations. They came to sit against its cool stone when they had to get out of the steam. Like the arch itself, these girls were known.

Travelers from all over Provence and Langue d'Oc knew about the Stews of the Arch, as the bathhouse was called, and about the women who worked there; not the fairest flowers of Orange, perhaps, for those were sent to Avignon; these were the gently flawed pretty ones that would have gone south but for a mole or the weakness of a chin. Girls who had not married because their fathers put them out to get money, or girls who had married, found it bitter, and came to live in the shadow of the arch. Girls who knew pleasure and taught it.

The sun had just gone down when Thomas approached the hulking Roman arch and the small town outside the town. He had little money, so there was no point in going up to the gates of Orange, which were closed in any case, or to the cluster of inns and wine shops just past the arch, whose lanterns advertised they were open for commerce. He did want a look at the town, though; he had first heard the name of this city in a *chanson de geste* called "*La Prise d'Orange*," in which a splendid Arab queen betrayed her husband and her faith to deliver the city to the Franks.

"You're all alike, aren't you?"

He was just about to leave the road and head into the countryside, hoping to find some fallow vineyard in which to sleep, but he saw a lovely young woman dash topless from a large house, laughing; a fair-haired young man, down to his breeches, stumbled out and fished her back in. It would do Thomas's eyes no harm if they fell upon a pretty whore before he took to his field, so he strayed closer to the Stews of the Arch, smiling a little. Ten years earlier, with a pouch full of deniers, he would have gone into this place, which steamed enticingly in the first cool of the evening, and which rang with laughter.

Now he was content to look.

He saw that one man sat outside the building, drinking from a flagon, swaying on his bench. A guard. He called inside to the others, but not in French, and not in Provençal.

His language was English.

And his weapon was a longbow, strung and propped against his bench, with a fence of three arrows stuck in the ground.

A stack of other bows leaned against the wall near him, along with a heap of quivers and a couple of poleaxes.

Thomas stopped cold.

These were the killers he had sworn to give God's justice,

drunk on wine purchased with the blood of the last village. They would enjoy these women and be on their way in the morning, before news of the massacre reached Orange and the girls of this place stopped laughing with them. From the number of dead in the last town, these archers were likely only one wing of the company—the others would have secured a camp and fanned out to find other entertainments. If this was the only brothel, they would come here in shifts.

Did they even care if news reached Orange while they were still here? It was unlikely the provost of the town or the local seigneur could raise enough men to challenge this band. The plague was on the wane here, but it had done its work. More houses were empty than not, and for every girl laughing in the stews, there were probably two shoveled under in a common hole nearby, or tossed in the river.

Thomas faded between two houses before the drunk sentinel turned his attention back to the road. The knight crouched down in an alley and watched, batting away an orange cat that purred and rubbed itself against him.

It was not long before the watchman went to piss.

The Englishman wove his way into the alley, seemed about to piss against the bordello's wall, then apparently thought better of raising a stink in the Stews of the Arch and turned to piss against the building across. He barely noticed Thomas, who was alone, walking rather than running, seeming intent on simply passing the man. Rather, he put one hand over the man's mouth and used the other to ram his head twice against a house beam. The man went limp, still pissing, and Thomas let him fall.

The knight unsheathed his sword and moved across the courtyard, stopping just before the door. "Saint Denis and glory," he whispered bitterly, and now breathed in and out twice like something between a bellows and a bull.

He stepped through the doorway and into a womb of flickering candles and steam. His knees were bent as he walked in, and his chain hauberk rasped against a beam.

He carried his sword over his shoulder, one hand on the pommel, the other under the quillons; he was ready to kill with it.

Several of the men in the tubs gasped. They all stared at him, none of them daring to speak.

They saw that this man was lethal.

He was huge and armored and they had seen enough fighting to know a killer's eyes, even through steam and in the flickering light of candles.

In an open field they would have stuck him to his death with arrows, but here they were drunk and naked and at close quarters; just so many heads bobbing in hot water.

A woman, who had been smiling at first, thinking him one of their company, now felt the fear of the archers and said, in French, "Please sir, do not quarrel here."

Another woman echoed her in Provençal.

He stepped farther in, moving so his back was not to the open door. One Englishman considered the plank spanning his tub, the remains of a game hen and two cups of wine upon it; could he wrench the plank up and wield it as a club and a shield? He would have no leverage in the tub, and he would be decapitated before he could get out of it.

The man in the tub nearest Thomas prepared to splash water in his face, clamber over the girl next to him, and roll over the edge, hoping to find his dagger on his belt among his clothes, drunk and in the half darkness; but the girl, sensing his tension, grabbed his *bitte* underwater as if to hold him fast by it. Even had she not, the plan seemed so clumsy to him that he couldn't gather the nerve to move.

Nobody moved.

One ruddy blond man spoke to him in English, telling him to do it if he was going to, but Thomas did not understand.

Or care.

It was then that it happened.

He felt something touch his heart, as though tiny fingers were on it, holding it as gently as one might hold a bird.

Voices came to him, as if from far away.
Don't kill him.
Don't kill anyone else again.
Thomas.
Sir Thomas.
We're going to pay for that.
Find my brother ... tell my brother ...
Do you swear to give them God's justice?
I swear.

He breathed in and cocked his hips, and the nearer men ducked under water, one of the *filles de joie* screamed, but he stopped. He had fully intended to start lopping and gouging these helpless men in their four huge vats.

But he just stopped, waiting until the submerged men came up panting.

He looked at each man, in turn, and each of them, even the ruddy one, looked away when his turn came.

He sheathed his sword.

"Not tonight," he said, and backed out of the room.

None of them mistook his actions for cowardice.

He had them.

All of them.

And they knew it.

Thomas slept that night in the belfry of a small, dead church that overlooked the road; he doubted the *routiers* would follow him, but it was always better to act as though the worst might happen. On his way out of the stews, he had walked by the stables and seen them full; how desperately he longed for the feel of a horse under him, but a little voice in him said *no* and he knew it was her voice somehow. He left the stable alone and veered off the road and into the fields.

This belfry was a good spot.

More than for the brigands, of course, he was watching for the girl, whom he suspected he had passed up. It had occurred to him that he might have harmed her indirectly by letting those men live—what would they do with her, after all, if they found her? Yet her wishes were unmistakable.

Her command.

Well, who is she to command me?

Who are you to resist her?

He tried to answer that, but only said, "Huh."

For whose sake did he keep pretending that she was not something like a saint? He had never believed that saints were anything more than figures in stories, no more a part of this world than basilisks or griffins or the other magnificent beasts nobody he knew had ever seen with their eyes.

And yet.

If he told anyone of this girl who spoke languages she did not speak and played instruments she did not play, they would say ...

Witch.

That was what they would say.

It was easier to believe in witches, after all. Their motives were of this world. Revenge, power, pleasure. Who has not wanted one or all of these?

And yet.

If any goodness remained in this world, it was in her, brat or not, witch or not. With her hair combed or tangled.

"She's holy," he said, the words strange in his mouth.

"Goddamn it," he added, and felt better.

A piece of the moon hung in the sky like a polished bone.

He would be able to see her if she came.

He fell asleep watching for her, then eased seamlessly into a dream about her walking down this very road; she had a basket of wildflowers, and she scattered them as she went. He felt as proud as a father when he saw what she was doing. It was brilliant of her to think of strewing wildflowers behind her; he smiled in his sleep. He would be able to find her now.

The traffic on the road to Avignon astounded him.

He had not seen so many people since the Death had fallen on them those few but very long months ago. A cart of mystery players went by, beating drums, two men in skull-faces dancing to show they were risen, an angel Gabriel blowing his horn while a ridiculous halo, painted gold but scratched to show the wood beneath, wobbled behind his head. An ox, of all things, pulled them.

"A whoring ox," he said, waving as they went by.

Later that morning he was walking in the road because the ground on the shoulders was loose and gravelly; he did not want to turn his ankle and hobble the rest of the way into Avignon. A man shouted at him to clear a path, and he obliged, shielding his eyes against the sun as the most recent of several military processions he had seen cantered by. Four knights headed this one, followed by a dozen men-at-arms.

This was, for Thomas, no ordinary procession.

This group of men and horses changed everything for him. It drowned his foal-legged love of mankind and his suckling desire to let even the wicked live in peace. It took him back to the days after the tragedy at Crécy-en-Ponthieu, when hate had draped the furniture of his soul and left him willing to damn himself for revenge.

One of the four knights was Chrétien d'Évreux, heir to the throne of Navarre, and the man who had stolen his land, his wife, his knighthood, and his soul.

TWENTY-EIGHT

Of the Affair of Honor

He trotted after the horsemen until the weight of his hauberk and the warmth of the day slowed him to a fast walk. He knew where they were going, of course. And he had no idea what he would do if he caught up with them, whether in Avignon or on the road. He would prefer the road.

I should have taken one of those goddamned horses.

But then I would have been in front of them.

It was when he came around a limestone bluff that he saw the stream. The road humped in front of him to form a small bridge that went over a stream feeding the Rhône. It was an old stream, then, one that soldiers had likely been stopping at for years to water their horses.

As these men bearing the quartered arms of Navarre had also stopped. Chrétien and his men were here, all sixteen of those Thomas had seen ride by. Putting on helmets and mounting their lovely Spanish and Norman destriers. They were just getting ready to take to the road again. If Thomas was going to do something, it had to be now.

But what?

A dense thicket and a sort of hill braced the clearing by the stream; it would have been easy to approach in force and deal these men an ambush, but what was a single man to do?

Stop thinking of ambushes and stealth.

You are a knight again, not a brigand.

Act like a knight.

"I seek an audience with Sire Chrétien d'Évreux. It is a matter of honor," he said in his war voice, walking up to the men, staring at the comte.

A squire, holding his helmet in one hand and leading his horse with the other, walked closer to Thomas, looked at him from his boots to his head, and then called behind him, "Sire, there is a sort of *routier* or raggedy-man here who speaks of honor."

Thomas stepped past him.

Men surrounded the comte now, unsheathing their swords and taking axes from their saddle-hooks.

"You should teach your squires respect, sire. It is unbecoming for a man to let his dogs bark for him. I have come here hoping that there is enough honor in you to grant a knight audience."

A big man reined his horse closer. He was nearly close enough to give Thomas a chop with his axe. Thomas's hand drifted for the pommel of his sword.

Don't.

It was Delphine's voice in his head.

Don't.

Thomas did not unsheathe his sword.

The comte, still three horse lengths away, leaned forward in his saddle to peer at Thomas. Thomas had never seen him before; he knew him only by his heraldry. He was a big man, like Thomas, but softer in the face and very young, not twenty-five. Had his wife really shared her bed with this puppy?

He was a resplendent puppy, though; that armor was the ransom of a village.

"I know of no knight," the young man said, "who goes alone on foot, with no surcoat, and a month overdue for a shave. Who are you?"

Some of the men-at-arms laughed to show their loyalty.

A boy of ten, a page in Navarrese red and yellow, leaned closer, his pale face excited; this could be the first time he saw blood shed in earnest.

The comte's horse was excited, too; it wanted to wheel about and get to open ground, but the nobleman reined it firmly and heeled it back the two steps it had taken.

The raggedy-man spoke.

"I am Thomas of Picardy, once seigneur of the little village of Arpentel, until it was stolen from me while I served our king."

"Hoooo!" one knight called out, apparently familiar with the story and aware of the implications.

Another of the knights near the comte blanched.

Thomas cut his eyes to this man.

It was André, his squire, the one who had saved him on the field; but he was a squire no more. He wore a fine suit of chain now, and had a moustache coming in. He rode a horse from the stables at Arpentel, one that Thomas had left behind when he went to war because it was too young and green.

What was the horse's name? He had ridden him only twice.

Jibreel, Arab for Gabriel.

Though this was a warhorse, no Arab.

My goddamned horse.

And my squire.

André. I hope your dubbing was the best day of your life. How could you serve this bastard now?

The squire did not lower his eyes, but those eyes moistened with shame.

The big man with the axe had cheated closer to Thomas and now nudged him with the head of his weapon.

"Leave him," the comte said.

Thomas turned his gaze back to the comte.

He knew what the young man was thinking: How could he be shut of this nastiness and come out looking honorable? Thomas had been respected. Everyone knew that his excommunication was unjust and that his lands had been stolen. Every man who served a king or a seigneur looked at Thomas's betrayal and wondered when an accident of loyalty and war would leave him vulnerable to a powerful opportunist like Chrétien.

His hands and more were up your wife's gown she loved it she loved a pretty young man in her bed and he is pretty not a scarred old bullock like you have you seen your ridiculous beard you look like a whoring prophet

Thomas blinked his eyes hard to bring him back to now; this was not a time to let his thoughts wander.

"What is it you want?" d'Évreux said.

Your Christless head lying in the grass for me to kick into that stream.

"Justice."

A crow cawed in the trees.

"And what sort of justice might I give you in a field, in Provence, away from my lands?"

Some of which are my lands

The crow again.

"I think you know."

"Hooo," the ignorant knight started again, but the comte shot him a look that cut it short. This was deadly serious business.

"Are you threatening me?" Chrétien d'Évreux said, leaning forward a little, hoping there was a trap here for the older man to stumble into.

"I am offering you the chance to redeem your honor, and mine, in an affair of arms. Here, in the sight of witnesses, both men and . . ."

"And what?"

"Those higher than men."

The crow again.

Now all eyes were on the comte. He had mishandled this —he desperately wished he had shoved this man aside before he could say his piece; but now the words were hanging there, and none of these men would forget them. Particularly not the young man, recently knighted, who had served as squire to Thomas of Picardy. Chrétien had once delighted in the theft of this man's fealty, on top of everything else he had taken; but now he thought the former squire's true allegiance lay where it always had.

He wished, too, that he had not ridden ahead in his eagerness to meet with the pope; another forty loyal men rode three days behind them with his younger brother, Charles.

He wished he were with them now.

If only that goddamned crow would stop.

"This man is excommunicate," he declared, "and cut off from honor, and the rights and privileges that come with it . . ." He felt the gazes on him now, and they were not kind. They weren't going to let him dismiss this man now that they knew who he was. If Chrétien opened the gates of Jerusalem with one hand and burned down Acre with the other, these men would remember his cowardice here, by this stream, and they would speak of it. His father had been cousin to the king; his blood was royal on his mother's side, too. He would be king of Navarre when she died. Death was promiscuous now; it was not impossible that the crown of France might fall to him, *him*, if he had enough support. If he was not thought a coward.

He would have to fight.

He might best this rustic fellow on his own.

If not, Don Eduardo would save him in extremity, out of love for his dead father.

"Notwithstanding that," he said, changing his tone, "I would not have any man here say that the Comte d'Évreux and the heir to the throne of Navarre would hide behind such words, especially from a man who insults him before his peers. Many who ask for justice are sorry to get it, and so shall it be with you."

Don Eduardo de Burgos, the oldest of the four knights, a Spanish vassal of d'Évreux's father and a veteran of battles with the Moors, shook his head at the young man's foolishness. It was always best to avoid a fight that would cost much and gain little. The man in the rusty armor was a serious man.

"Ay," Don Eduardo said, shaking his head again, and he dismounted, as did the others, all of them making their way back to the clearing by the stream.

The crow stopped cawing.

As Thomas had no horse and would not condescend to borrow his own, it was decided that the affair of honor would take place on foot.

The men squared off.

Thomas in his bad hauberk, bareheaded, his legs unarmored as his *cuisses* and greaves had sunk in the Rhône.

The comte in his thigh and shin armor, his arms likewise covered in steel, fine riveted mail under all of it, and under his breastplate, which gleamed in the weak sun—he had removed his surcoat so it would not be torn should the man's notched and snagged war sword cross it.

His own sword was beautiful, almost pristine, the shallower notches of the training yard having been easily ground out of it by his squire.

"Ready?" said the Spanish knight, who would reluctantly serve as marshal for this grotesquerie.

Thomas nodded.

The comte nodded as well, lowering the visor of his helm.

The Spanish knight lowered his baton.

"This is your last chance to think again," the comte said, his voice muffled ridiculously. He circled the older man but kept well out of range.

Thomas said nothing, holding his ground, his legs at a good bend.

"I will be willing to forgive your insults if you apologize and go your ways."

Thomas said nothing.

He knew the man would speak again.

"Then prepare yourself for the justice you—" he started, but Thomas launched himself at just the moment he knew the other man would have to inhale. He was stronger than the comte, much stronger, and lighter, too, since he had little armor. The comte defended himself, his training overriding his fear enough to keep from being killed, though only just. His breastplate deflected a thrust, aimed at the armpit, that would have broken his ribs through chain mail. He panted and gave ground, setting himself again.

"Anything else to say?" Thomas asked, but this time the younger man kept quiet. He licked out at Thomas with the point of his sword, and his reach was so long it might have caught a slower man, but Thomas batted it down, struck the young man a vicious upswing against his helm, and then knocked his sword down again. The comte managed to hold on to it, using it to block the blow that came at his legs. And so it went. Thomas worked at exhausting his better-armored foe, battering down his sword six times, causing the other knight, whose sword was getting very heavy, to panic and flail. Thomas ducked one fatigued upswing and this time planted his sword deftly in the comte's armpit; the chain kept it from killing him, but he tore muscle, and the comte cried out.

He saw motion to his side.

The one with the axe had gotten closer.

He circled away from that man and tried to close again with the comte, but the Spaniard interposed himself.

"Hold!" he cried.

"What?" Thomas shouted.

"I will make sure the comte can continue."

"The fight is on, man. There is no stopping it!"

"You will have your chance," the Spaniard said regretfully, "but I will make sure his armor is not damaged so as to prevent him from defending himself. Because this would not be honorable."

He took his time about checking the articulation of the injured man's armor, giving him plenty of time to catch his breath. Several of the squires and even the little page were shaking their heads at this, but it continued.

"If your lordship is quite ready," Thomas called.

The younger man nodded.

The Spaniard stepped away and, before he lowered his baton, gave the young lord a look that said quite clearly he could expect no more indulgences.

It started.

When Thomas beat down the exhausted knight's sword again, the man with the axe stepped too close for Thomas's taste; he spun just in time to raise his sword at the man, who had indeed shifted his axe in preparation for a swing. The man shrugged as if to suggest he had no such intention, but it was obvious to everyone watching that he had been about to strike. Now Thomas's former squire took that man by the shoulders and threw him down. The ignorant knight, seeing this, pushed Sir André away from the downed axe-man and drew his sword. André drew his in answer.

"Stop it!" the Spaniard barked, deeply ashamed, knowing that his lack of honor in defending his dead friend's cowardly son was to blame for the disgrace this was becoming.

Before the axe-man could get up, Thomas had a moment of inspiration about how to deal both with him and with the problem of the comte's armor. He kicked the downed soldier in the face, throwing his own sword out of reach and taking the heavier axe from the stunned man. He now rushed at the Comte d'Évreux, who, blinded by sweat and confused by all the motion, parried high, protecting his head, using his mailed palm to reinforce the blade near the point. He was right that the stroke would be heavy. He was wrong about where it would land. Thomas caught him squarely in the breastplate, his hips sunk into the blow; but the armor was

Milanese, and, though it dimpled with a loud clang under the war axe, saved the outmatched comte's life again. He fell backward onto his ass.

Thomas had no intention of giving the comte the time he would need to stand in that armor.

He circled now; it was only a matter of seconds before he would see the correct angle for the killing blow.

Chrétien, Comte d'Évreux, dug in with his heels to swivel on his ass, keeping his sword high to parry. The sword seemed to weigh as much as a small tree. The bearded cuckold had put the sun behind him and was about to kill him. With a whoring axe, as if he were a whoring capon. He tried to remember a prayer but couldn't think of one.

The ignorant knight's squire, who had stayed out of it until this moment, now saw his chance to earn the comte's favor at no great risk to himself; he walked up behind Thomas and clubbed him in the head with the iron-capped back end of his poleaxe.

Thomas went to his knees.

Curiously, the man who hit him fell down, too.

Thomas looked at his former squire, who had been shouting at the ignorant knight. He stopped now and looked at Thomas, seeing he was in need of help. He started walking toward his former master, then stopped as if another thought had occurred to him.

Something was wrong, though.

He tried to speak, but couldn't, and Thomas saw why.

An arrow had sprouted from the front of his head, all the way down to the fletching.

One eye filled with blood and he fell.

Thomas fell, too, his dizziness taking him as the clearing erupted with the whistle and crack of arrows striking home, and with the cries of those they struck.

The last sounds he heard were the brutish grunts and drawls of English as the *routiers* came out of the trees to finish their work.

Matthew Blount, the leader of the English and Gascon brigands, led his men down through the stand of trees that sloped to the clearing. He had counted twenty horses before it started, and fifteen still stood near the stream, waiting to be led or mounted by men now dead.

"Shite," he called, "Who shot the page?"

Nobody answered. The boy lay curled around his chest wound, still alive but dying. Matthew looked down at the tearful, shuddering boy and saw that his wound was hopeless. He knew of a monastery with a handful of monks still alive in it, but this little bird was stuck too deep to make the journey. He would die in minutes, and long minutes they would be. The brigand put his callused palm against the page's soft cheek and said "Sorry, lad." He punched his rondel dagger up under the boy's sternum and, when he finally lay still, thumbed his eyes closed.

"Christ!" he roared. "Did you see what I just had to do because of one of you blind pricks? And I'll do the same to any man that looses on a woman or a child again, understand? You *look* first. This doesn't fucking go, you hear?" The thirty Englishmen, many of whom had served under him when he was a centenar under King Edward, all said "Aye, sir." His Gascon second in command repeated the order in French, and the dozen Gascons nodded, too.

He walked to the body of a very rich knight, a big, young fellow in exquisite armor that had nonetheless failed to stop the arrow that went through his aventail under the chin. He sorted through the pouch on the fellow's belt and took the coins out, tossing aside a piece of rolled parchment bound with a cloth-of-gold ribbon.

"What were you quarreling about, then, eh?" he asked the dead man jovially. His Gascon was just picking up the dead knight's face-down adversary by the hair, meaning to cut his throat, when Matthew glanced over. The big man was still breathing, but not for long. The knife was under the chin, angling for the jugular behind the half-white beard.

That beard.

"*Attends!*" he said.

The Gascon looked at him, still holding a fistful of greasy longish hair, so comfortable with killing that he might as well have been holding a flower he was about to be asked not to gather.

"*Je regards son visage,*" Blount said.

The Gascon lifted the head higher, the eyes in it rolling white.

It was the man from the stews.

The big Frenchman who had walked into the Stews of the Arch like a goddamned bear and caused them all to piss their tubs. He could have killed half of them, maybe the lot, but didn't.

Blount had no idea what had stayed the Frenchy's hand, but *quid pro quo* was one of the few Latin terms he knew and he was a big believer in it.

"Not him," he said. Then, in case somebody else happened over, he shouted it and pointed down at the man.

Not him.

Now the *routiers* killed the rest, took their money and horses, and melted back into the woods.

The wind had started up.

Thomas woke with his head in a woman's lap.

Not a woman's.

A girl's.

Her luminous, almost lupine gray eyes looked down into his as she wiped his temples. It was hard to focus—everything looked blurry. Something moved behind her, and he thought he saw wings.

He had trouble remembering the last time he had seen her, yet it seemed very important that he should.

"You left wildflowers," he said.

"What?" she said, smiling.

He slept.

Near dark, he woke again, and smelled food.

Delphine had made a good, hot fire from blackthorn wood, and over that she boiled thyme, chard, and turnips in a soldier's wide-brimmed helmet. He heard a sound that at first seemed quite natural, but which he then remembered as wondrous.

A horse's whinny.

Jibreel stood eating grass near the stream, handsome and brown with white forelegs.

"He wouldn't go away," she said.

"He was mine."

She nodded.

"He remembers you. There's another horse hanging around, but it's scared. A little horse."

"We'll catch him," Thomas said. "Can you ride?"

"Just a donkey."

"That's something. I'll teach you."

He sat up against his tree, rubbing the back of his head and looking at her. He remembered being thumped now. Why didn't his head hurt?

And the girl. Was she just a cat's whisker taller? Was there the hint of a curve in her hips?

"You're different," he said.

"So are you."

She handed him a few sloe berries to eat.

He ate their flesh, then spat out the pits, making a face.

"They'll be sweeter after a frost," she said.

"You know what we've come to do now, don't you?"

"Yes. Mostly."

"I won't like it, will I?"

"Why should you? I don't like it."

"Oh shit," he said.

"You're not *that* different, are you?"

He shook his head, smiling.

"But you're ready," she said. "We're both ready."

He looked at her for a long while.

"What?" she said.

"I know what's different about you."

"What?"

"You've got tits."

She shook her head slowly at him.

"It's true. Just little ones, but they're there."

She threw a sloe berry, which hit him exactly in the middle of the forehead.

"I think you spout vulgarity all the time because you're afraid to see the big part of yourself that's good."

"And I think you're changing the subject. We have to hide those."

"I will," she said.

She came nearer to him now and showed him a piece of parchment rolled up in a ribbon of cloth-of-gold.

"What's that? The deed to a manor?"

"It's an invitation."

"To what?"

"To dine with His Holiness at a great feast of warriors."

"An invitation for the dead one over there, not for me."

"You are the dead one."

Thomas blinked at her, not understanding her game.

She went over to the dead comte and unbuckled his polished helm, pulling it off him. She brought it over to Thomas.

"How am I supposed to eat if I keep a whoring helmet on all the time? Or speak? Or . . ."

She held up the helmet to him.

The last of the light reflected in its fine steel, the color of smoke and lavender; the helmet also reflected a face back at Thomas.

But it wasn't his face.

The girl took the knight down to the stream and asked him to kneel.

She took water in her hands and asked him if he forgave the dead man whose face he now wore.

He paused; and then he said yes, and she poured water over his head.

She asked him if there was anyone else he carried anger for.

He paused again, and she waited.

"My wife," he said.

"Do you forgive her?"

"I can't."

She looked at him gravely.

"You can," she said. "If you choose to."

"No," he said, his eyes turned to the side.

"Then go back to Picardy," she said, and she let the water fall from her hands.

He looked down at his reflection in the stream; it was too dark for him to see clearly, but he could make out the outline of a bearded man with long hair. He was himself again.

The miracle was spent.

Delphine went back to where her makeshift pot of soup smoked and began to eat. She poured some for Thomas, and they ate in silence, although she looked at him the whole time.

She took his bowl and the helmet and walked to the stream to rinse them.

"Do you want to try again?" she said.

"Tell me she's dead. Tell me the plague took her and she died in a fever saying she was sorry. Maybe then."

"It doesn't work that way. That's not forgiveness, it's justice. And wretched justice at that."

"Why does it matter?"

"It just does," she said.

"Whatever we have to do in that city—and I'm frightened of that city, I'm not ashamed to tell you—it's going to get us killed, right? Isn't that enough?"

She furrowed her brow, thinking.

"No," she said, and handed him the clean vessels.

"What do you want me to do with these?"

"Put them somewhere, I don't know. I'm not your wife."

He tossed them down.

She started walking toward the road.

"Wait," he said. "Delphine."

She looked at him with that drowsy look he had come to dread; the look that meant she was about to speak words that weren't her own.

"Go back to Picardy and ask the bishop to pardon you, if he's still alive. He'll send you on pilgrimage to Santiago de Compostella, or maybe on crusade, if there's anyone left to make war on in the east; and back you'll come to the bishop, and you'll say words you don't mean and he'll say words he doesn't mean, and you'll get your castle back. If you can find anyone to run it. And be a seigneur, if anyone's alive to grow the wheat. And you won't have to forgive anyone or be merciful, or thoughtful or courteous, because devils will rule here. They'll kill the good ones first, and when all the good men are dead, they'll come for men like you, who were almost sound, but not quite; the bowls that leaked. And when you're gone, the worst of men will find themselves in the teeth of their masters, because those that fell have no love for man. And they'll take good and bad alike to Hell, because there won't be anyplace but Hell anymore. Not without love. Not without forgiveness."

Thomas stood and looked at her, and she at him, and night came on with a strong wind in the trees.

"We all fall short of perfection. You. Me. Père Matthieu. We all disappoint someone. Can we forgive only those who sinned against others?"

He closed his eyes and saw the priest's swollen, stung face, smiling weakly at the thought of his brother.

If you see Robert, tell him
Tell him
I don't know
Do you forgive her?

TWENTY-NINE

Of Marguerite of Péronne

Thomas de Givras married Marguerite de Péronne on a sleeting Candlemas Day, 1341. The daughter of a minor seigneur of the lagoons, she still brought a decent dowry: a cedar chest, three mares, two tapestries, ten gold livres, and a much-coveted recipe for pâté of smoked eel. Her true dowry was twofold. First, her connections—her mother's sister had married into the family of the great Enguerrand de Coucy. Next, and more troublesome, was her beauty. Many lords and not a few merchants had sought her hand, and yet her father had held out, hoping to thicken his descendancy with a drop or two of royal blood. It never came. By the time he lowered his standards, Marguerite was twenty.

Bad luck spoiled two near-matches. One knight of Abbeville died from a bee sting. The other, the very handsome son of a Ghent textiles merchant, hanged himself following an argument with his true love, a laundress, regarding his impending nuptials to a Frenchwoman he had never met.

Had he seen his betrothed, he might have only toyed with the rope.

Beautiful or no, Marguerite was on the waning end of her twenty-third year. Worse, it was widely rumored that she numbered among the nearly two hundred girls in Picardy to have been deflowered by the troubadour Jehan of Poitou, who was keeping count, if not naming names, in his verses. Even if this was true, she was a lucky catch for a foul-mouthed knight of low birth like Thomas de Givras. The father's agreement had been woven from three cloths: his desperation to see her avoid the nunnery; his love for the Comte de Givras, who had proposed the match; and the girl's own preference.

At first she had been wary of the match, disappointed to receive no letter from Thomas, rightly suspecting that his education stopped at the tiltyard.

It was October when he came to visit.

As soon as she saw what a *costaud* Thomas was, thin of waist, thick of chest, with his hair still dark on the fine head he had to lower to enter a room, his face still clear of the arrow-pit she would never see, she was dressed for the oven.

When she saw the impish humor in his eye, she was cooked. If he had few letters, he was neither stupid nor dull.

She was well matched for Thomas in this way, too—it was common for her to take the Lord's name in vain twenty times between confessions.

She did it the moment she laid eyes on her future husband.

"My God," she said, too low for anyone to hear.

And then she said it again.

On the cool October day of their meeting, Thomas had gone with a riding party that included the Seigneur de Péronne, the Comte de Givras, and Marguerite. From the moment she spoke, he was intimidated by her learning—this was no kitchen woman, as his mother had been; this Marguerite de Péronne not only knew Latin, she told jokes in it; following a hawk's near-refusal to come down from its tree, she said something to her paunchy, well-dressed abbot of an uncle that nearly made him tumble sideways from his palfrey. She sang, too, and not out of duty. Her voice was unfiltered joy. On the ride back, at any time the men ran out of words to say about the king or the war or the quality of the horses, she lit up her father's birch woods with snatches of carols, and sometimes looked at her suitor to see if he was moved.

He was, and that was good.

For at that young age, she still told herself she would never lie beneath a man who did not love a song.

On the day after their wedding, Thomas took his new bride to the top of the old Norman tower he had just received from the Comte de Givras. The February sky, gray, though no longer spitting ice, stretched above them, and the brown fields and few houses of Arpentel stretched below. His wife was smarter than he would ever be and prettier than he thought wives were made, and yet she was happy with him. Her pleasure in the marriage bed had seemed to touch even her soul, and her verdant eyes had rarely left his; three taps of her ring would always remind him of the three times he took her. "Once like a bull, once like a fox, once softly as a lamb," she said. He would be faithful to her. They would have many sons. He had risen. By God and by the grace of his beloved seigneur, he had risen.

His mother, a widow and a sort of handsome, dark-haired giantess, had worked in the comte's kitchens. She had told Thomas his father was a German knight on pilgrimage to Spain, ironic since she herself was the bastard of a Spanish knight, Tomás de Oviedo, whom she remembered in her nightly prayers though he was ignorant of her existence. She wedded young to a joiner's son who was already hurting from the kidneys that would fail before her daughter was three. She never married again. She came home smelling of grease and flour, bearing bones, cheese rinds, second cuts of meat, and stale bread from the comte's table, keeping Thomas and his older half-sister fed when others went hungry. Thomas had been such a large and physically gifted boy that the comte had taken him on as a page, and soon squire. He took to sword, lance, and horse so naturally that it was clear he had chivalry in his blood if not in his pedigree. After his accidental knighting at Cambrai, Thomas had distinguished himself at tourneys and in the comte's personal affrays; he had proven invaluable at training younger men and had endeared himself to the comte, despite the latter's godliness and his own coarse humor.

By the time his mother died, Thomas's sister was married and he was a necessary part of the comte's retinue. The gift of Arpentel and its crumbling, square tower to Thomas had enraged one better-born knight who, at a Michaelmas feast following Thomas's departure, got so far into his cups that he told the comte he felt himself more deserving of land than that "fatherless Knight of the Hare." The comte had kept his temper. The Comte de Givras never raised his voice. He coolly told the other man, toying with the mustachios that were his only concession to vanity, "If you covet Sir Thomas's land, fight him for it. To the death. I shall grant you the title if you win."

The man had found reasons that this would not do.

"Then hold your tongue. Wine makes men fools, and I myself have said foolish things in my cups. But if you wish to be welcome at my table, and in my house, you will never again let me hear you slander a fellow knight in his absence. Try me on this and you will think men lucky who sleep under roofs, let alone in towers. Am I understood?"

He was.

"It seems painfully obvious to me," Marguerite of Péronne, Lady of Arpentel, had said to her new husband on that morning, "that the Comte de Givras is your father."

She stood there, stunning in her fox-fur mantle, her greenish eyes alight with mirth, and he was no more sure whether she was jesting than if she had said it in Latin.

He had laughed at her, and she had never said it again.

And he had never thought about it again until Crécy, when he watched the great man die a man's death.

Wouldn't he have told him then?

No.

Not a man who would not cry out.

Was it a promise to his mother? To God?

He would never know.

But now he thought she was right.

Marguerite, who saw through everything.

Marguerite, who knew how to cut her losses.

She had chosen the son over the father.

Over him.

Over honor.

And she was right.

When Delphine saw the knight's eyes soften, she said, "Do you forgive her?"

He said "Yes."

She reached her small hand out, and he took it in his large one. She led him down to the stream, and, with its cool water, washed his head and his feet, and helped him wash the last of the anger from his heart.

His own face slipped from him once again, and fell in the water.

And again he assumed the aspect of his dead rival.

PART IV

The walls of God's kingdom held. And though the devils despaired of breaking the walls and burning the deep architecture of Heaven, yet were the angels stoppered in and could not come safely out; and so, unchallenged in the middle lands, the wicked ones delighted in what they wrought there. So they resolved among them to hold the plains and the mountains in their fist, and not to suffer the cities of men to live; but rather to reign there, on the thrones of their second Hell, with the first as their footstool and the angels of God trapped above.

They would weave sackcloth to mask the sun.

They would confound the father to kill his son, and then would they kill the father.

They would replace the beasts with clockwork things and the birds with dead hands that flew.

It had already begun.

And the angels of God stood at the walls of Heaven and sorrowed at the misery below, and fell out amongst themselves, some saying it was better to perish at once, in hot struggle for man's sake, lest the Lord return to find the earth empty of men; others cried that if they left their walls, He would return to find Heaven bereft of angels and smoldering, and Lucifer instead on His throne.

And the world was imperiled unto its death.

For now a call had risen up from he who held Peter's Chair in the west.

And a call had risen up from he who wore the sultan's crown in the east.

And men of great valor gathered in the city by the river and swore to take Jerusalem, and if they could not hold it, to put it to fire and sword.

And the valorous men of the deserts gathered in their tents and swore to hold Jerusalem, else to put it to fire and the sword.

And so were readied the armies of Armageddon, yet not at the hour long foretold.

And the dead stood with the living, and the living knew it not.

And the Lord made no answer.

THIRTY

Of the Priest's Brother

R obert Hanicotte stood in the stables, breaking up a leaf of hay for one of the cardinal's six black Arabian stallions. This one bore the name Guêpe because he was small and wasp-waisted, mean like a wasp; not as fast as the others at a straight run, but capable of breathtaking turns and giddy leaps. He was not the cardinal's favorite, but Robert loved him more than perhaps anything in this city. He would never let the old man know, though, or permission to ride him would be used as leverage.

He put his head against the horse's shoulder and took in his nutty, masculine smell, his own dark hair blending perfectly with the animal's coat. Guêpe wanted to move away from him, but not enough to stop eating.

"You're like me," he said, "small and beautiful and captive. We can neither one of us leave this place."

A nightmare had chased Robert from his master's bed; his older brother, Matthieu, the priest, had been laughing in a river with a soldier. Little black devils stood on the banks hurling rocks and spears at them, but they laughed on and on, Matthieu saying, "These are just our bodies! You can only reach our bodies!" At last Robert was pulled into this dream when his brother spied him in the bushes. He was suddenly ashamed because he realized he should have been helping but had chosen instead to hide. Matthieu stopped laughing now, and, looking remarkably like St. Sebastian, what with all the horrid little barbs stuck in him, pointed toward Robert and said, "But you're theirs, aren't you? All of you, inside and out."

"No!" Robert yelled, but now his brother and the soldier left, walking out of the river and ashore, leaving him alone with all the black devils. They looked at him, now, and the dream went dark until he could see only their yellow eyes burning like a hedge of malign stars. He understood that they would come now and take him to Hell.

He had woken up sweating, frightened at first, and then angry and not terribly surprised that Matthieu had found something else to make him feel guilty about.

"Boring old man," he said under his breath, meaning both his brother and this flaccid cardinal who could sleep only on his stomach, his ridiculous white ass pointed up to the top of the canopied bed. Robert was nearly thirty-five now, but taut and lean, not yet showing his age; Cardinal Pierre Cyriac was an out-of-shape sixty, and Robert intended to throw himself from a tower before he let his body look like that.

He heard a sound in the streets below, outside the high walls of the house, beyond the little grove of Spanish clementines the cardinal had planted every May only to have the mistral kill them each December.

A woman crying, now shouting "No! No! *No*," banging a fist on wood to punctuate each word, and another woman, crying more quietly, trying to hush her.

Another plague death, as like as not, all the more stinging because the disease was actually loosening its grip on the city, only killing scores a week instead of hundreds. Robert hated this time, less because he feared death than because the cardinal did; and because the cardinal did, he had forbidden his concubine to go out into the streets without him. He wanted to watch every move the younger man made, to assure himself that he kept a safe distance from strangers, that he did not go to the baths, that he did not linger too long in the market and risk bringing *it* home. He had sneezed once a few days before, and the old man had looked so coldly at him that he thought he might have him thrown from the house if he sneezed a second time.

He did not.

The Arabian had finished his hay now and would not suffer himself to be caressed further tonight. He didn't mind the saddle, but he seemed to hold men's hands in contempt. Robert slapped him briskly on the shoulder, earning himself a displeased whinny, and walked back toward the house, Guêpe nosing the door of the stall for a second leaf, which did not come.

Robert thought he might reread his boring old brother's last letter, in which he fell all over himself in thanks for the wine he had been sent. It was sweet, really, how easy it was to please Matthieu. And, however dull his company, he had been a comfort during the time of their youth in their monstrous father's monstrous house.

He would ask the cardinal for another small barrel, from the pope's personal vineyard this time, to be sent north when next His Holiness sent an envoy to Rouen. Lots of envoys were going north these days, asking for money and tradesmen and men-at-arms for the crusade.

What was the name of his brother's sad little town? St. Martin-something? It was a bother, but it would be worth it. He could see Matthieu's hands turning the tap, Matthieu's eyes lighting up when he saw the color of the vintage coming out of the spout, Matthieu's sad, grateful smile exaggerating the lines around those eyes. It made him feel warm enough to face going upstairs. One more goblet of something strong and he would crawl in beside the belly-sleeper, moving as lightly as a mosquito on the skin in hopes he would not wake him and be handled.

The marketplace off the rue de La Vielle Fusterie was nearly deserted. It was still too early. The military men who had been filling the city stayed up late doing what soldiers do in towns where they are not known, and they had set Avignon's hours back even further; he had passed two squires heading back across the Pont St. Bénézet who looked as though they had not yet gone to sleep. Now that the monks had all died, nobody rose before Terce anymore, and most waited for midday.

The cardinal had left the house, and now Robert had sneaked out for a vial of the cedar oil he loved to smell on himself—the pope had called for a grand feast tonight, another whoring feast, and he hoped to make good impressions all around—but the oil merchant's stall was empty. It was hard to know who was dead and who was simply out of things.

The swarthy little man who sold wine from the pope's vineyards was doing a good business, his loader rolling barrel after barrel under the emblem of the crossed keys, but the other wine sellers had closed up shop. Nothing was coming from Beaune or Auxerre but fantastical stories, and most of the vineyards near Mont Ventoux had also gone still. This year's harvest was dying on the vine, and last year's was nearly gone.

There just weren't enough people left to work.

Except in Pope Clement's vineyards.

He was a man who got things done.

Robert missed his days, only three years gone, working as cubicular to Pope Clement, who wanted no more from Robert than his help getting dressed, the lighting and snuffing of candles, and a little conversation when he couldn't sleep.

Everything had gone to hell since the Holy Father had made a gift of him.

With no oil to show for his walk across the bridge, Robert was determined to find some satisfaction. In the early evening he would have to look at the old man's disappointed smile as he failed to express a profound enough opinion on some religious matter, the smile that reminded him he was prized for his beauty, not his competence. He would have a few more hours until then, while the cardinal signed his papers and rattled his rings in the palace. The cardinals did little work, as far as he had ever seen, their duties spiritual rather than temporal; it was the apostolic secretaries and chancellors, and even the pontiff himself, who shouldered the real work at the palace.

Cardinals mostly discussed things, like some troop of self-important gossips in bright red robes and wide red hats. Sometimes one would go off as legate to this or that city, and could be gone a year or more, but in Avignon they sat on cushioned benches and talked about whether women went to the same Heaven as men, or if the queen of Naples had really strangled her boy-toad of a husband. They talked about Cola di Rienzo's thuggish uprising in Rome, as if they still had any business with that city that the papacy had divorced, or as if they meant it when they talked about the pope returning there, or as if they even had an Italian among them anymore now that Colonna had died of the Pest. They sat drowsing through canon lawsuits, saving their better selves for the evening's diversions. They waited for the pope to die so they could wall themselves in to squabble about which one of them would take his hat, and what favors he'd do to get it. They welcomed important men to their gardens and received gifts. They dallied with lovers far too attractive for them.

As much as he held them in contempt, Robert envied them more.

He often looked at his hands and wondered how they would look in fine white gloves, and rings of emerald and tiger's eye over those gloves.

Since the marketplace had more cats than people in it, he would have to find another way to kill the hour or two he dared to stay gone from the cardinal's house.

So he went to the apartment of the pope's second falconer,

a red-haired, smiling boy whose moss-stuffed bed crunched with dried lavender; he had a woman in that bed but, seeing who was coming up his stairs, woke her, sent her on her way, and put two shirts down over the stain they had left.

The cardinal's man was a rarer guest.

And a prized one.

"I know you value yourself highly," the cardinal said, as Robert counted his teeth with his tongue to prevent him from fully hearing the old man's words and letting his face betray his thoughts. "But I don't want you speaking tonight unless you are spoken to, and then it shall be to say 'Yes' or 'No,' followed of course by a few respectful words. Yes, my lord. Yes, Your Eminence. No, I have enough bread."

"Yes, Your Eminence."

"Have you eaten anything?"

"No, Your Eminence."

"Well, get some figs or something in you. It won't do for you to seem greedy at table. Vincent, bring some figs."

The boy who had been watching all of this while waiting to help the cardinal undress gladly left the room.

Three ... four ... five ...

"Furthermore, the tables of the Grand Tinel shall be full of knights, and highly placed ones. You won't be sitting near any, but try not to ... encounter them. They'll hear your proclivities in your speech and hate you for it."

The cardinal had imitated Robert at *proclivities in your speech*, and it stung. Despite his stately way of stamping out syllables, the old Limoges cunt had the same proclivities.

His father's face leapt into his head, and he nearly squinted.

Twelve ... thirteen ... fourteen

"Why are you pushing your lower lip out at me like that? Are you one of the Holy Father's camels?"

"No."

"No, what?"

"No, Pierre."

The older man pinched the younger man's cheek just a little harder than was friendly.

"Not until the hat's off."

"No. Your Eminence."

Robert Hanicotte entered the Grand Tinel for what must have been the thirtieth time in his life, but the great, barrel-vaulted room never failed to take his breath away. So many torches burned on their iron sconces and so many candles of the best wax glowed on the trestle tables that it was possible to make out faces even at the far end of the hall, where the pope would soon occupy his throne, near which a quartet of servants stood, and over which a canopy of crushed velvet the color of a shadow on wine hung, tasseled with braids of cloth-of-gold. He craned his head up to look at the false night above him; a cloth of gloaming blue covered the barrel ceiling, studded with gold stars only man would have measured out so uniformly. The steward showed him to his bench, next to the cardinal; eighteen of them were here, like vicious jabs of red in the mostly blue room. He took his seat facing the door he had just entered and watched the other guests file in.

The room got louder as it filled with knights and minor kings. He noticed that very few ladies came with these men, which made him wonder what entertainments the invitations hinted at. The youngest of these was a big fellow, handsome in a soft-chinned way, attended by a page in Spanish red. What made him stand out, however, was his quiet manner. His sobriety and bearing belied his youth.

The steward guided him right, toward the pope's cathedra and high table, and on they marched. He kept expecting them to stop, but this man was placed only two seats down from the pontiff.

"Your Eminence, may I ask who it is that just entered,

seated very close to the Holy Father?"

The cardinal smiled his weary smile.

"The man sitting just next to the pope is a Valois, cousin to the king. But he's too old for you to ask after, isn't he?"

"I was just . . ."

"Yes, I know what you were just. The one who caught your eye is the Comte d'Évreux, future king of Navarre. A sycophant and a coward with a capable younger brother everyone hopes he'll promote by dying. Any more questions?'

Robert looked down.

"Are you hungry?"

"No, Your Eminence."

"Good."

"Brothers, friends, honored guests," the pope began, standing before his cathedra of carved oak and gold leaf. "I welcome you all to the Feast of the Warriors of Our Lord."

As per the commands of his physician, the Holy Father sat between two great copper braziers, the brightest fires in the room, which cast twin shadows on the walls of the Tinel, shadows that moved forward as he did.

Robert loved to hear Clement VI speak—his every word seemed an artisanal gift selected especially for the listener and, with the weight of his office behind him, seemed also to suggest an intimacy not only with the man, but with God. Robert was too far away to see the lines at the corners of the pontiff's eyes, but he knew the power those lines had to punctuate the Holy Father's frequent smiles. His hands scooped the air as he spoke, like an Italian's hands, but gently, as though they were playing in water. When Pope Clement turned his attention on you, he seemed at once to overrule every churchman who had made God seem stern, and to forgive them their misunderstanding of grace. He also seemed to know your foibles, and that your virtues so far outweighed these that the Lord scarcely noted them. He forgave his own foibles with equal abandon. Clement was a pope of light penance, short pilgrimage, and stunning feasts, and his smile illuminated a far wider path to Heaven than you had feared to find.

If Robert stared at him with filial love, he was not alone.

Clement's voice flowed into the Tinel like mulled wine.

"For gathered in this hall are men beloved of the Lord for the charity of arms; when men take up the sword to further their own ends, they spill Christ's blood anew; but when they take up arms for His bride, the church, they heal His five wounds, and this is the profoundest charity. For too long now have Christian kings warred amongst themselves, each seeking to enrich his realm by impoverishing another. It is no accident that this killing Pest has followed wars, and that wars have followed famine; at each turn have we been shown, to greater and greater degrees, the displeasure of the Father whose Son lies abandoned, His Cross and His Crèche tread upon by those who will not drink his offered blood. I speak, of course, of the Turk, whose bloody crimes against the friends of peace are reviled in every decent land. In my left hand, I hold a letter from Edward, king of England and ruler of the Aquitaine. In my right, I hold a letter from Phillip, by God's grace king of France. Both letters, sworn to in the presence of bishops, pledge the crowns of England and France to a mutual peace, with one aim: Jerusalem, City of the Lord. Jerusalem, the holiest stone in the earthly crown. Even now the shipyards in Marseille ring with hammers. Let the believers in the lies of Mahomet tremble. We shall take Jerusalem back."

At this, the knights beat their goblets on the painted tables before them. One shouted *"Deus vult!"* and another joined him, and soon the Grand Tinel rang with *"God wills it!"* When the echo faded, the pontiff continued.

"The first ships will sail for Cyprus on Christmas Day."

Again they cheered.

"And," the pontiff said, stepping forward and opening his hands, "another matter concerns us. Our late words in defense of a certain quarter were, we now believe, in error. Many men, wiser men than we once thought, have said that we cannot drive the rat from the granary while the mouse steals in the pantry. I tell those very few of you who wear crowns or sit near them to ready yourselves and your kingdoms in secret; soon we shall recall our bull, *Sicut Judaeis*, in defense of the Hebrew race, and issue another which shall grant any Christian whatsoever the right to turn his hand against any Jew, and to take from such whatever goods he desires, even his house and chattel. Very soon now, from the feast day of Saint Martin of Tours, the murder of a Hebrew shall no more be a sin than the hunt of a stag. Remember this word, *stag*. For some of you shall soon have cause to love this word.

"In His holy name, and to His holy purpose, let us pull the weeds, both far and near, that have too long choked His garden.

"Yet I shall speak no more, for hunger makes men deaf.

"Let us eat."

Robert was disturbed at the thought of harm coming to the Jews of Avignon, who seemed a docile and clever people, and who were undeniably among the greatest artisans of Provence.

Yet he allowed the warmth in his heart to etch a small smile on his face. The pope's words had so affected him that he felt, perhaps for the first time in his life, a part of something immense and wonderful.

THIRTY-ONE

Of the Feast, and of the Hunt of Stags

The page of the Comte d'Évreux had turned so pale that the Valois Duc sitting to their right asked if the young man was well.

"Yes, my lord," the page said. "I have . . . I have not slept as well as I should have, for excitement at the chance to see the Holy Father."

"Eat a good piece of beef, boy; it will feed the blood. And throw a bit of wine on top of it, but not too much," the great man said.

"We are undeserving of such kindness, my lord," said the Comte d'Évreux, getting a hardy slap on his shoulder from the older lord just before they both looked up to see the feast that was coming from the dressing area.

It seemed that every creature that flew, swam, or walked had found its way to the trestle tables in the Grand Tinel. Swans with their necks twisted together as if in love floated amid armadas of game hens and quail, sails of swan, dove and peacock feathers jutting above them; these fleets cut through blue-plated "waters" of crabs and prawns and every imaginable fish, repeated every two yards so that each diner might reach his preferred dish. Before the diners ate, however, the steward walked both lengths of trestles, inclining over each plate a strange little coral tree hung with shark's teeth and the horns of narwhal; the pendants were said to shiver in the presence of poison. They did not shiver. The pope rang a small bell calling for the meal to start, and conversation died in the room as the sounds of eating rose up.

For Thomas, this had more than a whiff of the feast in the devilish Norman castle about it. He ate, though, and ate well. A serving boy filled his wine goblet, and he felt Delphine's hand on his wrist. He looked at her, with her shorn hair, wearing the livery of the dead Navarrese page, her nascent breasts bound tight beneath it. Her gray eyes speared him. She shook her head.

"What? Why?" he said.

She leaned close and whispered, "Just don't."

He whispered, too.

"Poison?"

"No."

"Will it damn my soul?"

"I . . . I don't think so."

"What, then?"

Exasperated, she said "Just drink it, then."

He didn't for a long while.

Then he forgot and drank.

It was good.

He heeled a drop from his lip just in time to see a viol player, who was introduced as the best in Aragon, stride into the middle of the hall, just at the end of tuning. He began, filling the room with his sad, exotic rhythms and complicated changes. Thomas knew the music, as well as the man. It was the very same one from the castle of the night tourney. As he had at that feast, the man went from guest to guest, and Thomas felt his insides go cold at the prospect of being recognized.

The musician did look Thomas directly in the face, but no longer than he had at the Valois Duc; he must have seen only the smug, youthful face of the Comte d'Évreux. When the man passed, his hips rolling with the music he bowed out of the viol, Thomas breathed out in relief and drained his goblet.

Delphine stepped on his foot and he glared at her.

She glared back.

Other musicians followed as the diners wrecked first this armada, then cross-shaped heaps of the finest pastries, nougats, and marchpanes Thomas or Delphine had ever seen. The tables were at last cleared of all but wine, and other entertainments commenced. A dancing bear capered to drum and fife; acrobats piled up on one another and tumbled. The steward apologized for the absence of a jester; a truly magnificent one had been expected from Dijon, but must have been delayed.

"I hope this will not dim your ardor, however, for, as baser men have said without error, a man may amuse himself without smiling..."

At this, the servers extinguished half of the torches lighting the hall.

"We should go," Delphine said, though she knew there would be no way to leave early without drawing unwanted attention. She was fighting a full bladder; she had not wanted to go through the kitchen and into the latrine tower, as other guests had, for fear of exposing her sex.

"We can't yet," Thomas said, and she nodded, casting her eyes down.

The steward spoke again.

"Now let the forests of Provence grow beneath the stars, and let God's friends have a foretaste of the delights that await them in the kingdom they have worked so hard to serve."

Servants wheeled out a number of trees whose leaves had been replaced with very thin, masterfully worked leaves of gold; golden and silver fruits and other precious objects winked in their midst. Now tapestried couches were rolled out and placed in nooks of the golden forest such that they were partly or fully hidden.

"Let those among you with cooler blood seek gifts from the branches; let those with hotter humors enjoy the hunt ..."

At that, the viol player returned and played a march that summoned forth a line of twenty women, all of them nude save for magnificent stag masks with golden antlers. Their bodies were perfect; lithe and firm, no one of them seemed younger than seventeen or older than twenty-five. They all struck poses beneath and among the trees, some leaning, some on all fours, one hanging upside down from a branch.

Thomas stared at this spectacle, a slow smile creeping onto his face.

Delphine shuddered.

Now the knights and cardinals began to file around the table.

Servants scooted back their benches.

"Come on, man!" the Valois Duc said, as drunk as any man still walking, "unless you mean to spend the whole night at whispers with your page."

Thomas followed him before Delphine could speak again.

He walked out into the dim hall, afraid and excited.

He entered the grove, melting in with the red-robed cardinals and resplendent seigneurs; a white-gloved hand plucked a pear of emerald-studded gold from a tree. A younger knight rubbed the backside of a "stag" who wiggled, and then led him off to the near-privacy of a couch. One girl's nude bottom now rubbed against Thomas's hip, and she turned her stag mask to him; the hall was so dim he could see nothing but blackness in the holes cut for her eyes.

A wall of strong perfume hit his nose, eastern scents he could not name as cardamom and sandalwood and patchouli, but which pleased and thrilled him.

He began to stiffen against his silk and woolen tights, pushing at the bottom of his red cotehardie. The stag noticed and lined herself up to grind the center of her on that. She was very good at it. Had he been nude, he would have entered her; the tip of his *verge* had nearly entered her even through the cloth.

It felt so good, and it had been so long since he had enjoyed that sort of pleasure, that full release was imminent. With some effort, he pulled back from her, another knight laughing at him and clapping at his now-obvious excitement.

"With your permission, my good comte, I shall take your place," he said. "I had an eye on that one the moment I saw her long legs." So saying, he fumbled up his outers and down his inners and slid into the girl with a frisson, not even bothering to four-leg her to a couch, but taking her against a tree, the golden leaves of which were soon rattling against one another.

Thomas saw that some had taken gifts and returned to their tables, so he reached up for a whitish something-or-other that turned out to be a finely etched ivory comb trimmed with golden angels. He took it and hurried back to his spot, just as he saw Pope Clement, magnificent in his red and cloth-of-gold robes and triple crown, enter the grove. With each step, a golden cross flashed on the toe of one of his slippers. He smiled at Thomas, and Thomas smiled back.

The knight bowed and said, "Thank you, Your Holiness."

"It is only a trifle, my son," the pontiff said, his words like warm honey. "Greater wonders await us all." And then he took a stag by the ear and led her in.

Thomas was half sure the pope had watched him leave, but he did not turn back to look.

Delphine knew she would never make it to the sumptuous apartment near St. Peter's where they were lodged, so she ran to a dark alley and squatted, pissing for what seemed like half a day.

Thomas turned his back and shielded her from view with his body.

"You didn't touch any of those deer, did you?" she said.

"No. Wanted to."

"Uck," she said.

"Uck, yourself. You don't know anything about it."

"I know more than you."

"Like what?"

She stood up and wiped her hands now, trying to walk like a boy.

"Let's just say 'more than you.' Anyway, I suspect more than I know."

So saying, she looked down, pulling Thomas's gaze down to his thigh, where something moved.

It was a maggot.

THIRTY-TWO

Of the Night Vintners

"What are you doing here?" Robert Hanicotte said.

He had come for his nocturnal visit with Guêpe and had nearly leapt out of his skin to see the small girl in her dirty gown hugging her knees in the back corner of the Arab's stall.

"You're going to get stepped on," he said. "Besides the beating you'll get if the stablehands find you."

"Why don't you beat me?" she said. "You found me."

"I just might," he said, but not even the horse was convinced.

She was an odd-looking little bird: long-legged with out-sized feet and short hair. A peasant girl, but not from here. She spoke to him in his own Norman French.

And the horse liked her. Goddamn if he didn't seem to *like* her.

Her words were lucid, but her heavy-lidded eyes looked half asleep.

"Robert Hanicotte," she said, causing him to start at the sound of his last name, which nobody had bothered to say for some time, "your brother died bringing me here."

"What?"

"You heard me, Robert-of-the-bushes."

Matthieu's name for him when he hid from his chores in the bushes behind their house. Matthieu, eight years older, who had done what he could to deflect their martial father's scorn from the younger and even more feminine brother.

She had used his childhood nickname.

He shook this off. Nothing he wanted to hear would come from this girl's mouth. He just wanted to be left alone.

"How dare you come to me and tell me my brother is dead? What can you know about it, you dirty little thing?"

He turned his head to shout down the stables for the napping boy who was supposed to be watching the horses.

Only when he turned his head, she was standing where he looked.

"Saddle that horse," she said.

He opened his mouth but said nothing.

"Père Matthieu opened his mouth like that when he wanted to speak but had no words. Now saddle your wasp. I have something to show you."

"I . . . the cardinal won't like it."

"The cardinal serves a devil."

"How do I know you're not the devil?"

"If you were not deaf to your own heart you would know."

He opened his mouth again.

"Robert, you're in danger."

"Who are you?"

"I don't know anymore. But I know my words are true."

"Where . . . where are we going?"

"To the pope's land."

"Why?"

"You'll see."

Delphine sat before the handsome, perfumed man as he cantered the horse through the steep streets of Villeneuve, just across the river from Avignon. It was in this city, away from the press of workers' houses, Jewish ghettos, market stalls, and ordure, that Cardinal Cyriac kept his great stone house with its tiles and garden and fountain. Most of the cardinals lived here. This was a city of ivy and warm stone and plane trees. Delphine closed her eyes so the beauty of Villeneuve would not distract her—it was going to be so hard to turn this man, she would need to be a clear vessel for . . .

For what?

For God

God is gone

For His angels then

But Robert had agreed to come with her, and she had not thought he would. He might yet do what she wanted of him.

What they want of him

I'm scared of them, too, almost as much as I am of their dark brothers; they're so bent against each other how can man matter to them?

I'm going to die soon

Delphine shook her head against her doubt.

There are far, far worse things than dying

And I'm about to see them

The horse stumbled on loose stones and jarred her eyes open just beneath the massive tower Phillip the Fair had built to menace the city of the popes some forty years before; Villeneuve was in France, not Provence, while Avignon had just been bought outright by the pope himself, making an earthly sovereign of him. The tower had been built by a bullying king to bully a weak pope; now both were dead and France and Avignon were in bed together, for good it seemed. The tower's murder-slits were dark, unlike many windows behind her; sleep was not coming easily to the city of cardinals, where important men could afford candles to burn against their nightmares. The people of Villeneuve did not know how close those nightmares were to birthing themselves in the world.

They rode across the torchlit bridge into Avignon, then took the northern gate toward Sorgues, and toward Châteauneuf.

Delphine had walked this way with Thomas after his trans-
formation; she had seen the handsome ramparts and great
square towers of Châteauneuf by day. She had seen the vineyards that provided the last wine in Provence lying still and
had not thought to return by night. Unlike Sorgues, which
lay dead and open, no part of it still working save the papal
mint, Châteauneuf was alive—alive enough to shut the Porte
d'Avignon at night as it had even before the plague struck. Delphine's business was not in the city, however.

It was in the vineyards that aproned it.

They steered Guêpe off the Grand Chemin de Sorgues and
onto the small paths between the *lieux-dits*, bearing names
like Bois Renard, Beau Renard, and Mont Redon; these were
among the most beautiful vineyards in the world.

But something was very wrong here.

Robert started to speak, but she pinched him to keep him
silent, pointing at the rows of vines lying under the nearly full
moon.

"What?" he said.

She got off the Arab and led him to a fence.

Robert dismounted, too.

"Tie him," she whispered, and Robert did.

She pointed again.

"I still don't . . ." he started to whisper, and then he did see.
The harvest was on. These vines were Grenache, an October
grape, sweet, the latest to go in the basket. Now the backs and
heads of men and women bobbed like so many black shadows
in the moonlit vines. They hunched to gather, then shuffled to
the next plant, shearing clusters of grapes off with the curved
iron knives of their trade.

"So what?" he said. "There's moon enough to see. Perhaps
they fear a frost and work night and day to save the crop."

She led them closer, creeping quietly down the row.

To Robert's surprise, however, she led them past the gatherers altogether, following three women with huge baskets of grapes on their backs. The women made for a stone farmhouse, just outside which a dozen workers tromped in a wine press.

The women dumped their grapes in as men in knee-length sackcloth switched out empty juice bowls for full ones, handing these off to men on ladders who funneled them into a giant tun.

The men seemed to be smiling, or making some other face that showed their teeth.

Robert did not care for this at all and did not want to know more.

"Let's get back before we're caught," he said.

"Do you see?" she whispered.

"I just want to go back."

"They're not singing," she said. "And they're not humming and they're not talking. Have you ever seen wine treaders tread in silence?"

He was fuming now.

This child who did not speak as a child was bewitching him.

He turned to leave and ran directly into a man bearing grapes on his back. Robert began to excuse himself, and then the smell hit him. He had walked directly into a dead man, whose lower jaw was missing and whose eyes had collapsed in on themselves. The dead man pushed by Robert, and then, as if it had struck him that something wrong had just happened, he turned. His black stub of a tongue worked and he pointed at them.

Neither Delphine nor Robert had to tell the other to run.

The dead man now drew air into his unsound lungs as best he could and made a dry, horrid sound like something between a busted cornemuse and a dying calf.

The treaders stopped treading and the gatherers stopped gathering.

All of them turned now to look at the fleeing man and girl who had intruded upon the vineyard. Whether by instinct or at some command, the treaders climbed out of their vat and the gatherers dropped their baskets. But not their knives. Now they ran, too, some of them falling as they blundered into vines.

They were gaining.

Guêpe bucked and reared at the smell of them, or perhaps at the sound of them rushing through the leaves and butting against one another, and his rope threatened to come loose— if he ran off without them, Robert and Delphine would be *hung like pigs with cut throats to bleed out into the vats* caught.

It was the girl who grabbed his reins, calming him while Robert fumbled with the knot.

"Hurry!" she said.

The rope came loose.

Robert mounted and nearly bolted without her, but he wheeled and scooped her up just as the dead swarmed over the fence. She would never forget their faces—even as their bodies rushed to do violence, what remained of their faces betrayed sadness, even apology for the murder they were being compelled to commit.

Their knives were out, and the first ones grabbed for the reins. Guêpe jumped one way and then another avoiding the flashing knives; he back-kicked one man whose head fell mostly off, causing him to flail his arms wildly, and then the horse found his footing and bolted down the Grand Chemin de Sorgues.

Behind them, the sound of threescore corpses shouting through blasted lungs and throats rose up, and, above them, the moon flirted with slow, ragged clouds as though everything below her had not spun wild.

The bridge was nearly deserted as Robert and the girl cantered across. She did not have long left to convince him.

"If you insist on blinding yourself to what you have seen, you'll have peace for a time. But they will come for you; and then you, too, will stomp in the wine press. Or you will go to Marseilles and sew sails with those who do not flinch when the needle pricks them. Or they'll strip your flesh from your bones for sport; you have no idea how much they hate you, though they smile."

"What do you want from me?" Robert said.

"The . . . Holy Father trusts you."

"Yes."

"Arrange an audience with him for my lord the Comte d'Évreux. A private one."

"Why does he not send the request himself?"

"Because the meeting must happen, and it must happen in the next days. There is no time to filter the request through secretaries."

Robert sighed heavily, pushing the air out, still shaken by the night vintners. He shook his head, though she could not see him behind her.

"Something about this smells."

"Yes," she said. "It does. And the stink is coming from the palace."

While Robert Hanicotte eased back in next to the belly-sleeping cardinal, Thomas sat on the edge of the linen-covered bed in his lodgings. He had not slept, worrying about the girl. He had stirred happily at the sound of footsteps once before, but those had belonged to a chamber boy bringing up a brazier of hot coals.

At last he heard her small, bare feet on the steps, and the door creaked open.

They looked at one another. His hands were folded like the hands of a father waiting to scold, but it was not his place to scold her, whatever she was. She was much more powerful, now, than she had been in that long-ago barn.

"You don't like me to be away," she said.

He shook his head.

She smiled.

She smelled like night air.

"It's good and warm in here," she said, putting off the harder thing.

He nodded.

"It's going to be tomorrow," she said.

"What is?"

"What we came for."

"And what is that?"

"We'll save the pope."

Thomas laughed a little at that.

"It sounds ridiculous when you say it like that. An orphan from Normandy and a thief from Picardy saving the pope. The whoring *pope*."

"You know when you swear that I'll say 'don't swear,' and then you won't for a while. Why not just not swear in the first place? But I suppose that's asking a horse not to whinny. Anyway, you're not a thief. And as long as you're with me, I'm not an orphan."

Thomas grunted.

"He doesn't look like he wants saving. The Holy Father, I mean," Thomas said.

"The man we saw wasn't him."

Thomas stood up and went to the window, looking up where a faint, reddish stain seemed to corrupt the moon. Subtle, but there.

"Who was he, then?"

"You know."

"The Devil?" Thomas said, with neither sarcasm nor disbelief.

"No. But one of his marshals."

She drew in a breath to say the next thing.

"And he's raising the dead. Lots of them."

Thomas's hand twitched, but he still could not cross himself.

"How do you know this? Dreams?"

"Yes. And I saw the unclean risen tonight, harvesting in his vineyards. And those girls . . ."

"Girls?"

"The stags in the Grand Tinel. They were readied before the great hearth in the *dressoir*, out of sight. They were perfumed and then filled with warm olive oil and honey, and then they were all backed up against the fire to heat their loins. Hot brass was put in their mouths and hands to warm those. So nobody would notice. That they were dead. The knights and cardinals had intercourse with the dead."

Thomas turned around now, his massive silhouette blocking the moonlight, but not the cool breeze that blew in the window.

"The devil in the pope's robes . . . does he have a name?"

The girl said something so faintly he could not hear.

He asked her to repeat it, so she wiggled her finger to make him bend down.

She said it in his ear, whispering as if the wall itself might hear her.

The wind blew the dead leaf of a plane tree into the window.

Thomas closed the shutter and lowered the bar.

"And what are we going to do with this . . . Baal'Zebud?"

"Zebuth."

"What are we going to do?"

"You know that, too," she said.

And his hand was already holding the pitted spear from Jerusalem.

THIRTY-THREE

Of the Pope's Garden

Robert Hanicotte held the bright little flower in his hand, noting its fragility; he had seen this variety before, of course, jabs of them clustered in vivid yellow in this garden or that, but he had never had a mind for herbs and flowers. He struggled to remember its name.

"Tansy," the pope said. "Crush it, Robert."

He did as he was told, then put his nose to the palm of his hand.

Pope Clement smiled at the face he made, which betrayed a reaction somewhere between revelation and distaste.

"That's it exactly. Its fragrance rushes at us, strikes us, and leaves us uncertain how to feel about it. So much power in something so tiny. Orange blossoms are similarly potent; I had the pleasure of smelling some brought from Naples when Queen Joanna was here; but they simply please where tansy bewilders. *You* seem bewildered, young Robert. What is it that you wanted to see me about?"

The air was cool in the garden, whose high walls thankfully sheltered it from the wind whipping through the alleys of Avignon and blinding its citizens with grit.

In the distance, in the duller section of the papal gardens where food was grown, women gathered onions and turnips bound for the *pignotte*, where the pope showed his magnanimity by feeding Avignon's poor. An easier task now that the plague had thinned them so; it had raged mercilessly in the poorer quarters, leaving some streets entirely empty of the living.

A lion roared.

A second lion, in a cage neighboring the first one, paced discontentedly and then curled up at the rear of his enclosure. The cardinal had been meaning to ask where the new one came from; it was larger than Misericord, the good-natured male the pope had received from the king of Bohemia before his death at Crécy, and Misericord did not like his neighbor. The new lion had too much black in its mane and its eyes were set too wide—something one might not notice without a well-made lion next to it, although Misericord was never precisely next to the new one; he tended now to sulk in the farthest corner of his cage.

Robert glanced over at Cardinal Cyriac, who was waiting politely out of earshot, watching a snow-white peacock trundle its carriage of feathers almost over his slippered foot. The cardinal did not like the intimacy between the great man and the man who once saw to his candles, not least because he feared that the boy (hardly a boy, but boyish in body and energies) would ask to be removed from his household. He knew he had been less than generous toward his concubine of late, but seemed unable to stop himself; intellectually, the boy had something about him of the dog who feared so much to be kicked that kicking it seemed obligatory.

"Your Holiness, I had a dream that troubled me. I should perhaps not let such matters disturb my peace."

The pope floated his hand before Robert's gaze, which was focused somewhere left of the Holy Father's foot, and lifted that hand gracefully, taking the younger man's attention with it until he found himself looking into the pope's ocean-blue eyes. It was a gesture he knew from his days as cubicular; this pope did not insist on the same sort of deference other powerful men did.

He wanted men to look into his eyes, which were very powerful instruments of persuasion, benevolence, or, more rarely, blame.

"Dreams are sometimes folly and sometimes fact. If we could choose between the two, we would not need our Josephs and Daniels, would we?"

Robert shook his head.

A manicured bush full of some exquisite blue-and-white flower moved in the cold breeze behind Clement's head. He was waiting to be told about the dream.

So Robert told him.

He omitted the fact that he had awakened in his clothes with his stockings wet from dew. The dew of the vineyards.

The pope tilted his head just a little, a paternal smile coming to his lips and his eyes.

"Are you sure this was a dream, Robert?"

"What else could it have been, Papa?"

Something tickled his hand, and he lifted it to see a fly with a body of brilliant gold rubbing its forelegs. It flew off again as if it had never been there. The smell of tansy welled up again in his nose.

"I hate to pronounce the word," the Holy Father said, "but I think you can guess it."

Witchcraft.

The word leapt into being and disappeared again as swiftly as the fly had.

The pope's eyes gleamed just a little as if in confirmation.

"It is no secret that we move in strength against the Arrogant One's hold on this world. Is it so unlikely that he would seek to stop our enterprise? And is it unlikely that he would seek to blacken our good name with his sorceries? The girl in your dream will have shown you her own villainies to confound you."

"Do you think they mean you some harm, Papa?"

"It would serve the Cruel One's purpose; I am turning

mighty wheels against him. Surely he trembles at the thought that we might seize from him the city of Christ and David. Surely he dreads the check he will suffer when we remove from us his agents, the Jews."

"I believe," Robert said, nodding, "I believe the little girl in the dream is pretending to be the page to Chrétien de Navarre, the Comte d'Évreux."

The pope's eyes registered something.

The older man stepped closer.

Robert watched the white, silk glove rise again, the weak sun flashing in the sapphires of the pope's rings as he laid his hand upon his former cubicular's shoulder. He was struck again by the majesty of this man, with his robes the color of aubergine, the pure white zucchetto on his head; he felt the warmth of the man even through the silk glove, even through his own vestments. His father had seemed mighty to him, but he only laid hands on Matthieu and Robert to strike them or yank them out of his way.

He wanted to cry at how deeply accepted he felt.

"You are perceptive and brave. And you are loyal, Robert. You have our gratitude," the pope said, the smile lines around his eyes deepening. "And you will have much more than that."

Robert's breath caught in his throat with excitement and gladness.

"Cardinal Cyriac," the pope said, calling the red-robed figure to him. "It is our pleasure to elevate this faithful servant, though to what position we have not yet determined; be as a father to him, and know that we shall return your every kindness to him tenfold."

Dismissed, the cardinal and the young man walked out of the garden, passing by the cages of the pope's zoo.

We shall return your every kindness to him tenfold

The cardinal moved his lips as he silently repeated the pope's words, trying to plumb them for their true meaning. He glanced past his self-satisfied lover, whose expression was not so bold it could be called a smile, and at the enclosures of the

Holy Father's bestiary. Something was wrong with the lions. It took him a moment to register what it was.

They were both in the same cage now.

The new, black-maned one sat kingly on its haunches while Misericord hunched miserably in his corner with something like fear in his demeanor.

A chill passed down the cardinal's left side.

Those cages don't communicate.

He blinked his eyes, sure they must have deceived him earlier.

He looked back at the black-maned lion, which yawned, curling its tongue lazily. When it noticed him looking at it, it did a very curious thing.

It stared directly at him, its mouth standing open, and moved its tongue over its teeth as if counting them.

THIRTY-FOUR

Of the Arrest

T he lodgings at which the pope had placed the Comte d'Évreux and his page sat practically in the shadow of the hulking palace, quite near St. Peter's church. The series of slanting and hunch-shouldered workers' houses that had occupied the place before had been pulled down four years earlier, the lumber carted to the palace and cheerfully burned in its kitchens and beneath its baths—it was as though the palace had eaten them. Pope Clement had continued his predecessor's policy of building up a stone Avignon to replace the wooden one, and the Elysium House was a fine example of the new extravagance.

Thomas and Delphine had sequestered themselves in their room, having excused themselves from the midday feast that an English duke was putting on in the courtyard. The sounds of revelry had been floating up to them for nearly an hour, and, as the revelers emptied pitcher after pitcher of the pope's wine down their gullets, more and more often the Valois and English lords who had once faced each other across battlefields now united in good-natured mockery directed at the window of the man they took for the Comte d'Évreux and his Navarrese page. This was precisely what Thomas had feared—though he bore the face and body of the dead man, he did not share his memories, and the world of high-placed men, though embracing all of Europe, was as small and incestuous as a village.

He was dangerously near betraying himself as an impostor.

"Is my lord of Navarre taken ill?" shouted the young William Montacute, Earl of Salisbury, in the boxy, snub-nosed French of English nobility. "For I should have liked to have a wrestle with him."

Delphine used the tip of her comb to trace the hem of a woman's dress on the wall hanging near the window. It was the simple comb of her mother's, brought from Normandy—she did not like the ivory comb Thomas had given to her.

"No, my lord Salisbury, he will not wrestle you. He was only wont to wrestle his little brother until Charles grew a moustache. Now he wrestles other men's wives."

"That is too much, my lord," laughed another Frenchman, though it was hard to hear him over the horsy guffaws of Sir William, who displayed a foreigner's overappreciation of French wordplay, as well as an Englishman's amusement at French adultery.

"I but jest. If our good Chrétien would poke his head out his window, he would see that I am all smiles."

Thomas felt vertiginously insulted and also pleased that the Comte d'Évreux was being insulted.

"Leave him be; he is ill from the other night's excess."

"Then how does he propose to face tomorrow's excess?"

A messenger had come the day before, crying the news below every window: Since the plague had killed so many cardinals, a new one was to be created tomorrow night; the celebration would be held outside, in the open courtyard of the palace, and open to all.

Now Delphine traced the legs of a knight, skipped chastely past his middle, and rejoined the outline at his belly. Past the tapestry knight, a young girl and her father bent in the field, their faces turned away, gathering sheaves. She traced them, too. It soothed her to keep her hands busy while she waited for a helpful thought to come. For once, Thomas would have been grateful to see the heavy-lidded gaze that meant she was about to use words that were somehow not hers. Neither of them knew quite what to do while waiting for an invitation to see the pope, an invitation that might not come at all.

He shuddered at the thought of trying to stab the false pope *in camera*, let alone in front of a table full of knights and a company of guards.

It doesn't matter.

I've come here to die.

"Give us at least your head, my lord of Navarre, so we may know you are not dead!" shouted up the English duke.

"You'd better," said Delphine, now tracing a little dog.

Thomas smoothed his unfamiliar, closely shorn hair and wiped at his beardless chin before thrusting his head out the window to general applause. He waved a hand at the celebrants.

"Come down," one said.

"No," Thomas said. "Our friend is quite correct; I ate more than a young man should at the warrior's feast, and have paid an old man's price for it."

The table below erupted with laughter.

"Where's Don Eduardo de Burgos?" another shouted. "He'll purge it out of you with *jerez!*"

Thomas swallowed hard at this.

"But," he continued, waving the last comment away, "with temperance and prayer, I should be whole by this evening. If my lord the earl does not throw me to the ground too roughly."

They laughed again.

"Well, get back to your sickbed," said the Valois, "and no more excuses tonight. Though you should send your page down for a bowl of this stew. It'll make a man of him. Oysters, ginger, and pepper."

Thomas made as though to vomit, provoking a cheerful "Hoooo" from the table, then withdrew his head and closed the shutter. It was struck by what sounded like a plum.

Delphine raised an eyebrow, impressed.

"Now go get us a bowl of that stew," he said.

The soldiers came an hour later.

Delphine had eased out of the bindings that flattened her modest unboyishness and sat upon her pallet near the window. The spear was around her neck. Thomas was scraping at the bottom of his bowl with a crust of hard bread, eager to get every drop of the spicy stew.

The sound of boots on the stairs froze them both.

They looked at one another.

These were not the light footsteps of the chamber boys, one of whom, Isnard, had made fast friends with Delphine in her role as page, nor was this a solitary messenger.

The knock, though expected, startled Delphine when it came.

She squeaked like a mouse.

The knock came again.

The hand that knocked wore mail.

"Who is it?" Thomas barked, sounding lordly.

"Servants of His Holiness," said an unimpressed voice. "Now open this door."

This was no invitation.

They were discovered.

Delphine confirmed her fears by peeking through a hole in the wooden shutters; two men wearing chain mail and the cross-key emblem of the palace stood in the courtyard below the window, one of them chasing off a kitchen girl who had been clearing up. Both men carried poleaxes.

Delphine clutched the case that held the spear.

"I'm sick," Thomas said. "My neck is swollen and my throat hurts." He sneezed loudly as punctuation.

"Amazing how many people we knock for feel the plague coming on. Open the door or I'll break it down. And you won't like your trip to the palace if I do."

Thomas took up his sword and Delphine shook her head at him, wide eyed.

"What, then?" he whispered.

"I don't know, but not that!"

The man outside the door flung himself against it; it was a new door, and solidly built.

"If you make me axe through this whoring thing, you won't walk out of here. *Open this door!*"

Delphine's eyes got heavy.

After the man yelled, she noticed a light coming from beyond the window. She put her hand over the spear and opened the shutter.

The courtyard was gone.

The window now gave on the bank of the river, outside the city walls, and it was as if the window had lowered; the drop from the ledge would be easy, not five feet.

An axe hit the door.

The man in the hallway was swearing.

Thomas would fight to defend her, but maybe not if she left.

He was to let them take him.

"Let them take you," she heard herself say.

Let them take me, Peter.

Come on, Delphine.

His ear's off! His ear!

She closed her eyes.

What about Thomas!

She smelled flowers.

Another one.

Stronger than mine.

It would protect her.

WHAT ABOUT THOMAS?
Come on, little moon.
She rolled out the window.

Thomas still had his sword in his hand, though sheathed.

Something like a wing flashed near the window, a very large wing, and Delphine opened the shutter.

It had been dark in the room, and the bright daylight dazzled him.

An axe hit the door.

"I'm going to break your goddamned legs, do you hear me? I'll drag you there by your balls if you make me chop this whole door up!"

Thomas drew his sword.

"Let them take you," the girl said.

Her cheeks were wet with tears.

She turned her face from him.

She rolled out the window then, but he never heard her hit the ground.

He thought he heard wings.

Thomas launched himself into the man who came through the door, thinking to bowl him down, hoping to find a smaller man behind him. He hit the big soldier, but not hard enough.

I thought I had him

I'm in the comte's body I'm not as strong

The man reeled back against the wall but gathered himself and gave the Comte d'Évreux the back end of his axe, breaking teeth.

His body but I feel it GOD

He fell.

He looked for his sword, but could not find it.

GOD

They hit him again.

He was not dragged to the papal palace by his testicles.

He was taken in a cart.
After they broke his legs.

THIRTY-FIVE

Of the Doctor

T he boy who served the pope's physician woke from his little bed at the other end of the room and brought a candle over to his master, who whimpered and thrashed in the grips of another nightmare. How many nights in a row had he seen him disturbed by of one of these? He knew the physician, Maître de Chauliac, to be a good man, and wondered what devils could trouble one so kind.

This was the worst nightmare yet.

He leaned close to look, but made sure he did not let the candle drip on the man's full cheeks or big nose. That would be like a story he had told him about a curious woman who drove away an angel. Was it an angel? Maybe just a boy with wings. The *maître* told him too many stories to keep them all separate.

"*Maître?*" he said, but very quietly.

He had learned not to wake him in these times, but he dearly wanted to end this particular dream. Did men die of dreams? He would try to remember to ask the doctor in the morning. Not tonight, though. He stood with the candle ready to light him to whatever the *maître* might ask him for.

Wine, the boy thought.

The worst ones always wake him and he asks me for wine.

But if I pour the wine and he does not wake, I shall have to put it back in the jug and clean the goblet so the little bugs don't get in it.

Pour the wine, Tristan.

He took a little enameled goblet from its shelf and poured wine from a pewter jug with three rooster's feet. He was fond of that jug, as he was fond of the smell of wine. Not lately, though. Something was off, like a hint of rot. Had they waited too late to get the grapes in? He had worked as assistant to a baker, and thought to work his way up to being a butler and minding the pope's fruit cellar at the foot of the kitchen tower, so good was he at ferreting out rottenness. His mother said he had the nose of a dog. But the great doctor had seen what a clever boy he was and pulled him from the kitchens to replace his former boy, who had died of the plague.

Actually, three of the doctor's assistants had died of the plague, but the good doctor had not caught it himself.

Not yet, he would have corrected. Or he might have said *insh'allah*, a word he had learned from Arab texts. It meant something like *So God be pleased,* but Tristan didn't understand why he didn't just say that.

"Tristan."

The doctor was sitting up now, his big, friendly eyes looking bugged and haunted. He rubbed a hand over them and they regained some of their reason.

"Tristan, help me dress."

"Yes, *maître*. Are you sure? It is still long before morning."

"Just get my clothes together, please."

The man and the boy went into one of the grand, vaulted hallways of the palace, and the physician stopped, considering. He looked left, in the direction that led to the pope's bedroom and adjoining study. The boy waited with the candle, looking very much like a small dog waiting for its master to open a door.

"Is the Holy Father well?" Tristan said.

"No, Tristan. I do not think he is, though I cannot say why. He seems in good health, but . . . he is changed."

"Is it to do with the wine?"

"Excuse me?"

"I thought, perhaps the wine . . . it smells funny."

He looked at the boy and narrowed his eyes, considering and rejecting this premise.

He turned on his heel now and went back into his room.

Tristan watched, fascinated, as the doctor sorted through the writs in his desk, many of which came directly from the pope. When he found one that seemed to suit his purpose, he fetched one of his chirurgical knives and, as delicately as though he were cutting live flesh, lifted the two separated parts of the wax seal from it. He then fetched a fresh sheet of parchment and wrote something in a very careful hand. When he had finished, he rolled it and, to the boy's astonishment, heated his knife in the candle flame and used it to graft the two halves of the seal together again.

"I see your mind frothing with questions, and yet, recognizing the delicacy of the situation, you don't ask them. Instead, you watch for yourself and come to your own conclusions. I think you have a future, Tristan. I think you will make yourself very useful."

Now they left again, the boy hurrying to keep up with his master's purposeful steps. He turned right this time and opened a door to a set of stairs the boy knew about but had been warned never to follow.

"I know you wonder why I'm going to this ghastly place, let alone taking you. The truth is I cannot say. Except that the people who work their art down here are the sort of men who might need two pairs of eyes on them to do the right thing."

A man groaned in the darkness ahead of them.

The dungeon.

This is the dungeon.

They put thieves and sorcerers here.

It had not occurred to Tristan, who had the deepest confidence in Maître de Chauliac, to be afraid until just that moment.

"We don't fix men down here, good doctor, we break them. I think you're on the wrong floor."

The dungeons, which had sat in such a state of disuse for the first years of the aptly named Clement's reign that old carts and tools were stored here, had recently come to life again. Sournois, formerly a blacksmith, had been singled out specifically by this changed and un-clement Clement to head up the new "nether wing" of the palace, which was where the enemies of God's peace would be stored and, when necessary, put to the question. The man hanging from his arms with his ruined legs dangling looked to have been asked a question of some gravity indeed—a question whose answer he could not or would not share.

The doctor noted, with some revulsion, that the man had neither nipples nor fingernails, and that his shoulders were out of joint.

Yes, this was the man in de Chauliac's dream.

"I'm in the right place. What is that man's name?"

"This geezer," Sournois said, standing up and patting the man's soft belly proprietarily, "is no less than a Norman comte and a future king of Navarre."

"The Comte d'Évreux," de Chauliac said.

"That's the one," Sournois said, sticking a thumb in the man's navel and pinching a handful of fat hard enough to make the barely conscious young fellow groan again.

"Get him down."

"And put him where?" the gaoler said, growing suspicious.

"In whatever you intended to remove him with when you were through. He's clearly not walking anywhere."

369

Sournois got closer to the doctor, but the doctor did not step back.

"I have it from the Holy Father himself that this man is to stay where he is. He's coming by personally before the feast tomorrow. Might even come tonight."

The doctor was aware of a cold sweat beginning under his robes.

He will not come yet please not yet insh'allah.

"And I have it from the good Clement that he is to leave with me. You might recognize that seal," the doctor said, handing his parchment to the other, who recognized his name on the outside and snapped the seal.

He frowned and stared at the writ with confusion and distaste.

"It says that you are to release your close prisoner to me so that he does not die. Which he most certainly will, and soon, if he keeps swinging from your ceiling."

"But why's it in Latin? It's always in French for me. I read a little French."

"Perhaps His Holiness forgot your lack of education. Shall we wait here for him so we may remind him? Frankly, I don't know if I can save this man, and I would much rather have him die in your care than mine."

Sournois put the writ in his pouch.

"To hell with that," he said, and went to fetch a handcart.

Thomas was cold.

He hurt so badly in so many places that a strange sort of numbness had settled into him. His chief complaint was the cold, which felt as though it would never be out of him.

He did not know who the man was that wheeled him out of the oubliettes and through a door meant for horses and carts, but he sensed that he would have died had he remained. Not of his injuries. Something had been coming for him, and he had just escaped. Had he remained, he would not only have died, he would have died spectacularly.

Horribly.

The man with the fly's head would have bitten him.

He shivered.

He looked up at the man wheeling him, and the man looked down at him with kind eyes. He wanted to ask him who he was, but he didn't have the strength.

When he saw that Thomas was still shivering, despite the garments that had been laid across him, the wheeling man stopped and removed his robes, revealing a long shirt that bore the irremovable stains of surgeries.

He placed this around Thomas, and Thomas smiled.

A doctor, then.

He might yet get home to Arpentel and see his wife.

"Don't speak," the man smiled down at him. "You have only one task, and that is to live. See that you do it."

He wanted to tell the doctor to get the arrow out of his tongue, but then he realized that was another doctor, another time. He wanted to ask him if angel's blood was made of egg whites, but that was wrong, too.

And no wife was waiting for him.

He wrinkled up his face as if to cry, but didn't let himself.

He lost consciousness.

When he came to again, a girl was looking at the wheeling man.

He was looking wide-eyed at her, as though he saw something Thomas did not see.

Delphine? Was that her name?

Her hair was short.

"Remember this, boy," the doctor said to a young man Thomas had not seen before, who also stared wide-eyed at Delphine.

What were they seeing?

Delphine put her fingers to her lips, and the man and the

boy left.

Now she looked down at Thomas, smiling.

Those gray eyes.

She cooled his brow with her sleeve, which had been dunked in the Rhône.

"I'm going to die," he managed.

"You already did die, remember? You're the dead one."

He felt his spirit coming loose, like a ship from its moorings, but she lifted his head and pointed.

"Hold on," the girl said, "just for a moment."

She put her hand behind his head and lifted so he could see.

Something was coming out of the river, lit by the moon.

A man.

A man in rusty armor, carrying a sword by the blade, cruciform.

A heavily muscled man with a graying beard and a scarred face.

Him.

He weakly shook the ruined head that was not really his.

Thomas de Givras stepped dripping from the river, eyes closed, a sleepwalker.

Delphine got out of the dripping revenant's way, and he came to the cart. Thomas was afraid. Was he already dead?

He watched himself bend over, getting closer.

Dripping on him.

He felt very dizzy; the world was going black.

He was being kissed now by his own mouth, not as lovers kiss, with tongues, but as true lovers kiss, sharing breath.

He breathed out of the comte's lungs and into his own.

The ship of his soul lurched away from his false body.

And into his true one.

He opened his eyes.

The body of the comte twitched now, once, then twice, only now it was under him. His mouth, his actual mouth, was on the dead man, and he pulled up. He breathed in, his strong lungs filling with air, his hands clutching, ready to grab weapons or levers or to brace against the pillars of the temple. He was strong again. He ran his hand through his full beard, and tugged on his longish hair.

He laughed, and Delphine laughed too, shushing him as he put the doctor's robes on over his cold, wet armor.

She now bent and kissed the cheek of the dead man in the cart.

"Give the river back its due," she said.

Thomas tipped the body into the water, and it floated for a moment, and then the darkness took it away.

THIRTY-SIX

Of the Arming, and of the Vigil

"Isnard!"

The chamber boy at Elysium House peered out the window and down at the street, the darkness of which still resisted the prying of the low morning sun between the close buildings.

"Here, Isnard!"

He wrinkled his nose and put down the piss-pot he had been about to chuck. Was that his new friend, the page? And had not that page served the arrested knight?

"Diego?" he called down in a carefully measured whisper.

"Yes!" Delphine said.

She, too, was an expert whisperer.

"What are you doing here?"

He looked behind him to make sure no hand was reaching to yank his ear for idleness.

"I need a favor."

"What is it?" he said. "And be quick!"

Why was Diego in his nightclothes?

"My master's things—have they been taken?"

"No. The room is as it was. The carpenter is coming tomorrow to fix the door."

"And my master's horse?"

"In the stables, eating twice his share of hay. The English lord means to take him."

"Open the door for me."

"What? I can't!"

"Yes you can. Open the door, and help me fetch out my master's armor and horse."

He looked behind him again.

"A horse? They'll hang me for stealing a horse!"

"It's not stealing. The horse belongs to us."

He considered this.

"All the same, they'll *kill* me! Then they'll turn me out, and my father will kill me again!"

"They won't turn you out. You speak French, Italian, and Provençal. How many times have they used you to translate? Just let me in, and I'll do most of it."

"They'll see you."

"Not if you distract them."

"How?"

"I don't know. Fall down the stairs with something loud. A pan or something."

This was beginning to sound fun.

He would get a beating, but some things were worth a beating.

And he liked the little Spanish page with the French accent, even if he looked a bit like a girl.

"Why should I?"

"If you do, I'll give you this ivory comb."

He licked his lips.

An ivory comb.

"It has angels painted on it."

Isnard liked angels.

In fact, he thought he'd seen one last night.

Delphine and Thomas rode past the tanners and parchment makers on the banks of the canal fed by a branch of the river

Sorgues, smelling the stink of their industry. He rode Jibreel and she rode her little palfrey. The horse felt good under his hips. He thought this might be the last time he ever rode a horse, but he didn't mind. He had died this morning, and he knew what it was now.

Tonight would bring more death, probably his.

He was ready.

This would be worse than Crécy, but sweet where that was bitter.

The fine armor he had worn in another body mostly fit him, though the chest was tight and the belly loose. The breastplate and leg armor were all Delphine could get out of the house, so his own rusty chain sat beneath them. He had also left behind the Navarrese surcoat and rode with his breastplate gleaming, though dented, and his head bare—nobody would take him for the Comte d'Évreux now.

They left the city by the Imbert Gate, but they did not travel far. In fact, they called at the first large building they found, just by the river.

The Franciscan brotherhood lived in a large, proud building, as befit the large, proud city it served; this did not sit well with all of the brothers, whose attraction to the order had more to do with Christian poverty than ecclesiastic pomp. And yet, here was the capital of Christianity, and here they could do the most to protect their order from charges of heresy. Better to let the popes build them fine churches than to be burned on humble pyres. They allowed the rich to bury their dead in the churchyard, as though the Devil were too simple to find a bad onion in good soil; and when the affluent tried to buy back their wasted lives, showering the monks with money from their deathbeds, the brothers used their wealth to spread the word of the impoverished Christ.

They never closed their doors to anyone, and their hospitality during these months of pestilence had exacted a heavy toll.

Only seven brothers remained of forty.

Brother Albrecht, an Alsatian with the beginnings of cataracts, welcomed the knight and his daughter.

He helped them stable their horses.

He showed them to a room where they could sleep through midday, and then showed them to the altar of the Virgin, where they could pray.

They told him they wished to have strong bodies and pure hearts.

They were going to the feast in the Courtyard of Honor.

Some lad of dubious merit was to be given a cardinal's hat.

It seemed curious that the knight wished to borrow a friar's habit, but Brother Albrecht was used to the vanities of the worldly—many men asked to be buried in the brown of St. Francis (as though a feathered stone might fly!). Brother Albrecht felt the man's chest and cheeks (was he preparing himself for the day he would need his hands to read faces as well as hearts?) and found no harm in him, but rather a long-buried goodness. So what if he wore rusty armor beneath his shiny breastplate; so what if his beard was unkempt and his fingernails long? Who refuses a gold coin because it has a little mud on it?

He gave him the new habit Brother Egidius had never gotten to wear, having caught the Pest the day it was given to him.

God knew they had more habits now than living men to fill them.

"You're not going to do anything to shame the order, are you?"

"No," the big man said.

"How about you, little one?"

She shook her head, smiling.

She had been smiling since she got here.

Brother Albrecht understood.

Blessed Francis just called some to him.

It was getting dark.

Delphine took Thomas's sword from its sheath.

"What are you going to do, break it so I won't hurt anybody?" he joked. She gave him that dry, tight-lipped head shake he knew so well. Then she did something that made him gasp.

She cut her hands on the blade.

Quite deliberately.

She smeared her blood up one side of it and down the other, massaging it into the runnel, on the point, on quillons and pommel, and into every notch it had gathered in the tilt-yard and on the field and in the furtherance of theft.

As if it were a holy oil.

It is.

He gasped again, but this was a gasp of recognition.

Jesus whoring Christ, do I have to watch you every second?

You bleeding all over my things doesn't help me, you, or anybody. Understand?

The thing in the murk had not been bothered by the billhook or the boar spear; it recoiled only when struck by his sword. His sword had killed it.

Her blood killed it.

Her blood in its heart.

The armorer at the night tourney would not touch it.

Christ, what the hell is on this thing?

I killed something foul in a river.

Hey, Jacmel, you want any of this?

Thomas kissed the bloody sword now, and put it in its sheath.

She took the spear from its case and gave him that, too.

He threw his dagger to the floor and wedged the spear into the sheath at the back of his belt. He smiled to think he had just shoved a relic worth the whole of Avignon into a piece of greasy leather near his ass.

She bent him down and kissed his cheeks.

Daughter witch page saint prophet angel what are you what are you You

Delphine
"What are you?" he said.
"Two things, I think. But soon I'll be just one."
He shook his head to keep from crying.
He could not, he *would* not watch her be hurt.
Not if it meant his soul.
"Am I still not to kill anyone?"
"Not men."
"What does that mean?"
"We won't be facing men."

THIRTY-SEVEN

Of the Visitation at Villeneuve

R obert Hanicotte spent the night before his elevation in a state of bliss only mildly tempered by the memory of the things he had seen in the vineyard. He ate the game fowl and sausages and even drank the wine, sweet from its late harvest, and with just a hint of something

dead feet corpses' feet

else. The something else was easily forgotten, though it tended to bob back up again, requiring further attention at inattention. So much of life demanded a kind of truce with perceived facts—one could not allow the suffering of the kitchen women, for example, to spoil the taste of capon. Neither would those women trouble themselves about the gnawings of a rat at the summer sausage; just cut that end off and serve the rest.

Silently.

He did not know, now, what he had seen at Châteauneuf-du-Pape, but it did not bear further thought. He had done the right thing warning His Holiness about the little witch.

goodness came from her she was benevolent like Matthieu her priest you betrayed one of your brother's flock

I don't know if she was good or evil I can't know that

Another thought that he had to step on from time to time

was the knowledge that he was completely unfit for high ec-clesiastic office. Oh, he had been a priest briefly; the pope liked to discuss biblical matters before bed, so it pleased him to seek cubiculars from among the monasteries and minor clergy. Robert's good looks inspired even those not given to love men to a sort of instant warmth and familiarity, and his years under a tyrannical father had clarified his mild, pleasant manner. His bishop had sent the newly minted priest south with Clement in mind. Now so long had passed since his stud-ies that he dreaded the first letter he might be asked to draft or, worse, the first Latin discourse he might be expected to give.

He might have despaired were it not for the example of Pierre Roger de Beaufort, the pope's dull-eyed, fatling nephew, as one of the last batch of cardinals created before the plague rose up. The boy was eighteen years old, and had to be re-minded hourly to shut his trapezoidal mouth and breathe through his nose. Robert could do as well as he, please God, at least that well.

He left the pallet he had set up in the study—he would not bed next to the belly-sleeper again—and walked down the spiral stairs to the garden. He had fought with the cardinal after the departure of their guests, making it clear to him that further indecency between them would be unbecoming to his new office. The old man wanted to throw him out on his ear, and would have but for his fear to displease Pope Clement, who had taken precipitate steps in Robert's favor.

The Holy Father loves me

That is not him and you know it

I don't know and I don't care

He heard one of the Arabs whinny and wondered if it was Guêpe; he wanted to go and see, but what if the little witch was there again, waiting to reprove him (at best) and perhaps to wither his manhood with some spell?

He shuddered at the thought and steered instead for the olive trees, running his hand through their slender, silver-green leaves and considering the pitted fruit hanging there. He wandered near the huge stone well, running his finger along its lip. He looked at the sky. The moon had a red edge now, much talked about in the city, like the rim of a drunkard's eye.

He did not pretend to understand the caprices of celestial clockwork; if these were, in fact, the end times, there was nothing to be done about it.

Something passed in front of the moon.

Quickly.

Not a bird.

He felt chill now; the cold hadn't taken long to work through his sleeping-gown and cloak. His feet might as well have been bare for the thinness of his slippers.

He looked toward the house, drawn to the warmth of the still-glowing hearth and the candles in the lower rooms. He would find another cup of wine and try again to sleep.

A small silhouette now eclipsed the doorway. Young Vincent, the serving boy, waited for him.

"Père Robert," the boy whispered, agitated.

While Robert had not held up the wafer in more than ten years, *Père* was the best title the boy could hang on his master's concubine.

"Yes?"

"There are men in the house."

Robert's blood ran cold.

"What men?"

"I don't know. It was too dark to see them well."

His mind raced.

He remembered the squire whose duty it was to protect the cardinal.

"Where is Gilon?"

"He drank a pitcher to himself tonight; I could not wake

him. But I have his sword."

He saw it now.

It was nearly as big as the boy.

"Put that down," he said.

He thought of the stable boy, a big lad, and he hurried to the stables, clutching his coat around him.

The horses whinnied and tramped about their stables; something had agitated them.

He found the boy, who normally slept like the dead at this time of night, sitting wide-eyed on his shoeing bench; despite the darkness, he could see the boy's outline, and saw that he was gripping a pitchfork.

"Come with me to the house," Robert said. "Vincent thinks he saw something."

The boy shook his head in the near-darkness.

"I command you to come with me."

"Command as you like," the boy said in a choked voice, "but I saw something, too. And I'm not going near that house."

"You'll force me to tell the cardinal."

"You can tell the Devil for all I care. And I think I know where you can find him."

"I command you..."

"Get out!" the boy said, standing now, leveling the pitchfork.

Robert got out.

Vincent was gone.

Robert found the sword the boy had left behind and picked it up, feeling ridiculous. He barely knew how to hold it, let alone swing it at someone. He put it back down.

He walked into the house now, going to the dressing area near the kitchen hearth and taking up a carving knife. He clutched it to his chest and stood there, unsure what to do. He listened. Hearing nothing, he made for the stairs, taking them slowly, quietly.

He heard a floorboard creak, but not from the staircase; it had come from the cardinal's bedroom.

He tried to think of where else he might go and hated his own cowardice; he could go the falconer's apartment, but what would he say? *I think someone may have broken into the house, but I decided to leave the cardinal and save myself?*

There was nothing for it but to go and see.

He crept down the hallway.

The door stood open, the light from a candle casting a wavering glow.

He edged up to the door and peeked in.

A man, or something man-shaped if not man-colored, stood over the cardinal. Impossibly, it had its arm down the cardinal's mouth all the way to the elbow. It looked up at Robert, its mouth full of dirty teeth, its eyes black but somehow luminous; were there twelve of them?

No, six.

Now two.

Its skin blushed from sickly white to baby pink and then began to sag and wrinkle.

It was becoming more like the cardinal every instant.

It spoke with the cardinal's voice.

"Go back to bed, my darling. Don't leave the house. Be sweet and you'll get your hat tomorrow."

The cardinal's eyes stared dead at the ceiling, his crammed mouth open so wide it bled at the corners, his soft neck wrinkled back on itself like gills.

"Please don't make me tell you again."

The cardinal twitched under the thing.

Robert dropped the knife and walked away.

He lay on his pallet listening to soft noises coming from the other room.

By morning, he had convinced himself he had not heard them.

The cardinal came to him near first light, asking if he'd had a bad dream. Yes, he most certainly had. The cardinal pulled him gently into his bedroom and he allowed it.

He allowed everything.

Everything seemed normal.

Except that Cardinal Cyriac now slept on his back.

THIRTY-EIGHT

Of the Rings of Lazarus, and of the Bathers

The large, hooded friar and the short-haired girl packed in with the poor of Avignon, who flowed toward the palace like a second Rhône of cowls and mantles and hats of many colors. If many wore the clothes of the wealthy dead, all of them bore their own hunger; it made them forget their fear of the Great Death, or, at least, to concede no more to it than rags held over faces while they pressed in together toward the pope's table. They had already tasted the pope's generosity at the pignotte, but there they got vegetables and bread, and not enough for all; here, in the square outside the hulking palace, beneath the little pointed towers that jabbed up like goats' horns, the smell of roasted meat maddened them and brought water to their mouths.

"At sunset," the criers had cried, and now they watched the sky in the west; the sun's departure was sweet to many of them already, as it called them every day to lay down hammers, scythes, and buckets and go to their hearths to eat and tell stories, but this was the first public feast since the Pest had fallen on the city.

This would be something.

As the last pale blue in the sky darkened to indigo, the herald bearing the crossed keys blew a trumpet note, and the doors leading to the Courtyard of Honor swung back.

The crowd surged in, managing not to trample one another, but edging as close to the front as possible for the first pick of the feast. Words came first of course, words in Latin, censers swung with strange and heady smoke, words in French about how the coming war would be seen from Heaven. Words about Cardinal Hanicotte and how the Lord knew his own and called them forward to be raised.

Now a commotion rose up.

Two men in yellow hats, bearing yellow circles sewn on their breasts, pushed forward, crying for help; they removed their hats. One of the men had dried blood on his head and a face streaked with grime from where he had hastily tried to remove plaster dust with his hand. They were Jews, they said. Children of Abraham and loyal citizens of Avignon. An abomination had risen. Something wicked had broken into the ghetto and was pulling down houses.

"It is made of men! A monster made of men!"

The crowd gasped, and, in the silence following their gasp, sounds of distress and terror sounded in the distance.

The crowd began to mutter.

"If we call God a different name, we share the same Devil! Help us against him, Your Holiness! We beg you!"

At this, both men went to their knees and extended their hands in supplication.

The people in the courtyard began to yell, "Yes," and "Help them!" and "Please!" and they moved and rippled like a living thing wanting to react to threat.

The Holy Father stood and calmed them, calling forward a small group of soldiers and speaking privately to their *sergent*, whose eyes bugged at what he heard; but then he lowered his head and nodded.

"Those are not enough!" the man with the bloodied crown despaired. "You have not seen it!"

Cardinal Cyriac stood and said, "If the Devil is here, soldiers of the church will give chase to him. If these were the hysterics of a deceived people, they will wish for the Devil."

One or two in the crowd laughed, but most were too disturbed by the sincerity and horror of the plea they had heard.

Now the soldiers marched off toward the Jewish quarter, bringing the men with them.

A woman's scream, far away but distinct, rose up past the new wing of the palace.

"If the Devil is in their quarter," said the pope, "perhaps this will be the argument that leads them to recognize that their Messiah awaits their recognition and stands ready to help them against him whose bidding they have foolishly done for so long."

Musicians came with drum and cornemuse, covering any further noise from beyond the walls.

And now, at a nod from the pope's steward, soldiers near the front uncrossed their pole-arms and let the crowd flow past them at something more than a walk but less than a run. The large friar waited patiently, letting others go before him. He favored his right side, curling around what might have been some stiffness, or some painfully withered limb, which he kept beneath his large habit. The girl he had entered with had slipped away some time ago, and no eye had followed her where she went.

Delphine made her way first into the garden, with its smells of night flowers and the calls of strange birds, and she skimmed the wall until she came to a door at the bottom of a tower.

Is it here?

Yes.

She kissed the iron lock and the studded door swung open.

The room she entered served as storehouse for the pope's wine; candles flickered on sconces (it would not be long before the butler's boy came to tend them), revealing graceful vaulted ceilings in the same exquisite limestone that composed the rest of the palace. Barrels hunched together, looking short beneath this ceiling, though each of them was taller than she. She stepped uncertainly to one barrel, laying her cheek against its cool oak and listening.

Quem quaeritis? the cool walls seemed to ask.

Whom do you seek?

You won't hear anything.

Feel him.

She now crawled on top of one of the huge tuns and curled on it like a kitten settling in for a nap.

Not this one.

She did this again and again until she came to one very near the back, one that had been waiting since August.

Here

He's here

You can't do this you can't this is a dream

She looked around and saw a rack of tools, pulling out a prying bar that felt much too heavy for her.

I'm too weak

No little moon not tonight

We're coming

Our strength is yours

She lifted the bar and brought it down with great force, nearly falling in as the lid began to give. She laughed at herself and stood on a neighboring tun to finish.

She got the lid off, throwing the broken disk aside, and a sour-sweet wall of scent hit her.

The wine looked black.

Splinters floating in it.

Say "Rise."

She opened her mouth, but no sound came out.

Say it he will hear

THAT CUNT FROM PARIS IS IN THE CELLAR WITH HIM

Hurry

"Rise," she whispered.

Nothing.

At first.
Then a ripple.
Nothing.
Another ripple.
Then a white finger.
The hand followed it.
Pinkish-white, waxy, shocking beneath its splendid rings.
She took it in hers.
God don't let it come apart in my hand I can't take it I can't
It squeezed.

That night in August. He could not sleep. The braziers on either side of him lit his bedroom with a fierce light, illuminating the curls and spirals of the fresco of the oak tree that embraced all four walls. Squirrels and birds perched there, and acorns, all on the slender branches that looped over a frescoed sky of the rarest blue. Pierre Roger, known as Clement, was sweating in his silk sleeping-gown, the cord of his sleeping cap wet beneath his chin. He called for Luquin, his cubicular, to bring him a little watered wine. The young man, an angelic blond from Bordeaux, had been charged by Maître de Chauliac not only to keep the braziers hot enough so fire might be seen (this to keep the Holy Father free of plague), no matter how uncomfortable the heat, but also, and more urgently, to watch that neither coverlet nor pillow should be pushed by sleeping hand or knee into the flame.

This was the hottest night since the fires had been prescribed. Clement felt he was suffocating and said as much, but then said, "Yet I withdraw my complaint; it is not for you to choose between love for me or fidelity to my good doctor's instruction. Is it, Luquin?"

"My first loyalty is to you."

"And mine is to God, whom I serve through ministering to his flock. And whom the doctor serves through ministering to me. It will not do for me to defy God's purpose by thwarting another of his servants, will it, Luquin?"

"Yet it seems to me, Holy Father, that by this argument no two Christians might honestly disagree. Could God not be served in different ways by men with different minds?" the young man said, wiping sweat from his face with his sleeve.

"Ah. Not wholly unsound. But your discomfort skews your argument, for you want the fires out. The maître's métier is fighting illness, a field in which I am ignorant; humility demands submission to those who know best. Keep the fires lit. I will go and nap in the room of the stag until I can stand to return."

His feet probed for the floor. Luquin rushed to bring his slippers, but he waved the young man off.

"The tiles are cooler than the air. My feet shall be grateful to feel them."

Clement shuffled through the stone connecting room with its staircase and then into his private study, fitted out with a small second bed for when he tired of the grand, canopied one in the bedroom. The walls of this room gave it its name, for its frescoes sang the glories of the hunt, not only of the stag, but of all manner of game; a man in parti-colored clothes let loose a ferret on a rabbit. Fishermen dangled nets over an embarrassment of fish. A naughty-looking boy took birds at the top of a tree. Some had grumbled that the pope should look upon scenes from Scripture rather than the delights of hunting and bathing and birding, but he had said, "God made earthly pleasures, too, which may be enjoyed without sin. Shall I affront Him with pride by thinking myself above them?"

Céleste was waiting for him.

Clothed modestly, as she always was, so that they might more easily separate and look guiltless at the sound of the far door opening. Might not a young woman privately visit her uncle by marriage to discuss a matter of Christian law? And as for sounds of pleasure, castle walls treat the ears capriciously. Do you know what you risk with this accusation? Are you very, very sure?

The entrance from the bedroom was safe; Luquin knew never to enter the room of the stag, and he was not so dull as not to know why. "They call it the room of the stag because that is where His Holiness mounts horns on his nephew's head," as he told his friend, the second falconer, and other friends besides.

When, with one warm, backward glance, Céleste slipped barefoot down the stairs between the rooms, her kirtle smoothed (if damp), her question of Christian law duly answered, Clement lay back on the bed, enjoying the air coming in through the window. Not cool, perhaps, but mild. A breeze from paradise itself compared with the furnace raging in his bedroom.

Sleep would come now.

It began to, at least.

At first he wove a nightmare for himself. Four soldiers of low rank and rust were on the verge of raping a girl in a barn. A donkey hung half-eaten from the roof.

Flies everywhere.

He woke.

The sound of high, girlish laughter had awakened him.

But whose?

And what a dream!

Guilt for his carnal sin, no doubt, the four soldiers Matthew, Mark, Luke, and John teaching him the grotesquery of his adultery with his niece by marriage. And the ass from Bethlehem or Palm Sunday, too.

He exhaled, considered returning to his proper bed.

No.

Cooler here.

Poor Luquin sweating in there, but he'll sneak out soon enough.

He closed his eyes again.

He slipped into a pleasant dream of children laughing.

What children?

Oh.

Those.

The tittering came from the wall next to him, where four boyish girls or girlish boys played and cooled their plump feet in frescoed waters. Not his favorite part of the painting, easy to overlook.

He had never really seen them before, these puti, *as they appeared to him in this nascent dream.*

So vivid and so happy.

He liked them very much.

That youth's endless pleasures must end had not occurred to the bathers, and he felt now that they were right. He saw, in the nave of his mind, one of them look at him with the shared, secret wisdom of immortality. Out of the corner of the eye, as befit the sly nature of the secret. He or she drew his or her feet out of the stream and stood on the bed next to Clement. The weight of the painted child was real somehow, somehow pressed down the bed.

More tittering.

Those watching from the wall.

Now that cherubic face bent to his, and he smiled in his half sleep, but the child's hand took his cheeks and made him soften his mouth, the better to receive the kiss. And what a kiss. It was spearmint and fennel, it was brandied and onioned and wild, it was water and the mark water leaves when it retreats from sand.

Céleste, he wanted to say, both her name and how this kiss tasted, celestial, an earthly pleasure upside down with its feet hung in stars.

But he could not speak, for he could not breathe.

This became urgent.

He pushed the bather's face away, and the boy-girl shrugged and returned to its fellows, one of whom bent to kiss it even more intimately.

Clement woke, gasping for air.

He looked and saw the fresco, which lay as it had been made, motionless save for the guttering of the candle that illumined it, and mute.

His lips tingled, though.

What of that?

"Céleste?" he said.

Nothing.

Only the sound of a fly.

He looked at the painting again and saw that he had been mis-

taken; it was not as it had been. He counted three children, not four.

He put his hand on the bed next to him and found it wet, whether from the loins of his niece or the feet of the bather he was unsure.

Enough of this.

He would return to his canopied bed and to the companionship of his cubicular.

He got to his feet in the shimmering near-darkness, and felt water under them.

As if something had dripped across the floor.

He took another step, but instinct slowed this one.

He nearly started out of his skin to see it standing near the doorway.

A child, neither boy nor girl but both, its skin pale.

Its feet wet.

It put a finger to its lips, but the man was too frightened to speak.

It pointed at the candle, which went out, though moonlight still lit the room enough for him to see it walking toward him.

Pierre Roger went to cross himself, but his arm cramped and froze in the third position, the useless claw of his right hand stuck to his left breast.

He backed up away from the boy-girl until his legs bumped against the frame of his bed.

The sound of a dog licking.

He half-turned to see one of the bathers on all fours, spiderlike, lapping at the love-stain on the sheet.

He inhaled a gasp of air, but another child, standing on the bed behind him, stoppered his mouth with a cool hand, aborting his shout in a spasm.

They pulled him down on the bed.

The one who had kissed him straddled him now, fluidly but with a boulder's weight.

Can God make something He can't lift? *its black eyes asked him.*

Now its arm down his throat, tearing his mouth.

He could not breathe.
He did not breathe again.

Until.

He sat up from his from his bath.

A small hand held his.

He could not see, and then he could, only shapes at first but his eyes were clearing. He could not tell who had his hand.

He needed to breathe out but could not.

His lungs were heavy and full.

He tried twice before he managed to empty them.

The dead man sat up.

He expressed thick, dark wine from his nose and mouth.

Delphine wrinkled her nose in disgust as it washed over her feet where she crouched on the neighboring barrel, but she did not let him go. His skin had the consistency of roseate wax; yes, he was a giant wax doll who had been held too close to a fire so that the features sagged and melted just a bit. She had to get him out of the barrel.

God, the stink.

The wine had covered it, sealed it.

But no more.

She felt ill.

Hurry.

She pulled, afraid that his arm would come off, but, though it did not, he was too heavy for her to lift alone.

She tried again, feeling more strength in her, and nearly got him out. He lifted his head and blinked what was left of his eyes at her. Then his eyes became whole. His features shifted and tightened.

He saw her for the first time.

Terror filled his eyes; not terror of her, but of what he had seen before.

She pulled again, with all her might, and this time he helped her. He clambered out in a great rush of wine, kneeing his way to the barrel next to her.

He covered his nakedness and shuddered, his mouth open, drool coming from it, but it was a living mouth now.

His teeth were purple.

When he spoke, he panted between words.

"I. Was. In Hell."

"You still are."

"Are. You. An angel?"

"No. But there's one here. And more are coming."

"Good," he said, crying, looking like a pale, adult toddler. "That's good."

"Maybe we won't think so. The war is coming with them."

PART V

The Lord made answer.

THIRTY-NINE

Of the Gemini, and of the Unmasking

J acquot squinted his eyes, waiting for the smoke from the pope's twin braziers to drift in another direction. His post as papal guard would not allow him to rest his loaded crossbow, nor could he wipe his tearing eyes. Neither could he fetch the untouched quail that mocked him from the plate of the new bugger cardinal just in front of him, despite its tempting crust of herbs and his desperately rumbling stomach.

Fuck off, smoke.

The smoke persisted.

He fought the urge to turn his head away, fearing to draw attention to himself. His duty was to remain still. Thus far, his duty was proving indistinguishable from that of a pillar.

He had not worn the crossed-key insignia of the guard for very long; it was less than two weeks since he rode into Avignon with the troop of Breton archers that had pulled him from his Norman tree, all of them slavering for Jerusalem gold and the absolution that going on crusade would bring. Yet his ability to quarrel a crabapple off a stump at thirty yards had so impressed the quartermaster that the captain of the guard had sent for him.

Now this.

Cunting, cunting smoke.

He had just wondered for the fortieth time how much longer this goddamned feast could last when he heard a gasp go up from the crowd. Several pointing fingers jabbed toward the rear of the courtyard, and the cardinals turned to look as well. Now the other guards looked, so Jacquot did as well.

What he saw bewildered him.

A second pope had entered the courtyard; Jacquot's watery eyes were unsure, but this pope seemed a perfect twin to the one who sat before him, save for his white robes and miter. A troop of soldiers in cross-key tabards, the captain of the guard among them, marched at this white pope's side. His right hand held a crosier and a peasant girl held his left.

The seated pope, wearing ruby-littered robes of burnt orange and a miter with three crowns of gold, looked right at his *geminus* but remained seated. The guards around the nearer pope, like him, were all new recruits culled from those who had drifted south, and none of them had the first idea what to make of this.

The men near the pope in white had their gazes fixed. They had been prepared for what they would see. Most of those were veterans of the palace, kept farther away from His Holiness these last months, but now standing together near the pretender.

Sweet Christ there's going to be a fight and fuck this fucking smoke.

He stepped back out of the smoke's path and wiped his eyes in case he had to shoot.

"False pope!" the pope in white shouted, his voice echoing off the walls in the Courtyard of Honor. "You know you are a devil! Show your true form or depart!"

Now the near pope stood, his eyes wide, pointing at the other.

"A devil in white cries devil at your Father! Lord protect us!" he shouted, but his fear seemed false.

"Tell them what lord you mean," said the little girl. Her voice seemed familiar to Jacquot. He wanted to wipe his eyes again to get a better look at her, but now the knight who had lately accompanied the pope and all but taken over the duties of the captain of the guard, a harsh seigneur with a leonine face and black teeth, growled, "Crossbows ready."

Jacquot raised his weapon.

The bugger cardinal, his upper lip dewed with sweat, turned on his bench and looked first at Jacquot and then at his crossbow, where his trigger hand partly obscured the ivory inlay picturing the Last Supper.

"No worries, Your Eminence," he said, knowing that a wink from his drooping eye was unlikely to inspire confidence but giving the young cardinal one anyway. He had found that steadying others steadied himself.

Peering from beneath his lowered hood, Thomas saw that the true pope had entered the courtyard of honor. All eyes had turned that way. The knight in friar's robes did not breathe like a bull before his charge, but silently readied his sword, curling his body around it to hide it from the poor of Avignon jostling around him.

He must slide it from its sheath and leap the first table in one motion.

He must be upon the higher table before they saw him.

He must kill the false pope before they could react.

He must surprise them.

At least two at the upper table were devils.

Now, he thought.

The sword leapt from its sheath and he leapt upon the first table, kicking a plate of dark bread aside.

The lion-faced knight turned, faster than Thomas had hoped, his axe already out. Recognition flashed in his little black eyes; he did not alert the others—he wanted to handle this himself.

YOU FUCKING THIEF YOU WANT DEATH AND HERE IT COMES

The devil-knight leapt upon the cardinal's table, just where Thomas had planned to jump. It squatted and slashed with its axe, but Thomas ducked and turned so it bit through his habit and glanced off his backplate, continuing his turn so the point of his sword wheeled around and into the lion-knight's face. It continued through the back of the head. The stabbed knight screamed, but it was also a roar.

Thomas yanked out his sword.

The impossible gash in the thing's head smoked.

It staggered back from the table, shaking furiously, like a wet dog.

It was growing larger, popping its armor.

Screams from the courtyard behind him.

Cardinals struggled to stand up, but some were too paralyzed with fear to move and weighed the shared benches down.

"Shoot him!" the new cardinal screamed, pointing at Thomas.

Now a crossbowman stepped forward.

Cheeked his weapon and triggered it with a flat but potent *whack* audible even through the chaos of crowd and devils.

The bolt shot true.

It struck Thomas in the chest, and he staggered back, stunned.

His cowl fell away.

Another bolt flew from farther down the table; this one clipped his neck, but got no cords.

The first one, though.

He looked down at the goose-feather fletching where the quarrel stood from the dimple in the comte's armor, the dimple Thomas's final axe-blow had made in their fight by the stream. It would have clanked off otherwise, for such was the art of the Milanese at curving and hammering their armor.

Dead dead I'm dead now

"Thomas!" the crossbowman said desperately. "I've killed you!"

Thomas saw his drooping eye.

"Jacquot?"

"Jesus Christ, forgive me," Jacquot said.

The old cardinal near him disliked his words so much he unhinged his jaw and bit Jacquot's face, dragging the skin from it and leaving his lidless eyes staring in disbelief.

Blood all over the young cardinal, his silk gloves.

Jacquot fell.

Thomas did not fall, though he expected to.

Through the bone the point tickling the heart I feel it

Panic in the courtyard.

It seemed everyone shouted or screamed at once.

People fled, running for the gates.

I can't I can't I can't

Thomas gathered strength in his mighty thighs and leapt up on the cardinals' table. Cardinal Cyriac grew larger. Blood on his face like a dog at the stag. Growing new eyes. Growing bird's legs beneath his robes.

Thomas ran past this monstrosity and made for the pope.

The thing that had been Cardinal Cyriac reached for him with one of its hands, snagging the sleeve of his left hand.

He turned and lopped the hand from it.

It screamed in rage.

The girl's blood hurt it.

Three more loping steps to the pope's cathedra.

Almost there.

The pontiff in orange stood with his hands out, magnificent, smiling.

Thomas's legs pumped.

Something awful behind him, the smell of sour milk and burning.

If he stopped, if he slowed, it would break his neck from behind.

The smoke from the braziers in his eyes.

ARE YOU SURE?

Yes.

Are you?

His sword fell and struck the pope's miter, cleaving the three crowns, and cleaving the head.

The crowd screamed in outrage.

His sword went all the way to the chin and the man's eyes rolled back white and dead, the wound smoking. The arms, though. One of them (not an arm so much as a fly's limb) grabbed the sword by the blade and yanked it. It spun in the air and away, over the walls of the courtyard. Thomas saw it for an instant, moonlight on it.

You'll never hold a sword again

Another head was growing from where the first one had split.

A wicked seraph.

A fly's head, but golden.

Baal'Zebuth.

One of the fallen.

A biting fly.

Shrieks of fear and horror.

The spear!

He pulled the spear out of its sheath.

The thing that had been the pope slapped him now with the arm that was still a man's arm.

Not in the face.

In the chest.

It hurt.

The peeled head smiled in its two halves.

Dizzy.

Into my heart!!! but i can still do this i can still

He blew out of his nose, bloody now.

This is what i'm for i do this i drive it home i'm strong strong please

He hammered down the spear in his fist with all his might, his hips in it.

It moved so fast.

It was as though it wavered in the air.

He missed.

Then something irresistible grabbed his arm.

Jerked it behind him, the pain dazzling.

Ripped it off.

His arm off still gripping the spearhead.

He looked around and saw it.

The other devil had it.

The lionish one, his wound almost gone.

i never had a chance did i

DO YOU KNOW WHAT WE ARE

ONLY ONE IS OLDER

ONLY ONE IS STRONGER

AND HE HAS LEFT YOU TO US

I'LL SHOW YOU

YOUR HEART HAS TWELVE BEATS LEFT

TRY TO LIVE LONG ENOUGH TO WATCH THIS

Delphine saw Thomas run for the false pope and her hands went to her mouth. She wanted to run toward him, help him, save him, but she knew she would never reach him. Could not stand against them. She kept her place near Pope Clement, holding his hand to strengthen him. He was shaking, but he did not run.

Delphine screamed with hope and joy when she saw her Thomas cleave the wicked one's head,

So strong he's so strong

but the nature of her scream changed as the thing in the orange robes changed. She screamed Thomas's name over and over again and fell to her knees watching his arm ripped from him, watching him fall on the table like a pile of laundry, then roll onto the flagstones.

Dead.

She screamed, "*NO!*"

She screamed, "*PLEASE!*"

They came.

She begged her Father in Heaven in Latin, then in Hebrew, then in Aramaic to stop them, but they came.

Six wings, six wings, and two wings.

Twelve-eyed thing, Fly-headed-thing, Lion-thing.

Tall enough now to look in second-floor windows.

They stank and a noise came from them, and heat.

Everything they walked past or over began to smolder.

They were coming toward her, toward Clement. One latched onto the brickwork of the palace and flung it over on a group of knights who had moved forward to fight, finishing some of them; the devils waded into the remainder, throwing them aside, treading on them, killing them like blind puppies.

Getting closer.

Clement's shield bearers began to fall away and run.

Not Delphine.

The twelve-eyed one, its mouth an O of fire, held its regrown hand over a dead man clutching a spear; the corpse jerked to his feet, his head lolling on a broken neck and his tongue out. The dead man now convulsed and threw his spear where the devil pointed.

At Clement.

The throw was true, but Delphine threw herself in front of it.

It went through her, into her abdomen, through her viscera, out the other side.

The worst pain she had ever felt.

Behind her, men grabbed the pope and ran with him for the palace.

She fell, bleeding so fast she could hear it spatter.

The twelve-eyed one picked the dying girl up by one arm like a poppet while the other two came near.

Careful not to get her blood on it.

The moon, blood red over them, wheeled madly as she dangled.

God, the stink of them.

Those twelve eyes drilling into her face.

The fiery hole singeing her hair, her gown, blistering her face.

WHAT ARE YOU WE'LL FIND OUT NOW

For the first time she knew the answer.

She smiled.

She looked sleepily at it, almost gone.

You know what I am.

OH.

THAT.

The lion-faced one used the knight's arm like a pick.

The fist still holding the spear.

THEN YOU SHOULD REMEMBER THIS.

It whipped the knight's arm, driving the spear into her side.

She clenched her teeth, still smiling.

It bit her legs off and flung her into the middle of the courtyard.

And she died.

FORTY

Of the Coming of the Host

Robert Hanicotte shook his head.
His mind was going.
His silk gloves were spattered with blood.

He crawled under the tables and ran for the gates, but he found himself pushed back as those who had tried to get out the gates now flooded back in.

An abomination chasing them.

So that's what was in the Jewish quarter.

A surge of corpses squeezed into the courtyard, not separately; they moved as one thing. Once inside, it re-formed itself. Four legs, or three, at its pleasure, composed entirely of stacked corpses. It moved around the courtyard gathering up fleeing people with its horrid mouth. It was fast. Human ribs as teeth. A light in the middle of it its sentience. When the bodies that formed the ends of its legs wore out, it left them behind and newer ones moved down, upside down, their arms clutching at whatever it wanted clutched at, their backs and chests taking its weight, unmindful of their broken necks. It fed found bodies into itself, or killed living ones. All manner of dead seethed in its frame; Jews and Christians, soldiers and midwives, the clothed and the nude; even a woman with a stag's head turned in the top of a limb, waiting her turn to be moved to the end to clutch at others and bear weight.

Robert's screaming turned into laughter.

Oh this is good this is really good Hell is here and here is its cavalry!

Off to his left, devils the size of towers killed soldiers.

He would almost prefer to face them than this living desecration.

No. I must run! I must live!

He ran with others, trying to get into the chapel, but the door was barred. Stone angels and devils looked impassively from the arch.

He was pressed in, smothering.

He turned to see where it was.

It stood alone in the courtyard, near what remained of the girl. The girl from the vineyards. She really was holy, then.

It picked her up, meaning to assimilate her.

That was a mistake.

Her goodness was lethal to it.

As soon as its inverted limb-corpses wrapped the nubs of their arms around her, those corpses fell away, as did all the others in that limb.

It was unraveling.

The light in the middle of it went out.

It toppled, gratefully.

Its dead all sighed at once, released.

Just another pile of dead in a dying world God had left behind.

And then.

And then.

A light came from the girl.

It shone into the sky, up and up, as warm and heartbreaking as the first finger of dawn.

She split down the middle and the light got bigger.

A wing came from her.

It was not hers.

It came *through* her.

An angel of God was born into the world.

Her blood on its wing.

The devils tried to stop it. They screamed their mind-killing scream, they flung blocks of rubble that would have sunk warships at it. They closed with it, the three of them, biting and lashing, desperate to block the gate by killing it.

They could not.

The glowing one absorbed their blows, but did not strike back at them.

It did wrestle them back, though, to make room for the others.

It was one of the strongest.

Zephon

Muscled and without need of muscle, ancient and exuberantly youthful, full again of the heat of stars and the patience of pushing mountains.

It shone its warm, moonish light all over the courtyard.

The horrid noise that broke minds was itself broken.

Another came.

Uriel

Its name in Robert's head as beautiful as a lost lover's name.

The light in the courtyard of honor redoubled.

Tripled as another birthed itself through the girl's ruined body.

And another.

And another.

The most perfect one yet, larger than the others and bearing a sword too bright to look at, a shard of the sun, now flew up and perched on the tower of the angels, the tower topped with a chapel.

The chapel named for it.

St. Michel

Robert could not see it where it landed, but he saw it fly brilliantly past on white eagle's wings the size of sails, prisms in its wake, prisms of new colors that made the old ones look gray.

Michael I'm seeing the archangel Michael.

It sang from its place on the roof, and it was the most beautiful thing Robert had ever heard. Now those who had survived in the courtyard made a noise of relief and thanks, a hoarse shout that lay beyond the power of words to contain. Some clasped hands and knelt, crying; some embraced one another.

And still the angels came, a host of them.

Their light casting wild shadows.

And yet the people were not safe.

The Archangel Michael, breaker of Lucifer's back, swooped down at the lion-faced devil, who feared it so that he flew blindly into the top floor of the great chapel, toppling the building and its wall on those pressed against its door.

On Robert Hanicotte.

Darkness and pressure.

The uncompromising weight of stone.

A noise like a squeal escaped him.

This was it.

Something had his hair.

A hand squeezed his as his life left him.

He thought it was Matthieu's.

I'm sorry, Robert-of-the-bushes.

I'm sorry.

The light of them was so bright it made a wildly careening amber day of sorts all over the city. Maître de Chauliac watched what he could of it from the windows of the pope's study, the pope himself raving that this was his fault, ordering his ermines burned. Ha! Who could carry all of them, enough of them to carpet the palace, and what would they be burned with? The candles, hearth, and brazier were out, so the men and women in this room huddled together in panting near-darkness, striped at times by lights from outside swinging as though on pendulums. The doctor ordered his men to keep the pontiff here, in this smallish room in the Tower of Angels. The singing from the roof had given him the idea that it, at least, might not fall.

A horrible noise came from the direction of Villeneuve, across the river. He could not see from his angle, and he was glad. He looked out the window, trying to control his breathing.

The spectacle he beheld was less a battle after all, and more an ineluctable pushing back of darkness, the habit of the sun, the birthright of light. More devils came, streaking down like stones on fire, trying to hold this earthly redoubt since the war in Heaven had soured. In their anger and impotence, they ruined the cities of Avignon, Villeneuve, and Carpentras, and killed men in the thousands, but their position against the angels was hopeless. They raged and bit at beings so calm, beautiful, and deliberate that it seemed they and the devils occupied two entirely different realities. One scene stayed with de Chauliac forever, obsessing him, even though, mercifully, the rest would blur; he saw a devil with wide black wings gripped by two angels, who drove it down and seemed to speak in its ears as they fell; they hit the bend of the Rhône, sending up a great, illuminated plume of water visible from Orange.

Two angels and a devil had tumbled into the water.

Three angels came up.

Forgiveness, then, was possible even for the worst.

FORTY-ONE

Of the Knight's Death, and of the Judgment

T homas went to his knees. The world swam with black. He knew he was dying, that unmooring feeling came again, and still he tried to see where the girl was, if she was safe. He could not see past the devils, their wings fanned out behind them, though he knew they were killing. Making more like him. Dead men. Ruined bodies. His vision failed him and a curtain of blackness fell; he felt the bricks of the court-yard flat beneath him now, his face on them. Cold. He smelled the stink of the wicked angels, brutal and nauseating. He lis-tened for his heartbeat but heard only silence in his chest. His arm was off, that he remembered, but he could not feel any of his limbs. He had the impression that his stomach emptied it-self through his mouth, but he was not breathing, so he had no fear of choking. Then he felt his bowels and bladder voiding. Then he ejaculated, barely feeling it, his body's final, muted pleasure. Images and words came to him in an urgent jumble, inside his head but louder than the sound of shrill madness that rose up outside, a sound that he had heard before, but now it was distant, receding, unimportant.

That's how the poor bastards sing

He smiled at that, or thought he did, but he was beyond the power to move any part of himself, even the tiny muscles that pulled his mouth. His hearing winked out, leaving only thoughts.

Is this it?

When does even this stop?

Is this how it was for the ones I killed?

Something in him broke free, and he got his vision back. He saw himself as if from above in a spreading pool of blood. His eyes, which he had thought were closed, were not.

I'm old, he thought. *When did I get old?*

Blood in my white beard.

Vomit under it.

I'm ugly.

He wanted to touch his face but had nothing to touch it with.

He wanted to lift his vision to see what was happening in the courtyard, he wanted to see the girl.

YOU CAN FORGET THAT

YOU'RE OURS

And the courtyard melted away as if it had never been.

"They destroyed my body. God made it, not them, and they destroyed it. What right did they have?"

"You might have asked that question yourself. You've destroyed a body or two."

Thomas was a small boy now, looking up at something sickening to look at, but which he thought would not hurt him.

That's not its job

It's just a clerk

The room was small and dim, and he was not sure where the light came from: no sconce, no niche, no hearth, no window.

No door.

How will I get out?

Will I get out?

He was not as tall as the table. The other consulted a book and other documents, hobbling around the table on its ankles, its feet turned on their sides like a cripple's; it carried a stool upon which it sat every third or fourth step, clearly in pain. Thomas had to keep moving around to see it past the big table. It was as if it wanted to hide itself from him, as if it knew it was hideous, its eyes just holes in its gray, formless head, its skin blotched and moldy. So it shuffled painfully and kept the table between them, checking the book, checking parchments against one another; its arms had two elbows each, so it was hard to tell what it would reach for next.

A sort of fishy mouth opened in the middle of its chest.

"You really did try at the end. To do the right things, I mean. You nearly escaped. It was your bad luck to die before the retreat from Avignon, when they took all the souls with them, regardless of innocence or guilt. A betrayal of their agreement, of course, but so was attacking Heaven. I suppose the worst thing about this for you, worse than the question of whether I am lying, and I am not, though a liar would say as much, is a question of intent. Will I tell you the truth out of sympathy, because I was naturally sympathetic in life and this part of my damnation is to damn the undeserving; or because your sense of outrage at being unjustly damned will heighten your pain? Hell, like prison, is worse when you don't feel you earned it. Eventually, of course, that goes numb. And they find something that's still raw and they work on that, or they give you something back only to make you feel enough to scream when you lose it again. I've even heard them make men think they were being pardoned, or born into new earthly bodies, or rescued by God himself. They're really quite good at it. It's all they've had to do for a very long time. That, and make mockeries of beasts and men. You've seen one or two, I think."

"I think so," he said.

His voice a little boy's voice.

He looked at his hand.

A little boy's hand.

A polished mirror on the wall, a stone wall as in a castle, let him see himself.

His son.

He was his very young son, as he looked the last time Thomas had seen him.

He was scared.

With great difficulty, the thing moved close to him and sat on its stool. It smelled like the bottom of a well. It looked like it wanted to cry.

"Thomas de Givras," it said, looking down at him paternally, "I damn thee."

"Where ... where will I go?"

"Out."

"How?"

"Don't you think I'm tired of that question? Can't you think of me?"

"May I just stay here with you?"

"I'd like that," it said. "But they wouldn't. And I'm more frightened of them than you understand."

Someone yelled in another room, in another language, and then began to beg in that language.

Hell's first floor, he began to grasp, was begging.

An utter loss of dignity, if not hope.

Not yet.

"Please."

"Well ..."

"Please?"

"No."

Silence.

It just aimed at him with the holes it had for eyes.

"How ... how do I go, then? Since I must."

"Through me, of course."

"How?"

"You're a smart boy. How do you think?"

"I don't know."

A bell sounded, deep like a church bell.

The begging in the close room turned to screaming.

"I'm sorry. It's time."

So saying, it grabbed the boy by a skinny arm.

Mouths opened not just on its stomach, but in many places.

"No! *No!*"

It ate him.

It hurt.

This scene played out innumerable times, with every sort of variation, but always ending the same way. Each time, he tried to reason with it, or to fight it, or to otherwise avoid the excruciating finale. He told himself not to try, that the end was inevitable, but even after he resolved to give up, still he ran away from it, or tried to use the table to block it, or any other ploy he could devise, because it hurt just that much. At length, when he gave up trying and even speaking, the interaction shortened to nothing more than its reading off his name and sentence

Thomas de Givras, I damn thee

and then chewing him down alive.

He shivered and let it.

I damn thee

He cried and let it.

I damn thee

And then he just let it.

Eventually he even stopped yelling, and that was when they decided he was ready for something worse.

FORTY-TWO

Of the Harrowing

He forgot his name. How long he had been there stopped meaning anything. He went from one torment to another, starting with bodily pain and going on to heartbreak; he was skinned and then made to drag his skin behind him, then made to sew this skin back on himself, with the dirt and gravel it had picked up now under it; he was shredded slowly, crammed with thorns and made to eject them, crowded in with naked throngs and scalded, made to fight for cool water or a glimpse of sky, and when they saw that he liked fighting, they made him fight again and again for everything, for years, until even his rage was broken, and he wept and succumbed when confronted; he was murdered and betrayed by those he loved, and then made to murder and betray them, then desecrate them, cannibalize them, regurgitate them. Nothing was left out.

No weakness was overlooked.

For pride in his strength he was made a plaything. For his carnality he was rendered sexless.

He was made to live each oath he'd spoken, no matter how ridiculous, lapping Christ's wounds, drowned with Christ in shit, boiled in Mary's sour milk, sodomized by the cocks of the Apostles, until he had been stripped of his capacity for laughter, or even the capacity to disbelieve the outrageous. They took his humor from him not because they themselves were humorless—they most certainly were not—but because it so offended them that man had been given this, too.

Hell was mutable and hard, banal and shocking, painful and numbing, burning and frozen, but mostly it was real.

He had become the butt of every joke he told.

Hell was real.

He was back in Paris.

Île de la Cité.

He lay against a wall, bloated, fat, dead of plague but not dead. He could not move except to blink. He could not close his mouth, which stood painfully open. To his right, a stack of empty, broken wine barrels. Arrows lay near him, stuck in mud, or lying with their points broken off from having struck the wall behind him.

An arrow hissed down at him from a crenellated wall, punching an agonizing hole in his gut. It burned. He yelled through his gaping mouth.

"That's it, Phillipe!" a man said to his companion on the wall.

More arrows flew, some missing, most piercing him. The last one went in his tongue and through the back of his throat.

"I work better with obstacles."

He shrieked.

Then he saw the light.

Coming from farther down the street.

The light in this infernal Paris had been dim, as on a rainy day or just after sunset, but now a proper light was coming.

The guards on the wall looked at its source, then began firing their arrows at it. They lost the lie of their human shapes, tails snaking out behind them. More devils came, leveling cruel, barbed weapons. A wheel of sorts made entirely of severed arms and legs rolled up and formed itself into something worse, taking up arrows with which to stab whatever was coming.

But it never got to.

He could not believe what he saw.

But then it made perfect sense.

He remembered that day, before they met the wood-carver.

The cart.

The girl drove it.

He tried to remember her name.

That girl.

Who was she?

Then he remembered her name and just as quickly forced it from his thought. It was not a name to be remembered here. It was a name that would kill with sadness and failure.

The devils spat at her and leapt, but none could touch her, nor the mule, nor the cart; a dome of daylight as golden as if culled from the spring of one's twenty-first year surrounded the intruder, and no unclean thing could tread where it shone.

She descended now, ignoring the hail of missiles and threats falling around them both, but powerless to harm.

She walked toward him.

It was the she of the girl's dreamy eyes, the maker of the words she had spoken that were not her own.

The thing that had been Thomas croaked through its open mouth but could not speak. This was the meeting of their souls, then—his withered, hers in glory, hers somehow not just her.

He had never seen a sight that looked so beautiful; he had forgotten what beauty was.

Another betrayal
These are false shapes sent to bring memory
And memory is pain
The only truth here

He shut his eyes against them and waited for the next tortures to begin. He sensed her drawing warmly closer, kneeling before him.

The arrow in his mouth came out, painlessly.

She pulled the others out, too, each one a candle flame of misery, now extinguished.

He wept at the relief, the pure ecstasy of relief.

Her small hand lay across his eyes and it felt good.

Beyond good.

Her hand went to his chin and shut his agonized mouth.

They were so devious, so low to do this.

She whom he had loved as a daughter, and more than that, if that were possible, had come again to give him hope.

He grew angry.

This was the best illusion of her they had sent, but it was not the first. How many times had they sent her to beckon and then abandon him, how many times had his limbs refused his commands to stop as he choked the life from her or violated her or butchered her like a lamb?

He opened his eyes, and still she remained.

I SEE THROUGH YOU YOU CUNT

He spat in her face and she smiled.

I understand.

Go away.

Not without you, Thomas.

What did you call me?

Your name. Would you like to hear it again?

I'm not falling for it.

I'll wait.

Horrid things raged behind her, bit at her, yet none came within the light that pooled around her and around the cart. He watched her for a day and a night, or what seemed like it in this place where time had been beaten beyond recognition.

At once, everything shook.

The horrors around them stopped raging and turned to see.

A sextet of Hell's princes, each as tall as a castle's outer wall, came down through the roof, bearing the smoldering body of an angel beautiful beyond imagination, drooping as dead as a martyr in their arms as they gnashed their teeth and descended with him through the ground and to the deepest, safest, most secret vaults of Hell.

His (her?) pale skin.

His wings smoking like paper about to catch.

Lucifer is fallen.

Mammon is Lord here now.

At last she saw a kernel of trust come into Thomas's eyes.

Are you ready?

He nodded.

Barely perceptibly, but he nodded.

She blew into his hands to warm them back to life. She kissed his feet. She kissed his forehead.

She smelled of cedar and of the sea.

You're Him.

There is no him or her.

Why did you not come as I would know you?

I came as you would follow me. I came as you would love me in innocence.

Why me?

That question has never been answered to anyone's satisfaction. But you were the last one. The last one I could still save.

And yet this is Hell. I'm here.

Not for long.

I'm damned.

Not anymore.

Night lay behind her head, but true night, with stars in their proper places, and no comets to trouble them. He was in the cart. She looked down at him.

I want you to answer a question, Thomas.

Yes.

Do you want to remember?

His eyes welled with tears and he shook his head, his

mouth contorting to sob.

Not Hell. I mean me. Us.

You?

Her. Delphine.

I don't know. What are you?

I was two things together. Then one. Now two again, apart.

I don't understand.

You don't have to. You just have to say yes or no. But it will be harder for you if you remember. Love is always harder. Love means weathering blows for another's sake and not counting them. Love is loss of self, loss of other, and faith in the death of loss.

Those gray eyes.

Those gray eyes through every part of him, loving what was strong and what was weak indifferently.

Yes.

I say yes.

She got in the front of the cart and took up the reins.

The cart rolled down a road near the beach.

Night was harmless here.

Someplace warm.

Provence.

Galilee.

No place at all.

He saw the stars above him, and something passed before them.

A seagull.

Just a seagull.

He slept.

FORTY-THREE

Of October's End, and of November

Thomas became aware of his body again, became aware of pain. Breathing was difficult because of the weight jostling on top of him as the cart rolled, some fabric half-covering his nose and mouth. Wet. Everything was wet. The stink of day-old blood and the ejecta of death were everywhere. A dog barked. Two dogs. The cart stopped.

"Ready?" a man said.

A boy answered, "Yeah."

Provençal, but Thomas understood that much.

The language of ravens rasped out as well, obscure in vocabulary but clear in intent.

Feeding time.

Vertigo as the cart was tipped and Thomas tumbled with the others. A dead thumb in his eye. Bewildering daylight. Pain again as he landed on his shoulder and neck on a pile of wet bodies, one of which farted.

He grunted loudly.

Provençal again, but beyond him this time.

I thought the big one's arm was off.

It was, I saw it too. He was deader than hell. Another miracle.

What do we do?

Help him, idiot.

Now arms hooked under his and lifted him out of the pit of bodies.

He was afraid to move his tongue—some dream of an arrow in it—but he did move it at last.

"Thank you," he said.

"French?"

"Yes."

He recognized the boy.

From Elysium.

"Isnard?" he said.

"Yes, sir. How do you know me?"

I had a different face then!

"I don't know."

"Lots not to know about these days. Did you see the angels?"

"No."

"An army of them in the sky. The most beautiful things. And yet I hope I forget them, for they are awful, too."

The boy crossed himself.

Thomas grunted.

Angels had come.

The war in Heaven had turned.

"We found you in the ruins of the palace. Along with these. Earthquake."

Earthquake?

Was that what had happened?

No.

But it was what men could stand to remember.

Thomas got to his feet, painfully, dusting himself off.

The man took a sack from the cart and approached the pit.

"Isnard, have you seen a young girl?"

"Lots of them."

"Or the page. Have you seen the page that served the comte in the Elysium House? Your little friend?"

"Not since. No. Not in the earthquake. But there are many dead. The Holy Father asked the whole town to help, as well as the soldiers who had come for the crusade. It was worst in the Jewish quarter. And in Villeneuve."

"How bad was it?"

The boy lowered his eyes.

The man began spreading lye on the dead.

Villeneuve had fallen into the river. And the river had diverted through Avignon. The city walls on the west side had crumbled, as had half the palace. Thomas looked for the girl, asked about her; nobody knew a thing. He returned to the Franciscan abbey, and the Alsatian told him the girl had not come back, but that his horse was waiting for him.

He took Jibreel into town; it was not easy to persuade a warhorse to pull a cart, but Thomas had a way with horses, he always had. He hitched Jibreel up with a team whose job it was to move the heaviest beams so that he and others might look for the living among the dead. He worked near the palace, hoping to see her walking, hoping not to see her under the litter of tiles and the nonsense of limestone bricks and tapestries. He became increasingly certain he would not.

Among the dead were three cardinals, one of them Hanicotte, the priest's brother, newly minted the night before.

Was it just last night?

So much happened since then.

But what?

Cardinal Hanicotte had been crushed near the entrance to the chapel, where many had tried to hide, his robes and fine gloves matted with blood. One of many, alike in death, wedded together under the stone angels and devils that had arched over the door.

But Hanicotte was at the center.

A stone devil had him by the hair.

A stone saint had him by the hand.

Thomas slept in a field with other workers.

He ate food from the *pignotte.*

He threw his coat of mail in the river and worked in the simple hose and long shirt of a laborer.

He looked everywhere for the girl, asked everyone twice, but nobody had seen her since that night, the events of which had dulled in all men's memories but his; he asked soldiers he had seen standing near His Holiness in the Courtyard of Honor, just as he confronted his false double. She had been with them then, they remembered her, but no one could say what became of her.

He thought about seeking an audience with the pope himself, but his station was so low and the pontiff had so many cares now.

He saw the Holy Father several times, blessing the dead, his breath steaming in the cold October air. This Clement was not the same man who had lorded over the feast in the Grand Tinel and called forth the dead stags. This pope radiated benevolence, and his smile now began in his heart, not on his face. He gave an address in front of St. Peter's asking all men to pray for God's mercy, and for a swift rebuilding. He said he had been in the grips of a long fever and begged their forgiveness for his folly. There would be no crusade in this time of pestilence, when seigneurs were needed in their demesnes. There would be no pogrom against the Jews, and any who harmed a child of Israel would be cut off from the salve of the church. The pope had already commanded de Chauliac, his faithful doctor, to marshal other doctors, Christians and Jews together, who were putting right a forest of broken bones and stitching the howls of countless lacerations into grim consonants.

On Thomas's last day in Avignon, he found his sword.

It had fallen in a gutter and broken.

He looked at the blade, the notches in it, trying to remember where the deepest ones had come from. Blurry images of brigandage and war came to him, but he did not try to sharpen them. He let them fall away. Thomas pressed his lips to the ruined blade, not in fondness for the harm it had done, but for the trace of the girl's blood which still remained on it. After a long crouch, he left it where it lay; some peddler would find it and sell it for scrap, all of it; blade, quillons, tang, pommel, the wooden handle and the deerskin wrap.

He hoped he would prove so useful.

He wandered north.

November came.

The plague left France for England.

Thomas sold his labor where he could; he turned down an offer to serve with a seigneur's guard, saying he had no sword and wanted none. Instead, he sold these men his horse and went to the fields, where working men, so scarce now, could come and go as they pleased, and sell their sweat dearly.

Money was lord here now.

Most were heading south for climate's sake, but he would go where the fewest laborers were.

And, eventually, he would go home.

He learned farming, making up in strength what he lacked in knowledge. But then he gained knowledge, too. He made friends.

Three of these came with him to Normandy.

She saw the four men in their rags and aprons coming down the road, bearing tools and sacks. When the rain came, they went to her barn to shelter. They could be forgiven for thinking her land deserted; the field was wild, and all the farms for miles around were silent. It had fallen on this part of Normandy in the summer, taking first her mother and then her sweet father. That was the last she remembered.

She had awakened in her tree this morning, bitterly cold.

It was August no more.

Her father still lay on the bed where he lost his struggle with the plague, but now skeletal, long dead. Where the months had gone was beyond her understanding.

She was hungry.

The clay and wicker beehives were burned.

Two pots of honey were all she had.

And Parsnip, heehawing by the willow tree.

She had to decide whether to seek her father's people in the south, though she did not know where to look beyond the name of a village, or whether to stay here and try to get through the winter alone.

But she knew what she had to do first.

She had to approach the strangers.

Her father had spoken with the neighbors in the spring, saying it was likely brigands would come, men who were once soldiers, but who now lived by robbery.

The men in the barn were none of these.

Just peasants.

She poked her head around the door.

"Hello," she said.

"Hello yourself," said the plumpest of them, amiably.

The tallest of them, a strong-looking fellow with long hair and a nearly white beard, had blanched pale at the sight of her. He looked familiar to her, as though she had dreamed of him.

"I need help burying my father," she said.

The tall one stared at her and cried, trying to hide it.

The plump one said they would help, and they did.

When the work was done, they made a fire in the barn and shared roasted chestnuts with her. They were warm and good.

In the morning, she left with them, riding her donkey as they walked around her.

The tall one walked nearest.

The one with the dark hair, just graying.

He wore a wide straw hat with a spoon through it.

She liked him very much.

It would be too bold to ask him on only a day's acquaintance, but she prayed for some sign that she could trust him;

her dearest and wildest hope was that this man would be a second father to her. She would need one.

He was not a learned man, as her father had been, but goodness shone from him as from an unseen sun.

"What is your name, good sir?" she said.

"Thomas. And not a 'sir.'"

"May I ask where you come from?"

He turned a mirthful eye to her.

"A town."

"Yes, but what is the town called?"

"Town."

"No town is called town."

"Mine is. Townville-sur- . . . Town."

She laughed.

"Is it near a mountain, this town?"

"Givras," he said. "I am from Givras."

"Which rhymes with Thomas. Would you like to know my name?" she said.

"I already do."

She smiled impishly.

She liked games.

"Then tell me."

He bent toward her.

This would be a secret.

Little Moon.

EPILOGUE

The old friar mounted the road leading up to the tower's gate. The guard called for and received permission to let him pass.

"The kitchens are that way," he pointed, but the friar didn't look up for directions. He just nodded at him and thanked him, making his way painfully around the west side of the keep, where a young boy in fine clothes waved a wooden sword at him. The friar mocked fear for the boy, making him giggle and gallop closer, pressing his attack.

"We don't charge at men of God," said a young nobleman. The lord of the castle, a minor seigneur. A big man, broad through the chest, fearsome in aspect, yet shod in the fashionable long-toed *poulaines* that had become the object of ridicule for older knights and a frequent subject of sermons. Perhaps he expected to receive one from the friar; his verdant gaze was wary, dismissive. Or perhaps he feared the itinerant might carry more than a begging bowl; the plague had returned, though not in its former strength. Only the lumps, not the blood-coughing. Villages were tithing a tenth of their number, not two-thirds, but the tenth it chose was especially hard. Some were already calling this the children's plague. Carpenters all over France had grown skilled at making small coffins.

"The door's there. Marie will fill your bowl. Prayers are

welcome, but keep them short. And don't touch anything."

The friar waved that he understood and went to the kitchen.

Marie, a youngish, formless woman with teeth in only half her mouth, filled the friar's bowl with soft turnips and leeks. She also filled his battered pewter mug with beer. She had seen him before, in town, though he had never come to the castle. She had seen him once, smiling a little through another friar's sermon about Hell, saying after the other left that fear of Hell is one of many paths to it. Forget Hell and love one another. That is all He wants of you.

He was the only friar she had seen who meant the things he said.

"I'm expecting," she said. "A prayer for the baby? And for the little ones at home?"

She placed his huge hand on her belly.

He smiled, then granted her a warm benediction.

"Father?" a chamber woman said from the kitchen door.

"Yes?"

"The lady of the house, my lord's mother, craves a word."

The friar blushed.

"She lives, then?"

The chamber woman laughed, then spoke low.

"Of course she lives! The reaper fears to bend his scythe on Lady Marguerite."

He closed his eyes and nodded.

"Of course."

The stairs were hard for him, but he followed his guide faithfully.

"Are you well, Father?"

"Ah. Yes. The injuries of spring are forgotten in the summer, but remembered in the winter."

She looked back at him, noting again the pit in his cheek. Injuries, indeed. Probably an old soldier. He had the size, even if old age had stooped him.

The lady waited in her parlor, an open book next to her, yet the old woman had the eyes of the blind. An impression in a near cushion told the friar the chamber woman had been reading to her.

She did not see him duck just a little to enter the room.

Not with those milk-white eyes with just a hint of green.

"Leave us, Jacqueline," she commanded.

The chamber woman left.

The friar entered the room alone. His nostrils flared as he filled his nose with familiar scents, bergamot chief among them. He glanced at the far door, which led to the bedchamber.

Now he looked at her.

"You wanted to speak with me, my lady?"

She tilted her head at the sound of his voice.

"I always ask those of Saint Francis's order to come to me. Although I myself have fallen short of Christ's example, I believe the cordeliers approach it quite closely. So I fill your bellies and solicit your prayers."

"My prayers are no better than yours, though I will lend them as you ask."

He waited. Her hands clenched gently in her lap, as though she wanted rosary beads, or a quill pen, or dice.

At length, she spoke.

"I do not want my grandson dead of this scourge."

"I will pray for his safety."

Silence.

"Would you like at least to know his name?"

"If you wish me to know it."

She told him.

"His father, my son, spoke rudely to you in the tiltyard. I will inform him of my displeasure."

"I did not find him rude, my lady."

"Then your hearing is not as good as mine. He is not so wise or kind as he is brave. His voice is harsh, like his father's before him. Did you know the lord of this place? My late husband?"

That head tilt.

The friar smiled.

"Scarcely. I knew the man's face, but little more."

Now the lady smiled.

"You have a kind voice, Father. Were you married, before you took orders?"

"Yes."

"And your lady wife?"

Silence.

"She has gone to her reward."

"Ah."

Though the eyes were blind, they kept the habit of looking down.

She spoke again.

"Did you have children?"

The old man fidgeted.

Now his hands wanted something.

"A daughter. She lives. We were farmers, and worked where we could. I planned to follow Saint Francis after I saw her wed, but she, too, wed the church. We took orders the same month."

Silence.

"Will you stay tonight, Father? I keep a comfortable room for men of God. You may pray unmolested."

"I am yours to command, though I am on my way to see her. My daughter. I visit her at her convent in Amiens each month, as I can, and I do not wish to be late."

"Then go in peace. She is lucky. To have such a father, I mean."

"Do you believe in luck, my lady?"

"The dart of the Implacable One struck your wife and my husband, and spared my son and your daughter. What divides the four?"

"God's will."

"And if God's mind is unknowable, how does His will differ from luck?"

"It is a question of faith. When I pray for the boy, shall I pray for luck?"

"I am a careful woman. I will pray for luck. You, good Father, pray for God's benevolence. Between the two of us, perhaps the boy will live."

"We are at common purpose, if our means differ."

Silence.

He rose.

"With your permission."

"Of course."

He was nearly out the door when she tapped her ring three times on the bench.

Bull.

Fox.

Lamb.

He stopped and swallowed hard.

He smiled despite himself, his eyes moistening.

He tapped his bowl on the wall three times.

And then the old Franciscan left the castle of Arpentel, and made for Amiens, where his daughter even now tended the convent garden, eyeing the sorrel she would pick for him in the morning.

ACKNOWLEDGEMENTS

I wish to extend my deepest thanks to those who helped midwife this novel: first, to Michelle Brower, whose positivity, energy and arcane agenting alchemy never fail to astound me. Next, and posthumously, to Barbara Tuchman, without whose masterpiece, A Distant Mirror, fourteenth century France would be much more distant indeed. Somewhat less posthumous thanks are due to Michael J. E. Reilly, whose knowledge of things ecclesiastical proved indispensable to this effort. Paul Dubro of Legacy Forge answered questions about armor, and, if you visit Youtube, you can watch longbow experts Nick Birmingham and Martin Harvey of Company Holyrood show how English archers used hundred-pound war bows to punch holes in that armor; these two also read and commented usefully on the chapter concerning the battle of Crécy. Allen Hutton, who knows more about the late medieval sword than a living man has the right to, helped choreograph the fight by the creek; and if the hunting scene seems credible, that's because I know Bob Haeuser, who makes Eastern Louisiana unsafe for deer. Teresa DeWitt, high-school French class neighbor, prom date, and now CSI investigator, turned me green with descriptions of what prolonged submersion does to the human body, and Professor Sylvie Lefevre of Columbia University graciously answered a stranger's query about medieval French names. Michael Gartner of Volgemut and Owain Phyfe (whose voice sounds as hot blown glass looks) were two of the many musicians whose work inspired my writing, and since I am lucky enough to call them friends, it is my pleasure to acknowledge their excellence here. (Owain has left us since the first publication of this novel, and many are we who miss the light and warmth he taught us to hear.) Thanks again, and always, to readers Allison Williams, Jamie Haeuser (expert on persimmons), Ciara Carinci, and to listeners Damaris Wilcox, Roxanna Wilcox-Keller, Noelle Burke, and especially Kelly Cochrane, who knows a thing or two about sewing, and about salt.

Lastly, thanks and adoration to Danielle Dupont, whose self-appointed position on this project was 'Advocate for Good.' Her counsel on the nature of angels seems more like first-hand knowledge than supposition, and she is, in many ways, Delphine's mentor and close cousin.

Made in the USA
Middletown, DE
01 October 2023

39880868R00260